The Hidden King

Book One of

The Brothers of Destiny

J C PEREIRA

THE HIDDEN KING

Registered with the IP Rights Office

Copyright Registration Service

Ref: 7682887933

Copyright © 2018 J C Pereira

All rights reserved.

ISBN:9781977037497

DEDICATION

I dedicate this book to my son, Nathan.

THE HIDDEN KING

CONTENTS

	Acknowledgments	i
1	Chapter I	2
2	Chapter II	Pg 9
3	Chapter III	Pg 15
4	Chapter IV	Pg 31
5	Chapter V	Pg 41
6	Chapter VI	Pg 50
7	Chapter VII	Pg 65
8	Chapter VIII	Pg 75
9	Chapter IX	Pg 83
10	Chapter X	Pg 96
11	Chapter XI	Pg 108
12	Chapter XII	Pg 131
13	Chapter XIII	Pg 158
14	Chapter XIV	Pg 172
15	Chapter XV	Pg 194
16	Chapter XVI	Pg 214
17	Chapter XVII	Pg 229
18	Chapter XVIII	Pg 241
19	Chapter XIX	Pg 265
20	Chapter XX	Pg 293

21	Chapter XXI	Pg 320
22	Chapter XXII	Pg 330
23	Chapter XXIII	Pg 346
24	Chapter XXIV	Pg 359
25	Chapter XXV	Pg 371
26	Chapter XXVI	Pg 400
27	Chapter XXVII	Pg 410
28	Epilogue	Pg 434

THE HIDDEN KING

ACKNOWLEDGMENTS

My thanks to my beautiful and wonderful partner Ornella, who encouraged and participated in every page which I wrote. To her brother, Daniele, and my good friend, Mary, who were my first readers and who seemed to have enjoyed my efforts, giving me much heeded and constructive feedback. And finally, my son Nathan, to whom this book is dedicated and who was the source of my inspiration.

Cover design by Ornella Petrone

THE HIDDEN KING

BOOK ONE

CHAPTER I

It was a night spawned for ghosts and madness. The ethereal black and silvered lunar landscape were both beautiful and terrifying; a place filled with false trails, dead ends, and dangerously distorted pathways. Released from the deepest of shadows, two horsemen emerged into the glowing moonlight, the hooves of their superbly bred mounts muffled by the seemingly white sand coating the craggy, blasted hillside. With a slight, musical jingle of harnesses and the soft creak of well used and oiled saddles, they pulled their horses to a halt. From a sandy mound of luminous light, they surveyed and scrutinised the dappled valley below them.

The men wore dark leather coats and leggings, covered liberally with a film of travel dust and hats which were thrust low on their heads. As a gust of dry, cold wind lifted apart their coats, a glimpse of metal winked in the moonlight, the metal of death, swords.

'See anything?' a young voice, soft, resonant, pleasing to the ear.

'Yes,' was the reply; older, more profound, almost lazy in its timbre.

Both horses snorted and tossed their heads as if sensing something on the thin, cutting breeze.

'Well?'

'Watch there. Can you see it? There is a movement to the left.'

The younger man's eyes were sharp; the world presented itself to him in clear, well-defined images, whether by night or day, near or far.

'Erh, no, can't see a thing.'

'There… Look.'

'Damn… you're right, old man. Something is coursing our trail, a man - on foot. The fellow is good, eh? He's keeping low and in shadow.'

They had been riding hard for a week now. Using every trick that they knew to make life difficult for anyone interested in finding them. They were seasoned campaigners and took nothing for granted, checking their back trail every couple of miles; and a good thing too, for somewhere down in that valley unwelcome company was coming eager and fast.

Reaching down onto his horse's shoulder, the young man freed the horn and wood composite bow from its sheathed resting place with an automatic and practised fluid-motion. With his boot firmly anchored in a flaring, wooden stirrup, he hooked the highly tensioned shaft around his lower leg, and with a casual flex of his broad shoulders and long powerful arms, slipped the looped bowstring over the curled edge.

Without even looking at each other, the two men separated, descending by different routes back the way they had just come.

Scratch was the best tracker in his village. Following the two clever, unknown horsemen was problematic, but not too difficult for someone as skilled as he was. The payment rewarded to him was handsome, and instinctively he caressed the money belt underneath his half cured vest with one hand and scratched the weeping sore on his scalp with the other. With well-minted coins, he would be able to buy Princess the best. He watched her with love in his eyes as she followed the spore, nose down and tail wagging furiously, running silently. He was still watching her when a straight, slender, wooden shaft seemed to mysteriously sprout from her neck, wrenching out a surprised yelp. She fell over, sprawling in the dusty dirt, her limbs and body stretching out rigidly and unnaturally. Alarmed, he stumbled towards her spasming form, reaching out to help, confused as to why he couldn't seem to get his legs to work. Baffled, he felt the cold sand underneath his head. His eyes fixed on the icy glare of the moon, staring right into his soul, bleak and uncaring until thankfully, blackness took away the nightmare vision as the goddess of night leached his spirit away and took it to her bosom.

Muttering a prayer for the departed the young man bent over and retrieved his arrows from the already cooling corpses, pausing to close the eyes of the dirty, scab covered tracker. This simple soul's paymasters will only be minutes behind. He felt a twinge of regret for taking such a pitiful life, but choices were not always yours to make. He and his mentor would have to move fast. Looking carefully around at the rock face, he listened intently, but only silence and emptiness greeted him. His commander would be moving into position and placing him wasn't really necessary as he would be already moving to where he needed to be. Finding a small, flat-topped boulder illuminated fully by the moon, he clambered up with ease and sat cross-legged, weapons placed neatly by his side, waiting patiently in the shimmering landscape for the hired manhunters to arrive.

Five horsemen cantered around the tight bend in the valley and sawed hurriedly on their reins, checking their horses in startled surprise at the sight of their quarry sitting calmly on a rock directly in front of them. As the abused animals bucked and bunched, the tall young man leapt to his feet and released two arrows in a breathlessly quick fashion, each barbed head finding its mark in a throat. Of the three remaining riders, two flung themselves from the backs of their heaving mounts. Rolling expertly to their feet, one rose with a notched arrow ready to fly, and the other sent a throwing axe spinning towards the target, whom they saw too late was no longer perched on the rock. The third was charging forward on his horse with a blood-curdling scream. As yet another arrow thudded into his chest, it was cut short, and he toppled like a sack of rotten potatoes from the back of his wild-eyed horse. The last two split on each side of the rock trying to get their prey back into their sights, and as a result, failed to detect the two throwing knives that after a brief silvery spin, sunk themselves tip first and deep, into the back of their necks just below their skulls. They felt nothing but fell headlong into inky blackness.

'That was almost too easy. It doesn't seem right.'

'No they certainly weren't the best, I admit, and to tell the truth, it worries me somewhat. I think our persistent hunters are testing us.'

The older man had seemed to have come from nowhere and now was quickly assessing the scene.

'Let's collect our things and move out of here. The game isn't over yet, and I feel a bit exposed standing here in plain view. If I were planning this, then I'd still have another card up my sleeve.'

High on a ledge above the valley, a gaunt figure crouched, unmoving. It seemed to be immune to the cold, harsh wind, and for the past three hours had not moved from its position, not even to twitch from an annoying itch. You needed to see your prey as it runs. A real predator is always patient and never fails to play the hunt out. Don't depend on rumours and gossip; always see and judge for yourself. The figure rose with a fluidity that was unnerving and unnatural. More like that of a reptile than a man, and removed the spyglass from his face. He had seen enough for tonight, and it was time to drop back and prepare the killing field a bit more. These two were not soft targets, especially the older one. He was an old wolf, and it was imperative to treat him with caution and diligence.

'You're brooding again, I see. A bit disappointed that the sad jokers didn't manage to get the drop on us? Come on, let me hear you say it; you were wrong, and while you're at it, please admit that you're also getting old and slow. Did you even notice that I got three to your two? Correction, four, if you count the scabby fellow.'

Grunting the older man glanced at the brightening sky. Both the sun and the moon were up there vying for control, the sun chariot racing hard on the heels of the silver goddess, and gradually, inevitably, the yellow warmth was slowly overcoming the cold majesty of the night queen.

He rubbed a strong, prominently veined hand across a lined, clean-shaven, angular face set with deep brown, thoughtful eyes; calm and fathomless. Removing his broad-brimmed hat, his hand continued to stroke his closely cropped, grey-streaked hair.

'It was a trap of sorts…just haven't figured it out as yet. We must keep our eyes open, especially now.'

With that, he turned slowly in his saddle and took a long, searching look behind them.

'There you go again, spooking me. Eh, old man? Is this some kind of lesson you think I should learn? I'm never happy when you start dusting off one of those shelves in that thing you call a mind.'

The young man was handsome. His smooth, open face filled with charm and mischief. In years he numbered around twenty-two, but in experience, well, it was probably fair to say that he had seen far too much, and sometimes when he was most unguarded, a haunting shadow surfaced in his sea-blue eyes.

At about noon they came upon a many rutted and grooved road, one that by all appearances carried a routine and regular commercial traffic.

'Looks like civilisation is out here after all,' mused the young man. 'Guess you're going to advise slipping back into the hills.'

'Not this time, Nat, my boy,' replied his companion with a wry and very rare smile. 'You're beginning to smell a bit like that nag you're sitting on, and besides, we need to get a few supplies. We've got next to nothing left.'

'Comedians, the world's filled with jokers,' grumbled the young rider with mock irritability, shaking his head and tutting like an old woman.

Turning their tired horses onto the deserted road the two trudged on, trying to ignore the dry thirst in their mouths and the cynical attempts by the burning midday sun to boil their brains in the bone pots of their skulls.

CHAPTER II

It had the feel of a carnival—the noisy crowd, packed with people from all walks of life. Small impromptu stalls lined the riverside right up to the stone bridge with its grotesque, carved statues, which was cordoned off from the heaving, unwashed mass by large, armoured, grim-faced soldiers. Hawkers called out their wares with bright enthusiasm. Urchins with dirty faces and bare, skinny legs, threaded their way through the jostling throng as they craned their necks, as best they could, for a good view of the centre of the bridge. These children of fortune were ever open to the opportunity of slitting the strings of an unguarded purse or two. The smell, the energy, the celebration of colours, the pregnant expectation all belonged to a grand fayre, but this festivity had an entirely different and dark purpose. On the opposite side of the bridge, a rotund, squat fortress sat brooding over the city.

The crowd fell silent and surged unconsciously forward, as a small, iron-gate set in the side of the fortress squealed open. Shackled between two burly guards strode a tall, dark-haired warrior. Despite the clear evidence that he had obviously received a severe beating, his finely chiselled face, now swollen and misshapen. He walked upright with great pride, studying the now baying crowd with steady, green eyes. A dirty, brown sack covered his broad, muscular shoulders, but he wore it like a king's mantle. He was marched up to the scaffold newly erected for this occasion, at the bridge's centre. Without waiting to be prodded and manhandled, he stepped smoothly and with great dignity onto the large, wheeled cart placed under the rough, hemp noose hanging from the scaffold; there he stood unmoving, unflinching and erect, his face unreadable. Not everyone was screaming for the hangman to snatch his life away - not everyone saw this as some cheap and macabre entertainment for the masses. They were quite a few, both men and women, high and low, who stood there solemnly, eyes brimming with tears and sorrow, come to say their last farewell.

Even the dark cowl executioner seemed reluctant as he took his place behind the cart. With a methodical, practised action, he made a loop and dropped the coarse coil of rope over the head and around the neck of the dignified warrior. Still, his victim did not give the roaring mob any satisfaction with a show of weakness or fear. In admiration, the executioner leaned into the unflinching man and whispered. The warrior registered the soft rebellious words impassively. He made no outward sign of acknowledgement even when the life stealer's warm, humid breath caressed his ear.

'May the gods' guide you home, King's Protector, for truly you belong among them.'

Instead, he smiled inwardly as an image of a young face with laughing blue eyes drifted across his locked-in mind.

'Hubris Aden, beware of hubris.'

He felt a sudden movement, and his world lurched, followed quickly by a vice-like grip around his throat, cutting off his air, his life-line to life. Using all the discipline painstakingly learned, he forced his body and mind to relax, embracing death, letting it flow in, denying his persecutors and condemners even the satisfaction of the last dance on the gibbet.

'Another of the great ones has fallen', whispered a stooped, grey-haired man, dressed in the expensive cloak of a noble. His two companions, one on either side, swallowed the painful lumps in their throats and nodded.

'Have we received any word on the last survivors?'

'None sir, they have fled. They remain yet uncovered, however, as far as we know.'

'Ah well, something to hope for in this mess, I suppose. Come on; let's leave this place of death.'

A fat, oily man with a shiny, bald pate marked by a blue tattoo of a sunburst on his forehead surreptitiously followed with small, shrewd eyes the departure of the three men. He had received enough payment to keep them in sight until after the execution, then report their actions. Pulling his grey, woollen cloak around his portly frame, he moved with surprising agility towards the still guarded bridge. When he arrived there, he stood in front of a brutish looking soldier and stared mildly up at him. After ignoring him for a slow count of five, the brute lowered his dim-witted but spiteful eyes and glowered down. Not intimidated in the least, the rotund man opened his palm and showed him a specially made coin, given only to those carrying out duties in the name of the city's new protectorate. Recognition sparked in the recesses of the soldier's primitive mind and with a guttural grunt, he quickly diverted his gaze. Taking this as consent to pass, the grey-cloaked man slipped past with smoked ease, his bare, dirty feet caressing the stone cobbles of the bridge. He did not lift his head to peer at the slowly swinging corpse, but his demeanour seemed to betray a hint of sadness as he drifted by. Twice more, he had to show the coin before he gained admittance to the cavern-like interior of the fortress. After being left to wait for a very long time, he was finally beckoned forward by a priest of this new and aggressive religion brought to the mother city by these equally aggressive and ominous invaders. Ushered through in an unfriendly silence, they showed him into a small side chamber on the second floor which contained one window overlooking the sacred river. A large, square-jawed man with close-cropped, white hair sat with his back to the window and behind a pitted, wooden desk, reading through a pile of official-looking papers. He didn't look up as the tubby man stood in front of him, his face still mild and unperturbed as ever. After another few, heavy minutes of silence, he snapped:

'Report, I haven't got all day!'

Without even a slight change of expression, the bald man responded in a light, musical and very cultured voice that betrayed not a hint of nervousness.

'Our gentleman mark did as expected from all citizens issued with a warrant of house arrest. He only left his residence today to attend state affairs as commanded. With him were his two attendants of long-standing. He did not take part in celebrating the death of the condemned, but this is usual behaviour considering his standing in our society. He left right after the execution and returned to his home. There is nothing more to add, I'm afraid.'

The white-haired man looked up and studied the calm, chubby spy with undisguised disdain.

'I do not like you people. I do not like you. I do not like your supposed guild. Thieves and beggars, that's what you are, we pay you good money for information, and you bring us dung. Left to myself, I would root you out, every one of you, and hang you all! Get out of my sight!'

'Excellency,' echoed the mild and respectful reply.

Turning smoothly, the round fellow glided past the glaring priest. The latter had positioned himself behind him throughout the short meeting. He then made his way quietly back the way he had come, out of the fortress, across the bridge, back into the city. As he walked through the foreign quarter connected to the once again busy and industrious port, his thoughts turned to the questionable and dangerous activities of his guild. Yes, outwardly they collaborated with the conquerors. Yes, they sold them information, for this was the ancient occupation of his guild. Yes, they did betray the whereabouts of Aden Greylock, originally prised away as he was dragged unconscious from the battlefield, and given dangerous refuge, but this was after only they had become aware that his situation lay compromised anyway. They would have to progress with even greater caution as they balanced on that fragile line of what was ethical, mere expedient or a downright act of betrayal.

CHAPTER III

'Not much to write home about, eh?' muttered Nat, short for Nathaniel, a legacy from his father whose religious adoration and alcohol addiction competed with each other up to his dying day.

From their hillside vantage point, they could see the hard-packed, dirt road winding down onto the plain below. As it neared the village, more a hamlet really, it divided into two at a crossroad. One branch headed for a beautiful, incongruous, stone temple built on a little mound. The other meandered through the village with its collection of rude huts and hovels made of daub and mud walls with thatched, sunken roofs on one side. On the other, a neat row of fields separated by dry-stone walling and fed by a dirty looking, sluggish stream which followed the village's seemingly main road along its full length and on into the distance. The houses were of varying sizes, one, in particular, was much better made than the others, reaching up to two levels, with an in-built chimney. At the back of this building was a large, wooden barn. Running through and interconnecting the whole affair was a series of dirt paths which signified the level of activity and communication in the village. On the scrub-like verges in between and in parched fields surrounding could be seen bony livestock of varying types grazing greedily on whatever hardy vegetation was available.

Around the whole thing, not including the temple, small stretches of rotting palisade were sticking up with overgrown ditches in front of them, remnants it appeared, of some earlier attempt at fortifying the settlement.

'Interesting place when the winter rains come,' mused Nat's older companion. His rugged, brown face slightly creased in contemplation.

'Why do you say that?'

'It looks like they've built their settlement on a floodplain. Good planning when the ditch and palisade defences were in action, but now the place will be a quagmire; a pig's heaven.'

'Ah, well let's go down and greet the happy porkers, shall we? Maybe they are serving roasted dinner.'

As they slowly walked their horses towards the large stone marking the centre of the crossroad, still not a living soul could be seen on that hot, dusty afternoon. Turning left to follow the road into the village, a huge man with hulking shoulders and dressed in a dirty, brown smock and green leggings, stepped out from behind a lean-to and blocked their path. In his ham-sized hands, he held the long shaft of a long-bow to which a black-feathered arrow lay already notched and partly drawn.

'Oh, how nice,' muttered Nat sarcastically, 'here comes our invite to evening aperitif.'

'Good afternoon, my good fellow,' he called out cheerfully, taking off his hat with the flourish of a dandy, and offering a broad, white smile.

His efforts received a hostile, glowering stare.

'More bows to the left and right,' observed his companion, seemingly to no one in particular.

Glancing at him with an annoyed, 'I can do with some help here,' frown, Nat tried again.

'I wonder if you might indicate to us how we might buy some travelling provisions. We just need a bite to eat then we'll be moving on.'

'Show us your coin first, sonny!' came a thin, quavering voice as if from nowhere.

Glancing accusingly once again at his mentor Nat whispered, 'Was that you… sounded like you?'

Ignoring the flat gaze he received in turn, he responded to the unseen voice.

'Of course, good sir,' lifting a small leather bag from which he poured a few silver coins into his palm.

After a short, greedy pause an old, withered man, sporting a straw hat with a hole in its crown, hobbled into view from around the corner of a tiny cottage. Bent almost double he made his way to the big man with the bow and shouted.

'Let them pass, Ivan.'

'By the gods,' whispered Nat, 'reminds me of you when you were younger; spitting image!'

'So where you folks from?' shouted the old villager, shuffling alongside Nat's horse. 'No one comes this way any longer… unless likewise, they be running from something.'

'There is nothing so romantic about us, honourable sir. Someone reliable told us that there is a fortune to be found in the Black mountains, so we thought that this might be the shortest route to get us there.'

The old villager gave out a loud, humorous cackle. He enjoyed a lie as much as the next man. Taking another tack, he said. 'Your friend doesn't say much. Your pa…?'

'More like grandfather…but no…not that I know of. We're not related, but then again, in these times one can never be too certain.'

The older man nodded as if this was the most important truth he had heard in many a year.

Turning his head as if to admire the broken back cottages they passed, Nat took in the small assemblage of armed villagers now following behind them.

'Ten bows, two pitchforks,' drifted a dry, calm comment from his side.

'What's that you say, sonny?'

'Nice village you have here. A good place to settle down.'

Again the cackle cracked through the dusty air.

The old man led them to a neat, white-washed cottage about mid-way through the village. Attached to its side was an open-fronted shed stocked with an assortment of goods and tools. A thin, young, leather-aproned man bearing a remarkable resemblance to their host, timidly came out and peered at the two strangers with a near-sighted frown.

'This squinting idiot is my eldest son Drake. He looks after the village store. Tell him what you need, and he'll fetch it for you,' quavered the old man.

The older of the two companions dismounted in a smooth, economical motion, now free of his heavy coat. He wore a rough, close-fitting, black shirt, with the sleeves rolled up to just above the elbows. The elderly villager, who seemed to be the equivalent of the headman, studied with ever-shifting eyes the rock hard body of the stranger. His muscles snaked under his shirt, and the sliced, dark healed scars on his sinewy fore-arms flexed and flowed with his movements as he lowered his hands from the saddle. He produced a crumpled piece of paper which he handed to the old man's myopic son.

'Can you read, young man? Here is a list of the things we need.'

'Of course, I can read!' replied the storekeeper testily, studying the list with deep concentration.

'No offence intended, son.'

Turning to the ever-watchful, canny village elder, he continued:

'My name is Morgan Heston and my young, handsome friend there is Nathaniel Woodsmoke. We thank you for your hospitality.'

As the names were given the head man's eyes steadied for a split second and then flicked over the sheathed short sword and throwing axe draped comfortably from the stranger's hips.

'Welcome to our village, sonny. I'm called Hatch. Guess you must be hungry, especially that big, young fellow with that pretty sabre hanging on his back. My wife Becky will fetch you the best bowl of stew found in these here hills.'

'What lovely music for my ears, me old mucker!' beamed Nat, leaping from his horse with athletic exuberance.

As the two men turned to lead their horses to a large, stone, water trough sheltering under the only tree in sight, the old man saw a further two throwing knives sheathed at the back of the shorter of the strangers, just by the kidneys and easy to reach. In addition to that, the handle of a dirk poked out from the top of his left boot. Sitting on the cool stone, the companions took off their sweat-stained, leather hats and enjoyed the slight breeze caressing their heads and faces.

At this, the assembled and impromptu, village, defence brigade began to break up except for a small group huddled around the hulking figure of the man named as Ivan.

'I'm surprised that you gave them our names. You just happened to have left out the 'Ap' from yours. Still, I think the old bugger sniffed something.'

'No point in lying… we're the last of the King's Truth Sayers.'

'Last I saw the King is dead,' muttered Nat under his breath, a grim look surfacing on his habitually open face.

A dark, rainy day filled with noise and blood, a noble, bearded face, pressed into the oily mud.

With a small shake of his head, Morgan dismissed the unwelcome flash of imagery from his mind.

'Oh, no. Trouble,' mumbled Nat, suddenly taking a keen interest in his fingernails.

'Oi, you two, I'm sick of your slick lies. Tell us what you're doing here! So help me, if you don't speak truth, I'll beat the crap out of you!'

'Leave it out, Ivan!' shouted the old man from across the road. 'They've been offered guests' rights. Leave them be!'

'Shut your mouth, old man!' tore across the nasty reply. With that, he reached out with his oversized hand, intending to grab Morgan by the throat and haul him to his feet.

Lazily deflecting the meaty paw Morgan slid effortlessly upright, stepping neatly to the side of the giant thug and held up an open placating hand, palm outwards.

'Take it easy, son,' he said softly.

'Oh dear,' mumbled Nat.

'Shut your face, pretty boy! Your turn next!' snarled Ivan, turning and swinging a vicious blow at Morgan's head with a meaty fist.

Almost leisurely Morgan stepped past the punch, raising his left hand behind his ear and smashed the point of his elbow into the brute's biceps. With the same motion, his other hand flew out straight, heel palm connecting solidly with Ivan's nose with a crunching sound. Swivelling his hips in a continuous flow of movement, he blocked the next wild blow with his right wrist and punched Ivan's left biceps with an extended, middle finger knuckle. This hand then formed a hammer fist, hitting the confused giant with a stunning blow to the neck junction just below his ear. Flowing like water, Morgan ducked underneath Ivan's armpit. Spinning smoothly, he smashed his forearm into Ivan's triceps, and, at the same time, caught the bully's wrist, extending the arm and twisting the thick joint simultaneously. He then stepped back with his left leg, keeping his centre of gravity low. As Ivan bent forwards, breathing heavily through his mouth, Morgan reversed his right hand, cupping Ivan under his chin, yanking his head backwards and in the same instance, kicking his leg from under him. Ivan crashed heavily onto his back. With a roar of frustration and a spray of blood from his torn nose, he stumbled to his feet, only to fall again, glass-eyed and unconscious, as Nat thudded a fisted blow into the back of his neck.

Looking at the quiet, questioning face of his older friend, he said:

'Sorry, couldn't help myself. The big fool called me a boy. For heaven's sake, I'm a pretty man, not a boy.'

'Not seen that style of fighting since I was a young man in the old King's reunification army, sonny,' quavered the old villager. 'Seem to remember some of his elite bodyguard training somewhat similar.'

Giving the older man a steady, sidelong glance, Morgan commented:

'Memory can be a tricky thing, my friend and the time of Kings is long gone.'

'Yes, yes, you're right there, sonny. I seemed to have forgotten what I just said.'

The three men stood for a few moments looking down on the supine form of the large man.

'Stupid lump of a fool he is - always was. Best fighter in these here parts though, all brawn and fists, undefeated until now. I never did even get the time to make a bet, what a downright shame.'

The old man shook his head regrettably as he mused out loud.

'Dumb bastard though he is, his dad's lord of this here shire, and has gone and bent the knee to our new protectors. He's a fearful but vengeful man. He will have already heard of this little mishap.'

On saying this, he looked absently at the now-abandoned space where Ivan's friends had been just moments before.

'Time to see if that diligent son of yours has our purchases prepared,' said Morgan calmly, turning and walking across the road with the old villager in tow. 'I noticed a fine-looking donkey tethered to your wall. Is he yours and would you be willing to part with him for a fair price?'

The old soldier cackled with delight.

***

'Two men, you say? In the Badlands, south of the Black Mountains!' snapped the square-jawed man, his closely cropped white hair catching the morning sun as it shone through the open window.

'Bastards are moving fast. Who sent you with this message and how many days ago?'

'The one called 'the Krarl' your Excellency, about five days of hard riding.'

Despite his stern military bearing, the man charged with the governance of the newly conquered territory in the name of the Protectorate, hesitated, a look of unease passing swiftly across his eyes.

'Abomination before our lord god,' he muttered under his breath.

The informant kept his expression neutral. He knew what precisely the governor was thinking. They all thought the same.

'How is your father, soldier? Is he keeping well?'

'Yes, sir, thank you for asking, sir. He is working hard at getting his new dukedom working efficiently in the name of the Protectorate; the god is our keeper.'

'God is our keeper. Good-man, your father. We served together when we were both young.'

After a brief, reflective pause, he continued.

'It will take men like your father, like you, to show these heathens the true path!'

'God is our keeper; we are his flock,' replied the young soldier.

'What's your opinion, soldier? Do you think that our prey is the infamous commander of the special guard? Reputed to have served the upstart heathen and his father, wasn't he? Rumour even has it that he coordinated the so-called reunification wars. Impressive if true.'

'Well sir, to be honest, all I can say for sure is that they are a bugger to catch. Even 'the Krarl' is wary. Saw the evidence myself of a hunter pack of five wiped out by ambush faster than a cat can wink an eye.'

The two men, despite the differences in their ranks, were comfortable with this straight talk, soldiers' talk. For a brief refreshing moment, the politics and hypocrisy of the situation sat thrown out of the window.

'Yes…hmm…. If that one is staying his hand…then…then, he might well know something we don't,' contemplated the governor. 'Is your elder brother still with the unit supporting him?'

'Yes, sir. He is the titular commander.'

Ignoring the dry bitterness in which the young man said this, the governor ploughed on.

'I want you to go to your father's estates and assist him. Do not return to your unit. I will call on you when it is time. I need, the Protectorate needs, young men of your talents, especially in the next few months to come. I sense things are not yet at the finish line in this godless country.'

'As you command, Excellency, the god is our keeper.'

An ill wind had blown politics right back in again. It was his sacred duty to obey without question.

***

'Don't you ever sleep man!' loudly grumbled the stooped, elderly lord, his wrinkled skin still marked with the impressions formed by his pillow. 'It's the middle of the night! Even the gods' are resting at this time.'

The portly, bald fellow, his face expressionless and his posture as still as a hunter's shadow regarded the dead King's ex-counsellor in his rumpled, nightdress and cap, his white, shoulder-length hair, a rat's nest of wispy disarray.

'My apologies, but visiting you unobserved is not a simple matter, especially since I'm they give me payment to watch and report on you,' he replied in his soft, cultured voice.

'Yes, yes. I still have the suspicion that you simply have a perverse pleasure in waking old men from their much-needed rest, Timothy. You've always had an odd outlook on life, even as a boy.'

A ghost of a smile played on the round man's lips.

'The King Maker and his companion have been located. The hunt is hot on their heels led by that cursed Krarl.'

All humorous eccentricity disappeared from the old lord's eyes as he focussed on his long-term friend and associate, the intelligence of the man beaming through them.

'What are his chances?'

'He is formidable…and if they corner him…well, you know what happens when he becomes cornered.'

'Yes, Kingdoms are changed forever,' whispered the old lord with a sigh. 'He now belongs to the past, revered yes, but a relic. Could he prove jeopardy to our plans? At the moment he is a much-needed distraction, but if he turns and attempts to influence events - then maybe we should consider him expendable.'

The portly man remained silent for many heartbeats, wrapped in his grey cloak, wrapped in his unreadable thoughts.

'We do not know who this man is. He was here even before the first King. Yet he mysteriously remains unchanged. His long-term presence is disturbing. Let's be very careful before we start playing expedient politics on his head.'

'Are you afraid of him, Timothy?'

'Yes, we all are.'

The silence of the room dragged out, both men staring into the spaces between the flickering candles light.

'Our order is making attempts to reach him. I shall keep you informed.'

The old lord wasn't even aware when the grey shadow disappeared.

The man named Timothy was born into the noble class, whatever that meant. Men, given positions of importance and titles, which in turn enabled them to enrich themselves, buy property, educate their children and elevate themselves above those who they should be serving. He was a guild master and without doubt, a supreme negotiator in the selling and buying of information. It remained a commodity desired both by the rich and poor alike. Kingdoms and nations coveted it, and so did the godly and ungodly. His guild was old, and he was a continuation of a long line of abbots. The guild was there, dressed as beggars, when this stubborn nation, now on bended knee, struggled to raise itself under the guise of a republic; ruled by a council of ten good men, elected every third year by its martial population. The guild was there when greed and corruption entwined itself around the hearts and minds of the ten good men until they began to forget their real purpose.

The guild was there when a young noble, brimming with outrage and confidence, railed against the fallen ten, won the support of the people and the guild who worked in the shadows to protect him. The guild was there when this noble made himself king and started a fledgeling dynasty. The guild was there when this king's grandson fell into the mud on a sodden hilltop. The guild continues.

The Beggar Abbot clambered up and flipped over the wall shadowed by two pine trees on the corner of the ex-king's councillor's town residence. He dropped barefooted into a dark alley and was immediately shrouded in the stinking smell of urine, both of animals and men. He had no fear as these narrow, dark streets were patrolled and controlled by the members of his guild. The guild kept records. Its temple was a vast library three levels below a run-down, seedy quarter of the city, with passages opening into the original sewers, built-in hard stone since the early days of the republic, now long forgotten or ignored by the good citizens above. These records mention through time a mysterious, iron-grey man who guarded the first king and organised his armies and his battles. He remained ever in the background, never seeking rewards, riches or recognition. He was never present in the King's council meetings; he never attended state functions or private parties. No one ever found him shadowing the throne. Written records find him standing close to the Reunification King.

They also reveal him standing by the side of this king's son, holding a position as commander of the Royal Bodyguard. Indeed, did this post have a royal grant? A title handed down to successive, capable men? Or so he first thought.

He needed to get to Morgan Ap Heston. This man held answers to many mysteries. He felt that time was working against him. He did not want to arrive too late.

Keeping close to the poorly illuminated side of the buildings he arrived at a small, unobtrusive, metal studded, wooden door, slipped through it silently into a small, stone-paved courtyard and disappeared into a tiny damp recess on the other side.

CHAPTER IV

These cat and mouse games seemed unnecessary. Watching, peeping and planning. For what! The prey was right there under their noses. Numbers, equipment and skill were all on their side, yet this endless prevarication. Roasted and burnt by day, frozen and chilled to the bone by night. Dirty, always dirty! Oh, what he would give right now for a bath and a good massage by soft knowing hands.

Using all of his willpower, he tried not to stare daggers at the back of the unnaturally tall and motionless creature. The thing didn't seem to need eyes to know what was going on around it. And those eyes, when they did fall on you, it made you want to soil your pants. God is our protector. What did he do wrong in life to be allied to a devil? At least he had got his brother out.

Under the boiling sun, it stood. Dressed head to foot in a long, black, hooded robe fashioned from some sort of rough, durable hemp. Under this garb of a priest at mid-winter service, the creature wore a heavy, chain-mail hauberk accompanied by thick leather boots, but no leggings. Disgusting! As usual, it was peering through its ever-present spyglass, tracking the movement of the 13 country yokels, commissioned to bring down the fugitives. What was that all about, anyway! The large, fat lord of squalor had insisted that they had besmirched his son's honour. It was his right, he claimed, as the manor bred lord of this land, to bring the culprits to justice on behalf of the Protectorate. Instead of dismissing the fat fool's pretensions 'the Krarl' seemed all too happy to play along. For four days now they had been riding a parallel course, all except the vile creature who ran afoot as no horse would stand to bear him on its back, to the peasant idiots, always staying well out of sight. He could see the unease in the eyes of his nine-membered hunters unit, all seasoned warriors, accustomed to operating in enemy territory, now reduced to a silly games brigade.

Krarl felt the unit leader's distaste. He resisted the urge to reach out with his consciousness and squeeze him just a little. The time wasn't right yet. He didn't want them running off into the night like frightened, little girls; couldn't spare the time to turn and kill them. He needed to concentrate on his age-old enemy; the hunger in him made him tremble and his fanged mouth slavered with saliva. Soon, finally, he would drink his warm blood, thwarted so many times before. Once again he suppressed the wild urge to howl and run into the hunt. Not yet, not yet!

He knew the village peasants didn't stand a chance. But he needed to tear the sheep's skin off the wolf's back. This wolf was a pack leader, the best of the lot. He needed him in his proper form when he ripped his throat out and drank his blood. He had to be careful, though, for the pup with him was not fang-less, and he must keep in mind never to turn his back to him. He was counting on the unit sent by the Protectorate to survive long enough to keep him covered from the mishaps of fate. The Protectorate was under the misconception that he worked for them, but they were irrelevant, transient even, this was personal and deadly.

'Lord Krarl, should we not be moving on? Night has already fallen in the valleys. We need to find a safe place to bed down.'

'Weak, succulent, little girls,' thought Krarl, nodding his head in acknowledgement and loping off with a long-limbed, fluid pace.

***

The cold rain was sleeting down in torrents from the thunderous sky with black, heavy clouds hanging ominous, pressing down on the struggling men. Water was streaming off of his helmet and into his eyes. He looked around, trying to assess the state of the battlefield. On the highest point of the hill, he stood in the slippery, oozing mud, at the centre of a ring of iron disciplined, chain-mailed warriors forming a circle around their King—a ring of grim steel, two-hundred strong, three layered deep, unbreakable. On the left-wing, stood the Earl of Greendale, forever a man of questionable intentions. On the right, the stalwart army of the Lord Constable of Highwater, his men, already engaged, throwing back time after time, the heavy cavalry charge of the determined and ferocious enemy; their snarling shouts of 'Out, out, out!' echoing around the gloom-shrouded hilltop. At the centre, below the guard, stood the compact shield wall of the Earl of the Marches, a commander tested many times in battle. A piercing scream drew his attention, frowning he tried to place it, but somehow it seemed out-of-place. Again the cry, high, female, filled with raw passion and despair...

His eyes flew open, quickly marking his surroundings. The cold starlight softly illuminated the landscape outside of the natural rock overhang where they had found shelter for the night. Next to him, the bundle of blankets revealed where Nat was comfortably sleeping, his quiet breath pulsating across the intervening space to his alert ears. He sat propped up with his back against the hard stone, legs folded in a meditation stance. Somewhere during deep meditation, he had fallen into a dream trance, which seemed to be happening more and more often these days.

Something from the waking world had found him there - something urgent. Opening his senses, Morgan searched, spreading his awareness outwards. There, he had it...

'Nat,' he whispered, 'wake up, we are needed.'

He was already moving, heading for a now dried up, run off ravine that wound its way upwards in shadow. He didn't look behind. He detected the questing senses of the quickly alert young man, who did not waste time in useless questions. Instead, he stealthily followed his commander; young as he was, he was a seasoned brother of war, practised, efficient and in his deadly element. After about ten minutes of rapid climbing, they emerged onto a plateau covered with sparse, stunted trees.

'Struggle ahead,' whispered Nat fiercely. 'I'll take the right side,' and surged past without a sound, a long, wicked, knife-blade winking liquidly in the starlight.

In a small clearing, just before a cliff's edge, a desperate struggle for life was in play. Two bodies were already lying unmoving on the cold, hard ground, but next to them came the heart-wrenching gasps and grunts of a woman who knew that the last of her strength was fading rapidly. Yet she fought on, not knowing that help was at hand, twisting and turning against her two male attackers, not allowing them to do what they intended once an ounce of breath was in her body. Her lips, bloodied, her blouse ripped to shreds, revealing a pale, lithe body filled with womanly curves. Her leather trousers lay half pulled off, but her eyes gleamed with a fierce light as she raked her nails at the twisted faces of her attackers, driving elbows and knees into soft flesh, her breath rasping and hoarse. Morgan stopped, still as one of the watching trees, and folded his arms.

Without warning, a form streaked across his vision from his right, soundless. As it passed the two men, one head was yanked back violently by its greasy hair, and a blurred, silvery motion, followed by a dark spurt of blood and a harsh musical sound reminiscent of wind blowing through a pipe. Before his companion of wickedness could react, an iron forearm was wrapped around his throat, followed by a vicious wrench and the cracking sound of a dried twig. The two bandits, bent on rape, fell headlong into the dark everlasting night.

Scrabbling backwards the young woman pulled her trousers back over her nakedness and grabbed at a rock, holding it threateningly before her, her eyes locked frantically onto Nat's. Slowly he backed away.

'It's over, lady. The bastards are dead.'

At his soft words, the woman drew back even further, raising the rock with intent.

'Nat, we have to move now. Others will be drawn to this night's sordid fracas, like scavengers to a kill,' cut in Morgan's even voice. He still hadn't moved, but his eyes had already read all the evidence.

'Come lady. Trust us. We will protect you,' beseeched Nat with a soft voice.

Her answer was to snatch up a nastily curved, slashing short sword from one of the corpses, holding it cutting edge first towards Nat, her eyes wild with shock.

'Girl,' grated Morgan's firm voice from across the distance, 'you will have to take a leap of faith and trust this young man. His words are his intention. Believe you me; you will not find a man more trustworthy than him in all this world. Decide and decide now, for time is not our friend tonight.'

After a moment's hesitation, the girl, and girl she was, staggered to her feet, one arm held across her breasts and the other clutching the wicked, curved blade.

Without another word Morgan turned and drifted back along the path, they had come, followed silently by a frowning Nat and a shaken half-naked girl, trembling from both deep shock and the energy-sapping cold.

Within three minutes of arriving back at their campsite, the three were picking their way through the dark. They worked their way roughly still towards the Black Mountain ranges, the girl sitting on an unhappy donkey, her head and torso wrapped almost entirely in Nat's blanket.

Dawn found them winding upwards to reach a long, flat, dry plain dotted with gnarled, hardy scrub. Nat was sunk in himself, unusually subdued and only the girl's breathing could be heard, making a strange whistling sound. Morgan knew what was going through his young companion's mind.

Riding hard on the King's road, Morgan had been drawn down a side track that followed a pleasant, clear water stream, by a feeling unexplained. His companion of old, Aden, long accustomed to his commander's strange mysticism, trailed him in silent attention. After about twenty minutes of careful riding, they had come upon a sorrowful scene. On the porch of a roughly made, but homely log cabin, lay the broken and twisted remains of a ravaged young woman. Holding her hand sat a small boy, dry blood caking his soft, blond curls and his round blue eyes wept tears that broke the heart.

As the men slowly approached, he stood on firm, pudgy little legs, fixed them with a look of determination and gripped firmly in his small fist a stick that must once have belonged to some now long-forgotten toy. Aden, who had a strong affinity with all living things, climbed off of his horse and gently got down on his knees in front of the little boy. With a warm, soft voice, he asked:

'Your Mam?'

The boy nodded, moving slightly to put himself between Aden and his mother.

'She is gone, son. May I help you to put her to rest?'

'Bad men did this…why?'

Making sure that his eyes did not look away, Aden answered:

'I do not know son, but if you are willing, we will help you to find these answers.'

The boy nodded again, looking down at his dead mother, he sadly seemed older than his handful of years.

'What's your name, son?'

'Nat.'

'Well, Nat, let us help you to free your mother's spirit to the heavens. This day will be the first day of the rest of your life. Together we will find answers. Welcome to the brotherhood of the King's guards.'

From that day on, Nat had been fiercely protective of women, even those who did not particularly deserve it. His view of women was formed from the smoke of his mother's funerary pyre as her spirit rose into the sky.

The whistling grew louder, breaking into Morgan's reverie.

Twisting in his saddle, he looked back at the girl just as the donkey crested the ridge, bathing her in a golden light. It was the first time his eyes had seen her properly. She was beautiful; her hair a halo of golden red and her eyes a piercing green. He nearly smiled as he saw Nat staring, his mouth open and wonder in his gaze.

'Girl,' he said, 'that infernal whistle is driving me to distraction. We have to do something with that broken nose of yours.'

Despite himself, Nat grinned broadly.

'Don't take too much notice, my lady. He is famous throughout the land for his charming bedside manner.'

Dismounting in the welcomed warmth of the morning sun, Morgan strode over to the girl perched on the diminutive donkey and peered at her nose, which had a livid black and purple discolouring around it.

'Try not to scream,' he said, placing both hands up to her face with fingers extended and lying alongside both sides of her broken nose. To her, his hands felt peculiarly warm but bafflingly pleasant. Gradually, Morgan increased the pressure of his fingers until there was an audible snap and flaring warmth flowed from his hands into her nose and face, numbing the pain.

'Done,' he said, turning away and remounted his horse. The girl stared after him with her startling green eyes, tentatively exploring her nose with her long, elegant fingertips.

Nat grinned even more broadly and shook his head, turning his mount to follow Morgan's. The girl kicked the donkey into motion, pulling the threadbare blanket up over her head, as the little animal lurched into action, giving an annoyed whisk of his tail.

CHAPTER V

The old lord was irritable. For his sins, he stood related to the Earl of Greendale, Kingslayer, traitor, informer, and collaborator. Was he similarly tainted? Is that why Timothy was so quick with his rebuke? Had he succumbed so much into the treacle of political intrigue that he had lost sight of what was evident and just? Lord of no titles, that's who he was. He once carried the grand title of Lord Chamberlain, a man close to the King's ear. More like his arse, if truth be told. Lord Yesteryear, now that was a fitting title, or maybe Lord Fool was better. What became of the court fool, he suddenly wondered.

'Get on with it, you senile old man!' he muttered under his breath.

'What, sir?' exclaimed his long-serving secretary as he looked up startled from his search of the official records, rescued from the palace after news of the King's death had reached the city.

'Not you, Franklin. I was just engaging in an old man's past-time of berating oneself. It's much better than picking my nose, eh?'

'As you say, lord,' replied the old secretary in a neutral tone.

Maybe Lord Jackass.

'Found anything yet, Franklin?'

With a look that seemed to say, 'Maybe you should try helping,' the secretary responded in a dry, academic tone.

'The absence of written accounts and records is an official statement in itself. For such prominent figures or figure as I think you suspect, unlikely as it seems, as our mark will have to be well over a hundred years old, to find hardly anything is highly suspicious. Each of the three Kings would have had to have sanctioned this extreme editing. The next question is, why?'

'Yes, indeed. There you have it. Let's leave it there, for now, Franklin. Thank you for your efforts in trying to satisfy an old man's curiosity.'

'King Maker, now that's a title,' muttered the old lord. Left on his own to contemplate and reminisce in front of the warm fireplace, he became lost in his memories.

The guard ringed the throne room, silent, unmoving, like statues of a bygone age. Ominously, they faced inward, not out. Tragically, the old King, fallen into sickness after his efforts to unify the warring kingdoms, had retired to his bed. His eldest, trained from birth to take the helm, had been acting as regent in his father's stead, but he had squandered his inheritance, spurning all sage advice in a headstrong and arrogant way. Now the Kingdom was in jeopardy. The populace at large was in riot, burning, looting, raping and pillaging. A civil war was at the palace's gate now that news of the old King's passing was out.

'What shall I do Morgan? I trust you. What shall I do? My father lies in bed stone-cold and his Kingdom, his dream, is breaking apart. What is there to do?'

He said this with the King's councillors all present, but the question lay not directed at them. The iron-grey man stepped out from the guard. They all knew that without him, there would have been no kingdom at all.

'Abdicate.'

The word echoed around the chamber like the tolling of a fell bell, resonant and deep.

'And so it came to pass that they chose the younger son to rule…and a better king was he,' muttered the old lord, taking another sip of his expensive and imported brandy. 'Here, here!'

***

He stood firm in an island of calm on that drenched, forsaken hill. The King's guard captain, general in all but name, of the King's armies, noted that a determined and wily foe was subtly drawing the right-wing under the valiant command of the Lord Constable of Highwater down the treacherous mud banks. The archers who had been sending wave after wave of black arrows into the enemy ranks stood bedrenched, hampered by wet bow-strings, poor visibility and an intertwined foe and friend. He despatched the glorious Aden Ap Greylock, some say the best of the guard, to warn Highwater to err on the side of caution and hold his position. The centre, under a rampant Earl of Marches, was being sorely *pushed by the full force of the invaders' infantry. His men raged with shield and short sword. They had taken up the hue and cry of Highwater's men, 'Out, Out, Out!' Amongst the din of hoarse shouts, screams, clashing steel and the churning of mud and blood under a pissing sky, the ever-watchful captain noticed the left-wing of the centre beginning to bow inwards from the constant pressure. To stop the gap before it formed, he signalled for Greendale to move his men forward and set the plug.*

What happened next was the first exhibition of high treason on that fateful day. Greendale sat fat arse on a horse and did not move. With a snarl, the captain peeled off fifty companions and marched through the squelching, slippery mud to carry out the treacherous dog's work. The guard detachment with their unleashed leader at the head of their flying wedge leapt at the enemy with a savage roar. It was heard clearly by all on the field as it echoed around the low hills. What held witnessed on that day is hard to describe in this short account, and had I not seen it with my own eyes, would have had it dismissed.

It was not the first time that Lord Abbot, Timothy, had read this account, written by one of his most trusted disciples, of the day that the Kingdom and its King, fell to the invaders, the Protectorate. But even now it took his breath away and caused goosebumps to rise on his neck and arms. Rubbing a hand across his tired eyes, he continued reading.

Abandoning shield for a two-handed battle axe and short sword the captain, a battle lord of days of old, surged into his prey with a cold ferocity matched only by his seemingly inhuman strength and skill. Seasoned warriors fell beneath his onslaught as if they were children brandishing toys, sliced open, brushed aside and ploughed under by his following, chain-mailed entourage of war. The quietly spoken and unassuming captain had transformed before my very eyes and that of the King - a death demon unleashed. The movement of both his weapon-wielding arms was too quick to follow, and his reflexes were lightning fast, as he twisted and turned, ducked and slipped his way through the enemy, untouched and feared.

The awe-inspiring success of the guards ironically was the catalyst that caused the King's army to unravel on that day. As dread terror gripped its cold hands around the hearts of the men so ravaged by the guard captain and his companions, a rout ensued, triggering a ripple through the attacking army. This ripple resulted in a pause by the skilled and relentless enemy cavalry tearing time and time again at the King's right-wing under the now harassed Highwater as he struggled to control the over-enthusiastic aggression of his men.

Despite the best efforts and loud exhortations of both Aden Ap Greylock and the Lord Constable, the blood of the defending soldiers was up, pounding in their veins, and they interpreted the pause in the enemy horsemen as a turn of fortune. Howling for retribution, they forgot hard-earned discipline and in a mass frenzy, broke ranks and seethed down the slippery slope, throwing certain victory into the mud. Seizing this long-awaited boon, the fast, mobile, Protectorate cavalry, darted around what had now become a floundering mob, flanked and slaughtered.

At this point, the second act of high treason stood committed. Seeing the danger, the King himself sent a clear signal to Greendale to release the reserve horse held under his control, to counter. The traitor turned a blind eye to his King.

Even in the midst of mortal combat, the guard captain became aware of the dire situation. Under his guiding commands, the wedge flowed backwards into a hard battle-line, adjusting smoothly from offence to defence. Leaving the fifty under the capable leadership of the young and promising Nathaniel Woodsmoke, Ap Heston disengaged and made haste back to his King to coordinate his protection. It was plain to his eyes that all sat lost on this final cast of the die. The fickle tide of fate had turned. We all knew it, especially the King. Standing at his elbow, I could feel his sadness. It was he who had insisted and pressed on Ap Heston that Greendale receive the gifted command of the left.

Despite all, I could see the captain assessing the field, his face calm, and his demeanour unhurried. I followed his gaze with mine. To the right Greylock and the Lord Constable fought on doggedly, with a fighting square of around one hundred stalwart soldiers, inching their way back towards the King. He could not lend them help even though he so much wanted to. Their fate stood sealed. The fearless centre held their discipline. The Earl, now lost of voice, croaked out steady orders, as they withdrew in good order back up the hill, the enemy barking and biting at their shield gates. To the left, the traitor still sat unmoving on his spiteful horse.

Giving a terse, crisp command the captain led his men, the elite guard, into a contracting manoeuvre, forming a circle around the king - a ring of hardened steel forming a crown at the summit of a rain-soaked hill, to protect the crown of our nation. This action marked the moment of the third and final act of treason committed on this day of sorrows.

Eyes filled with tears, Timothy could no longer see to read on, no matter how much he wiped them away. The librarian, noticing his anguish, drifted quietly to his side.

'May I be of service to you, Lord Abbot?' he asked softly and respectfully.

'Yes, my old friend. Are you able to find me any battle transcripts or records that relate to the court of the first king?'

'I will do what I can, Lord Abbot.'

'Thank you, my friend.'

The night was going to be a long one.

***

The governor had summoned the Earl of Greendale to attend him without delay some three days before. He had not yet appeared. The governor was not an overly patient man when it came to the people of these heathen lands, especially those who turned on their own. Still, this so-called Earl had played his part, claiming loyalty to the true and rightful heir, so the governor should give him the benefit of the doubt; for now at least. These fools liked to follow Kings, so the Protectorate, the god is our keeper, having taken one away, would provide them with another; be it one more susceptible to the good god's directions.

Without knocking, a pinched, hawk-faced priest, dressed in the white robes of a servitor entered.

'Yes, Father. What can I do for you?'

'The foreign collaborator is waiting below. He sends profuse apologies for his tardiness and begs forgiveness,' replied the priest, his sour, disapproving expression seemed to be saying that in his opinion the foul sinner stood ripe for purification on the wooden stake even now. It was never too late for burning repentance.

'Thank you, Father. God has a use for him. Please show him up.'

Muttering under his breath, the priest departed with ill grace.

Waddling into the antechamber which was currently being used by the governor as a working office, the traitor Earl looked somewhat ill at ease, mopping his sweating brow with a sodden, silk cloth which, at the same time, acted as a miniature security blanket. The governor fixed him with a piercing, steady scrutiny.

'Good day to you, your Excellency. You honour me by calling my humble person in to offer counsel,' oiled the fat man obsequiously, his red, veined nose and puffy face betraying his recent turn to alcohol to seek comfort and hide guilt.

'Your counsel is not required here, Greendale, nor is it needed,' replied the governor flatly. 'You are tolerated merely for the timely service you have provided to the Protectorate, god be our keeper.'

'A service that is still in wait of the promised reward, Excellency,' creamed the greedy response. 'My lands and title were to be left secure to me in recompense.'

'Our valued guest has been given and left in your care. That is a reward enough for now. What follows next depends upon your conduct henceforth.'

'But…'

'Please, Lord Greendale. Let's not pursue this dead-end. Would you prefer to be given back to the people you once swore to serve? I think not.'

'I stood sworn to serve the true heir!' stuttered the ex-Earl indignantly.

'Be that as it may, we called you here to undertake the preparations for the crowning ceremony according to your customs. Do not fail us in this. Please, see yourself out.'

CHAPTER VI

There wasn't a single point on which they could agree. Every order, every suggestion, was met with dissent, argument and grumbling. Most wanted to go home, but were afraid to do so. Ivan saw himself as the sole appointed and rightful leader, seeking to impose his will on every decision. Most wanted to listen to the advice given by old Hatch, who seemed unperturbed by the glowering and threatening antics of Ivan. These villagers were simple people, but they were hardy, and if they made up their minds collectively, they could be fearsome and bothersome indeed; even the dull, brutish Ivan knew this so he never truly over-stepped the mark. Hatch, on the other hand, seemed reluctant and unwilling to assert leadership. His suggestions were limited to the safest route to take. How fast to travel, where to find water and the best place to stop for the night. His duty, as he saw it, was to keep his people safe, until this fool-hardy venture - which most of them stood pressed into - ran out of steam and they could all go back to etching out a living. They were not hunters of men, especially when those men were supreme predators. He knew who they were, even if the others were too addled and parochial to recognise those two men. Ivan, the fool, wanted to lead these simple folk onto a certain death.

THE HIDDEN KING

He also knew who that creature was. He had learned many things during his scouting days for the old King's army. It was a nightmare from elder days - from the days when men with power and forbidden knowledge did things that should not be done, just for the sake of seeing what they could do and get away with doing. An abomination, that's what it was. And it was watching them, day and night; waiting to see if they would do its bidding. The last thing he wanted was for that thing to decide to start hunting them.

Two days after Heston and young Woodsmoke departed, that creature strode into their village. Ignoring their bows, it cut a path directly for the manor, almost taunting the villagers to let loose their darts. No one did, no one dared. The thing looked just too wrong. A good thing also that they had allowed it to pass unmolested for just minutes later, a Protectorate's hunting pack followed the creature in, riding hard. No one knew what they said behind the closed doors of the manor, except fool Ivan, but soon after, the lord cajoled them to bring in the horses from their pasture, form a party and ride down the fugitives in the name of the Protectorate. Lord Fool! They're nothing but lambs hunting wolves. Now they sat caught between a rock and a hard place.

Anyway, from their tracks, he could tell that they were moving fast, even though they seemed to have picked up a third member. At the rate the villagers were going they would never catch them, unless, of course, Heston and his party all fell into a ravine and broke their legs. It was only a matter of time before the creature lost interest in them and surged onwards to hunt his own game, or so he dearly hoped.

***

Krarl had already decided to do just that. The stupid villagers were just too slow and incompetent to provide the entertaining distraction he craved; the softening up, so to speak. Gnashing his large, powerful teeth together in wet annoyance, he upped the pace, loping off well ahead of the pack. Two nights ago, he had been drawn to the sounds of a struggle but had arrived far too late. His prey had got there before him and had joined in with the killing. They had picked up a third person, a female by the smell, but instead of slowing them down, it had spurred them to move faster. Now they were using bush-craft and evading tactics as well as greater speed. The real hunt was on. The One knew he was on his trail.

***

The girl was tough. She did not complain, nor did she speak. They left her with her thoughts and concentrated on covering their back trail. Her name was still unknown; who she was, why she was out here, who was the man that had died trying to protect her? To these questions, all yet remained unanswered. Nat felt that Morgan was doing more than attempting to cover their physical passage. At certain places, usually high points, he would get down off of his horse and enter a meditation trance. Nat had never seen him take these measures before when evading trackers, so there was something beyond the norm on their heels.

He was well aware that his companion was able to sense things that ordinary men did not. When he was a boy, he used to try and question Aden as to what these things were, but Aden would only smile and shake his head. In the end, he just stopped asking questions and just trusted.

The girl's fair skin was being burned raw by the unforgiving sun, and the animals were getting tired, so Morgan had called a halt to shelter until the mid-sun had passed over. They had found an overhang at the side of a canyon wall, and although it was boiling, they remained shaded. Morgan was once again in a trance. The girl would not respond to any of his attempts at conversation. Lying back on the comparatively cool sand, he tried to recollect when last he had seen his co-mentor.

He felt proud. Morgan had given him his first command, in the very heart and thick of battle where the heat was at its highest. Given control over of fifty fearsome and war-seasoned men. Like the true professionals they were, they rallied to his cry, caring not of his youth, acknowledging that only he was the one who held the baton of command. He wished that Aden was in a position to see him now, but the gentle warrior was probably fighting for his life on the right - fighting to carry the day. It was the first time he had truly seen Morgan freed of all constraints, his warrior soul unleashed. It was an incredible spectacle - a manifestation of a demi-god of war. It had taken every ounce of his youthful strength and spirit to keep his place in the wedge, yet Morgan, at the point, bore the full brunt of the enemies force without missing a stride. This paragon of men was his mentor, a man of legend, a king among kings; the

King Maker. Now with a hand clapped to shoulder and a nod of a grim, helmeted head, he had passed him the command and melted back through the ranks to protect their chosen king. At first, there was a welcome respite as the shocked enemy took time out to regather their flown courage. But then they all felt it, like a sudden wind bringing a shiver down your spine. Something unseen and unexpected had happened over on the right - something that swiftly emboldened the foe to leap back into the fray; savage and slavering. With bended knee and hunched shoulders, the fifty took the strain of this new violent onslaught without giving an inch of churned mud. Over the heavy, gasping breath of the labouring combatants, their cursing, sometimes pleading, their screams when sharp weapons found flesh, and their shouts of rage when their efforts of intent were frustrated, he could hear the gravelly, booming voice of the Earl of Marches. He was steadfastly grounding out commands and encouragement, keeping the whole line fused as one fighting force; 'Hold or die, you bastards!' He almost smiled.

'Who is he?'

Snapping back through time, Nat flung open his eyes, quickly looking around, disorientated.

'Who's who? Where?'

His darting gaze came to rest on the girl, captured by her arresting green eyes.

After a moment's pause in which he felt she was deciding whether or not if he was a simpleton, she said:

'Him, the old man, who is he?'

'He is a hard bastard who will keep us alive.'

Another intermittent pause stretched between them where she searched his face with her penetrating eyes, she said again:

'He seems to have strange abilities.'

'Yes, girl, that he does.'

There followed another pregnant pause.

'I'm no girl, boy. We're almost of the same age.'

With that, she turned her back to him and lay down.

Nat chuckled. At least she was now speaking.

Fighting to keep his mind focused on the task at hand, Morgan painstakingly erected walls with his consciousness. If his mind wavered, even a little, he would have to start all over. It was tiring, but very necessary. He knew what was tracking them and although it would be impossible to lose it, his efforts would frustrate it and waste its time. He had hoped never to confront this complicated, nightmare creature again, but it seemed that the sisters of fate couldn't resist meddling in his affairs. With a sigh, he pulled his consciousness back and re-entered his body. Immediately, a wave of heat hit him, followed closely by the sound of Nat chuckling. Opening his eyes, he regarded his young charge fondly. He was the closest thing he had to a son.

'Shouldn't you be resting instead of laughing to yourself like a madman?'

'You're right, grandfather, but I've learned awfully well from you, it seems. I even picked up your questionable mental state and habits.'

Listening to them, the girl smiled for the first time since that horrible night. Poor Hamish, he had been her bodyguard and friend since a little girl. Now he was gone. His body, rotting on a cliffside without proper burial or even a chance of farewell. Warm, wet tears followed her smile.

***

'I still think it's better to have one of ours than one of them!' exclaimed the old, ex-chamberlain, waving his thin arms about in exasperation while pacing up and down restlessly.

'A puppet is still a puppet, no matter which way you choose to look at it. They want this only to legitimise their rule and keep the people quiet,' replied the Earl of Marches.

One of the few to survive the massacre after the battle of the Hill of Sorrows, gravely wounded, he had been in hiding ever since, moving from one safe house to the next, all orchestrated by the Beggar Abbot and his shadowy guild. In reality, they sat gathered for their meeting in one of these very same safe houses at this very moment; a damp basement, stone-built, and stone cold.

'But he will still be one of us! We will be able to exert some influence…'

'Lord Chamberlain, if you remember correctly, this so-called one of ours of whom we speak, did not do so well for us last time around…and he wasn't anyone's puppet then.'

The Earl's voice was still strong even though he was still not fully recovered and remained very frail.

'Yes, yes…banished before he had a chance.'

'That statement is unworthy, Lord Chamberlain!' rebuked the ex-Lord Privy Counsellor.

All six other heads huddled around the rough table nodded in unison and agreement. Of the dead King's ten advisers of state, eight had made it to this secret conclave. If they fell afoul of discovery in this suspect setting, they would merit summary execution in the eyes of the Protectorate. There would be no hearing, no trial, and no appeal. They knew the dangers intimately and understood the penalty.

'Please accept my apology, esteemed colleagues, but the fact remains that the rightful heir stands exiled on the authority of someone, a foreigner I might add, who did not have the proper rank to do so…and done without consulting the chosen King's councillors!'

'I truly do not like the sound of this or its intended direction!' objected the Earl of Marches.

'Please do not miss-understand me. I am not challenging the legitimacy of our beloved King, may his soul rest in peace. We all feel his loss deep within our hearts and sorely wish that he was still here with us. However, he is not. We need to make some hard choices.'

'I regret to say that you remind me tonight of your cousin, Lord Chamberlain,' the Earl said sadly.

'I am not a traitor, Earl! You will not find a person more loyal to our nation, but we have to play the best hand that fate has given us to survive as a people much less as a Kingdom!'

'Here, here,' muttered the council, all except the Earl.

'Shall we vote on this, esteemed members of the chamber?'

The Earl's eyes were brimming with tears as all hands stretched raised in favour. His was the only one left grounded on the lap.

Some two hours later, the Lord Chamberlain was the last one left in the basement, besides the silent Abbot. They were awaiting the night disciples to return to guide the lord through the shadows and unseen, back to his residence.

'What is your opinion on this night's work, Timothy?'

'Your eloquence carried the day, Lord Chamberlain.'

'I hear in your words, disapproval, Timothy. Why didn't you voice your concerns?'

'It was not my place to do so, Lord Chamberlain. I was never a member of the King's council.'

The old lord sucked air through his teeth to sound his annoyance.

'Be that as it may, man, but none of us would be here without you.'

'What value is that, Lord Chamberlain? The council almost to a man voted against a great man to whom the entire nation is gravely indebted. In fact, without him, we would not have a nation in which to make these secret votes.'

'Look, Timothy…'

'Enough, Lord Chamberlain, I am not subject to your politics, and if you do remember, I once warned you of playing politics on Ap Heston's head. He is far from dead, and I do not think that he is fleeing in the manner that we all think he is. Be wary, be very wary.'

'Is that some sort of threat, Timothy?'

'No threat at all from me, Lord Chamberlain. I continue to serve. My words stand as they are. Come, it's time for you to be safely home.'

***

'You are telling me that some of these so-called members of…of some so-called council, broke curfew orders and met at dead of night!' barked the governor, his square jaw clenched in aggressive anger.

'Yes, Excellency, they did.'

'To what purpose, do you think?'

'Rumour has it in order to vote on whether or not to support the coronation.'

'Ah! That news is out of the bag, is it! Where did they meet?'

Meeting the governor's eyes, Timothy answered without preamble.

'We were unable to discern this, Excellency. They are receiving help from one of the other guilds.'

'Do you know which one?'

'Not yet, your Excellency, we're trying to find out.'

The governor gave Timothy a long, flat stare.

'Your hands are dirty, little thief. They are so dirty that I can't see what you're hiding in them. Be careful, or one day I may decide to break every one of those nasty fingers of yours to have a good look. Collect your purse from the priest outside and get out! Oh, by the way, don't take too long in finding out who is helping our good counsellors.'

'Yes, Excellency, we will be looking into it immediately.'

The governor turned and gazed out of the window at the racing, green waters of the river. He felt the warm sun on his face and enjoyed the sensation. He hated being trapped indoors and itched to be out on campaign again. He knew who these counsellors were. For the moment their little games were useful. He knew how they would vote. It was all working out nicely so far. Those who played in politics were always predictable. It wasn't they who he needed to watch. It was this paid informant of his. There was something about him that made him uneasy. As soon as he had a spare moment, he would get to the bottom of it.

***

Earl Greendale was not a happy man. Promised so much and given so little. This mixture of unjust grievances seemed to be his lot in life. The King had promised to bring him to court and make him one of his trusted councillors; that never happened. The King had promised the hand of the Earl of Marches' eighteen-year-old daughter to link with to his thirteen-year-old son. With this bountiful union would have come much-needed estates; this never happened. The condescending Earl had promised to bring his precious heifer to court when she reached her majority; of course, this never happened. Nor will it ever happen, as assassins stood sent to all the strongholds to eliminate any potential heirs. The Protectorate was thorough. In the end, the King did instruct the upstart Ap Heston to give him command of the left, more the fool he.

He made his way to the palace, which now had the air of a deserted place left behind by events. Showing his official coin to the seemingly uninterested Protectorate guards, they let him through the iron gates. He immediately headed for the previous King's old quarters. Here he was challenged by a quartet of alert, professional and serious-looking guards, who checked his coin carefully, then requested his papers of passage and checked the governor's signature against a sample that they held. He then received further questioning as to the purpose of his visit. Finally satisfied, he was allowed to pass through into the royal rooms. He wondered if these guards were mostly there to keep someone in or to keep others out.

Two young women -whom he did not know- and an old, dapper gentleman, who he did know, greeted him. The old fellow spoke for them.

'Welcome, Earl Greendale. Fate has preserved you well.'

'Hello, Alfred. As usual, you're very clever with your words. Pity the Protectorate didn't clip that glib tongue of yours.'

'I'm not important enough to warrant a notice, my lord. Please follow me through.'

Sitting in a green, leather, padded chair was a tall, thin man at the near edge of his winter years, his long hair, tied back, and beard, neatly trimmed to a point, was heavily streaked with grey. His eyes were closed. At his feet sat yet another young woman who seemed to be in the act of massaging his naked feet.

'The Earl of Greendale is here to see you, Your Majesty,' toned Alfred.

The man's eyes flew open, revealing piercing grey, haunted mirrors with which he fixed the Earl.

'Greendale, you've become fat!' the dead King's older brother shouted.

'Yes, your Majesty, fortune's jest. Worry and discontent have led me to eat overmuch in search of comfort. Welcome home, your Majesty.'

'Along with betrayal and regicide, no doubt,' the King's brother said drily but without any apparent rancour.

'I was always loyal to you first and foremost, my liege.'

'I know what I am, Greendale, and I know what you are,' was the sharp reply.

'I am here to arrange your coronation, your majesty, so that you may take your rightful place once again.'

'Yes, I know why they sent you, Greendale,' the past and the future king replied absently. 'Do you know where my brother's body has been laid to rest, Greendale?'

'No, your grace, he was spirited away by the upstart Ap Heston.'

The King to be fixed the Earl with a studied, emotionless gaze and remained silent, slowly becoming lost in a memory thought long forgotten.

'Where shall I go, Morgan? Where shall I go?'

'You have coins and guards to protect you. Now is not the time to heed my advice. That time has gone. Go somewhere where you are not known. Do good and learn from your mistakes. Your brother will welcome you home when you prove yourself ready. He loves you deeply.'

Those were the last words of his old friend and teacher.

'I would dearly love to say goodbye to my brother. I have dreamt time and time again of receiving his welcoming embrace. In the end, even Morgan could not keep him safe from the hands of fate.'

'That man will soon be brought to justice, your grace. It's only a matter of time.'

The thin, haunted man merely smiled.

CHAPTER VII

Krarl was frustrated. For the fifth time that day, he had had to backtrack. The hunting pack had started to look at him with open questions in their eyes. He did not like that. He preferred awe and fear of any other emotion evoked. The fools were increasingly witnessing his now many mistakes, and their crushed spirits were rising out of the dirt. They saw his frustration. Yes. They would soon feel his anger if they continued to regard him in that condescending way.

He could no longer sense his prey except for infrequent occasions. Why this was so, he wasn't sure, but he was beginning to suspect that the One had learned of a way to block him somehow. He didn't know that such a thing was possible. So night hunting was now a thing of the past, and his prey was very, very good indeed at hiding their trail or even worse, leaving a false trail. So hunting by day was also a problem. Sometimes he just wanted to howl at the sky, sometimes he just wanted to kill something, but he needed the cubs in the pack to stay with him. He didn't want them to run off back to their mummies. He needed them when the final kill came.

'Lord Krarl, have we lost them again? The horses are beginning to tire. In this terrain, they will break their legs if they become too tired.'

Krarl involuntarily bared his fangs at the pack leader and immediately regretted it as the succulent pup recoiled with fear in his eyes. Krarl did not like talking. It took too much effort and was unnatural. However, he attempted to reassure the frightened puppy.

'All grood. We rrest soroon,' he slobbered, wiping drool from his mouth with the back of his hand.

From the look of horror in the pack leader's eyes, he concluded that the attempt was a failure. Maybe he should just kill the stupid baby. This sudden idea was the simple solution - perhaps later.

A guttural, choking sound came out of Krarl's mouth with a sudden force. It took sometime before the unit leader realised that Krarl was laughing. He slowed his horse as much as he could to keep his distance.

'Sir, I think the thing's going mad.'

'Shut your mouth, Henderson. Do you want to be torn limb from limb?'

Krarl heard them and stopped laughing. Yes, he would kill them all, but not yet.

***

The dark, icy evening found them still riding. It was almost impossible to see anything with the naked eye except elusive shadows and shades, yet Morgan, riding lead, picked his way slowly but confidently along unseen trails. Guiding his mount next to his, Nat leaned over in his saddle and stared as hard as he could at his face. He had a strange sensation that his teacher was riding with his eyes closed and shook his head in wonder. Better not to ask, he thought.

The girl, as usual, was silent again, but he didn't worry about her for the little game donkey, except for the occasional heehaw of disapproval, was very much at home in these barren, rugged canyons; whether night or day, cold or hot. He envied the plucky, sure-footed, little ass. Thinking of the beautiful girl it carried on its back, he decided, yes, in more ways than one.

After about two more hours of the same, the chilly, thin wind that had been harassing and aggravating them continually, trying its best to get into every minuscule gap in their clothing, suddenly stopped.

'We'll shelter here. It's a good place to camp for the night.'

Nat and the girl looked around. They couldn't see a thing.

Nat could hear Morgan dismounting, followed by the sound of him gathering up firewood. In a short interval of a few minutes, a small blaze illuminated their campsite with an orange glow. A strange formation of rocks had formed a shelter on almost all sides. It created a natural windbreak, and already the rocks were radiating the heat from the campfire back at them. Morgan was right; it was an excellent place as any to spend the night. Nat and the girl dismounted now that they could see, and started the task of unpacking the animals. Morgan began to unwrap a brace of rabbits from their skins, which earlier that day, he had brought down with deft twirls and flicks from a rawhide sling-shot. He soon had them roasting on the open fire.

'Not worried about being seen tonight?' Nat asked.

'Not so much. Our tracker is no longer having an easy time of it.'

'I'm not going to ask how you happen to know this. You have some knowledge of who is on our tail, don't you?'

'I have a fair idea.'

'You're him, aren't you?' blurted the girl.

Both Morgan and Nat stared at her. Morgan recovered first.

'Maybe you should give me a little more, girl, if you want me to answer that.'

'You're him; the King Maker.'

'Ah!' said Nat. 'A thinker.'

The girl eyed him with a deep, annoyed frown. Nat busied himself with putting stones around the fire.

'You have the better of me, girl. Why in all the world, would you even suspect such a thing?' asked Morgan.

'My father has told me many things about you.'

Nat stopped doing his busy doing nothing task.

'I see,' replied Morgan in a measured way. 'And who might your father be?'

'The Earl of Marches.'

Nat started to cough uncontrollably.

The girl fixed Nat once again with her frown, specially made for annoying idiots.

Nat broke off in mid-cough 'Sorry', he croaked, 'dust.'

'And anyway,' he continued, clearing his throat. 'Why in heaven's name, would Earl of Marches' daughter be running around this barren wilderness all on her lonesome?'

'Assassins,' said Morgan in a flat tone.

The two youngsters looked at him in silence, one with a questioning look, the other with a sad look of acquiescence.

Morgan continued.

'It is standard practice for the Protectorate. As their armies break and plunder, they send out assassins to all the ruling houses, eliminating all possible heirs, reducing the possibility of future rallying points.'

Then with a more sensitive tone, he turned to the girl and said.

'Is this what happened to you, girl?'

She nodded silently, with tears in her eyes.

'They murdered mother in her bed. Then they came for me. If it weren't for Hamish, I would be dead.'

'The man to whom that curved sword once belonged? The man we found next to you? He was your bodyguard?' Nat asked.

'My protector and my friend, since I was a child,' replied the girl sadly, but they noticed she no longer cried. 'They chased us, till the only place to run to was here, but they still caught us in the end. I guess you are running to?'

'Of a sort,' replied Morgan enigmatically.

This evasive response drew a glance from Nat.

'What are we going to do?' she said with determination in her voice.

Nat looked at her and raised an eyebrow. '*Like father, like daughter*', he thought. '*All spit and brass.*'

'Well, first we're going to eat and rest,' replied Morgan in a no-nonsense tone. 'Tomorrow is another day.'

With that, he returned to turning the roasting rabbits.

The girl started to say more, but Nat looked at her with a serious expression and shook his head slowly. Something in his face showed her the man who she first thought was just a boy. She bit off her words before they could escape her tongue and stared into the flickering fire.

Later that night, as his two companions slept the sleep that only the young are capable of, Morgan slipped into another dream trance.

The fighting square was sundered and scattered. Slogging through the bog-like mud, the man he named his true friend, Aden Ap Greylock, ran for his life. With him, ran the Lord Constable, his movements telling of profound exhaustion, and two surviving men at arms. As they ran, their heaving breaths misting in the frigid air, they revolved around each other covering one another's backs with their swords.

As he watched their mammoth struggle, he felt his spirit raging and resisted the compelling urge to fly to their aid or join them in death. Still, he could not, for he knew that every move he made would be instinctively picked up in the mood of the King's army, deciding whether they stood firm in the face of adversity or fled in mass panic.

He stood ten feet clear of the battle line, his eyes and consciousness focussed on his friend, lending him courage, fortitude and energy. His heart leapt in his chest as he saw his companion of old, his noble spirit unbowed, turn back time and time again to drag the staggering Constable out of the path of harm's way. His selfless actions, making a myriad of blood-seeking horsemen sway away from certain death themselves as his sword weaved this way and that. Had he a mind to save himself only, he would have, without doubt, made it to the firm, waiting lines of his fellow guardsmen, but Aden's heart stood made from better stuff. He did not think ever to abandon his striving companions. Cut down savagely from behind, the two remaining men of arms, first one, then two, fell spiralling into the rain-soaked earth. Then the Lord Constable himself, driven far beyond the limits of his stamina fell on hands and knees into the mud. Without hesitation, Aden returned for him, standing with legs splayed and sword singing, until he too was eventually overcome by sheer numbers. Morgan kept the link, feeding his friend his indomitable strength, watching as even ten men struggled to keep him down, but then recognising the hopelessness of his comrade's position, withdrew, feeling the loss as Aden slumped into oblivion.

His friend lay lost, but not dead, as he could still feel the afterglow of the link, so Morgan turned to secure his King's position. Something crashed in on his senses, a heavy, demanding weight of dread. Without further thought, he shouted, as loud a shout as he had ever made:

'Shields! Up Shields! Testudo! Testudo! Cover the King! The King!'

At this fell moment, the fates sprang free the third high treason of the day like a carrion bird unleashed from its cage.

Slicing down with the cold rain, came a deluge of black-feathered arrows, hammering on shields, cutting through armour and burying into unwary flesh. On the left, the traitor lord had, at last, climbed down off of the fence of indecision. With a deceitful heart *and willful intent, he turned his darts onto his liege lord, his anointed king.*

'Close shields! Close shields!' roared Morgan, but the empty place in his consciousness radiating from where the king once stood told him that it was too late.

Racing towards the royal chariot, Morgan pushed through a huddle of shocked, motionless guards, to find the thin, wet form of the royal scribe trying to cradle the body of his king, trying to keep the noble face from sinking into the oily mud.

With a shiver, Morgan climbed up through and broke the surface of his dream trance and emerged into the chilled night air. The fires had burned low, and his heart was heavy with memory. Closing his eyes, he tumbled into a deep sleep, pulling a healing blanket over the past.

They were up and moving again before dawn could reach the bottom of the deep ravine. Stiff, cold, sore and dirty, but filled with resolve after the King Maker's veiled hint that he was not merely running for his life. True to his reputation, there was a purpose in his every action.

'So we're not just running after all. You have a plan?' Nat stated the obvious.

Morgan glanced at him but didn't reply immediately.

'Of course, he has a plan!' the Earl's daughter piped up from the rear. 'He's the famous guard captain. My father always said that he was never without a plan.'

Nat heard the heavy sigh that Morgan emitted and thought to himself that the female copy of the Earl of Marches had transformed herself from the silent princess of tragedy into a loquacious Morgan supporter.

'What's your name, girl?' asked Morgan wearily.

'Elaine, Lord Captain, my name is the Lady Elaine of Bloomsbury.'

Nat coughed loudly.

'Well, my Lady Elaine, the first part of my plan is to find shelter from life-threatening persecution. Then attempt to negotiate a speedy response. Not an easy task, bearing in mind the hard-headed nature of our potential allies. Lastly, I must leave the two of you behind whilst I slip back along our trail to confront my past. I'll fill you in on the rest after that.'

So saying, Morgan spurred his horse forward, pretending not to have noticed the confused glance his two young companions gave each other. As far as they knew, all that lay ahead was a burning, barren land inhabited by lizards, snakes, scorpions, stinging ants, wild beasts and desperate bandits.

CHAPTER VIII

The market was in full swing. Everyone that you might happen to ask would answer that it had always been so. Way back in living memory, every start to the week, even in the official records, you will find it mentioned. But nowhere would you see that it was ever officially approved or that a tax ever levied on its trading. The people saw it as their right as a people born of this land. It had nothing to do with their rulers or their kings. Just one day in every weeks' cycle; Market day.

Things started as was usual and commonplace. It was only two hours after sunrise, yet the large square -situated not far from the river, at the far end of the foreign quarter- stood packed with country farmers and local, city entrepreneurs. The usual noise and bustle of a thriving market were in full cry. Matrons with heads thinly veiled, sporting colours of every variant. Unmarried, young women, mostly raven-haired, but dotted here and there with dyed mops of red and yellow, sashayed from one stall to the next in girly groups or chaperoned by stern-faced widows, sampling and examining various items on sale, mostly without buying. Local toughs and educated young men belonging to well to do families stood idly occupied admiring and soliciting admiration. Pickpockets and beggars wandered about hoping for some opportune opportunity or unguarded offering, all enjoying the only event in this foreign-dominated city that remained unchanged.

A few alert eyes, mostly those belonging to beggars, noticed a few groups of Protectorate soldiers, drifting in at irregular intervals and stopping as if by accident at the cobbled side roads feeding into the market square. They did not offer any threat, but their positioning to the more than casual observer warranted questions on intent. One or two wary beggars slipped away through the milling crowds and disappeared back into the city.

At somewhere nearing mid-morning, the loud stomping noise of iron-studded boot heals carried an early warning of what was approaching. Vendors and buyers at first remained unperturbed as this sound was now daily in their conquered city. However, as a heavy phalanx of armoured, shielded soldiers thundered into the square, gripping thick wooden staves in gauntleted fists and carrying sheathed swords at their hips, turmoil broke out as panicked citizens rushed to get out of their path. Peeling off martially, three separate groups headed for the first stalls they encountered. As the frightened stall owners looked on in trepidation, many would-be bargain hunters attempted to beat a hasty retreat only to find aggressively stationed guards blocking their escape routes at every exit.

There stood, positioned within each of the three military groups, a pair of officious, unsmiling men bearing heavy ledgers. As each group cordoned off and isolated a stall, the officials approached the petrified shopkeepers and demanded.

'Give your name, address and type of wares sold!'

One brave owner stammered back in answer.

'We are all free citizens here! We don't have to answer no questions! We have nought to say.'

'Your claim to freedom lies washed away on a muddy hill. Now answer my questions!' said the tax collector dismissively.

As people started pushing more and more to get out, several grey-robed men slipped in. They immediately began to surreptitiously coordinate the toughs in the square, sending them into the crowds as agitators. Slowly the mood of the market throng began to change. Where there was minutes ago fear, there was now a growing mood of outrage.

The tension was building. You could feel it like a living thing, yet the tax collectors, secure in their civic duty, continued to press.

'If you do not provide what the state requires, we will arrest you forthwith and your goods confiscated!'

'We don't answer to your kind!'

'Why don't you go back to where you came from?'

'We don't want your kind here!'

'Stinking foreigners!'

A flurry of unidentified yells and catcalls streamed out from within the crowd.

The feeling of unrest was beginning to build; palpable, like something deep within a volcano. The crowd was starting to turn nasty. They began to edge forward, hemming in and separating the three divisions of the phalanx. At first, whispers of 'out, out, out' echoed ominously around the confined space. Then, gradually, like rolling thunder, it grew into a calamitous roar of 'Out! Out! Out!' A cry which broke around the square and over the city in a wall of sound. Alarmingly, the Protectorate soldiers, disciplined as they were, started to have a hard time of it and the commanders, belatedly issued the orders for them to withdraw, but it was too late.

From the shaded shutters on the two-storey buildings overlooking the square, came a sudden and devastating hale of steel-tipped arrows. A fifth of the Protectorate's soldiers crumbled under this unexpected assault, many screaming in agony. This hidden attack only fuelled the crowd, who, sensing a weakness, turned into a frenzied mob, ripping savagely into the belly of the hapless soldiers. Even the matrons who some minutes earlier were the epitome of model behaviour and their nubile, young daughters who were playing the game of innocent flirtation, were transformed into harpies. Spitting profanities at the troupers in a guttersnipe, shrill dialect, they tore at them with their very nails which came away bloodied after raking over chain-mailed shirts.

Swinging viciously with their staves and even their swords, the soldiers closed ranks. They did not think that this morning's work would end in conditions equal to and worse than any battlefield. They were mentally unprepared. The guard soldiers, whose job it was to hold the exits had already fled, bent on saving their lives from the ravening mob. The men guarding and protecting the tax collectors, three of whom had already been torn apart by the howling crowd, struggled vainly to retreat in good order. In the end, they dropped their weapons almost to a man, and raced off panic-stricken, with the mob slavering at their heels.

***

'Who gave the order for this debacle to take place?' rasped the governor, his jaw tight with controlled anger.

'The treasury priests, your Excellency,' came the careful reply.

'I see.'

After a short, grim pause, he continued.

'Make sure that the officer who carried out this order of madness without informing me first, is here in front of this desk before this day ends!'

'As you command, Excellency. The god is our keeper.'

The governor studied the short, grizzled sergeant standing in front of him for an icy moment.

'You ran with your detachment, sergeant,' it wasn't a question.

'That or die, sir.'

'I see.'

Another studied pause.

'You hinted earlier that the whole thing smelled of orchestration. Explain.'

'Someone planted agitators to stir up the crowd, sir, plain as my face.'

'Do you have any suspicions, sergeant? Did you detect anything or anyone out of the ordinary?'

'Some conspicuous grey-robed men, conspicuously doing nothing,' the sergeant forgot the title, but the governor didn't seem to have noticed.

'In your opinion, were they behind the orchestration?'

'It's hard to say, sir. As I stated, they weren't doing much.'

'I see.'

'I want notices up informing these people of the immediate imposition of martial law. Make it clear that any public gathering of more than two is forbidden and we will punish any insubordination with incarceration and flogging.'

'At once, Excellency.'

'I also want you to prepare your men to carry out house to house searches on my order.'

'Yes, sir.'

'Thank you, sergeant. You're dismissed.'

'Yes, sir. God is our keeper.'

Left on his own, the governor placed a callused hand to his forehead.

'God spare me from priests!' he muttered. 'Forgive me, god. I know they are your children, but that's the thing. They behave like bloody children!' An interesting thing about those grey-robed men though - something may come of this yet.

***

'You had no choice but to act, Lord Abbot.'

Silence.

'If you hadn't, we would be no different from those who still call themselves the king's councillors. Senile, impotent, all talk but nothing to show but political expediency.'

'You don't have to try to convince me, Patrick, of the rightness of action. The course lay set,' replied the Beggar Abbot gravely. 'However, the price we paid and the toll yet to come was and will be costly.'

'It's the price of war, Lord Abbot.'

'What do we know of war, Patrick? Our general has still not returned.'

'If we wait for him, Lord Abbot, there may be nothing left for him to return to.'

'The opposite is more likely to be true. We have forced their hand. Have you seen those posters?'

'Yes, Lord Abbot.'

'The governor is a hard, arrogant man. A man of action, but he is also a clever man. This skirmish is only the beginning. More will soon follow.'

'We have information he needs, Lord Abbot.'

'Value is relative. Besides, he has a king to play as a pawn, and people, in the end, are fickle.'

CHAPTER IX

They were no longer distant, looming above them, dominating the flat, dust driven plain. The small band of lonely riders felt insignificant as they trekked across the barren expanse, held cupped as they were, in nature's hands. Their faces wrapped in cloths to smother the gusting swirls of spiteful grit and sand whipped up by an unforgiving wind. The majestic, snowcaps of the Black Mountain ranges seemed omnipotent and unassailable, towering above their petty discomforts, blind to their transient ambitions. Animals and men alike heads down, they slogged stoically onwards towards their goal.

The sand and dirt gave way to scrub. Then suddenly, beautiful stretches of copper beech trees, separated now and again by thick, green carpets of fern magically appeared as they climbed, twining upwards between broken boulders laced together with lush, vibrantly coloured vegetation. The pure, otherworldly silence washed their souls and cleansed their minds. Stopping by a stream made for fairy tales, they dismounted and made camp, the tired horses whinnied in relief and drank deeply from the cold, clear waters; the donkey whisked its tail and chomped away oblivious to all.

'Well, here we are at last,' said Nat brightly. 'What next, old man?'

'Onwards and upwards in the morning,' replied Morgan, coaxing a flame into life.

Nat glanced up at the impressive mountain, then back at his mentor.

'All tales say there is no way through these mountains; many have tried, and many have died. So speaks the legends.'

Morgan looked up from his efforts and grinned. A phenomenon Nat had seen only once or twice before. He was taken aback as to how young Morgan's face suddenly appeared.

'Well, young brother, tomorrow will tell,' Morgan said enigmatically.

Nat looked at him closely, shook his head but didn't say any more.

The girl sat silently watching them.

'I'm going to take a bath and wash these clothes. I smell. By the way, so do you two.'

Nat immediately sniffed his armpit and Morgan smiled and replied.

'Tell us when you're done and we'll follow suit. Now is as good a time as any to try to be human again.'

In the ethereal mists of the morning, they continued their climb. It hung eerily over the stream. It drifted between the trees like shifting curtains dividing the land of living from the dead. As they moved higher and higher, the beech trees gave way to pine, filling the air with a lung-clearing scent and a myriad of pine needles blanketed the forest floor, muffling the hoof fall of the animals. Morgan led the way, taking them up one ridge then, without warning or visible sign, changing direction and heading off along what appeared to be a disused animal trail, following the contours of the mountain. After two days of following this seemingly erratic and winding route through pine-covered mountain and valley, Morgan suddenly turned upwards on a rocky, treacherous track.

The trees soon surrendered to hard rock, snow and ice, forcing the travellers to dismount and continue on foot, guiding their mounts behind them. As the journey became increasingly difficult and dangerous, Nat took up position in the rear with the girl Elaine in the middle and Morgan at the point, leading them unerringly on a path that only he knew. Not once did he hesitate or seem unsure. They crested over two snow-filled mountain passes and the third day found them picking their way carefully down a narrow, ice slippery track on the side of a ravine, a path so tight that it would have been difficult for two men to pass each other on it. Making it even more hazardous was the cold, which numbed them right down to the bone. They hardly spoke to each other anymore, just making brief hand gestures when it was time to stop or change direction. Elaine started to develop frostbite on the fingertips of her left hand, the hand she repeatedly used to grip the side of the ice-coated cliff for fear of skidding off the edge of the tiny track.

Somehow Morgan noticed that she was in difficulty and turning, made his way back up to her. Removing the rags protecting both their hands, he covered her delicate fingers with his hard hands and stood motionless for a few minutes. Incredibly, she felt a warm tingling sensation in her hands which, for a brief moment, started to become painful. Then after a spell, the discomfort changed to a delicious warmth which began to spread throughout her whole body, suffusing her with energy and filling her with renewed strength. Without a word, he spun, surefooted and agile, on the narrow track, and continued to lead them downwards. At her back, she felt the reassuring presence of Nat walking behind her donkey and carefully leading his frightened horse.

On the fourth day, they came down onto a damp, moss-covered valley that had tall, pine trees growing on its banks on either side. Morgan followed the winding path of this little valley until they finally emerged onto a small grass-covered plateau overlooking a serene, green lake.

'The Watchers will have seen us by now. It won't take them long to intercept us,' said Morgan in a matter-a-fact voice. 'Ah, here they come.'

They came at them from both sides, bearded men cloaked in green and wearing green leggings. Instead of boots, they wore tough, raw-hide moccasins, and in their hands, they all clasped half-drawn longbows with arrows in fletchings green and purple. They sat their rugged, hardy looking ponies with easy confidence and their eyes were stone flints as they surveyed the trio sat calmly on their mounts.

'How did you find your way through these mountains?' demanded their leader, a curly-haired, middle-aged man with a barrel chest and short muscly legs.

In a steady, polite voice, Morgan replied.

'We rode through the Adamite Pass.'

The men regarded them with a very still silence.

'That pass is only known to the sworn watchers and a few others.'

Morgan did not respond but remained patiently waiting.

'Well!' demanded the leader.

'I was not aware that you had asked a question, son,' replied Morgan evenly.

Before the leader could say anything else, he continued.

'We are refugees from the Kingdom of Granehold. We are here escorting the Lady Elaine, sole surviving heir to the Lord of Marches, into the protection of your King and Queen.'

'The Earl of Marches' daughter astride a donkey!'

'As I said, son, we're refugees.'

'I'm not your son, old man!' spat the barrel-chested leader of the watchers, pushing his chest out a little further.

Nat sniggered.

Bowstrings creaked as tense arms pulled back on them a little harder and barbed arrowheads lifted towards the perceived intruders.

'Easy, gentlemen,' said Morgan without change of tone or expression. 'If I remember correctly, it has always been the policy of your rulers to welcome those bereft of home and country. In truth, it lays enshrined in marble on the walls of your Piazza della Pace.'

A shocked silence travelled through the watchers.

'What do you know about our laws, stranger? And who are you?' demanded the leader with some unease in his voice.

'The answer to those questions are for the ears only of your King and Queen,' replied Morgan with a hinted timbre of command in his voice. 'I formally request that as ambassador to a foreign and sovereign state that you carry out your duty as a border watcher and escort us into their presence without further delay.'

The leader tightened his lips in anger but made the formal reply of acknowledgement.

'As you request, so shall it be, Ambassador.'

Uttering a quick succession of terse commands, four young watchers moved their ponies forward and around the party and started to usher them forward.

Halting his horse for a moment, Morgan directed his words directly at the prickly leader of the watchers.

'A word of forewarning, captain, keep your eyes open extra wide and your bows strongly drawn for the next visitor to your nation from this path is a thing out of every man's nightmare. If you cannot bring it down from afar, give it a wide birth. Do not let pride be your fall, captain. Heed well my words.'

With that, he wheeled his horse about and spurred it forward before the bewildered captain could comment.

Three days later, a bored gate sergeant on his second posting to the walls that week was hailed by a private onto the parapet over the city gate.

'Hope this is good!' he grumbled. 'I've just made myself a cup of good, strong tea.'

'I think those are Watchers coming, sarge.'

Shading his eyes from the hot, mid-day sun with his hands, he muttered again.

'By my grandmother's hairy tits, I think you are right!'

Seeing the elusive and legendary Watchers in the capital was a rare sight, as they only appeared when there was real danger or threat to the nation, preferring to send messages to the rulers via third parties.

'Wonder what brings these dandies down our road?'

'It looks like they are riding escort.'

'Well, kick my arse, Mr bloody Hawkeye! I think you have it right again!'

Racing down the stone stairs, the sergeant bellowed out for a welcoming detachment to assemble at the gate. He wasn't going to miss this for all the world.

'Show a leg, ladies!' barked the sergeant. 'Let these boys in green see what true men look like! Form up! Form up! Two columns, one on either side of the gate posts. Come on! Look lively! Quick march!'

Assembled smartly in front of the city gate, luckily the quietest time of day as most people had just started their siesta, the sergeant keenly observed the approaching party. At the centre rode a man of middle years, with deep, sun-browned skin, of about 5' 10' in height, and a sinewy, rock hard body. 'Not a man to mess with,' thought the sergeant. Next to him rode a broad-shouldered youth, athletic and robust, his handsome face carrying a natural smile, but his eyes missed nothing. Next to the youth, incongruously rode a beautiful, elegant, red-headed girl on a little donkey, her full, lustrous head of hair pushed through a thin make-shift poncho, which lay belted off at the waist. On either side of the small party rode two Watchers on rugged ponies, sporting faces devoid of all humour.

'What brings the Watchers to our gates in this time of peace?' greeted the sergeant, invoking the age-old greetings for the sentinels of the kingdom's borders.

'Peace still reigns,' drawled the reply from the young Watcher riding on the left. 'We are here to present an ambassador from the Kingdom of Granehold to our Majesties.'

'May you pass through our gates and find shade and water,' responded the gate sergeant, ending the ritual. Then his face froze in shock for as they passed the lean, middle-aged man, the ambassador he presumed, gave a quick hand signal of greeting. The shock was not for the hand greeting in itself. The surprise lay in the delivery of the secret code of the Guardians of the Wall. This closely guarded signal belonged to the guild to which the sergeant belonged, and no one expected a stranger to use it. The companions soon found themselves hastily escorted to the palace guest quarters. After giving further introductions to the officials there, the Watchers hastily departed without so much as a farewell.

'Friendly bunch,' Nat muttered.

They were well treated, greeted courteously, taken to the bathhouse and given fresh, clean clothing, fed a delicious, hot meal, then showed to private rooms adjacent to each other.

Lady Elaine was in excellent spirits, despite being tired. Without knocking, she bustled into the room that Morgan and Nat were sharing and joined them on a polished wood balcony, raised above a wonderfully fragrant herb garden.

They sat together in companionable silence as the late afternoon wore into evening, breathing in the scents of the little garden.

'I must say, Morgan,' said Elaine, 'I've never seen you so relaxed as this before.'

'And very familiar in a place that should be strange,' muttered Nat.

Morgan smiled at them but did not offer a comment.

'When do you think their majesties will give us an audience?' asked Elaine.

'Courtesy requires that they do so sometime tomorrow morning,' answered Morgan.

'You see, there he goes again,' muttered Nat. 'Too darned familiar.'

Halfway through the following morning, true to Morgan's prediction, a court official arrived with the summons for them to attend the King and Queen. Lady Elaine was excited and set about organising and fussing over the appearance of the two patient men.

'You have to give an impressive first impression. Remember we are supposed to be ambassadors.'

'We?' enquired Nat with a raised eyebrow.

'Well, Morgan is. You're just a ruffian,' flew in the tart reply.

With another brief smile for his two young charges, Morgan turned and strode purposefully away, the court official hurrying to catch up with him.

'This way, Ambassador,' he stuttered, flustered by the odd turn of events.

As they approached the double-winged and guarded doors leading into the throne room, Morgan stopped, allowing the harried official to adjust his robe of state hurriedly and take the lead.

With a pompous 'harrumph', he knocked three times on the ponderous, wooden doors and pushed them open with long, skinny arms. With a surprisingly loud and deep voice, he boomed:

'The Lord Ambassador of Granehold, the Lady Elaine, daughter to the illustrious Earl of Marches, and company.'

Nat rolled his eyes.

The throne room was large, filled with light and gleamed of polished wood; a favourite of this court it seemed. Directly across from the door, on a raised dais of two steps, stood two thrones side by side, on which sat two elderly monarchs - on a third throne, placed on the lower level, primly perched a veritably ancient, royal looking lady. More like a withered bird of prey than a lady, if truth be told.

Ushered forward by the spindly court official, the companions walked across the mirrored floor, giving them the impression of gliding over still water. As they neared the dais, they noticed four motionless guardians standing in the shadows of four ebony pillars between which the thrones sat broodingly and over which lay stretched a large, green canopy, linking them. The guardians, armoured in a manner reminiscent of that of the 'Brotherhood of the King's Bodyguard' created to protect a regent long dead and a kingdom many miles away. Unusually, these four guardians did not stare straight ahead but followed the advancement of the trio with watchful eyes.

'Bend the knee,' instructed the court official.

No one paid him any notice.

'Bend the knee! Bend the knee!' he whispered urgently and frantically.

Morgan, his eyes studying the royal trio in a fashion which must have broken at least one of the rules of protocol, bent from the waist and executed a perfect, elegant and courteous half bow. Beside him, Lady Elaine dipped into a sweet and proper curtsy. Nat hovered behind them with an open grin on his face.

The elderly, royal couple remained impassive; their thoughts laid hidden. Still, the ancient was studying Morgan with an intense stare. Even for a person held in such an august position, one could interpret her regard as rude. Morgan, however, seemed unaware. Addressing the king and queen, he said:

'Your Majesties, we have fled here to your borders seeking protection for this young lady, sole living heir to the valiant Earl of Marches, and with the death of our king and many of his nobles, a possible heir to the throne of Granehold.'

In a dusty voice, the queen answered:

'The Kings of Granehold are now ashes, Ambassador. Their kingdom, scattered before the winds of an ambitious Protectorate. Why should we risk their ire by harbouring this fugitive; this mere slip of….'

The queen cut off her words as the ancient woman seated next to her tottered to her feet, and on creaking knees moved slowly and purposefully down the step of the dais, her hawk-like eyes riveted on Morgan.

'Grandmother?' said the queen with confusion and concern in her voice.

The old woman, now clearly identified as a mother of queens, ignored her. Stopping in front of Morgan, she stared luminously up at him for an uncomfortable breadth of time. Suddenly, and to the shocked astonishment to all present, she fell to her knees before him and cried:

'Your Majesty, welcome home!'

CHAPTER X

Krarl felt burning rage building rapidly inside him like hot magma boiling upwards, bursting into his chest.

'There isn't a path through these mountains, Lord Krarl. The fugitives are fleeing to certain death. Our remit stops here,' said the unit leader, trying his best to reason with the disturbing beast.

'He Knoores. We folloore,' growled Krarl in response.

'Be that as it may, our orders were to hunt them down within the borders of this godless land. Not to encroach on other guessed at kingdoms and risk nervous retaliation. On this unfortunate crossroad is not the time to build escalation.'

Krarl had had enough. His only warning was a chilling, wet snarl.

With gnarled hands, tipped with dirty, dark brown talons, he ripped out the throat of the unit leader in a messy spray of arterial blood. The movement was so fast that the cavalry soldier did not know that he was dead, and was still trying to understand why he was falling from his horse when he thumped headfirst into the dirt. The other eight members of the unit stood frozen in shock at the sudden and unexpected assault. Krarl did not wait. With a howl of savage glee, he bounded onto a large rock then flung himself sideways into the nearest horse, knocking the hapless animal off its feet and into the other horses standing next to it. The result was a pandemonium of rearing, snorting, wild-eyed animals, doing everything they could to escape this primitive attack. Krarl followed the horse down as it fell, and as it hit the ground with a bone-crushing jar, he stomped on the trapped trouper's head with a heavy, booted foot and leapt at the remaining seven, who sat so distracted in trying to control their panicked mounts, that they offered little resistance. Like a demon from the pits of hell he leapt and twisted among the desperate unit, ripping and slashing in a gore-filled frenzy till they all lay dead and twitching in the dust, their spirits fleeing their cooling bodies in horror. Krarl remained still for a moment, absently licking his bloodied fingers, and calmly surveying the brooding mountains towering above him. Now he hunted alone.

Three nights after that gruesome event, on the other side of the mountains, three young Watchers on night patrol noticed a slithering movement at the entrance to the pass.

The night was chilly, with a crisp hoar frost coating the ground and the leaves of the bushes. The hard, glacial, crescent moon above, glared down sharply from a black sky dotted with a few diamond stars. Pulling their green cloaks close, they scanned the terrain below them with eyes trained to sift and identify any anomaly. There was something slightly out of place. There, in the shape of an unmoving shadow. Crouched eerily beneath a stunted tree at the bottom of the valley, lurked an oddity. Everything had a rhythm, a rhythm that breathed with all things in nature around it.

This shadow did not have a rhythm; it was far too still, unnatural. With slow, careful movements, the three Watchers eased arrows from their oiled, leather sheaths and notched them to the durable strings of their longbows. Taking a deep, even breath, they extended their bows to the full extent with their hooked fingers holding their bowstrings taut just below their earlobes. Releasing both breath and bowstring in a smooth fluid motion, they sent their barbed arrows cutting straight at the strange shadow. With a blur of movement almost too fast to follow, the shadow ducked and twisted right, the shafts meant for it thudding into the rough bark of the tree behind.

Now exposed by the eye of the icy moon, the Watchers beheld a sinewy, man-like shape, with its head covered by a dark cowl. Luminous eyes glared up at them balefully, even if no normal man could see them, given their superb cover and the conditions of the night. Grimly the trio sent barrage after barrage of swift darts lancing after the creature, but fiendishly it evaded them all. Even so, it was driven back up the mountain path until with a chilling howl of frustration and rage, it dropped onto all fours and bounded back to whence it came.

'Fuck!' breathed one of the watchers, wiping with the back of a shaking hand the clammy sweat running from his forehead.

'Not bloody human!' joined in his companion. 'Better warn the captain to double the patrols. The ambassador's caution lies understated.'

Two nights later, Krarl made a second attempt to break through the cordon of Watchers. The first sign that something unusual was happening was at about 3 in the morning. One of the veteran Watchers, a rough man with a thick neck and built like a wrestler, a man who never exhibited signs of fear under any condition, suddenly started to look around him like a harried sage fowl. His eyes wide and darting, and his bald head glistening with sweat, he stood rooted and trembling, holding onto his yew shaft with a white-knuckled grip. Through a clenched jaw, straining with the effort to reassert self-control, he ground out words only expected from the mouth of a madman, with a harsh, rasping whisper.

'Something is in my head, Captain! It's coming! Coming for me!'

'Weapons out!' commanded the captain in a tight, tense voice.

Krarl came at high speed. His plan was simple, terror and swiftness.

With no attempt at stealth, Krarl came tearing down the mountain trail. His hood flew back, revealing a big, heavy-boned face, covered in coarse, chestnut hair and a wide mouth filled with large, yellowed teeth with disconcertingly overlong canines. He made no sound, and the kingdom's border guardians fought the urge to run as he closed the distance between them at an inhuman rate.

'Hold. Hold,' commanded the Watchers' captain.

Krarl's entire focus was now on the narrow path that would take him past the Sacred Lake of Birth, where all spirits passed through the parted legs of the goddess before taking the form of men, its black waters now mirroring the night sky, revealing the presence of that alternate world. Once through that path, he could lose these annoying guardians with ease. The captain and his men had another take on this objective.

Standing on high ground, the Watchers sent shaft after shaft down on the streaking creature, until finally, two arrows struck its chest with a glancing blow, and a third embedded itself into a naked thigh. With a yelp like that of a beaten dog, the thing veered off. Executing an impossible swivel, it headed back towards the safety of the mountain with even greater haste, zigzagging all the way.

'I think I've pissed myself!' drifted across an anonymous voice in the dark.

Relieved and nervous laughter followed.

Krarl sat on a rock high up on the mountain track. Mewling to himself, he gripped the arrow in his thigh and with a deep insuck of breath, ripped it free, making a muted yowling sound as he did so. With the barb free of his flesh, he ignored the torn and bleeding wound and examined the broken links of his hauberk on his chest. He seemed more concerned with the damaged metal links than the weeping flesh underneath. With a grunt, he settled back onto the cold, hard rock, licked his fingers and fell into a deep sleep. He would wait for the One to come to him since he couldn't get to the One.

***

Morgan was never just merely a man. His presence had always seemed to be everywhere. In his first memories, he was there. In his sword lessons, he was there. He taught him the art of statecraft - the art of being a king. He taught him too well. When the mantle had finally fallen onto his shoulders, he thought that he knew it all. He was very wrong. With every action, there is a consequence. A king must always remember that his purpose is to serve his people. He could still hear his old friend and mentor saying those words. Why did he not heed them?

The tall, thin man sat in a finely crafted rocking chair in front of the open window with a leather-bound book lying open on his blanket-covered lap. His eyes were half-closed as he enjoyed the warmth of the morning sun playing across his bearded face. He considered himself an aesthete. For a long time now, he had devoted his life to beauty. He hated ugliness; the ugliness of thought, the ugliness of action, the ugliness of being. Through ambition and hubris, he had become a prisoner of deformity - a passive prostitute to other men's schemes. All he wanted was the peace of mind to contemplate all that was beautiful. Deep down inside, he knew that like beauty, this wish was an illusion.

'Your Majesty, I have some disturbing news that you may wish to hear.'

'What news is this, Alfred? Please, do tell. Reality has a way of finding me wherever I may try to hide.'

'There have been rumours of disturbances among your subjects, Sire. They protest against the imposition of taxes, and many deaths and fatalities have occurred. Now the blanket of martial law smothers them and leaves them even more to smoulder. This land is in dire need of their king and his guiding hand.'

'The king they will get, Alfred, is only a figurehead. His hands lie at his feet, amputated.'

'This is not so, your Majesty! In three days hence your coronation stands set to take place. The people and preparations lie ready and waiting to receive your grand entrance. The occasion will be a spectacular rebirth, sire! You will lead us again like your father and your grandfather, once did'.

'Leave me, Alfred,' wearily replied the king yet to be crowned. 'Oh, and Alfred!'

'Yes, my liege?'

'Thank you.'

Riot, civil disobedience, oppression, selfishness and war; ugliness! They had a way of finding him, just like dog shit on his doorstep. I only wish to say goodbye to my brother. I want nothing more but to have my family again; to have my home once again. The sun had lost its beauty for the day. Ugliness always seems to win in the end.

***

'He has to be removed.'

'That would be a dangerous action.'

'Is it not more dangerous to have the people drugged with false hope and misdirection?'

'You are right, of course, Lord Abbot, but this brings to mind the phrase 'stirring up a hornet's nest'.

'Time is not on our side. We have to do this necessary thing before the puppet has a crown fixed on his unworthy head. Our hand, once again, has been forced. I don't like it any better than you do, Elisha, but over careful consideration is not an option.'

The tall, athletic and elegant woman sauntering beside Timothy nodded, her long, jet black hair falling like a curtain over her furrowed brow. As she brushed it away absently, she said.

'Morgan would not take kindly to such an action.'

'Ap Heston is not here with us. He is running for his life with a monster on his tail! Look, Elisha, regicide does not sit comfortably on my conscience, but the Protectorate is trying to force poisoned honey down our throats.'

'He is of the true line of kings. There is no one left more legitimate than he. Why not abduct him? Killing our very own king sticks cloyingly in my throat.'

'He is not our king! If I remember correctly, ineptitude led to his abdication. We cannot kidnap him. The governor would tear this city apart stone by stone to find him, and many of our own would help him do so!'

'You refer to the councillors?'

'Yes, them and more, ambition and grasping greed makes strange bedfellows.'

They walked in silence for a few minutes, their footsteps echoing on the stone paving of an upper floor balcony surrounding and overlooking an inner courtyard. No one could see them there even if they were to clamber up onto the baked, clay tiles of the roofs.

'I take it that you already have a plan, Lord Abbot.'

'Yes, Elisha, I have a plan. You are the best that we have, dear girl. You will have to do this personally.'

'Yes, I knew this when you called me here.'

'There is a strong possibility that you might not be able to get away.'

'Yes, this too I already know.'

'I am sorry, Elisha. Come, we have lots to discuss.'

'Yes, Lord Abbot, we have.'

***

'Yes, Excellency, we have received and are continuing to receive official requests asking to be guests at the coronation. In fact, not only this morning I sent a refusal to that interfering ex-chamberlain, asking for permission to visit the king in his chambers for a private meeting and show of support.'

'Ah, and in whose name did you send this denial, Father?'

'I sent it in the name of the Holy Conclave, Excellency, with their seal of authority stamped on it.'

'Ah, I see. God is our keeper. Thank you for your diligence, Father. Please send out another reply rescinding that of the Holy Conclave forthwith. And Father, my stamp of authority will be in the ascendancy on this one.'

'But Excellency! I must protest, the…'

'These pretenders swim and connive in murky waters, Father. I need them to surface so that I can see them. I also need these foolish, riotous people to feel a sense of national unity. This distasteful display is important for us to govern them. Do you understand? Send the letter granting acceptance.'

'Yes, Excellency.'

'And Father.'

'Yes, Excellency?'

'Always inform me first before acting.'

'Yes, Excellency.'

'Is there anything else that I should know, Father? What of the hunting pack? Any news?'

'The express messengers sent to communicate with the unit leader have not yet reported back, Excellency.'

'This is causing me some concern. Entrusting anything into the hands of this creature Krarl, causes me concern. Let me immediately know as you learn anything.'

'Yes, Excellency.'

'One more thing, Father, prepare and despatch a scouting unit to have a closer look at these Black Mountains. They give me an annoying itch.'

'They are a dead-end, Excellency, the end of the world. The records of the Holy Conclave asserts…'

'Humour me, Father. Send out the scouts.'

'Yes, Excellency. Is that all, Excellency?'

'Yes, Father. Thank you.'

***

The Earl of Greendale had been working excessively hard on the arrangements for the upcoming coronation. Although exhausted, he was pleased to see that he had lost some weight. He was even more delighted to see that his stubborn, pig-headed cousin had come around to some degree to his way of thinking and was beginning to rally around the rightful king. His aid and that of the council had made his exertions much more bearable.

The Protectorate too was very co-operative. They had provided nearly everything that he had requested. Supplies, equipment, even the required labour, were all at hand. Everything foreseen was on schedule. The only flea in the ointment was, in fact, the king himself. He seemed somewhat vacant and at times dismissive of the whole grand affair, not taking the considerable import of it at all seriously. Still, he was confident that he too, in time, would come around. Life was beginning to be as it should. Whistling to himself, he waddled off to prepare the meeting between the king and some members of the council of chambers, something that the governor himself had put his seal of approval to.

CHAPTER XI

Morgan sat in their assigned quarters with both Nat and Elaine facing him. He tried to ignore their open stares, Nat with a perplexed frown on his face, and Elaine with a concerned and troubled expression of uncertainty on hers. The day had not gone as expected.

You could have heard a pin drop. In truth, the scarecrow dressed up as the court official let fall his baton with a loud clatter. Morgan stared down at the unmoving, venerable mother of queens at his feet; a quizzical expression etched on his face as if he were struggling to remember something. He smoothly got down on his knees before the kneeling, royal grandmother, and took her frail hand in a gentle grip. Leaning forward, he looked deeply into her eyes.

'What is your name, child?' he asked softly. 'Something in your eyes tells me that I should know you.'

'You are my king. You promised me that you would return. I sat on your knee on that last day. My name is Deema. Princess Urchin you called me then.'

Morgan's memory, like the stuck hand of a clock, clicked back in time.

'Here you are my little princess urchin, why such a sad face?'

'Why must you leave, grandfather?'

'People, my child, even the best of them, will understand and accept only so much. Then superstition and fear take over. I have to go before this happens.'

'I don't understand, grandfather.'

'You will, my little urchin. And when you do, I shall return to visit you. Remember, always, you were born to be a queen.'

The warmth of Morgan's smile filled the room with calmness.

'Ah, little urchin, I've kept my promise then. I'm back.'

A collective intake of breath vibrated throughout the chamber as the mother of queens, with a huge sob, wrapped her arms around Morgan and buried her face into his neck.

'Leave us now!' commanded the king, surging to his feet.

Immediately, the bemused bodyguards snapped forward, ushering the uncertain courtiers outside of the throne room and closed the doors firmly behind them. The only ones allowed to remain were the now frozen, open-mouthed court official, whom everyone it seemed, had forgotten. Positioned around him were the royal guards, the reigning monarchs, Nat, Elaine, and of course, Morgan and the queen grandmother. These last two were still locked in an embrace, oblivious to all around them.

'What is this nonsense all about, grandmother!' continued the king, stepping down from the dais with indignant disapproval stamped all over his face. 'And you Ambassador, this is unseemly. Who in the name of heaven are you? Get up, man, and release the royal person whom you are holding in such a familiar manner!'

'Shush, Clarence,' said the queen distractedly, now, in turn, studying Morgan's face intently.

'But Harriet, this behaviour is most improper!'

Ignoring the king's pomposity, the dignified queen turned to one of the royal bodyguards and commanded in a quiet voice.

'Go to my royal chamber and fetch me the painting hanging over the side table, would you please?'

Snapping his heels together and spinning on the balls of his feet, the guard left in haste. The king's eyes followed his departing back in befuddlement, but he kept his mouth closed this time.

'Ambassador,' the queen continued in her quiet, dry voice, 'are you acquainted in some way with our royal grandmother?'

Morgan flowed to his feet, bringing with him the old lady who still refused to let him go as if she were still that little girl of ages past, caught up in a time-bubble within the circle of his arms.

'This is not a thing easy to explain, your Majesty, but yes, we once knew each other in a past life.'

'She's probably his wife, the old bugger,' muttered Nat under his breath.

Morgan turned slightly to look at him.

'My granddaughter, actually,' he said matter-of-factly.

Nat turned white, and the king sputtered, outraged.

The queen continued to regard Morgan steadily, filling the room with a very uncomfortable silence, broken thankfully, by the noisy return of the guardsman as he manhandled a large, golden framed picture through the heavy doors. No-one moved to help him.

'Good, finally,' said the queen. 'Let's see what we have here. Be a good man and hold this portrait next to our honoured ambassador, would you please?'

Quietly looking out from the portrait was a royal personage with the exact likeness of Morgan.

'Well kick my bum,' muttered Nat.

No one else could think of anything else to say.

After a long pause, the king exclaimed.

'This is madness! Look, it's not possible! There must be some logical explanation.'

The queen looked at her husband and said.

'Fair enough, Clarence. Please, tell me what it is.'

'Well! Well! It's obvious that… Well, it's clear that…'

'I see,' said the queen.

'Ladies and gentlemen,' said the queen, moving swiftly on, 'you see before you the true likeness of King Leonidas the Lawbreaker. Why such a strange title? Well, it wasn't because he had little respect for legal matters, but because he was a reformer. He ruled and re-fashioned our little, sheltered kingdom for ninety years. Then one day, so the records say, he passed the crown onto his youngest daughter through a written and signed deed and disappeared. No one knows what became of him. Through the line of women, we have ruled in his name ever since. Once beset by many savage enemies, now none can cross our border, and if they did, they would find a trained army that has not seen defeat since this man ascended the throne. I am sorry, but this little history was necessary for as you can see, our ambassador bears a remarkable and uncanny resemblance to our beloved king of old. My equally remarkable grandmother, queen in her time, believes, unlikely as it seems, that the two are the same. I am of the leaning to dismiss this belief, but my grandmother is no one's fool, and her mind remains one of the sharpest in the kingdom, so we are bound to look closely at her claim. I, therefore, ask that our valued guests return to their quarters while we take time to deliberate this unexpected matter more closely. This audience is over.'

'Always knew you were an old bugger,' Nat said to Morgan in a voice laden with gravitas and wisdom. 'Your joints, you see. They give the game away. Stiff and slow…'

Before he could go any further in this vein, Elaine cut in.

'Morgan is all this true? I mean…This would mean that you're terribly old? I mean, is it true?'

'Yes, child,' said Morgan simply. 'I am different from most. In reality, there is only one other like me.'

He did not say this in a manner of boasting. He said it calmly, almost with a heavy sadness.

The two young companions glanced at each other, lost for words.

'What shall we do now?' asked Elaine.

'Do? We wait. I am here as an ambassador to a foreign court. You are here seeking sanctuary as heir to the crown of an invaded kingdom. Nat is my companion in arms and one of the last survivors of a foreign king's royal bodyguards. We make no further claim than this. We wait for now.'

'How long?' asked Elaine.

'The Queen is wise, competent and capable. Events caught her by surprise. So were we all. It won't happen again. She will re-call us when she sits prepared. It won't take her long.'

This statement proved to be correct for within two days a very subdued court official, he of the skinny arms, turned up at their door with a royal request for them to attend the court for a private meeting within the hour. The poor fellow was even more flustered than before and seemed very uncertain as to how to address Morgan. Seeing his obvious discomfort, Morgan said:

'You have the look of a young scribe from the Hariban mountain stronghold. His name was Hector if I recall correctly.'

Reluctantly turning his shifting gaze on Morgan, the nervous official answered in a wavering and tremulous voice.

'My great, great grandfather's name was Hector, and he came here from Hariban keep. My family has served the royal court ever since.'

'Ah,' said Morgan, giving the official a warm smile.

This last proved too much for the old fellow. Without another word, he turned and bolted down the passageway, his gown flapping.

'That one was not made for the battlefield,' observed Nat in a mock-serious tone.

'Don't make fun of him. All of us are not ruffians like you,' responded Elaine with a smile.

It didn't take long for them to get ready. In reality, the companions had already been waiting for a few days. Morgan led the way to the throne room as the old official had failed to reappear. It was clear that the man had been traumatised by the possibility of dealing face to face with the legendary king from the time of his great, great grandfather. But then again, none of them at this moment wanted to confront this possibility. It created too many questions, and hearing the answers might prove to be a very uncomfortable experience. Only Morgan really knew, and was he prepared to tell?

The Queen watched the iron-grey man stalk through the winged doors ahead of his two charges. His movements were controlled and calm, yet she had the impression of a hunter, a ferocious and powerful jaguar, a jungle cat, hidden under his skin and rock-solid, sinewy muscles. He was dangerous; she could feel it, palpable. What was the real reason for him being here? Her grandmother, a queen of steel in her time, still had a formidable mind. She had made it clear that she was not some impressionable, old woman who had let her dream overcome her, a desire to see her king, her great-grandfather, fulfil his promise. A promise made to a little girl.

'Think what you like, child. Act as you will as reigning regent, but my business with my grandfather is mine to pursue as I see fit. Rule your kingdom, but stay clear of my private affairs.'

She would do just that, but she would let no man, risen ghost king, imposter or sorcerer, hurt her grandmother despite her straight-talking words.

'Welcome back to our presence, Ambassador, Lady Elaine, royal guardian.' She favoured Nat with a smile.

All three bowed in unison.

'Ambassador, what is it that you want from us? I will be honest; your appearance among us is a source of some discomfort.' Her smile disappeared.

'Your Majesty, I understand, but as you already know, we represent the assaulted Kingdom of Granehold; assaulted by an aggressive state bent on devouring others in the name of their god. They do not respect borders, they do not respect independent kingdoms and their people, and they do not respect secular governments. Their god drives them ever onwards.'

'We already have information on this, Ambassador. At the risk of repeating ourselves, what do you want from us?'

'I request your protection for our Elaine. I request that you lend us aid in establishing a bridgehead to our nation in order to drive out these invaders and not allow them the time to cast a jaundiced eye on your peaceful kingdom. As for myself, I ask nothing, but you allow me to play a part in coordinating the reclamation of our country, and return it to rightful rule.'

'Very laudable, Ambassador, but if we were to grant you royal arms in this venture what guarantee do we have that you would not retrace your steps with mal intent driven by self-interest at some later date?'

'None but my word as a man, your Majesty,' replied Morgan grimly. 'Your Majesty, I ask a boon, if I may. I would like to have your permission to address your royal guard captain?'

'Towards what end, Ambassador? Your request is most unusual.'

'Please, your Majesty, grant me your forbearance.'

After a pause through which she regarded Morgan steadily, the Queen replied.

'Very well, Ambassador, but there had better be a point to this,' she warned.

With a respectful nod, Morgan turned to face the captain of the Queen's bodyguards, his fingers weaving a silent message which said:

'Greetings honourable foe; grant me fair combat. Two others of your choosing against me.'

The captain started, visibly off-balanced by Morgan's knowledge of the secret, hand code of the initiates to the Queen's bodyguards. He was slow to react, his eyes staring at Morgan's hands. With an effort of will, he returned the ritual response in code.

'Well met, honourable foe, your challenge is accepted.'

Without preamble, the captain and two of his men drew their swords and flew with deadly intent at the unarmed Morgan. The King, ignorant of the exchange between the two, staggered to his feet. A look of horror painted on his face. The queen held up a calm hand to forestall him. Nat swiftly guided the alarmed Elaine back out of harm's way. He knew what his mentor was capable of.

At first, Morgan did not move. His gaze was fixed on nothing as if he stood lost within himself. Nat watched unfooled – he recognised Morgan's stance for what it was, remaining open on all sides. The guard captain reached him first, his sword slashing down in a violent blur of motion. Morgan was no longer there. Faster than the eye could follow, he pivoted under the downward slash of the sharp-edged weapon, then straightening alongside the surprised captain, Morgan caught his wrist. With his right palm, he pressed firmly down on the back of the unfortunate fellow's sword hand, locking his wrist and stripping him neatly of his weapon. Continuing in a smooth flow of motion, Morgan glided sideways, hitting the captain in his back and side with his shoulder, sending the floundering warrior flying across the chamber, crashing to the floor. Again, without pause, he spun back, deflected the downward stroke of the following guard with his newly captured sword, and turning in such a position that the final guard could not get at him, disarmed his second opponent with a circular, flick of his wrist. Stepping forward, he seized the surprised fellow by his armoured chest and hurled him into his companion as if he weighed the same as a child, sending them both sprawling heavily to the polished wood flooring to join their captain.

'Three seconds to end game,' muttered Nat.

The other onlookers, King, Queen, Elaine and the other guards were stunned into astonished silence by the utter dismantling of three of the most elite and highly trained warriors in the land.

Morgan, his breath even and calm, turned to the queen and said.

'This is who I am. Who I was lies buried in the Mausoleum of Kings underneath this palace. My word and my sword are things of iron. My word I have given to you. My sword lies given in service to another kingdom.'

'You have made your point,' said the queen quietly. 'We will think carefully about your requests. This audience stands concluded.'

Morgan spent the next few days gently fending off questions from his two companions, mostly from an anxious and even more bewildered Elaine, but also a couple of frivolous ones from a curious Nat.

'So how old are you, then, old man?'

'I'm not actually quite sure, but definitely older than you, without a doubt.'

With this, Nat would nod his head slowly and sagely as if it were the wisest answer he had ever received. Morgan knew that if Nat had suddenly learned that he was, in fact, the goddess of fertility it would not affect his opinion of him in the least. He was a very rare diamond. You would have to look far and hard to find another like him. As far as Nat was concerned, Morgan was family. And that was that.

'Nat, I need to return to the mountains for a few days while the queen and her advisors deliberate.'

'You are speaking of the tracker on our scent? Is he perhaps someone from your past?'

'Yes. He needs confronting. By me.'

'Ask, and I will walk beside you willingly as always.'

'With my eyes closed, I know this, but I do not ask. I must do this alone.'

Nat looked intensely at his mentor for a moment, then nodded, offering no further comment.

'Stay next to our Lady Elaine whilst I'm away. Guard her well.'

***

The city was a hive of activity, by night, by day, things that were accepted and likewise, others that stood unacceptable. The citizens remained polarised. Partisanship was the order of events, or better yet, the disorder of the day. What on paper was a small thing to implement, had mushroomed into the undoable. Everything seemed transformed into a nightmare of law and order for the governor. He had expected the rise of factions for and against the crowning of a new king. However, what he now had before him was a powder keg of a city. In his mind's eye, he could see a slow-burning match heading towards it. Adding to this explosive cocktail was the increasing interference of the Holy Conclave, side-tracking the myriad of administrative priests on agendas baffling to his ordered, military mind. Then there was the king to be himself, who showed very little enthusiasm or indeed, interest in this grand opportunity, treating it like that of a reluctant bride forced to marry her cousin for the sake of the family honour - unwanted but inevitable. Twice already he had had to send out his specialist, urban squad, trained to correct civil disobedience with brutal efficiency, to quash rioting in two separate quarters. This foray was since the debacle in the marketplace, sparked off by priests with their very own fanatical objectives.

At least the collaborator, Greendale, had done a marvellous job with the organisation for the coronation, and everything was in place for the event. The painted temple devoted to their heathen goddess of order and civic pride already seized by the Conclave days after the city had fallen. It would now be the setting and show-piece for the crowning; a crowning with a brand new ceremony in the name of the true god, created to accompany it. Tomorrow was the big day. Already, brightly coloured bunting danced energetically in the fresh, morning breeze, strung from rooftop to rooftop, crisscrossing noisy thoroughfares crowded with revellers, their festive spirits buoyed up by illicit alcohol and forbidden minstrels. The priests were unhappy, but let the ungodly have their moment of fun. Give them a little of what they want; then they will be ripe for us to take what we need.

'Excellency!'

His thoughts flew out the window. Turning, he forestalled the sour twist that was starting to form around his mouth, with a mental effort.

'Excellency, the Conclave is wondering why the decree forbidding married women to traipse around in public with their hair unbound is not yet issued! It's a sin before god for them to go around freely, bearing the sign of prostitution!'

'All in good time, Father. They are but wayward children. We will guide them step by step. And father,' he continued, holding up his hand to stop the priest whose mouth had opened in the prelude to ploughing on. 'Did the rehearsal with the King go well? Did it proceed as planned?'

'The Conclave does not like the idea of sanctioning kings, Excellency. It is ungodly! The rehearsal went well, however. The King said his words without fault.'

'Well done, Father. Please relay my thanks to the Conclave for their wise advice and patience.'

In a sign of dismissal, the governor turned his back to the priest and looked out of the window.

Yes, at first glance, the citizenry seemed to be gaily celebrating the prospect of gaining a new king, but they had also rejoiced at the execution of one of their heroes. They were an unruly and troublesome lot, given to passion, and what in one instance appeared to be joy and happiness, could turn at the drop of a hat, without any visible provocation, into an ugly destructive mob. It happened before, and he was sure it would happen again.

The next day, Coronation day, started quietly. It was an official labour free day, and people had stayed up well into the night celebrating in whatever form they chose. As the sun's warmth slowly spread along the deserted streets, stray individuals visibly meandered along, making their way to their homes or wherever it is that they were wont to sleep. Curfew and martial law lay relaxed for this national occasion, and so far only drunken fights had broken out here and there. Street cleaners were already about, tidying and sweeping the public thoroughfares, their carts and brushes making subdued noises in the morning light. As the day progressed, unit patrols were becoming more and more visible, and hawkers who despite the work free decree, were setting up stalls, happy with the opportunity to fill their pockets with coin. At about mid-morning, the public spaces were becoming increasingly crowded, especially along the route that the royal procession would take, with citizens dressed in their holiday fancies and with the hope of finding the best vantage point to view the proceedings. Unusually, the commonplace beggars were rigorously targeted by the patrols, who kept them moving on, not allowing them to settle anywhere.

 Greendale was brimming with energy and happiness. The governor had granted him extraordinary, if temporary, civic powers, allowing him to get things done. Even the priests, most of the time, did his bidding. The temple of the goddess had been scrubbed from top to bottom in a very fanatical way, then white-washed with lime. Trappings of the new god had now taken the place of the goddess whose images and statuettes had been broken up and dumped into a refuse pit. The Earl did not care. He had a job to do, and this job was the crowning of his rightful king. If only he could find the way to give some of his enthusiasm to his liege lord. A regent in waiting who did everything that was required of him perfectly and flawlessly. However, the way he did these things was disturbingly vacant. He had even heard rumours coming from the palace servers that the Protectorate priests had exorcised his soul - King Soulless. What nonsense! He needed to get to the palace where the royal procession would both start and finish, following a circuitous route through the central marketplace then onto the temple where the crowning ceremony would take place officiated by the high priest himself, to end finally, back at the palace. His position to and from the temple would be to ride at the right hand of the crowned prince, king to be, an honour, the beginning of his future, rightful station.

The King stood composed, his thin face bearing a faraway look, as he waited patiently for the groom to bring his steed to him, a white charger bred on the plains to the north. As he saw Greendale bustling up, a ghost of a smile played on his lips.

'Ah, Greendale, I had thought that you might have decided to join the clergy of this new, magnanimous god, instead of wasting your time with my earthly preoccupation,' said the king dryly.

'Not at all, your Majesty, there is no place more worthy to serve than at your side.'

The King did not seem to have noticed his reply, for his eyes had turned inward once again.

A priest was busy blessing the prancing, charger who appeared to be overly interested in taking a nip out of the loudly chanting white-robed apparition in front of him. It took the groom quite a lot of trouble to restrain it.

The King looked on placidly, his expression unreadable. Greendale was anxious.

The crowd hemmed in on all sides, the twisting street connecting the royal palace to the temple. The cheers turned into a roar as the vanguard of the procession came into view. First to be seen, were troupes of jesters, liveried in red, green and yellow, all-in-one outfits, with three-pronged head-gears tipped with tingling bells.

They cavorted, spin-wheeled and somersaulted along at a dizzying speed. Behind them marched a brightly coloured band beating on kettle-drums with a huge man in their midst beating time on an equally colossal drum, their yellow tunics and red leggings flashing in the sunlight. Following close behind came the brown jerkin and metal men-of-arms, with the insignia of the Protectorate, branded on their chests. The crash of their iron-shod feet keeping time with the beat of the band.

Next came the sombre court officials, wearing dark grey tunics, tights and cloaks, representing the gravity and seriousness of the rule of law. Behind them, on his own, strode the ex-chamberlain proudly, all in black and with a black cape edged with white ermine. In his hands, he carried a red, silk cushion on which rested the golden orb of authority. On his heels, rode the King astride a high stepping, white charger, resplendent in a tight-fitting red tunic and tights, with his red, velvet cape edged with white, fox fur, blowing in the wind. His greying hair lay tied back into a ponytail, and his beard, trimmed to a sharp point. On his feet, his calf-length riding boots, glossy black, gleamed in the stirrups. On his right, on a roan stallion, rode the Earl of Greendale, attired all in green, fashioned after the legendary forest rangers of days of old. His girth, however, made some ironic mockery to that claim. Held over and covering the two horsemen was a red canopy with yellow tassels, held aloft on red poles by four members of the previous king's Privy Council. In a cacophony of fanfare, trumped another band, with matched livery to the first, blowing lustily on horns. Striding behind this noisy display came the king's new royal bodyguards, selected from the best fighters amongst the Protectorate army, their simple armour of chain mail hauberks glinting under white cloaks. Still yet after, rode the king's cavalry in name only, but in fact, a division of the Protectorates cavalry. A military display to awe and inspire the crowd.

However, not all were impressed. As the procession climbed the slight hill to the temple, perched on a mound in which stone steps were carved, surrounding the whole edifice, it entered an open square. Here, traditionally, was where the people gathered on certain feast days to witness the offerings and sacrifices made to the goddess in return for a good harvest. On reaching this point, the energetic and colourful jesters spread out like butterfly wings on either side of the following marchers. Three of them with exceptional skill, led by a tall, distinctly female figure, whose tightly clinging outfit left little to the imagination, tumbled in intricate unison towards a roaring lion, stone sculpture, brought to bay in the basin of a fast-flowing fountain.

The crowd cheered even louder, riveted and enthralled by their daredevil antics as they leapt up onto the stone lion. The King, ever the one for beauty, paused to admire the fantastic figure of the female acrobat, who, seeing his interest, began a display that was extraordinarily spectacular, daring and revealing. The King guided his horse out from under the canopy and edged closer to the fountain to get a better view. Although this was against protocol, the square had already been sealed off by guards so only Greendale, with his mouth hanging open, and his eyes shining with lust followed him.

The woman, clearly enjoying and revelling in her moment of glory, flipped off of the lion's head, somersaulting twice in the air, and landed neatly on the edge of the fountain's basin, eye level to the King. Here she pirouetted elegantly on the balls of her feet, stretching her arms upwards. The large silver stars that adorned her outfit from wrist to elbow flashed in the sun, and gifted the King with an angled view of her taut, perfectly rounded and sculpted buttocks and the clear evidence as to her sex, outlined graphically against her costume.

As she turned slowly full circle, she ended by collapsing into a graceful bow, one shapely leg extended, perfectly balanced, and head almost prostrated. The King sat enraptured on his prancing horse; joy brightening his face. The acrobat then slowly crossed her arms before the King, head still bowed, and gripped the bright stars on both her arms. With a movement, sudden, quick and deadly, she straightened both arms and body, hurling with glinting speed, the disguised shuriken at the shocked king. The King was rooted, unable to move, and would have been impaled fully in the face and neck if it wasn't for the swift and selfless reactions of the Earl of Greendale. In a response unpredictable, based on past actions, the Earl flung himself across the king, dragging him off of his horse and onto the ground, taking the full brunt of the wicket spikes on the back of his head, neck and shoulder. The three would-be assassins, seeing their plan foiled, turned at great speed and fled into the crowd, with angry guards, belatedly awake to the danger, hot on their heels, only to become entangled in the confused and shouting onlookers. The King, with eyes for once, alive and shining, clambered hastily to his feet dragging the shaky Earl with him. Briefly clasping the round man in an embrace, he held him at arm's length and with a voice breathless with barely controlled excitement said:

'My thanks, Greendale! Why I think you have become a hero! The man who saved his king! Are you hurt, man? There is blood on your face…'

'Not really, your Majesty,' laughed the Earl. 'It will take more than a few pin-pricks to bring me low,' he added, reaching up with shaking fingers to pluck loose a bloodied shuriken from his fleshy neck.

The King clapped him on his shoulder and started to return his laugh, at which point the Earl's face turned a deathly white, clammy and sickly to the look. His eyes rolled up into his head. Then, with a terrible shudder and a deep moan, collapsed to the hard, rough flagstones like a sack of flour.

A short, broad-shouldered sergeant of arms appeared at the king's side and pushed him back into the protective custody of some of the guards under his command. He then bent over the stricken Earl to examine him. By now the unfortunate Greendale was frothing green slime from his mouth and shivering uncontrollably.

'Poison,' said the sergeant in a grim, cold voice.

With a cry, the Earl, his body shuddering in a rigid spasm, went very still then with a soft sigh, died.

'Poor, bugger,' muttered the sergeant.

Straightening hurriedly to his feet, he turned to the men-at-arms surrounding the king.

'Check his royalty for wounds! Quick man!'

'He's untouched, sarge,' came the reply after a pause. 'Not a scratch on him.'

'Thank god for small mercies,' muttered the sergeant. 'Bring his royal his horse and let's get on with this bloody show! Pardon me, your royalness. And somebody, get the Earl out of here!'

The Earl's corpse was dragged away unceremoniously, his boot heels grating on the stone pavement.

The King remained silent for the rest of the journey. He did not even recall his crowning; going through what the organisers required of him without much emotion or feeling. Surrounded by white, robed priests, a band of gold was placed on his head amidst much chanting and wafting of fragrant smoke. The crowd cheered even more wildly as he emerged from the temple and climbed back onto his white charger to complete the circuit back to the palace. He did not show any care when the High priest hauled himself onto the back of Greendale's beautiful, roan stallion and took the Earl's former position on his right.

He was now the blessed, anointed king; invulnerable to even assassination attempts. But something had changed, something stood awakened deep down in his soul; you could see it swimming behind his grey eyes, giving them the colour of steel. Greendale's death had breathed life back into the body and mind of a dead king.

'The king is dead,' he whispered to himself. 'Long live the king.'

CHAPTER XII

From his high vantage point, the guardian watched. A runner had already brought news, so he had a fair idea of who the lone rider was. He sat astride his horse in a relaxed, off-hand manner which hinted at familiarity, confidence and consummate skill, moving through the narrow, leaf-strewn, forest path at a slow, even pace. The Watcher was young but experienced. He knew bush-craft and the art of concealment as well as any forester. His protector was the god who faced both ways, and this god demanded that his followers were always aware, and so, he couldn't shake the uncomfortable feeling that the rider too, was watching him. This reality he knew should have been impossible. It was the second time this month that he had experienced such a thing. The first time had not been pleasant. Making the sign of the horn with his fingers, he prayed that this new meeting would not be the same. He heard the slight rustle as his captain, alerted by prearranged signal, climbed the promontory where he lay on the eastern side of the Sacred Lake, a noise as subtle as a gentle breeze would make in the trees.

'Is it him, do you think?'

'Can't think of whom else it could be, Captain.' After a pause, he continued. 'Do you believe the rumours to be true?'

'If old two-face knows the answer to that he hasn't confided in me.'

'Captain?'

'Yes.'

'I have this strange feeling… that he is watching us… like that other night…'

'Don't you go jumping at shadows, young Watcher!' rebuked the captain tersely. 'Let's go and meet our guest.'

'Yes captain, sorry captain.'

They slithered down the slope together where they met up with three other Watchers sitting silently on their sturdy ponies and holding the reins of the captain's and the young Watcher's mounts. As he straightened to walk over to them, the captain grumbled irritably:

'By the way, I have the same feeling.'

Lashing their ponies into a gallop, they thundered around the lake and stopped at the far side facing the kingdom. There at the bottom of the incline at the edge of the trees, the lone rider waited patiently, absently stroking the neck of a beautiful, piebald, Watchers' pony. Reining in their horses to a show-stopping halt, the captain and his men descended at a cautious walk, leaning back over the haunches of the animals as they did so, their eyes never straying from the man sitting calmly on the little, painted pony.

'Riding one of ours, I see,' said the captain. 'What brings you back here so soon, Ambassador, and all alone?'

'It's good to be amongst the company of the followers of the two-headed god once again, captain, but I ask your leave of safe passage to cross your borders for a brief period.'

'You have plans to return?'

'Yes, captain. In short order, if fate allows. I have to return to the presence of your queen.'

'Does your business in these mountains present any danger to our realm, Ambassador?'

'You have met that which courses my trail.' It wasn't a question.

The Watchers to a man, shifted on their mounts with visible unease, losing for a moment their veneer of certainty.

'I know something of this creature and have a great need to send it on its way. It is very dangerous, and needs to be diverted from its course before it hurts those close to me just for the joy of it.'

'It is a foul creature. Not of this earth. We will not ask how you come to know it nor will we assist you in hunting it.'

'I would not think to ask such a thing, captain. I hunt alone.'

The captain knew that some of his men did not agree with him. These four at his back was the best of them. Some were curious to the truth behind this enigmatic man who claimed only to be an ambassador of a foreign state, but rumours from the court said otherwise. Others wanted an opportunity to hunt the fell creature roaming on their borders so that they could return to sleeping peacefully in their bedrolls.

'Go then Ambassador and good hunting. However, I need to tell you this. If I find any collusion between you and this monster, I will spare no effort in stopping you, no matter the personal cost.'

Morgan fixed the captain with a steady, calm look, nodded once, and clicked his pony into motion, steering it up the slope that led to the lake and a long-delayed meeting beyond.

The group of silent Watchers turned and shadowed him, their captain's threat to the man who may be their legendary king, hanging in the air.

Morgan climbed agilely and swiftly up the side of the craggy mountain pass. He had left his little pony with the Watchers. He could move much faster without it, and it was, of course, one less life to worry about. The mist swirled about him and among the rocks. A natural occurrence as the frigid air from above met with the warmer air from below. He moved within this shifting whiteness like a ghost, a force of nature. As always, when free of the eyes of others or under extreme conditions, he became free; free to be what he was. He could feel the familiar yet at the same time, the alien mind of Krarl, who was still unaware. Worryingly, at the edge of his awareness, he could sense at least three Watchers, one of which was the young Watcher among the group who had met him at the lake yesterday, a young man burning with questions in his eyes. He was not sure of the other two. They were following his tracks, struggling to keep touch. He must not let them distract him. Not now. Suddenly, he felt a force, like a tunnel narrowing, an awakening, the exultation of a long-awaited prey, the joy of the hunt. Krarl knew he was coming. Morgan increased his speed, bounding upwards from rock to rock, with impossible swiftness and power, an elemental.

'Waelcome broothaar,' the mangled greeting echoed in his mind.

Leaping up onto a plateau of rock and ice, Morgan froze. Krarl was here somewhere, but he could not pinpoint him. He had scattered his essence within the cracks and fissures. A subtle trick, he had learnt much. Opening his five other senses, Morgan patiently began to quarter the area, questing for Krarl's hiding place.

'I knoor you corm. Hav stolen wart izz mine. I take it bark now.'

The wind shifted slightly, and a dry reptilian smell drifted into Morgan's nose; from the right coming fast. He just had time to drop to his knees in the snow, rounding his shoulders and covering the back of his head and neck with cupped hands. An avalanche of fury tore through the snow-filled space he had just been standing in, but even so, granite feet crashed into his ribs, and although his protective arms and elbows had cushioned the force, the shock of the blow took his breath away and rolled him to his side. Krarl, however, was catapulted over his body and crashed in a tangle of limbs and spraying snow. A roar of pain and rage tore from his mouth. Both gained their feet at the same time, a split second, and began circling each other in the swirling mists. In the crack of time when the fog thickened, Krarl hurled himself at Morgan with a wet snarl, the talons of one gnarled hand streaking for his face and the other, fast after, tearing for his stomach. Morgan ducked the first with lightning reflexes and twisted away from the second without slowing his counter-attack. As his body slipped sideways, his left fist swung around in a vicious hook, powered from his hip, crashing with force into Krarl's maw, snapping his head sideways and back. Spinning into the forward momentum of his move, the point of Morgan's elbow came full circle, connecting solidly with the creature's throat. Any human opponent would have died from a crushed larynx with this assault, but Krarl merely staggered backwards a step and lunging at Morgan, grabbed his head in a vice-like grip between forearm and chest. Still committed to forward momentum, Morgan powered into it the headlock, driving his opponent backwards, shoving him with a jarring force against the rock face. At the point of impact, he allowed his body to go limp, forcing a distracted Krarl to re-adjust his grip. With this small opening, Morgan surged upwards smashing the top of his head into Krarl's chin, cutting into his tongue. As the creature roared with the sudden agony, Morgan wrenched its elbow upwards savagely and slipped under its armpit, circling his body in a pivot motion. Clear of the stranglehold, he transferred his forearm between the joint of elbow and arm of Krarl, and stepping back, brought his left hand up and violently depressed the creature's overly broad hand in a downwards wrist-lock, pulling him forwards and off-balanced.

Before Morgan could complete the sequence of this move, an enraged Krarl thundered a blow on Morgan's shoulder, sending him flying sideways, torn and bloodied. He hit the ground hard, but rolled smoothly, charging right back into the fray as soon as he regained his footing, even before Krarl could regain his position to follow-up his attack. Morgan leapt like an angel of death under Krarl's defensive arms, bounding upwards and clasping the creature's head with both hands in the grip of iron, pressing his thumbs under its blood-stained eyeballs. Krarl yelped and roared at the same time, tearing frantically at its tormentor's back with its talons, realising the immediate danger of having its eyes forced out of its skull. Morgan was relentless. His face fixed in a rictus grin of determination, he smashed his forehead into Krarl's bulbous nose time and time again, not releasing his grip on its head for a second. The creature fell backwards into the snow and ice, its nemesis riding it down like a pit bull, clamped and intent on victory. Twisting desperately, with all of its remaining strength, Krarl tore free in a spray of blood, colouring the snow with its brightness.

The young Watcher felt the icy, cold air tearing at the inside of his lungs. He was probably the fittest of all the company, but following this man who, taking normal consideration into the calculation, appeared old enough to be his father, was killing him. His legs, shoulders and arms, filled with the build-up of lactic acid, burned like a thing on fire, and his whole body trembled with the effort of the fast-paced climb. Glancing back he could just about make out the figures of his two companions as they laboured stoically to keep up, the thick mist alternately covering, then revealing them. He knew they wouldn't stop. Potter was a singular individual made of rock and who knew no fear. The only time he had ever seen him assailed by this emotion, was during the supernatural attack of the night creature. The other, Trapper, was his life-long friend, both given over to the Watcher's guild at the age of fourteen. He would follow his friend till death took him. Anyway, neither of them had a choice but to see this thing through. They had disobeyed their captain, a capital offence among the Watchers. Command, obedience and trust were everything.

Blowing on the gusting wind, he could hear the faint sounds of a primaeval struggle, grunts, snarls, yelps of pain and the skittering of ice and snow as feet and hands grappling for purchase, grew louder as he ascended. Flopping over the icy lip of a plateau, he stared at a savage and bloody scene in sheer, shocked disbelief. The creature of the night, hairy, massive chest bared in the freezing cold, wrestled in a titanic struggle with the ambassador, whose clothing hung about him in bloody tatters, flapping erratically in the frigid wind. Both were gasping loudly for breath, but where the ambassador fought on in grim silence, the beast snarled, mewled and twittered gutturally. Suddenly, the ambassador dipped at his knees and twisting, flipped the creature over his shoulder and brought it crashing on its back to the rocky floor with a bone-jarring thud. With a growl deep in its throat, the beast rolled furiously away, narrowly avoiding the vicious stamping foot of the ambassador, meant to crush its head.

Swirling to its feet, it swept up a rock and swung it at the ambassador's head for a killing blow.

The ambassador ducked with quick, honed reflexes. Then ran in low, smashing his forehead into the creature's groin. Grabbing it with both arms behind, at the top of its thighs, he heaved it into the air with prodigious strength, racing it backwards and slamming its spine against the jutting, ice-coated rock face. Howling in pain and rage, the fell beast brought down clubbed hands on the back of the ambassador in a crushing blow which brought him to his knees. Then, swinging its knee upwards, the creature smashed the exposed face of the fallen ambassador in a splash of blood, sending him spinning and reeling away. Like a consummate fighter, the ambassador flowed with the forced movement, and cat-like, regained his feet and balance in time to send a terrific, reverse, knife hand crushing into the throat of his attacking opponent. The timing and placement of the blow were perfectly executed, especially in the abused state the ambassador was in, for with a strangled cry, the creature grabbed its throat and staggered away. It was at this very moment he heard the twang of a bow-string by his ear. Both Morgan and Krarl twisted away, impossibly, even before the sound could have reached them. The arrow meant for the creature's heart, flew inches wide, clanging on bare rock and spinning off into the empty air. With incomprehensible speed, the two were in movement, one tearing off up the side of the mountain and the other flying across the intervening space to where the three men lay. The surprised and petrified Watchers peered up at the snarling face of Morgan, his hands poised in mid-space, inches from doing them fatal harm. Potter, his fingers frozen on a half-drawn bowstring, looked as if he were about to vomit. Suddenly, a veil lifted from Morgan's eyes which seemed to have been burning with a golden flame, and recognising them, the iron calm that they knew him for, slowly spread across his face.

'Ah, it's you,' he said.

***

The captain was furious. The three errant Watchers sat in a circle on the grass before him, surrounded by a curious group of their fellows. Morgan rested on a flat stone under a tree, the remnants of his clothes stuck to his body by dry and congealed blood; some of his wounds were still weeping. No one so far had offered to tend to his lacerated and bruised body. He didn't seem to mind but idly sat on his stone, munching on a piece of dried bread, and watched the unfolding proceedings.

'Are you children! Our code is everything. Serve queen and country, revere the two-headed god, obey your captain, be stalwart in the face of mortal danger, be aware, be one with your brothers. Are you children to have forgotten this?'

Silence.

'We are Watchers, for god's sake, the first to engage, the last to fall! This mantra is our charge, our duty. Why did you abandon your sworn duty to undertake this forbidden venture?'

Potter, well respected by his peers, rose smoothly to his feet.

'Captain, you know well that we are not children. To be aware, we must first get information. These improbable rumours about that man there carried too much weight for us not to actively chase down the answers. So we went hunting and what we found still staggers us.'

'So then Potter, tell me again from the beginning what happened on this hunt of yours?'

'That tale belongs in its telling to our young leader of this venture.'

A bit self-consciously, Tam climbed to his feet. In an unsteady voice, he started recounting his tale. His tone, growing stronger in confidence as it unfolded. He told of convincing his companions as to the opportunity to be witness to a strange and mysterious meeting - the gruelling, whirlwind of a climb up the mountain pass. He recalled the epic and savage combat that took place on the plateau, the scale of it never seen by any of them before. He described the journey back down the mountain in the company of a man who although wounded from top to bottom, moved faster and more sure-footed than any of them on the treacherous trail.

At the end of his accounting, they all glanced a little nervously at the still silent Morgan. No one invited him to comment, nor did he ask to do so.

'Like it or not, this man's short presence in our land has upset the apple cart of our long peace. Whoever he turns out to be, he has set us on a path that we stand forced to follow to the end. The Watchers, as always, will flow with these changes. This guidance has been the essence of the training handed down to us by our last king. You three will be assigned to the company of this unlikely ambassador until further orders, in the name of the Watcher's guild. Fate and your actions have chosen your path. May old two-face guide your sword arm.' With these words, the captain turned and left the clearing.

***

Sweat glistened on his strong, youthful body as he countered his opponent, flowing smoothly from one move to counter-move, the way Morgan and Aden had taught him. Eyes closed, mind and body relaxed, he blocked, deflected, twisted and turned, ever-challenging and challenged. His breath was deep and even, pulling balance through the nose, and smoking it out through the mouth. He could feel the fresh morning air on his naked back and chest and sense the rising sunlight on his glowing skin. Everything was in perfect harmony. He tried not to let the intense gaze of the shadowed figure, her scent hauntingly familiar, distract him from his ritual practice. He had heard her as she had softly called his name and receiving no answer, the slight scrape as she opened the door to his room and let herself in. He had heard the whisper of her moccasin-clad feet as she crossed, searching for him, until, emerging onto the porch, she spied him at his morning exercises. Pulling back into the shadows, she had silently watched him for the past twenty minutes. Eyes still closed, he pivoted elegantly and executed a perfect bow in her direction. As he opened his eyes, with a beautiful and radiant smile rewarded him. 'Like the sun,' he thought. She took two purposeful strides towards him, and leaning down to where he stood on the square flagstone space in the herb garden, said a little breathlessly:

'Teach me. You must!'

Nat grinned up at her.

'You're a bit late for lessons, Miss Slug-a-bed. It's now time for my wash and breakfast.'

'Certainly a wash,' she replied, wrinkling her nose and following it with another smile, her eyes twinkling.

He grinned again.

'I was thinking that we could go for an early morning ride in the hills and watch the sun come up. If you hurry, we could still get a ride in before it becomes too hot.'

'Good idea!' he said cheerfully, grabbing a waiting bucket of cold water and dashing off to a hidden corner of the garden.

She listened to his breathless splashing and blowing with a wistful smile on her face and toyed with the idea of taking a peek. Good sense over-ruled, and she decided that it probably wasn't the best thing to do. Give the fool ideas above his station.

It wasn't long before he re-appeared, half-dried, clothed and grinning.

'Are you ready, princess?'

She smiled, and surprising him, reached out and took his hand.

As they spilt out of his room, happily hand in hand, they spotted the old courtier, like a crow, moving towards them along the corridor with a sense of purpose. Since the absence of Morgan, he had regained his confidence and place in the universe.

Eying them suspiciously, he croaked in his high crow voice.

'The queen wishes that you join her forthwith for breakfast, young lady and gentleman.' As he said this last, he cocked an eye at Nat disapprovingly.

Nat, as usual, grinned.

With his trademark 'Harrumph' the old crow set off, leading the way to the queen's quarters.

The queen was having her morning repast on a sunny balcony situated on the second floor of the palace. She sat looking at the game park spreading out at her feet, sipping a pale wine from a delicate, pale blue, glass cone beaker. A side table next to her was laden with three different types of fish, an assortment of freshly baked bread and some seasonal fruit. To Nat's nose, the aroma was mouth-watering.

Without turning or rising, she said absently.

'Lady Elaine, guardian, thank you for accepting this late invitation. Please be seated, and help yourself to whatever you fancy. I like to be alone at the start of the day. It helps me to think.'

Nat immediately started to pile food onto a clay platter, ignoring the disapproving frown that Elaine flashed him. The queen smiled.

'Lady Elaine, I needed to speak with you privately. Your ambassador's presence fills us with unease. He has turned our peaceful kingdom on its head in a mere few days. We are not happy with this. He has asked us to participate in a war. It is a thing we prefer to avoid. Diplomacy is the sword of every great kingdom; war is for morally bankrupt leaders. We do not like conflict.'

Elaine sat silently, hands-on lap, watching the queen. Nat munched away on the sidelines, his keen ear attuned to every word.

'My dear husband, myself, and our advisors have deliberated long and hard on your ambassador's request for armed aid. It hurts me to tell you this, my dear, but we are going to refuse him.'

Again Elaine did not comment, but Nat noticed that she stiffened slightly.

'You are welcome to stay under our protection for as long as you deem fit… you too young guardian…and woe betides any person or persons who attempt to do you any harm whilst you are with us, but we will not enter a war on your behalf.'

'Thank you for your words of shelter, your Majesty,' said Elaine respectfully. 'May we be permitted to leave?'

'Of course, child, this will be a clear and sunny day. Go out there and enjoy it. Remember we are only young once. Oh, and guardian, if you count the ambassador as your teacher, your skills must be prodigious. A place of service awaits you if you wish it.'

'Your offer is a great honour, your Majesty, but at this moment in time, my place is alongside the lady Elaine.'

Elaine quickly glanced at him and the Queen's visage transformed into a natural and fond smile for the two of them, prompting Elaine, whose face suddenly took on a pink flush, to depart quickly, trailed by a still munching Nat.

'Oh, dear!' the queen called after them. 'Bless me, I almost forgot. A ship arrived early this morning carrying a party of diplomats from the Holy Protectorate - brave souls. They had a harrowing voyage through the Straits of No Return. It took them weeks to get to us. This evening I have granted them a royal audience. I would be most pleased if the two of you were there.'

Elaine's face, this time, turned as white as a sheet and Nat's eyes took on the look of an eagle, sharp, deadly, poised to hunt.

That evening, a grim-faced Elaine and Nat marched towards the royal audience chambers. Elaine wore a flowing gown fashioned in the traditional colours of the House of Marches, burgundy and white. Nat was garbed in the manner of the Royal Bodyguards of Granehold, shining, chain-silver hauberk, dark green leggings, and a blinding, white cloak trimmed with white fur. All gifted by the royal household.

They stepped in time, and something about their demeanour made passers-by and palace service staff, move warily out of their path. Elaine carried herself like a queen and Nat, all boyish charm vanished, strode confidently with the air of an experienced and dangerous warrior; which is what he was.

Arriving at the throne room, the heralds immediately announced their presence and admitted them. The spacious chamber stood filled with courtiers and nobles decked out in a variety of multi-coloured state costumes. Their tardy entrance must have interrupted something important, for the room had become pregnant with silence and the group of men arrayed in front of the royal dais, were staring at them and glowering. The first to catch their eye was a tall and rather large, black-bearded man, attired entirely in black and possessing a distinctly salty look. Surrounding him like pigeons in a town square, were priests. Protectorate priests, dressed in brown and white habits.

'The Protectorate dirty business brigade,' muttered Nat under his breath.

'Welcome!' announced the queen in her firm, dry voice. 'It pleases us that you were able to join us. Emissaries, may I introduce the royal lady Elaine of Granehold and her guardian, Nathaniel Woodsmoke of the king's bodyguards.'

Mischievous amusement leapt into the eyes of the large seaman, probably the ship's captain, as he had been allowed to join the delegation, but the sudden venom in the glare of the priests was startling to Elaine. A particularly viper looking priest spun back to the queen and declared:

'This girl is no royalty, your Majesty, but a vile fugitive bearing false witness!'

'Your information runs contrary to mine, emissary Sidevinder. Would you care to explain yourself?' the queen responded in a voice straight off of the desert.

'Your Majesty, the so-called king from the land whence this woman comes, and how she got here we do not know, usurped the crown from the rightful heir, his older brother, forcing him to flee in fear of his life, to our bosom. Hearing of the foul deeds of this ungodly usurper, we answered the call of his oppressed people in the name of god and freedom. These two are but fugitives of this evil and unlawful governance. We formally request, your Majesty that you give them over to us in the name of god and law!'

'I was not aware that I was conducting a trial on this good evening, emissary. Surely, I was not mistaken in that we were welcoming new friends to our shores? These two are our guests, and honoured guests they shall remain. Are my wishes on this clear, emissary?'

'Forgive me, your Majesties. Passion overtook my words. We offer only friendship.'

'Well said, Emissary. Let's put this unfortunate misunderstanding behind us and retire to the banquet and cheerful celebration.'

 During the rest of the evening, the nest of priests avoided Nat and Elaine. It was as if they stood infected with the Black Plague. They shot daggers at them with their eyes at every opportunity. However, this vitriol did not seem to be part of the make-up of the large, black-bearded, sea captain. The queen had seated the youngsters near her table as an emphatic statement of favour. However, this did not put the fellow off in the least. Getting up from his table, from which he was the architect of loud guffaws and laughter, he sauntered confidently over to them, with a half-filled tankard of ale gripped in his calloused paw. Beaming down at them, he carried out an expansive and over-blown bow.

'Good evening, me birdies', he said, with a gap-toothed grin.

'Birdies?' enquired Nat, looking squarely and unsmilingly into his eyes.

'Birdies indeed, young guardian, for you must have sprouted wings to have gotten here so quickly,' answered the jovial fellow, helping himself to a bench.

 Neither Elaine nor Nat offered comment.

'Are you truly one of them? Saw them on the crown of the hill from me ole ship's deck. Bless me soul. The bastards could fight! Were you there?'

'I was there,' Nat replied flatly.

'Left on this bloody voyage soon after,' said the captain with a nod, his face turning serious. 'I never thought we would make it. Worse time at sea I've ever had. More whitewater than blue.'

 Again neither of the two ventured anything.

'I take it you didn't come by sea?'

'You ask a lot of questions, captain,' said Elaine dryly, sounding very much like the queen.

'Just being friendly and sociable like, lady,' he countered, throwing back his head and emptying his tankard in one draining gulp, spilling some into his beard which he then used to groom it.

Lurching to his feet, he said. 'Been a real pleasure, me birdies. Hope we meet again.' Winking at Elaine, he strolled back to his table.

The king and queen retired early, after which, following the unwritten code of court protocol, guests began to leave, Nat and Elaine being some of the earliest. As they threaded their way through the banquet hall, they could feel the baleful stares of the Protectorate priests marking their passage.

'As soon as Morgan returns, we will leave this place!' Elaine said emphatically.

Nat only nodded in response, recognising her frustration at the unfortunate and unexpected turn of events. They walked in silence to the wing where their quarters lay, each preoccupied with their separate thoughts, and eventually when they arrived at the doors to their rooms, Elaine surprised Nat by suddenly turning to him and stretching up on tip-toes, gave him a swift brief kiss on his lips. With a little, girlish giggle at his shocked expression, she whispered a quick goodnight and hurriedly disappeared into her room, closing her door with a soft click. Nat stood there gazing blankly at the door for a few seconds, then shaking his head, strode off into his room.

Some hours later, at that time of the morning when the whole world seemed to hold its breath, Nat flew awake. Yanked out of a deep, dreamless sleep, by the out of place whisper of a slither of sound. As his mentor had trained him since childhood to do, he relaxed and sent out his senses, quartering the spaces, searching for what was there and what should not be there. In a spot too dark for shadows, the air moved. With lightning reflexes, Nat twisted away, hearing the double thud of sound as two throwing knives, a split second apart, embedded themselves where his body had been a mere moment before. His sword slipped into his hand with practised ease as he rolled off the futon, just in time to deflect the slashing stroke of an invisible, sharp-edged weapon with a clanging, metallic noise; splitting the night. With a reverse stroke of unimaginable speed and power, Nat felt a wet tug as his counter met living flesh, sending whoever was there screaming into death. Moving, always moving, Nat slipped sideways, feeling the ill breath of another sword's deadly passage tearing a whisker away from the tiny, light hairs on his naked shoulder. Nat's sword, held in a high handed, vertical stance, was already moving. His sword came hurtling downwards and diagonally, powered by young, steel-like muscles, ripping through the throat of the second unseen attacker.

Nat fought instinctively, not challenged by this assault in darkness. His mind was on the safety of Elaine. If they had come for him, it was only a delaying tactic. She would be the real target. Before the body of the last assailant could hit the floor, he was already through the door, a feeling of deja-vu settling around him.

He raced on silent feet across the intervening space, shoulder charged through Elaine's door, going down and rolling smoothly to his feet, senses questing. The assassins were caught by surprise by his speed; interrupted in their nocturnal intent. Two more he thought, his body already in motion. He dropped low onto one knee, pulling his head down between his shoulders, and propelling his body forward, sword extended in a straight line. He felt the breeze as the cutting edge of a blade sheared through a few strands of the long hair on his head. A slight punch followed that flowed up his arms as the tip of his sword punctured the living flesh in front of him. He felt it writhing and squirming like a speared fish before darkness took it and left it limp and lost to the land of the living. He flung himself to the right, spinning and cutting low, as an entangled and cursing assassin stumbled past - the cursing giving way to a loud, shrill screech as his weapon sliced through the unfortunate's thigh, hamstringing him. The drum of iron-shod feet and the lurching, chaotic glow of burning torches filled the corridor outside as the palace guards thundered up in response to the commotion.

A helmeted squad sergeant stuck his head around the door jamb and quickly took in the scene. In the flickering light, he saw a wild-eyed and dishevelled Elaine, crouching against the back wall of the room. On the floor in front of her was a moaning and sobbing man, covered entirely in black. He lay half entangled in the broken ruin of a futon and clutched a profusely bleeding leg in both hands. Standing over him stood a nearly naked blond warrior, a sharp, wicked longsword held loosely in his hand, dripping drops of dark blood.

'All under control here?' he asked Nat.

Nat nodded and replied.

'You may want to take this bastard away for a chat before he dies on us.'

Two guards stomped in and grabbed the would-be assassin roughly by the arms and dragged him away, leaving smeared bloodstains on the floor and screams ringing in their ears. The guards then withdrew to cordon off the wing and gave them some privacy.

'You okay?' asked Nat as Elaine busied herself with lighting candles.

'You did well. Pulled the futon up as a shield and threw it on the bugger. Nicely done.'

'Watch your language, ruffian!' said Elaine absently. 'Who the bugger were they, Nat?'

Nat lifted an eyebrow but didn't comment on the obvious.

'No doubt we'll find out from her Majesty in the morning. We'd better get some more sleep. Tomorrow will be a long day.'

With a slight wave, he turned and left. Despite the situation, Elaine found herself admiring his broad shoulders and taut buttocks.

'Calm down, floozy!' she muttered to herself.

The following morning, Nat and Elaine were having a late breakfast of fruit, bread and fish, in their favourite spot on the porch overlooking the herb garden. The chaos and blood in the darkness now lay efficiently ordered and removed.

'I suppose I have to thank you for twice saving my life,' said Elaine quietly.

Nat looked up from his assault on a slice of river pike but didn't offer a response.

'If it weren't for the noise coming from your room, I wouldn't have heard the two assassins sent for me. I guess we know who sent them.'

'Sounds a bit familiar,' replied Nat, but before he could venture more, a polite knock echoed from outside their door interrupting them.

'Visitors?' enquired Elaine.

'More like our summons to court,' said Nat.

Once again, they found themselves being escorted by the old crow, as Nat had taken to calling him, towards the royal audience chamber. Without announcement, the old chap ushered them in to find the room already filled with people. Some wore faces of excitement, some anxiety, others puzzlement. However, what struck them most was the burning gaze of the gaggle of Protectorate priests as their heads swivelled towards them; they were assailed by a wall of hate, like a wave of forest fire surging across the open space between them. Elaine met this with cold indifference, and Nat didn't seem to notice at all.

The queen, noting their entrance, called out dryly.

'I bid welcome to my royal wards.'

Nat and Elaine glanced at each other. Such a title was certainly a surprise to them.

'As we all here well know, these two, who are under my personal protection, were attacked and assaulted under this very roof, in the early hours of this morning. Due to the alertness and fortitude of our royal guards, we stand successful in thwarting this gross attempt to foment dark mischief, and seized a prisoner in the bargain.'

Elaine once again glanced at Nat who gave a small, non-committal shrug.

'Under our persuasive questioning our guests, recently to our shores by ship, has been implicated and accused.'

With this, all eyes turned to the Protectorate priests who were corralled in by strategically placed guards.

Their spokesman, Father Sidevinder, stepped forward arrogantly, and with a strident voice declared:

'Your Majesty, it is our sworn duty to eliminate any troublemakers or pretenders that threaten the security of our fatherland and our god's order, may he protect us. We offer up no excuses for this as we answer only to his call.'

'I see. You make no denial then that you are behind this dark deed to attempt murder on the persons of our two wards?'

'This was no murder attempt, your Majesty, but righteous justice. We demand a second, time that you deliver these two fugitives into god's hands.'

'I see. Thank your god priest, that we follow civilised codes and do not bring harm to those who visit our shores on diplomatic missions. Your captain is presently preparing your ship for departure. See that you are all on it before night falls on our land.'

'What of our god's servant who you hold unwilling in your hands, your Majesty? He too is part of our mission.'

'His life is forfeit.'

With these final words of power, the royal guards stepped forward and escorted the party of priests out - their brisk and martial demeanour, brooking no prevarication.

As the guards marched the Protectorate party away, the queen beckoned over both Nat and Elaine.

She then spoke, not only to them but to the whole assemblage,

'Having welcomed these vipers into our bird's nest, we have been placed at a disadvantage. We have revised our original decision. We will now offer our help to your kingdom's representative in the body of your ambassador. The Protectorate will soon discover that they have awakened no mere bird, but a bird of prey. From this moment onwards, our nation is on a war footing. Royal soldiers, your last king, once asked this of you. Now I, your queen, requires your reply. Please, will you answer the call? Are we ready!!?'

The chamber trembled with the martial reply, 'Ready!'

The queen stood up tall on her feet, her voice, now vibrant and powerful, rising to a shout.

'Soldiers, are you ready to defend your kingdom!?'

'Ready!!!'

'Soldiers, are you ready for war!!!?'

'READY! READY! READY!!!'

The watching Nat and Elaine experienced a moment of shared astonishment. They were indeed looking at the great, great, great-granddaughter of Morgan Ap Heston. Like her grandsire, when things got tough, the queen's warrior spirit sprang released – a tiger inside a caged breast.

CHAPTER XIII

'There are no survivors?'

The governor's voice was calm and quiet, his face relaxed, without expression.

'No Excellency. We found what could be nine bodies.'

The messenger was nervous. His eyes kept straying to the corner of the room, where he seemed to be seeing something that no one else could see.

'Why 'could be'?'

The voice now deeper, with a hint of insistence, pulled a wandering gaze back from a faraway place.

'Yes…yes, Excellency. We could not be certain. Most lay badly eaten, rotting. Wild animals - we think.'

'You think? Explain.'

'It's hard to say, Excellency. Limbs were missing, even a head or two. The stink was overpowering, disgusting! It was hard to tell which was mortal injury and what sat caused after. Of a struggle, we were certain. They were surprised as there were few signs of defence…'

'Ambush?'

'Maybe… we are not scouts Excellency, merely messengers. We do not have the training to read the signs. We lack the necessary knowledge.'

'I am aware of this, man. Try your best. Why 'maybe'?'

'Something, someone, hit them hard…even the horses. Seemed to have taken them one at a time, but fast, very fast - They did not defend themselves.'

'Why did you say 'something'?'

'No weapon marks on the bodies…just slashes and tears.'

'Not the fugitives then? And the abomination called Krarl?'

'Not a sign, your Excellency. He was certainly not among the dead.'

'Very well, you've done the express service proud, despatch rider. Go and get yourself some food and a well-earned rest.'

'Thank you, Excellency.'

Here lay another perplexing puzzle. Either the fugitives had launched an ambush using some unknown beast or that creature, I rue the day that I employed his services, had a hand in it somewhere - unpredictable, unwholesome creature. Did it turn on the hunting pack for some base reason of its own? And if so, where has it run off to? Is it still chasing the fugitives or has it fled off into the barren countryside? He needed answers. He needed them now. Well, he had better start by penning a letter of condolences to the unit's families, beginning with their leader. His brother and father will be devastated.

With an effort, he sat down at his desk and tried to compose the necessary condolence letters, but his mind was irritated by the current events. First, there was this assassination attempt on the king. Brazen bunch! In broad daylight! During the heart of the procession itself! Surrounded by soldiers and guards, the villains achieved clean escape! Then came the death of Greendale, an insufferable buffoon, but useful. What next!? No doubt the priests will have a thorn ready to poke into his side.

***

'Where is the King, Alfred?' the elderly Lord Chamberlain was annoyed. They, he and three members of the Privy Council, had arranged a meeting to discuss court affairs and the way to move forward with the new administration in a direction so as not to irritate the governor. Now the king was absent.

'Practising the sword, my lord.'

'The sword? I had thought that he had put aside such boyish pursuits! A king has bodyguards and soldiers to prosecute such enterprises on his behalf. Where exactly is he, Alfred?'

'He left word as not to be disturbed, my lord.'

'Alfred!'

'Very well, my lord, he is in the temple cloister with the Earl of Marches.'

'Marches! Isn't he supposed to be in hiding? Swords in a cloister. What next!'

Like a hungry vulture, the Lord Chamberlain and his flock scuttled hurriedly to rescue the king from foolishness and of course, the potential influence of the Earl of Marches. Fifteen minutes later they broke noisily into the hallowed emptiness of the palaces' temple cloister, greeted by the echoing sounds of sword on sword, and the breathless laughter of the king.

'Your Majesty!' the Lord Chamberlain shouted to make himself heard above the metallic din. 'Urgent affairs of state await your presence.'

The King did not pause in his efforts but continued in his labour of swinging a heavy-sword at the Earl of Marches who deftly deflected and blocked the king's attempts. Both men were blowing bellows through their mouths, but also wore insane grins on their screwed up faces. They seemed to be enjoying themselves tremendously.

'Your Majesty!' shouted the Lord Chamberlain once again.

With a sour twist of his mouth, the king broke off, leaning heavily on his sword and panting hoarsely.

'Ah, the new Earl of Greendale, like a phoenix risen to scold his king as if he were but a boy,' said the King to Marches between quick breaths. 'Not to be disturbed, means not to be disturbed,

Greendale!' he continued, turning towards the Lord Chamberlain with flecks of steel glinting in his grey eyes.

'Your Majesty, this unexpected title was not my ambition's aim, but sad circumstances presented it. I merely try to serve where my talents lie, as best as I can.'

'Of course, you do. As you say, Greendale, we must all ride masterfully this steed called ambition, or else it runs away with us.'

The king's rebuke echoed through the cloister as loudly as did the din of swords, and reverberated in the minds of all present, causing halting reflection.

'Your Majesty, my humble apology, but ambition is honey that can tempt the best of us,' replied the old chamberlain, glancing at the Earl of Marches.

The king missed nothing.

'I sought out one from my arrogant youth who speaks his mind plain and does not mix his words in honeyed wine. Do you understand the simplicity of this, my lord? I needed a companion to exercise my limbs and lungs and to exorcise my spirit. A king's prerogative, don't you think?'

'Your Majesty,' answered the chamberlain quietly.

'Uncle, thank you for the fresh air of sword practice today, I hope to do better tomorrow. Same time, the same place?'

The Earl of Marches gave a smile, a slight bow, turned, and limped away without a word.

'Come, Lords of the Privy, let's discuss state business,' said the king.

***

'You do know that the governor still wants you imprisoned or even worse?'

'I am well aware.'

'Yet you risk all to do this puppet's bidding?'

'I have always considered you a man cool of judgement and balanced in action. I may have to change this notion, for your recent decisions are showing more fire than water. First this ill-advised assassination attempt, now partisanship which ill becomes you.'

'You may be right, Lord Earl. Finding balance is difficult in these days. So what is it that this Protectorate king wants with you?'

The Earl sighed heavily, then answered.

'Sword practice.'

The Beggar Abbot regarded the Earl with a deep frown.

'That's it!? No offers in return for support? No political manoeuvring to elicit your cooperation?'

'Just sword practice. He knows I don't and won't support him.'

'A strange man,' mused the abbot.

'A changed man,' responded the Earl.

'We will all see the truth of that soon enough. Farewell, my lord. You had better get the physician to check those old wounds of yours. Sword practice! What next.'

Timothy watched the Earl of Marches limp away down the damp corridor. The Earl was probably one of the last nobles left in the land who he could call honest. He held Morgan's trust and had proven that this faith planted in him did not stand misplaced, demonstrating this fact more than a dozen times and more. It would be wise to listen to what this paragon of men had to say as the Earl was no man's fool. Still, he did not like the idea of this king, but maybe he could find a way to work with him and thwart the Protectorates will in different and subtle ways. He would try to offer contact, but now he had loose ends to tie up.

Taking a burning torch from its holder on the wall, he turned and walked into a rounded, stone-lined passageway, which appeared to have once been part of the city's sewer system in by-gone days. Eventually, he came to an iron, oval door which squealed, protesting his efforts as he struggled to push it open. With a grunt he stepped into a large, natural cave, which although spacious, had the air of prison about it, and running around its top, in the shadowy, flickering depths, a dimly discerned wooden walkway stood in evidence – a circular platform from which to spy and control. An identical iron doorway lurked directly opposite and in between, on a wooden bench, sat a dark cloaked figure, head covered and unmoving.

'Thank you for waiting,' the Abbot said simply, seating himself.

'My options are limited,' crabbed in the non-committal reply.

'You have placed me in a difficult and uncomfortable position,' continued the Abbot.

'Likewise,' was the returned comment.

'Levity was never your strong point, Elisha. You have failed me.'

'Yes, remaining alive was never part of the plan.'

The Abbot sucked air in through his teeth as a show of annoyance.

'Don't be petulant! Your failure has got the governor crawling through every nook and cranny of this city looking for you. Many are happy to take his coin to volunteer information. We must not underestimate this man. He is clever, efficient and brutal. These evident attributes, we all know well. He will not stop until you stand found. Why should I not hand you over to him?'

The professional assassin, moving for the first time, purposefully glanced upwards at the shadowed walk-way hovering over their heads.

'Two of my fellows, who once shared my childhood games, have found their way into his hands; strangely dead. You have come a long way, Lord Abbot.'

'Their sacrifice has allowed you to remain alive. You should not think to judge me.'

'For how much longer, I wonder?' mused aloud the assassin.

Silence settled momentarily around the two except for a faint creak coming from a wooden plank above.

'What now, Lord Abbot?' continued Elisha with a tone of resignation in her voice.

'I have secured a berth on the Night Owl for one person. No questions asked. It leaves at midnight.'

With that, the Abbot stood swiftly and glided from the room, closing the metal door with a resounding bang.

Elisha's ears were listening only for the several creaks now coming from the planking over her head, mimicking the slow release of the crushing, constricting weight on her mind. She hated the sea.

***

Morgan arrived at the gates of the queen's city at high speed and in a swirl of dust. His hardy pony was sweating heavily on its neck and flank. So were those of the two Watchers who had attached themselves to him like fleas on an old dog. The same sergeant who had greeted him previously was once again on his post and saluted him through with a grand ceremony. He seemed to be one of those men who was quickly bored in times of peace and did everything possible to find entertainment. In times of war, such men were invaluable, for they led by example. He would keep him in mind.

'What's your name, sergeant?' he shouted down at him over the chaos of the traffic of commerce at the gate.

'Sergeant Joshua Honeycut, first-class, of the 6th squadron, Sir,' he shouted back.

The city had changed in his short absence. It buzzed with activity and had to it a martial air. Even the Watchers seemed to have been taken by surprise. With eyes narrowed, they gazed about them with a slight look of incredulity. Artisans were particularly busy. The main trading street rang with the sound of blacksmiths hammers, and bare-legged lads were enthusiastically pulling carts laden with newly fletched arrows up the slope to the palace's army barracks. Soldiers drilled in the open fields outside the walls on horse and foot. Archers, mounted and dismounted, practised with their bows, launching wave after wave of arrows into straw-filled targets.

'Are we at war with someone?' exclaimed young Tam.

No one answered, but Morgan spurred his painted pony into a faster clip, heading straight towards the palace-fortress, the war centre of the city. At the inner keep guarding the fortress proper, Morgan and the Watchers had to wait for a security check and clearance before, with a wave, they passed through.

'First time that Watchers have had to show what's in their pockets since, since…well, since a long time ago,' observed the habitually unsmiling Potter, to which his fellows chuckled softly. Tam turned to Morgan and commented:

'Potter here is the Watcher's historian. We rely on him heavily for the dates of important events from the past.'

On their arrival at the inner courtyard to the keep, they were met by a very dignified court official who greeted them politely and informed them that the queen and her consort were presently in the war room and would meet with them immediately.

A court attendant guided Morgan, and the Watchers to a very functional, stone-lined room, bare of all decorations except for a sturdy, battered long table, strewn with opened maps. Seated at the near end, were the king and two older men with the bearing of generals, discussing what appeared to be supply logistics. At the far end, was the queen, Nat and Elaine, who stood concentrating intensely on a very detailed map of the Kingdom of Granehold. The queen was indicating several areas with a pointed finger and firing searching questions at Nat who responded in a very measured, knowledgeable and competent voice.

As Morgan strolled in, the Queen glanced up and said in her standard dry way:

'It's about time, Ambassador. We decided to start without you. Watchers, welcome as always.'

All four gave a respectful bow, and Morgan answered.

'Your Majesty, events delayed me longer than estimated. Nat, Lady Elaine.'

Nat stepped forward and gripped Morgan by the forearm in an energetic greeting, studying the still not healed slash marks on his neck and cheek."

'Having difficulty shaving these days, old man?'

Morgan knew that these light words were Nat's way of showing grave concern.

'Something like that. I'll explain at a more convenient time.'

'Please include me at the time of telling, Ambassador. I think that it would be a most interesting tale,' said the queen.

'And me,' piped in Elaine, rushing forward to hug Morgan.

'We three will gladly fill in what he misses,' volunteered Tam.

Morgan grimaced slightly and quickly changed the topic.

'May I ask, your Majesty, what catalyst galvanised such a strong and positive reaction to my request for aid?'

'Let's just say that an unexpected embassy blew into my harbour and soon revealed the true colours of their underwear in the wind.'

Morgan raised a quizzical eyebrow.

The King, who had sauntered over to join them, laughed and said:

'Let me explain. My royal wife has become very colourful with her language in these last few days. Your nemesis, the Protectorate, has reached its arrogant hand to our shores, threatened the lives of our precious wards, in words and deeds, and showed no remorse when cornered. My wife and queen demanded their immediate departure, but we saw enough to realise their inevitable intent.'

'Threatened?' enquired Morgan.

'A long story,' said Nat quickly. 'We both have tales to tell later, it seems.'

Morgan nodded and didn't inquire any further into the matter. Instead, he turned to the king and queen and took another tack.

'They came through the straits; I take it? A hazardous voyage and not a decision one takes lightly. Did zeal or desperation drive them, I wonder?'

'Both I would say,' replied the king. 'They are driven to conquer for their god. In his name, they do not respect borders, and so they are desperate to intimidate before others unite against them.'

'Let's carry the fight to them, Morgan,' said the queen.

They all turned to look at her.

BOOK TWO

CHAPTER XIV

They streamed out of the foliage covering the mountain as if from a cavernous, green, bearded mouth, and fanned out like a small army of hunting ants. They made minimal sounds, alert to everything: their green cloaks, jerkins, and leather leggings blending into the surroundings. Lean and athletic, they flowed down the slope, weaving through the ferns and vegetation rather than cutting through it. In their hands, were gripped stout bow staffs of yew, and on their backs, quivers filled with steel-tipped arrows. At their head, was a tall, blond, long muscled youth, whose blue eyes took in everything with a sweep. They were all on foot, carrying just about two days rations in a leather bag swinging at their sides.

Stopping in the deep shadow of a pine tree so as not to be outlined on the horizon of the slope, the leader, using hand signals, called two bearded and tough-looking warriors over to his side.

'Daniel, Tobias, select ten men each. Scout east and west for a day's march. Check everything, stay hidden, but move fast. Meet us back here at this same location.'

The men nodded and slipped away without useless questions.

After scanning the Badlands rolling away from the mountain very carefully with his keen eyes, Nat moved further back into the trees and joined a small group of silently waiting men, one of them being Sergeant Honeycut from the city wall.

'Spread the word. We camp here. Cold rations and water only. If anyone stumbles this way and sees us, make sure he doesn't leave. No one is to stray beyond the treeline, understand? Our job is to lock down, prepare and secure. Go!'

The team leaders melted away to carry out their orders.

Meanwhile, high up in the mountain passes behind them, teams of engineers toiled and struggled in cold, icy and hazardous conditions to widen the track-ways, cutting and chiselling at the rock-hard stone faces and carving, rough-hewn stairways at the most treacherous inclines and declines. The freezing, incessant wind cut into their sweating flesh seemingly from every angle, causing them to shiver uncontrollably, as their perspiration froze on their skins. Morgan was among them and with them, heaving boulders into the abyss, securing loose rocks and scree in strong rope nettings to prevent them from crashing down on the yet to follow food baggage and troops, guiding them, encouraging them.

They worked in shifts throughout the day and at night even, if there was enough light. Men suffered frostbite and other minor broken bones, but they were doing the work at a fast pace. After a week of back-breaking, bruising effort, Morgan left the engineers and headed back up the pass. It was time for the next phase to begin. As he climbed back into the mountains, much more accessible now after the engineers' exertions, he kept sending his mind out, questing. The last thing he needed right now was for Krarl to take it onto himself to join the party and carry out a surprise attack. He could find no trace of him and wasn't sure whether this was a good thing or not, but it would serve.

Morgan descended into what, for all intents and purposes, was a large, sprawling army, base camp. The once virgin, green and tranquil landscape was now transformed by the rough abuse of loud, uncaring soldiers into spoiled, worn and bruised scenery, like the fate of a lost and forgotten woman. The prickly captain and the few Watchers left of his original command looked particularly unsettled and greeted Morgan with resentful, but not hostile eyes. He was the catalyst. He had changed their chosen posts and lives. Still, they recognised in him the manifestation of both their past and future.

'Hurry and get these ignorant townies over on the other side before there is nothing left here for us, Lord Ambassador,' pleaded the captain. 'They are like locusts in boots. Heaven help us all! Just their presence at camp should be enough to send the enemy packing.'

Morgan gave the captain a nod and a grim smile.

'I'm happy to oblige you in this, captain.'

After a brief meeting with the section commanders under him, Morgan had the baggage train, transporting food and equipment, winding its way up the mountain trail within three hours. A small unit of guards led the way, and another group protected the rear. Their safe passage was crucial to the campaign.

The infantry cohorts would be next, followed by the cavalry units. By the end of the next day, Morgan wanted the whole enterprise to be on the mountain. Heavy mists were beginning to form above the peaks, and he was concerned that this might herald lousy weather. Already the small team of volunteer camp workers were dismantling unused tents and tidying up the area. This effort, at least, should please the captain. Suddenly, a wildly riding group, but expertly so, horse riders came swooping into camp, streaming around the tents, jinxing left and right, heading for the command centre denoted by the flying wolf on the queen's colours. Morgan once stood and fought under this very same emblem.

'What now?' thought Morgan, walking towards the unexpected commotion.

As the small horde neared the clearing before the command tent, they put on a display of abandoned horsemanship. The seemingly mad horseriders leapt off their horses, bounded back up, then down again on the other side in a daredevil swirl of motion. Turning backwards on their rudimentary saddles, they hurled throwing knives, spinning back and forth between them, gleefully yelling all the way.

By the time Morgan managed to arrive at the command tent, a harassed camp aid was desperately trying to restrain a group of playfully aggressive, now dismounted, riders from barging into the tent. His efforts were being watched in amusement by the idle trio of Watchers who had become almost inseparable from him, appointing themselves as his unofficial bodyguards.

'May I be of any assistance here?' asked Morgan in a deep, commanding voice. Before the aid could address Morgan, a tall, leather-clad woman, with a lined, weathered face, dark of colour, and long, randomly plaited hair, decorated in a mishmash fashion with small glass beads and ribbons, spun on him, and fixed him with a piercing gaze.

'Take us to your General Morgan Ap Heston, immediately!'

With a cursory glance, Morgan realised that the riders were all women, tall, rangy and similarly dressed. They also smelled strongly of horses.

'Ah, certainly,' replied Morgan. 'And may I ask your stated business with him?'

'That's for his ears only, little man!' said the tall rider, taking an aggressive step towards him.

Amid the sound of soft sniggering emanating from the Watchers, the aid stepped between Morgan and the woman and spluttered indignantly:

'You are speaking to Lord Morgan himself, woman!'

The rider stared at the fellow as if he were a fly that had just landed in her soup. Then ignoring him, altogether, spoke over his head to Morgan.

'The queen said it was okay for us to join in with your fun. So here we are.'

'Ah,' said Morgan. 'Welcome. Please, would you tell me where it is that you're from? I hope my question is not impolite? Your warriors are not familiar.'

The warrior woman regarded Morgan as if he were a not very smart, small boy, but one who she had to tolerate anyway.

'Our home is the sea of grass, a great journey from the north. We heard of a sister queen who takes charge and shows lazy men how to do the necessary things without whining.'

As she said this, she looked pointedly at the three Watchers, who shifted their feet uncomfortably under her scrutiny. In her heavy accent, she continued.

'We decided to take our horses on the long gallop over the sea-grass and pay her our respects.'

'Ah,' said Morgan. 'And for how long have you been galloping your beautiful horses?'

Once again, the warrior paused, studying Morgan as if trying to discover why this unlikely general should ask such a silly question but pleased at the compliment nevertheless. Finally, she answered.

'For many, many nights, we slept, woke, yawned, and carried on till we got to where we wanted to be.'

'Ah-ha,' responded Morgan. 'Thank you. Please feel free to tag onto our cavalry when they depart in the morning. Can we offer you anything by way of food and refreshments?'

'No, General. All we need is water for our horses and a place where we can await tomorrow undisturbed.'

With that, she turned and sprang onto her horse, spinning it in a rearing pivot, and galloped away followed by her whooping warrior troop.

'I noticed she didn't mention bathing whilst on her travels,' observed Tam.

'That's true, but she did mention bedding down with her horse,' responded a serious-looking Potter.

'Maybe for the sake of unity and cohesion, I shall ask the queen to make a decree that all unmarried males be joined to outsiders in matrimony,' mused Morgan aloud.

All three gave him a disconcerted glance.

At dawn the next morning, things were as Morgan feared. The heavy mists now covered the entire mountain, gloomily and ominously. Leaving the cavalry commander in charge, as he would be one of the last to depart, he immediately headed for the mountain, trailed by his three erstwhile bodyguards. The temperature got decidedly colder as they climbed swiftly and on the second peak, which was not the highest, they encountered the straggling, back end of the baggage train. They also met steady snowfall. The drivers and guards sat hunkered down, seemingly intending to wait out the bad weather. Morgan changed. He strode forward snarling.

'Up you fools! You will find death here rather than a shelter! Up and move. Who commands here!?'

A stocky, disgruntled sergeant stepped forward.

'I am, sir. With this snow, we won't be able to move far.'

'You're relieved of command. Potter, take over, and see to it that everyone is up and moving immediately.'

'Yes, General!' came Potter's crisp reply.

Stepping towards the huddled men, he shouted in a startlingly authentic parade ground voice.

'Up you bastards! No time for squatting on your arses till it freezes! Up! Up!'

He reached down and yanked two men to their feet, sending them staggering towards the waiting mules. Still shouting, he kicked another two to their feet. One lashed out at him only to have Potter's vicious back-hand send him reeling sideways with a bloodied lip.

'Move it! Move it!'

Morgan continued onwards with the two other Watchers. Twice more, he met sluggards, waiting to die in the snow. Twice more, he met men in charge who were not fit to command. Twice more he left a Watcher to take over, first, the young, but competent

Tam, then his friend and faithful companion since childhood, Trapper.

Morgan moved on through the blinding snow-fall which was beginning to develop into a blizzard, encouraging, cajoling, pulling slipping, disorientated men and mules back into line before they could slide off of the narrow track and into their doom.

On the last ascent, on the final peak, while helping a desperate and cursing line of troupers wrestle their protesting mules up the steep, winding path, Morgan encountered Nat and a squad of Watchers with a grinning Honeycut in the forefront. Nat had made the instant decision to climb back into the mountain and assist. This position made, after taking a quick assessment of the glassy-eyed condition of the baggage train vanguard wobbling into base camp on rubbery legs. He had begun to notice a new resolve in the struggling men and wondered the cause. Then he spotted the reason hauling both men and animals by his sheer presence up the steep, treacherous track.

Morgan was a force of nature; tireless, seemingly to be everywhere needed, assisting with abounding energy and iron strength.

'Well met, Nat,' he shouted over the roar of the wind, 'all in hand on the other side?'

'Yes, General,' Nat shouted back, leaning in close to the shorter Morgan. 'The water stashes are being laid.'

Morgan nodded his head vigorously and waved a hand in acknowledgement.

'Good. Talk later. Take over here. I'm going back.'

He turned and loped back down the trail, bounding sure-footed, from one jutting stone to the next; a snow-covered wraith that soon disappeared in the flurrying snow and whiteness.

It wasn't long before Morgan came across the engineers who were once more hard at work trying to keep the trail open. As he trotted past he slapped their captain on his shoulder and shouted:

'Well done, Duncan! Good work, soldiers, rum for you on the other side.'

He was gone before the 'Thank you, General!' replies sprang uttered from cracked lips - blown away by the wind.

The entire line had steadied again and was moving stoically with good pace. This feat was thanks to the timely leadership of the three Watchers and the indomitable presence of their general. After an interval, he passed the infantry, holding their long line of march in good order. He was pleased with them. The first of the cavalry that Morgan came up to was the wild and hardened women warriors from the northern plains. They were leading their horses up the path, heads bowed and talking gently into their mounts flicking ears as they climbed. Morgan watched them in silent admiration. These women of the horse were extraordinarily disciplined and competent despite their savage appearance and would serve a valuable addition to his campaign.

Their leader lifted her head and eyed him standing there. He could almost hear her thought of 'Idle man!' as she walked past, giving him a sharp nod of her head.

Morgan took up a position with the rear guard consisting of short, tough soldiers, moving on foot. They were part of the queen's exclusive, mountain assault squad, who were also siege specialist. They saluted him but did not speak. Their eyes remained ever watchful, checking the back trail, checking the mountain slopes for potential danger, monitoring the condition of the cavalry's progress ahead of them. These men were professionals.

The engineers had prepared strategic, night, stop-over points, so of the three nights that the army had spent on the mountains, each division only had to spend one night. Morgan himself spent two, with hardly any food, and very little sleep. In the end, when he arrived with the disciplined rear-guard into Nat's carefully prepared bridgehead camp, he was happy to see his small army settling in. They had gotten there without any significant losses. Nat's neat, professionally presented, written report, noted only three dead, ten severely injured, twenty others with minor broken bones and frostbite, eight mules lost, and fifteen horses temporarily lamed. It was an outstanding result.

***

'What, man! What did you say?!'

It was the first time, in a very long time, that anyone had seen the governor so alarmed.

'Green cloaked, armed men, your Excellency, they have appeared out of the burning Badlands as if from nowhere.'

'Who are they? And how many are they?'

His voice now back under control.

'Not sure, Excellency, strangers all. About fifty or so of the buggers, they told us. About half of the villages picked up and headed north. We assume they went off to join them - ungrateful bastards!'

North, you say? Didn't the villagers put up any resistance?'

'Well, in a fashion, Excellency. The local lord's son, a brute of a fellow by all reports, attacked their leader, a tall blond youth, with his sword, but was despatched bleeding in the dirt in the same time it takes for a dog to cock its leg on your boot.'

'Very poetic,' replied the governor sarcastically, 'and what of this lord? Why didn't he organise resistance?'

'The bugger was strung up by his heels in the sunshine before he had the time to fart from his fat arse, your Excellency, sir.'

'Thank you, sergeant. A colourful report, as usual, god is our keeper. Why didn't our scouts detect anything of these men?'

'What scouts, Excellency? Don't know of any scouts. Bunch of frightened despatch riders brought me the news. Like rabbits, they were.'

'No scouts you say? Thank you, sergeant, start assembling a hunter squad of two-hundred men. We need to find these green-garbed men and determine whether they are bandits or otherwise. And sergeant?'

'Sir?'

'On your way out would you send in that servitor priest who acts as my secretary, immediately?'

'Yes, sir, right away, sir. God is our keeper.'

After a few moments, a priest, dressed in dazzling white and with burning zeal glaring through his eyes, walked confidently into the governor's work chamber without bothering to knock.

'God is our keeper, Excellency. How may I be of service?'

'My scouts, Father. Where are my scouts?'

'Scouts, your Excellency? What scouts?'

'That's my question. The ones I ordered dispatched to the Black mountains.'

'Ah, those; I deemed it an unnecessary venture and a waste of good men's time. I sent them to the south-east along the river to locate villages to add to the records of the Treasury Fathers.'

'I see, Father. Did you know that a band of unnamed and armed men have accosted the good citizens at the nearest village to the Black Mountains? I only belatedly heard of this today.'

'Mere bandits, Excellency, if I were you I would send a troop of hunters to bring them to justice.'

'It's already done, Father, already done.'

'Perfect, Excellency, now if you will excuse me, I have to file some reports to the Holy Conclave.'

'Of course, Father, of course,' said the governor mildly. 'Oh, Father?'

'Yes, Excellency?' replied the priest, with a trace of irritation in his voice.

The governor continued, his voice soft and his face, mild and calm.

'If you ever disobey a direct order from me again, I will have you stripped and flogged till you no longer have flesh on your back. Am I clear in this? Leave me.'

The priest started in shock, made as if to say something, then darted out of the room.

Taking his sword down from off the peg on the wall behind him, the governor strode determinedly through the door. He'd had enough of this little room of endless reports and disappointing news – fed-up beyond forbearance. Today he would make a surprise visit, both for politics and to get some fresh air.

As he stepped into the cavernous inner chamber, three armed men stepped away from the dimly lit wall and fell in behind him. They were his appointed bodyguards for the day. He barely noticed them. He had grown accustomed to having these anonymous shadows guarding his life. This everyday situation was the usual and commonplace order governing every aspect of his working day.

A young cleric in the brown robes of the researchers appeared anxiously at his elbow, trying to consult a scroll in his jiggling hands.

'Excellency, you have a scheduled meeting with a direct representative of the Conclave in ten minutes… He has travelled many miles from the homeland to meet with you.'

'Have I? Has he? Oh, yes. Please inform him when he arrives that I had other urgent matters to attend to.'

'But…'

'Since you are here, please be a good man and run ahead and ask the castle groom to have my grey saddled and ready immediately. My legs are not as young as yours.'

'But…'

'Now, young Brother Jacob.'

'Yes, Excellency,' breathed the young monk as he scuttled ahead with panic in his eyes.

By the time it took for the governor and his three protectors to arrive at the stables, the head groom was waiting in the yard holding by its halter a large, powerful, grey horse that was stamping, snorting and tossing its head with spirited impatience.

Behind him, two stable-hands held three other lesser animals in check.

'He is in a bad mood today, your Excellency. He may want some watching,' offered the groom.

'He's just bored like me, Cutter. Old warhorses like us are not very fond of four walls,' replied the governor, patting the neck of his favourite charger.

The last time they had seen action together was at the so-called 'Battle of Sorrows', as the locals had become so fond of calling it, but it lay written in the records as the 'Battle of Victory Hill'. Much better, and this is how history shall remember it. As he mounted the heaving animal, time stood still for a brief moment, and he sat transported back to that momentous day.

He watched his famous cavalry, rebuffed time and time again. Black arrows mixed with black rain cutting them down and sending them crashing and sliding into the black mud. He was at a disadvantage. The usurper king and his bastard general held the high ground. There was no way around. His only hope lay with the collaborator, but the fool was not committing. In the meantime, his men were dying. Just as he was contemplating an ordered retreat, the over-zealous enemy made an error. Instead of moving their battle-lines down the churned slope by steady gradients, they charged pall-mall after his near defeated left-wing. His god had given him the opening he sorely needed.

'He needs a fast gallop to settle him, Excellency.'

'What? Ah, yes. Good idea, Cutter!'

With these words, the governor spun his warhorse and raced out of the stable yard with the animal's iron-shod hooves clobbering the cobblestones, the echo making a thunderous din as the other horses bolted after him. They pounded around the castle walls and over the bridge, scattering alarmed soldiers and petitioners alike. A few guards moved forward to stop this outrage, then realising who it was, checked themselves and hurriedly saluted. Without slowing, the governor tore through the narrow streets causing vendors to snatch their trays of goods hastily out of the way, throwing panicked curses in the air left behind by the reckless passage of the governor and his men. Pedestrians leapt left and right, some narrowly avoiding having their skulls cracked by war trained hooves. The governor showed ill regard for the safety of the people he claimed to govern.

Five minutes later, the governor ended his irresponsible dash through the city in a flurry of hooves at the very gates of the palace. He leapt from his saddle in a show of physical prowess absorbing the impact of his landing on thick, powerful legs. Without pausing, he strode through the gates ignoring the surprised salutes of the guards. He headed directly for the old council chambers; his mouth, twisting in a grim, humourless smile and his eyes gleaming with a hint of cruelty. Palace staff and officials hurriedly stepped out of his way as he made no effort to avoid them politely as they went about their duties.

He brushed aside the efforts of sycophantic court officials. He knew, well enough, that they sought to delay his inexorable and uninvited march towards the meeting - held, at this very moment, behind closed doors. He watched others scuttle ahead of him in the vain attempt to give warning of his approach, but his advance was unchecked.

'Cockroaches!' he thought in disgust.

With an action that spoke of controlled violence, he slammed open the doors to the council chamber and stood rewarded by the sudden turning of startled, white, scared faces; mice who have belatedly realised that the cat is amongst them, he thought with satisfaction - all except one. The king, sitting at the head of the dark, ebony table, regarded the governor with quiet, calculating, grey eyes as if weighing the value of his rude intrusion. The governor's mind clicked a gear upwards, suddenly forced to re-estimate this man. His spies' whispered warnings were correct. The king had changed like a bloody chameleon – transformed into a worthy adversary. He brought all of his dominant personality and force of bearing to focus on the king. But, even so, the degenerate remained unfazed.

'Welcome, Excellency,' he greeted the governor with a tight smile. 'Had I known you were coming, I would have left the seat of honour open for your esteemed presence to occupy it.'

'An on the spur decision only, your Majesty. Please, do not let me disturb. I'm here merely to observe and learn. You have already given me an honour.'

With that, he placed a chair behind the circled councillors, his back against the wall. His men closed the door and took up positions before it, giving the added psychological impression of being imprisoned.

'Please, continue,' said the governor, smiling in return, 'and do not let my presence interrupt.'

'So then,' said the king in a lazy drawl, 'we were discussing our response to some valid questions put to us by a large section of our citizens, the main one being 'How do we justify our rule when we are subject to the guiding will of a foreign power?''

The council members jerked their heads up and blinked nervously. They had been discussing no such thing.

The newly re-confirmed Lord Chamberlain hesitantly took the floor.

'Ah-hem, your Majesty, due to the shortage of time left to us maybe it would be better if we pursue less weighty topics and try and sort out instead the problem of the malfunctioning city sanitation system.'

'A very worthy subject, Lord Chamberlain, but as we all know, the unsavoury backups we are experiencing are mostly due to sabotage. So let us lance the boil before we apply the dressing.'

An uncomfortable silence hung like a shroud over the council.

The governor's chair creaked as he leaned his bulk forward into the silence.

'My apology for intruding, good councillors, but I am very interested in hearing your thoughts on the matter put forth by your king. Please, humour me.'

'Excellent! Thank you, Excellency! Let me start with some suggestions. We could politely ask the governor and his army to leave…'

The king turned to the governor and gave him a slight bow and a smile. The governor smiled back pleasantly.

'But we all know that that won't happen. We could abdicate for the second time. But that won't solve anything. We could limit ourselves to repairing and improving municipal things such as aqueducts, fountains and road repairs. And laudable as this is, some few good citizens will only continue to destroy them behind our backs - a circular problem. We could, of course, pursue these citizens and deliver them to Protectorate justice, but I'm afraid we'll only be stepping on the toes of our good governor here. Finally, of course, we can pluck up the courage and support our citizens in freeing our nation from the sword held at our throats. Unfortunately, as I know you are all dying to comment, time, as our good Lord Chamberlain has pointed out to us, has run away from our deliberations. Let us adjourn to contemplate these things so that we may prepare a timely report for our esteemed governor, informing him of our decisions.'

With a hasty scrape of chairs, the noble privy councillors fled the room, squeezing past the stationed guards, and disappearing through the door.

'You're playing a dangerous little game, your Majesty. I am hoping you did it just for the sheer joy of annoying me. I hope for your sake, as I love a good jest as much as any man, but I will give you a word of caution anyway. Don't play any more games, unless you aim to have your clever head used as a football to entertain the masses.'

Having issued his threat, the governor heaved his mass from the protesting chair and stalked out of the chamber. Behind him, the king wore a wistful smile on his face.

***

'He did what!'

'Turned the tables on the governor, if all reports be true,' replied the Beggar Abbot, as they ambled through the dimly lit, stone-clad corridor. 'Not many can make such a claim.'

'This King is beginning to grow on me. He's got balls', grinned the Earl of Marches, limping heavily alongside the abbot. 'I can't say the same for my council peers, though. Gutless wonders, all of them.'

'Well, I did think that the Lord Chamberlain had a straighter spine, but he ran just as fast as the rest. Are you telling me, dear Earl, that you are ready to accept this king?'

'I didn't quite say that. But his majesty's recent actions would make even Morgan smile in approval.'

'Yes, I am sure. I think we should work with him. Do you agree?'

'Yes. I'll try and sound him out a little tomorrow after sword practice.'

'Thank you. I can no longer risk going out as the governor is arresting any fellow unfortunate enough to be wearing a grey cloak. However, I beg you to bear in mind that he still wants your skin decorating his wall.'

'How can I forget? He has been particularly nasty since the hunter pack chasing Ap Heston, and Woodsmoke lay found slaughtered to a man.'

'Morgan, do you think?'

'Naarh! More likely that monster Krarl, can't trust the bastard as far as you can throw him! Rub him the wrong way, and you're dead.'

CHAPTER XV

Hot, burning sand sprayed whitely in every direction as a laboured and sweating horse came lurching over the sandhill, its mouth foaming with thick saliva, tinged pink with blood, its eyes wide and nostrils flared and blowing. Clinging to the desperate animal's back was an exhausted, but excited Protectorate scout, waving frantically.

'One of ours!' shouted the hard-bitten sergeant to his captain, a clean-cut young man with good connections within the Protectorate hierarchy.

Holding his arm up the captain brought the column of two hundred riders to a sliding halt.

The scout careened down the crumbling slope of the sandhill, leaning well back over the animal's haunches, and then hitting solid ground, thundered over to the hunter pack.

'Found them, sir!' he exclaimed breathlessly. 'About forty men dressed in green, trotting in a dry river-bed and trying to keep out of sight. Not more than three miles west of here.'

'It's got to be them! Come on you laggards! Let's hunt!' the captain shouted enthusiastically, spurring his horse into a sudden gallop.

It wasn't long before the fast-moving pack crested a ridge of baked clay and coarse sand, to find below them a straggling group of men jogging in the dead sand of an old, dry river creek, just as the scout had described. On seeing the horsemen silhouetted on the ridge, the runners increased their pace, twisting their necks frantically to see if the sudden newcomers were chasing them.

'Bring them down!' shouted the energised, young captain, plunging his horse down the embankment.

Although the fleeing men had a good lead, the all-out pace of the horses would soon bring them to ground. The captain screamed out a strident command.

'Lances to the fore!'

At the same time, he jerked his from its leather holder under his right leg and couched it tightly under his arm, the wicked, steel tip pointing at his intended victims. His men replicated his action.

The sergeant, a man who had fought in and survived many skirmishes and campaigns, was the only one glancing around him with unease. The others had a look of concentrated, savage glee on their faces, like a pack of wolf-hounds with the blood scent of a lone wolf in their nostrils. Finally, they would make the kill; no questions asked.

The green-clad, bandits were now sprinting for all they were worth, seemingly every man for himself, with no thought to unity or cohesive defence. Some of the hunter pack were already standing in their stirrups anticipating the spearing of a green rabbit or two;

breaking the hard training rules of cavalry riders. They could smell the sweat of panic on their scampering prey. Still, the sergeant was unsettled. He noticed the narrowing ridge on both sides of the dry creek. He saw how the galloping horses were blowing loudly and slowing noticeably in the energy-sucking, loose sand underfoot. He noticed the quick hand movements as the striving men threw something from leather bags behind them before scrambling up a steep sandy incline, dead ahead; what! Why? He edged his horse next to his impetuous captain's and yelled:

'Captain, captain, it's a trap!'

The captain turned his head and looked at his sergeant wearing a puzzled frown on his face; a loud-mouthed, uncouth peasant, that is how he saw him. Suddenly, his horse's hooves hit the firmer ground, and it surged ahead. The captain quickly put his sergeant's wild assertion out of his head. Not noticing as his junior officer roughly pulled his mount aside, taking two men with him. The others tore on past in the frenzy of the hunt.

High pitched screams of horribly wounded horses penetrated the ears of the alert sergeant from out of the swirling dust. A place of bewildering chaos as both horses and their riders inexplicably crashed into the dirt, those coming after catapulting over their comrades, screaming and yelling in agony as bones snapped and flesh tore from the unexpected impact. The sergeant and the two men who followed him sat their horses impotently and watched. The hitherto, seemingly panicked men in green, turned in smooth order and discipline, and sent shaft after shaft of black arrows tearing down into the churning mass of horses and men, adding to the turmoil of pain and terror.

'What the fuck happened, sarge!?'

'The bastards used caltrops! Spiked our fucking horses and brought them down!'

'What shall we do, sarge?'

As these last words leapt from his subordinate's mouth, a vision of unbridled horror came ripping down the crumbling dirt bank from the left in the form of a horde of screaming and yelling enemy riders, their long hair streaming wildly in the wind.

'Run, fools!' roared the sergeant, spinning his horse back down the dry creek before they too, fell to the encircling demons.

'Bloody gorgons of hell are on us! Ride!'

The three surviving members of the two hundred hunter pack sent by the governor fled for their lives. Their comrades were as good as dead already. These fuckers aren't bandits, was the fleeting thought in the sergeant's head as he bent low over his horse's neck, coaxing even more speed from it.

***

'Good plan! Wonderful ending! Great fun!' grinned the leader of the wild, warrior woman band down at Nat.

He nodded acknowledgement to the grudging compliment, trying to avert his eyes from the dripping scalps hanging from the saddles of every warrior in the troop. Some had even finger smeared their victims' blood on their faces. This graphic display, combined with their happily grinning faces, proved to be very unsettling, even to the skirmish seasoned Watchers.

Wide-ranging scouts had detected the Protectorate hunter pack well in advance. This pre-warning had given Nat ample time and opportunity to lay his trap; a larger and more elaborate version to the one that he and Morgan had laid many, many moons ago in this very same territory. The arrogance and impetuosity of the pack had made it all too easy. Morgan had split the army into three fast-moving, penetrating prongs. The middle one, which had passed through old Hatch's village on the way to the rendezvous point, was under Nat's command. It lay comprised of the majority of the Watchers, local villagers and frontiersmen who had joined them, and of course, the band of fearsome women warriors to provide cavalry support. These last stood charged with the task of shutting the door of the trap. The speed and reckless disregard for their personal safety were astonishing, and their off-hand and gleeful cruelty to their foe was terrifying to behold. Standing on the sandy slope, Nat had felt somewhat sorry for the hard, put-upon hunter pack. The ferocious women did not take prisoners. Win or die was their motto. They tore into the enemy and shredded them, slashing across the foreheads of the fallen with sharp knives and ripping free their scalps - some were still alive when they suffered this savage mutilation. The goddess, have mercy on their souls. How these horsewomen avoided the sewed caltrops, he would never know. Leaving the bodies of the dead to rot in the burning sun, Nat didn't allow his command to rest. He led them, moving swiftly onwards. The Watchers loped alongside the trotting horses of the warrior women, one hand holding onto the saddles for support, forming teams of two or three for the sake of speed.

***

Morgan sat quietly on his horse; hands crossed over the pommel of the saddle and watched the heavily laden infantry trot past in squadrons of fifty. Each man carried on their backs three days' supply of rations, water to last a day, basic cooking utensils, an axe and a shovel. On top of this, they were in full armour, except for their helmets, which were also on their backs. They travelled by jogging for 100 metres, walking for fifty, then jogging again - all under a burning sun. Every four miles they would stop for a ten-minute rest and a few sips of water. It was gruelling but necessary. Speed was paramount. They had to get to the rendezvous point, undetected if possible. Last in line, smothered and breathing in the biting dust churned into the air by three thousand stomping feet, came a small group of supply mules carrying top-up rations and water followed closely by a troop of cavalry who provided more mobile protection and cover. Another cavalry troop roamed ahead acting as trailblazers and scouts for the marching infantry. Of the three prongs despatched by Morgan, his was the most vulnerable. It was the slowest and because of this, the hardest to keep supplied. It was also the most susceptible to being trapped and isolated if detected by the enemy. Therefore, Morgan's detachment was furthest away from the river and the city which it supplied.

The sparsely separated watering holes dictated their route of march. Flanking him on either side were two of the ever-present Watchers, Tam and Trapper. Potter and the irrepressible Honeycut stood newly promoted to master sergeants, prowled the trudging line tirelessly, kicking flagging legs back into quick motion. The hard-pressed men both hated and loved them at the same time. Morgan smiled inwardly. He found that he was having less and less to do on this venture due to a few outstanding men and acknowledged that If they could keep moving like this, it wouldn't be long before they would be leaving the Bad Lands and pushing into the cultivated parts of the country. Here is where the fun would begin. Here is where he would be expecting those with rebellion smouldering in their hearts to join and swell his ranks, and where the enemy would start throwing themselves at him. Both would slow him down. Both would endanger his plan.

A lot depended on the success of the detachment under Nat. Him winning through would reflect directly on the fortunes of the Queen's General Hadrider and the bulk of the cavalry under his command. Nat's goal was to get swiftly to the rendezvous point, secure it, and then send out support to guide Morgan's foot soldiers there in one piece. There was a considerable risk inherent in his decision to split the army, but he needed to pick his battle position as the enemy could and would field a much larger army than he could. He required a telling advantage, and he could not obtain this without taking risks.

***

General Hadrider was an astute leader. He had studied all the tactics of the last king very carefully, developing a philosophy around his battle decisions. Talking to Morgan though, was like shining a burning torch into the past. Things long puzzling and seemingly running contrary to the accepted move and countermove of battlefield tactics became apparent. First, be informed of your enemy, his movements, his goals, his traditions, and his pride. Second, always know the land around you from all sides, how it folds, its rivers, its hills, its ravines. Use scouts, use spies. Melt before the enemy, appear where he least expects. Confuse and demoralise him. Stand when the advantage is yours only, be patient, punish him mercilessly when he makes a mistake. Encourage him to make mistakes. Pretend inferiority and let his arrogance defeat him. The horse squadrons under his command had moved exceptionally and unexpectedly fast. One of his objectives was to shield and warn the infantry divisions of any impending enemy movements that may threaten to tie them down, but his primary mission was to first get to the rendezvous point. Due to the peculiar contours of the land, his equestrian prong was the first to emerge into the rolling countryside. In this landscape of scattered farms and Hamlets, the locals hid in fear and wariness. They were suspicious of such a large group of horsemen, one thousand five hundred strong, as their colours were unknown. Likewise, such a large group could not fail to draw notice, and it wasn't long before two enemy cavalry patrol squads were coursing their trail in an effort to intercept and identify them.

'Rider coming, General!'

The sharp warning pulled the general back from his thoughts. Turning, he saw a black horse, moving at a dead gallop across the freshly weeded verge of a ploughed field. The rider lay over its neck, up in the stirrups - his bum in the air like a race jockey. As a jockey, he was small in stature, and he seemed one with his flying horse, effortless.

The man was a superb horseman. The general could feel the admiration of the troops behind him, and some gave a small 'whoop' as horse and rider sailed over a hedgerow in a smooth, spectacular leap, landing on the other side without a pause in their headlong gallop.

'That'll be old Hatch, without doubt,' laughed his aide-de-camp, 'no mistaking the old bastard!'

The beautiful, spirited horse charged down on them making their mounts shy with nervousness. Hatch brought it expertly to a rearing, skidding halt.

'General,' he quavered, in his old, high voice.

'Hatch,' replied Hadrider, nodding at the old scout, 'you've got news for me, I take it?'

'They are making to close the door on you, sonny.'

'How many?'

'More than we've got.'

'Suggestions? You know this land more than any of us could ever hope to, and certainly not from studying maps.'

'Split and run. Just like Ap Heston said we should.'

'I agree, three squads of five hundred! Hatch, you're with me! Let's run before the wind! The last group to the rendezvous cleans the stables for a month!'

Guided by Hatch and two other local scouts, the three squadrons separated and melted into ancient Holloways and byways known only to those who had grown up with an intimate knowledge of the land. They worked their way around the waiting enemy patrols, hiding by day in copses and woods and riding mostly by night.

Twice discovery found the squad led by Hadrider and guided by Hatch. The first time was an unfortunate accident. Taking advantage of dawn's light, they were riding hard down a Holloway that cut through ancient woods. In times of old, this was once the main road leading to a now long-forgotten village. As fate would have it, a Protectorate patrol of three hundred riders seeking to bring their presence into the homes and consciousness of the country folk had risen early and was making its way down the dimly lit route. As the floor of the Holloway lay covered in the mulch of damp leaves and earth the sound of the horses' hooves were muffled and muted, and only on turning a moulded, tree-lined corner did the two sides come face to face.

It was the quick reactions of old Hatch that saved the day. The Queen's riders were tired after their long night in the saddle, and the Protectorate patrol was still sleep drugged from their fitful night of dreams, so both sides hauled in their reins in startled surprise. Hatch did not wait to stare, but with a loud warlike cry spurred his black horse into the foe, slashing one man across the face with his curved sword, slicing his cheek open in a spray of blood. His scream woke his companions to action, but it was too late. The general and his men were on them as a cat onto a mouse, cutting and slashing in hot passion, their warhorses rearing and crushing skulls with iron-shod hooves. Men do not like one to one combat. It is naturally terrifying, but in the surreal, misty, indistinct light of the early dawn, men gritted their teeth and swung their weapons blindly for all they were worth. The advantage lay with those who had moved first. Thanks again to old Hatch. The Protectorate squad was the first to break, turning in wild panic and scattering back up the way they had come. This time the general did not stop to hide and rest but pushed his tired men and horses on through the day.

 The second incident happened just forty-eight hours later. Sheltering in the shade of a leafy copse, the exhausted general made a mistake. Throwing caution and good sense out of the window for the sake of expediency, he sent Hatch and two others riding into a sleepy village to negotiate the purchasing of well-needed rations. Villagers had to be persuaded, sometimes forcibly, to part with their food as the winter months could be hard on them, but Morgan had insisted that they receive as much compensation as possible for their loss. There slap bang in the middle of the shaded and picturesque common land just beyond the village green, were camped three platoons from the governor's crack division of mounted shock troops. Hatch immediately took in the situation. Two village men swung gently in the breeze from the ropes noosed around their necks and looped from sturdy branches. Five young village women, tied like goats, naked, their blank eyes staring unseeingly with loss of hope and dignity; used for the communal pleasure of uncaring men. The old scout spun his black horse on a coin, shouting a warning to his two comrades, but the Protectorate soldiers were just as quick. Before the running horses could make three strides, iron-tipped arrows were streaking towards them, three of which buried themselves with meaty thuds into the fleeing backs of Hatch's companions. They fell rolling in the dirt like broken dolls. Hatch did not look behind him. He raced out the way he had come in, knowing that deadly pursuit would only be minutes behind.

'Shit! Something's wrong, General!' came the warning from the lookout.

Forcing his bone-tired body to stand, General Hadrider, made his way over on aching knees to see with his own eyes. He felt old.

'What's up, soldier?'

Then he spied Hatch's racing black tearing across the patchwork fields with a posse of mounted enemy soldiers thundering after him.

'Shit! To horse! We've got bad company coming fast! Captain Turnbridge, peel off a hundred and fifty lances. Make your way to the gathering point as best you can. May the gods go with you. Go! Go now!'

As they brought his charger to him, the general pulled himself into the saddle and awaited the fast approaching Hatch.

'Brought some friends with you, I see! You now stand promoted!'

 Turning back to his men, he shouted.

'Two hundred horse with me! The rest follow Captain Hatch! Meet you at the rendezvous, bless your souls!'

 Without another word, he wheeled his horse away and galloped off. Similarly silent, Hatch charged off in another direction, followed closely by his newly acquired command. Not much surprised old Hatch anymore.

***

'Who are these bands of riders running around the countryside flying unknown colours?'

'We don't know, Excellency.'

'They aren't raiding, and they don't seem overly keen on fighting.'

'It doesn't look that way, Excellency!'

'Melt away and run like greyhounds at the summer fare when discovered.'

'Yes, Excellency, they sure do.'

'How many of the bastards are they?'

'Of that, I'm not sure, Excellency, their true numbers are hard to garner.'

'Not much to go on, eh, corporal? Why don't you tell me what you do know!'

The governor leant over his desk, calloused, swollen hands gripping its edges, beefy shoulders hunched forward, and square jaw clenched in barely controlled aggression.

'Well, sir, reports are still coming in, but two patrols picked up the tracks of a substantial contingent of horsemen. The tracks showed that they were all iron-shod and ridden in brisk military fashion. We sent messages ahead and attempted to box them in, but they split into three factions and evaded confrontation. Seem to have a better knowledge of the land than we have. Further reports mention a skirmish between a small band of very mobile horsemen in a forest somewhere in the mid-country and us. We didn't fare so well. No fatalities, but we received a thrashing and ran for it - although five of that patrol will never be fit to serve again. The latest report sites another small contingent of armed riders. They seemed to have stumbled onto a division of your crack, shock troops in a small village in some chalk hills south of the first skirmish. We did a bit better here. Got two of the bastards, but the rest split into three and fled into the countryside. Dividing by three seems to be the fashionable tactic these days.'

'Were the prisoners put to question?'

'They were all killed on the spot, sir.'

'I see. All moving roughly south,' observed the governor, 'and in a great hurry. I wonder why?'

The intelligence officer remained silent.

Suddenly, his white-robed secretary burst through the doors in a very flustered and unpriestly manner.

'Excellency, please pardon my intrusion, but a very rough, uncouth and dirty sergeant of arms is outside! He is demanding immediate access to you.'

'Did you take a name, Father?'

'I tried to note it, Excellency, to book an appropriate appointment, but the ruffian threatened to shove my scribbling, well you know where, if I didn't personally inform you of his presence.'

'And did Sergeant No-name say what exactly this urgent matter was?'

'He said that it was a military matter and not one to bother the god about, so he didn't need to talk to a weak-eyed, knock-kneed priest.'

'I see. Show this sergeant in, Father.'

'Are you sure, Excellency?'

'Please, Father.'

'Right away, Excellency.'

A few moments later a brief commotion at the door revealed a rather dishevelled and dirty sergeant, fully armoured and belligerent. He shoved the spluttering priest out of his way, leaving a mucky handprint on his immaculate, white robe and stomped into the small chamber, stamping to a sudden halt and saluting the governor smartly.

'Ah, it's you is it? What a surprise. Didn't I send you out with a hunter pack of two hundred? Report sergeant!'

'Yes, sir! Yes, you did, sir, but also with a novice captain, who wouldn't take sound advice, pardon me, sir.'

'Criticizing your superiors is bad discipline, sergeant. Now, where are my two hundred?'

'Dead, sir, barring three.'

The governor stared at him. The corporal's jaw dropped open in dumbfounded astonishment, and the room fell silent.

'Dead, you say?'

The governor's voice was like ice.

'I hope you're not going to tell me that bandits in green killed them?'

'No, sir. Not bandits.'

'Small mercies…'

'Not bandits, but the bastards stood dressed head to foot in green alright—green-clad professionals and harpies. Drew us into a trap, they did. Closed the door tighter than a gnat's ass and wiped us out.'

'Slow down, sergeant. Please tell us your tale from the beginning.'

Standing rigidly at attention the sergeant regurgitated the harrowing details of his experience over the past seven days. Starting from the time the scout brought news of the men wearing green up to his harried entrance into the castle just twenty minutes before.

'Each time I see you standing before me sergeant, you've come helter-skelter, running from something,' observed the governor.

'No need to die uselessly, sir,' replied the aromatic fellow, the stink of his stale sweat filling the room.

'Yes, that's one viewpoint. What were their numbers, sergeant?'

'About fifty to seventy, sir, not including the harpies, but they could have been more. Lured us into a bottle-neck and stuck us full of arrows.'

'Yes, so you said. And what of these even more mysterious warrior women?'

'Not women, sir. Demons! Never seen such antics done from the back of a galloping horse! So fast, your Excellency; fast and rollicking furious.'

'Numbers sergeant?'

'Roughly equal to ours, sir, but we didn't see them until it was far too late.'

'Thank you, sergeant. Go and get yourself a bath, food and rest. I'll soon have another task for you.'

'Yes, sir, thank you, sir.'

As soon as the door closed, the governor turned to his intelligence officer.

'What do you make of all this?'

'One group working together, split into small units for stealth and speed. Comprised of rangers and mounted units. They have an objective, and we can assume that they are more.'

'Those are my thoughts exactly, corporal. Enough parts to make an army when assembled, you think?'

'We should make that assumption, sir.'

'On my orders, double the patrols, especially to the south, fore and aft of the river, and, corporal… prepare to mobilise.'

'At once, Excellency.'

***

'My Lord Abbot, a moment of your time, if I may?'

'Good morning, dear Earl. What gets you up so early on this cloudy day?'

'Life, good Abbot, and faith in the rising sun. Strange rumours have been finding me recently.'

'What rumours are these, old friend. And you never did enlighten me on your conversation with our new king.'

'He was very enigmatic, and said something to the tune of him being an old dog, and if you threw him a bone to chew on, his dull teeth may yet again stand sharpened for the hunt.'

The abbot smiled.

'And don't switch the road of our conversation on me, young guild leader. Our topic was that of rumours!'

The abbot's smile turned into a grin.

'Yes, I've heard these rumours. Our guild is trying to add meat to them.'

'Ah, we're still on bone analogies. Ap Heston, do you think?'

'It's too early to tell. It fits his style, movement with set purpose, risk, and aggression. They have been moving too fast to engineer contact but, the reported leader of a group of rangers bear close a resemblance to our young Woodsmoke. As for the horsemen, we do not recognise their colours. Nor do we understand where they could have entered our borders. We remain cautious but optimistic.'

'There you have it! I can feel the sun on my face already. I'm off to convince the king to double our hours of sword practice.'

Suddenly, a dark, troubled cloud moved across the face of the Earl, and he paused hesitantly.

'Any further news on my daughter, Timothy? My dear wife is gone, that is certain, but I still cherish hope for my beloved daughter.'

'No. Sorry, my friend. She has disappeared into the Badlands with old Hamish. He loved her like the daughter he never had. You know well that he would give his life for her. Many strange things are happening in the parched lands these days. Let's continue to hold on to cherished hope.'

With a nod, the Earl walked away. Timothy noticed that he no longer limped.

CHAPTER XVI

Morgan twisted his head away, feeling the soft breeze on his cheek made by the sword blade passing a whisker's breadth away from drawing blood. So much for remaining undetected, he thought. Tucking down his chin, he stepped back onto his right leg, tensed his back muscles and pushed aggressively with his shield. He coolly watched the surprise on the face of the hugely muscled, Protectorate infantry soldier as he was hurled back into his fellows. The dust swirled in the air as hobnailed boots, tightly packed in a churning defensive square struggled to keep form against the oppressive odds. Three squares each of fifty battling men strove to keep the rear guard, allowing the main force to keep marching without being assaulted.

'Move to my mark! Move! Move! Move! Hold! Shields up! As one! Heave! Forward! Stab! Back! Move! Move! Move!'

He called out the cadence of an ordered, holding the retreat in a deep, rough, commanding voice, feeling the men moving together, taking courage from each other.

He could hear the parade ground voice of Master Sergeant Honeycut doing the same thing, but using much more colourful language.

'Common ladies, dance back a bit. These no-good bastards are trying to fondle you. One step! Two-step! Three! Hold! Skirts up! Stick them now that they are blind! Stick! Stick! Dance away, my lovelies! Dance! Dance!'

Master Sergeant Potter led the third square. His no-nonsense commands were terse, coarse and to the point.

In the tight squares, the men were close to exhaustion. Their left arms trembled with the effort of keeping their heavy shields up, and in their right, their swords felt much heavier than they should have been. Salty sweat mixed with dust and dirt, dribbled into their bloodshot eyes, blinding them. Their legs wobbled, and their nerves, stretched to breaking, many casting furtive and sometimes panicked glances over their comrades' heads, weighing up the odds against making a desperate dash back to the enfolding arms of the main body of the army. Driven to the edge of their strength and stamina, their gasps for breath turned into gut-wrenching sobs with tears of anger and despair, cutting hot rivulets under their metalled cheek guards. Only the steady voices of their commanders and the fellowship of their fellows kept them in place. They held together grinding on through the rigours of their situation. Outnumbered, they stood defiant, and only the favourable terrain kept them from being surrounded, overwhelmed and defeated.

The three armoured divisions were moving upwards on a steady incline, constantly manoeuvring on a broad, dusty stretch of chalky land separating roughly cultivated fields on either side. Six hours ago, the scouts had brought word of massed infantry forces marching double-quick at their rear. Morgan did not want to slow for engagement, so he had peeled off this hundred and fifty manned team to try and stem the Protectorate tide and stop it from chewing into the army's backside. Now they sat caught in hell's grinder.

'Here they come!' shouted Morgan. 'Shields tight! Shoulder it, lads! Shoulder it!'

With a crushing sound and the weight of a tonne of rocks, the enemy bore down on them. Its thunderous assault, forcing the front ranks down almost on their knees.

'Hold! Hold!' came Morgan's deep, bass voice over the grating of iron bossed shields, over the grunts and sobs of over-burdened men, the hoarse gasping of parched throats, and sometimes the occasional whimper of a man at the edge of his strength. Saliva drooled from open mouths, and thick snot from blowing nostrils dripped onto dirt-covered boots, turning the chalky dust into a muddy paste, slippery, waiting to betray the next step.

'Hold or die, lads! Hold! Hold! Wait for it! Wait for it! Now! Heave! Together! Forward! Stab! Stab!'

In the front ranks, where the biggest, the strongest, the meanest, and the downright craziest crouched in belligerence, all tensed as one. Their back and shoulder muscles, bulging under the enormous strain. Then with a roar of pure aggression and fury, they surged upwards and forward on Morgan's powerful command. Their shocked assailants flew backwards, shields wrenched, thrown high, leaving a gap. Into this won space sprang the defenders, their short swords stabbing viciously into the now exposed bodies before them. Before the screams could fade, before the bright blood stopped gushing, the iron-rimmed fence of shields snapped inwards, shut tight, and with shuffling boots, the armoured squares retreated further up the incline.

The attackers hung back. None wanted to fling themselves on the iron tips of death after being repulsed in such a bloody fashion, time and time again. Despite the loud railings of their commanders, they hung back, shouting and posturing after the steadily withdrawing, chillingly, faceless enemy.

Throughout the day, they withdrew in order before the Protectorate forces, ignoring their taunts and bluster, withstanding their eventual assaults, weathering each storm. Worryingly, men were beginning to falter, falling asleep on their feet, and had to be jolted awake and supported by their comrades in arms. Morgan was the centre point for all three squares. His iron strength held them together, his deep voice welded their concentration and will, his timely commands carried them onwards. He was their squad leader, their commander, their general.

As the shadows of dusk fell around them, men, despite everything, began to feel the fingers of gloom and lost hope entwining themselves around their hearts. Once again, Morgan's steady voice found the last vestiges of strength left in their souls.

'Our time is here, soldiers and comrades! Be ready! Help is at hand!'

Moments after, faintly in the distance, came the sound of a cavalry bugle. Joy and renewed energy surged into the hearts and limbs of the battle-weary defenders. In the enemy, there was only dread.

'How the bugger did he know help was coming,' gasped Honeycut, drooling blood mixed with saliva from a smashed mouth.

'Ready, soldiers!?' came Morgan's cry.

'Ready, General!' came the quick response. 'Ready! Ready! Ready!'

'At my mark! Quick march! Double time! Up, up, up!'

With drumming of metalled soles, Morgan and his men trotted off into the growing darkness, leaving behind an uncertain and reticent Protectorate infantry who were unwilling to test the new oncoming threat, especially in the black of night.

It wasn't long before the stomping troopers, still in their battle squares, were drawn to a halt by Morgan. Arrayed on the road ahead of them sat several cavalry riders, sitting silently on their mounts. The shield wall opened, and Morgan strode out and confidently walked up to the man leading them.

'Well met, Nat. It's good to see you again.'

'You too, General.'

The formality of their words lay belied by the warmth in Morgan's voice and the broad grin on Nat's face.

'Made it to the rendezvous already?'

'Yes, General. Slipped right through the Protectorates skirts then decided to ride over and see what was keeping you.'

As he said this, a yipping group of about a sixty riders smoothly galloped around the stationary troops like smoke in the shadows, not bothered in the least by the darkness.

'Brought the ladies with you, I see,' observed Morgan.

'They brought themselves, General. There is no controlling them. Guess they're technically off to harass and harry the enemy, but to them, they are just off to have some fun with silly, no-good men.'

'I see. Well, we had better chase after our army before they lose us again.'

'They've encamped about two miles ahead, General, awaiting your return.'

'Ride ahead, Nat. Tell them that my orders are to break camp immediately and march through the night. We'll follow as best we can.'

'At once, General.'

As Morgan turned to re-join his rearguard, something crashed powerfully into his mind causing him to stumble slightly. Frowning, he sent his senses out. 'Krarl!' He was out there somewhere, dogging his heels once again. Would he never give up! He already knew the answer.

After a sleepless night of nervousness, disorder and sudden attacks by fast-moving ghosts and she-devils, the Protectorate infantry units were very relieved when three divisions of the governor's own mounted, shock troops arrived just after dawn. The night devils had mysteriously disappeared, and the infantry commanders were much embarrassed when steely looks and silent stares met their questions as to their whereabouts. Joining together in battle formation, they moved in double time to engage the enemy before they could break camp. Naturally, when they got there, the invaders and already gone. As they sat in a nearby farmyard having a collective scratch head on what to do next, heralds arrived with burning news from central command to regroup immediately ten miles upriver from the city. They were to move at all speed. The governor himself had taken to the field.

***

The city was alive with rumour and counter-rumour. Some said that the country had been invaded by a second as yet unidentified, foreign force. At the head of this invasion was the captain-general who was intent on seizing the kingship and claiming it as his own. Others insisted that he was here to support the new king. Some others even vowed that the old king was still alive and was back to liberate the kingdom from the god-bothering Protectorate. 'Peasants!' fumed the old, Lord Chamberlain. They are just plain common folk with no common sense whatsoever. There was an atmosphere of unrest settling over everything causing unnecessary disruption to smooth governance.

He was late for a secret meeting of the Privy Council, one being held without the knowledge of the king himself and lacking an invitation to the troublesome and contrary Earl of Marches. Lately, the actions of the king were becoming uncontrollable, putting all of them in harm's way. This meeting stood convened to hear proposals of how best to guide him. Of course, it goes without saying, for the betterment of all and the future welfare of the kingdom. The gathered ministers of state would also have to use this opportunity to make decisions on how to limit the growing influence of the Earl on the king. Of equal importance, was the matter of how to curtail the dangerous machinations of the Beggar's guild under the gung-ho leadership of Timothy. Some people seemed genuinely incapable of making practical adaptations. The world stood filled with dream chasers, ever racing after elusive ideals. It always came down to a few good men to keep steady hands on the tiller of events. As he had feared, the old warmonger, Ap Heston, if indeed it was he, was back again tearing the country and its traditions apart with his antiquated ideas and methods. There was something inhuman caged inside that man's breast; something that does not belong to the world of men. He had warned Timothy that this might happen, and lo and behold; he had been proven right. The man knew nothing about how to conduct peace negotiations and engineer constructive compromise. At the first hiccup, his hand would fly straight for the sword. Why the Beggar Abbot was so hell-bent on giving him full-hearted support he would never understand.

'A moment, if you will, Lord Chamberlain.'

The old lord froze, arrested by the softly spoken and unexpected voice, which penetrated his thoughts, leaving behind an unpleasant feeling of guilt.

'Your Majesty, I am…'

'In a hurry. This fact is obvious, my lord, but I promise not to detain you for longer than is necessary.'

The king strolled along the passageway, flanked by two scarred and grim, white-robed bodyguards. The Lord Chamberlain peered at them suspiciously.

'Do you like my two latest recruits to the royal bodyguards, my lord? They are genuine survivors from the Battle of Sorrows. Served under our beloved Earl, they tell me. Impressive, don't you think?'

'Your Majesty, we must try not to aggravate the governor too much, especially at this time of uncertainty.'

'Uncertainty, yes…' the king responded thoughtfully.

'Tell me, Lord Chamberlain, did my brother hold you in his trust?'

'Why, of course, your Majesty, I was a valued member of his inner circle of advisers!' spluttered the lord, puffing up his chest in indignation.

'My pardon, my lord, everyone testifies to this, calm yourself. And now, you are one of my trusted advisors, are you not?'

'Without any doubt, my King!'

'So good to hear, my friend. What advice did you give, my lord, when you first received the news of my brother's fall?'

'I...I...I suggested...'

'That it was best not to aggravate this grave situation any further, I have heard this as well. Who had charge of the city's defences, my lord?'

The king's voice remained soft and calm, almost friendly.

'The Privy Council, I have been told,' the king answered his own question. 'Did my brother not leave contingency plans behind, my lord?'

'Yes, my King, but we did not expect to have to put them to use. Ap Heston was very confident...'

'Ap Heston is always confident. He is a confident man who instils confidence. So tell me again, my lord, did the Privy Council put the royal contingency plans into action?'

'No, your Majesty, Ap Heston fled the battle to save his skin...'

'Ap Heston spirited the body of our dead king, my brother, away when all sat lost to prevent its abuse as a trophy. Don't be boorish, my lord,' the king interrupted with a patient tone. 'So again, Lord Chamberlain, what was the decision of the Privy Council?'

'To disband the reserve army and remove the city's defences. We sent a peace envoy instead to the Protectorate's general. We did it to save lives to...'

'Was this the last command of our brother, your king?'

'No, sire, it was not.'

'Thank you for this little historical chat, my friend. I hope I haven't kept you overlong.'

As a visibly relieved Lord Chamberlain turned to go, the king called out.

'Oh, one more required advice, my lord. Do you think a king should always know what happens under his royal roof?'

'That's a strange question, your Majesty, but yes.'

'Thank you, my lord, go in peace.'

Hurrying away like a brigand fleeing the scene of his crime, the Lord Chamberlain's old limbs shook with terror. He couldn't help but think of his now-dead cousin, the then Earl of Greendale.

***

'It's him with dead certainty.'

'Wherein lays this certainty, Lord Abbot?'

'My envoys sent to catch him these many months past, have finally reached their goal. He heads a force of infantry many miles upriver. It is not enough to bring sound completion to his tasks, and his hopes lie in our countrymen's will to bolster his fledgeling strength.'

'He has taken a bold risk!'

'He is a bold man.'

'Are we yet positioned to show our hand?'

'Not yet, we need Ap Heston to pull stronger on that septic tooth which is the governor. When his attention sits narrowed, then we can unsheathe our hidden knives.'

'Is our dear Earl healed enough and ready to lead?'

'Our Earl is as tough as old leather, Patrick, and he has never been slow at stepping forward,' laughed the abbot.

'When the time is right, will we be fast enough to make an impact?'

'You are correct in this, of course. Timing is everything, and our forces lie scattered for safekeeping. That is why the Earl is the heart of our effort. The governor knows this. I'm afraid he will take action against us very soon. We must remain prepared.'

'And the king?'

'That's another worrying matter. Without him, unity of action will be much more difficult to achieve. He speaks only with Earl Marches, and in riddles at that. He knows well that he lives in a house of spies, busy eyes and wagging tongues. We cannot be certain of his support. Unfortunately, we can no longer risk the Earl's safety, so contact has in all intents and purposes, stands severed.'

'What shall we do?'

'We do what we must. We wait for Ap Heston to make his move, then act quickly, with or without the king.'

***

The governor placed his grey at the head of a five thousand strong force of cavalry. Of these two thousand were his personal, highly trained, shock troops; battle-tested and battle-hungry. He loved the scent of war, and his nostrils were now full of the intent of the bastard general; he knew his objective and was moving fast with his vanguard to meet him head-on. He had sent out the call and the far-flung, newly gifted, Protectorate lords would be bringing their warbands to join him within the next few days. Yes, the wily bastard had chosen and secured a favourable position to make his stand, but the numbers were in his favour as well as war trained troops. He would on a conservative estimate outnumber this Ap Heston three to one.

The majority of his patrols should already be ahead of him heading for the designated base camp, adding another four thousand to his starting total. To put up any type of fight Ap Heston would have to rely on a significant number of his countrymen to join his army.

'Outriders, approaching, Excellency.'

A dusty pair of scouts, sweating under their mail shirts, cantered up to the governor's party and saluted briskly.

'May the god protect you, General. A large force of eight hundred horse warriors sent by Lord Neville awaits you in a dale two miles ahead. They are under the leadership of his younger son, who sends his greetings and asks permission to join his forces with yours.'

'Ah, young Neville, I knew he would be one of the first to answer my call. I have done well in singling out this future lord. Ride back and bid him to sit tight and rest. Tell him we will camp where he is and that he must join my advisers and me in our talks when I arrive.'

In a small, flat, grassy plain surrounded by a series of low lying hills used by the locals for the grazing of sheep, the governor set up his encampment to discuss strategy with his commanders. By late afternoon most were already gathered in his tent when Lord Neville, the younger, dipped his raven head through the tent flap.

'Permission to enter, Excellency, the god is our keeper.'

'Young Neville,' beamed the governor, with genuine and rare warmth, 'welcome, we require fresh eyes for an age-old situation.'

A gaunt, hatchet-faced man with the sides of his head shaved, and a scar running through his lips giving him a permanent sneer, interjected roughly.

'What has stood defeated once is ripe for defeating twice.'

'True, true,' responded the governor coldly. 'Lord Neville, meet Lord Otto. He has commanded my right-wing through many of our recent campaigns. What do you think of his assessment?'

'Our lord has it right in that defeat bleeds bloated confidence, but some are very good at learning from a fall and become twice as dangerous, given a second opportunity.'

'Well said. We cannot become complacent with this Ap Heston. He knows what he is engineering. A position strong atop a high point between running water and bothersome wood, with a foot squarely placed on the sole crossing within leagues of our castle fort, which we must keep to guard our rear against undesired fortitude and surprise. He invites us to come to him and go to him; we shall.'

CHAPTER XVII

Food was becoming a problem. Foragers and hunters alike were ranging far and wide. Although over the past few days, their circles stood pushed into ever-decreasing spheres. The steady march of the Protectorate army was limiting their effectiveness. Now many were staring with some trepidation, as the growing ranks of the enemy kept flooding onto the plains below, throwing up an increasing number of tents and camp defences. Already they sat outnumbered despite many country-folk joining their effort. People were unsure if trusting this foreign army was better for them than the Protectorate, and if Morgan's intentions weren't just straightforward and blatant opportunism. Yes, correct, he was a long-serving and trusted general to their kings of old, but he was a foreigner himself, and certainly not their king. Was he making a bid to make himself one? For the last seven days, the full company had been labouring around the clock, to fortify their position. The commanders stood not excluded from this work due to rank. Everyone had to pitch in. At the bottom of the hill was dug a gaping, sharp-angled pit, topped on its upper side by rows of sharpened stakes, firmly embedded into the hard earth. Above this was a palisade with a walkway running along the entire western circumference and crossing the ford by a wooden bridge.

Commanding each side of the river were three, sturdy towers. All along this edifice, archers, slingers and men armed with light, throwing spears, patrolled. The heavily forested area on their right flank lay blanketed with nasty traps of varying types, and only troop leaders and hand-picked scouts knew the safe passageways between them.

Now the supply of food was becoming a problem. The foragers and hunters had been increasingly coming into contact with their opposites, leading to growing, running clashes, harassment and counter harassment. This activity soon developed into a tit for tat raiding. In response, the governor issued orders for a scorched-earth policy. This decision forced the displaced villagers to seek shelter amongst the fortified army, which in turn led to more mouths to feed with dwindling resources and food supplies.

Morgan knew that time was not on his side. He had to tempt the governor into battle sooner rather than later, to draw and tie down his attention, but the man was no stranger to war and was carefully working out his strategy. It was time to pull his tail a little.

'Nat, I need you to take the ladies out tonight to play a bit with the governor's men.'

'Must I? Surely, Tam is much more the ladies' man than I am.'

They both turned from surveying the enemy's activities to study a now perturbed looking Tam.

'Now, now gentlemen, you know well that these shy girls do not like me or trust me, for that matter. It is Nat here who they always invite to their little parties.'

'Actually, he's made a good point there, Nat,' responded Morgan. 'You are the only one who seems to have won their respect. It has to be you, I'm afraid.'

With a heavy, weary sigh, Nat said.

'Okay, what do you want us to do?'

'Harry them. Raise hell along their supply lines; cut it if you can. I want to distract them from burning more villages. Tam, I've got an equally important and dangerous task for you. You too will have to leave tonight.'

***

Fear lay over the village like a heavy blanket. Huddled in their draughty, vermin-infested, straw-thatched hovels and huts, the poor of the land hunkered down in the darkest hours of the night, hoping that the uncertain world around them had forgotten their existence. It was not to be. Suddenly, the thunder of hooves, reverberating through the bare ground of their rude shelter, called home; drumming up from deep in the earth that primitive, wide-eyed terror, possessing the superstitious soul, driving it out of a warm hearth, dispossessed, into a blind land of hobgoblins and demons. In smocks still soiled with a hard days toil, strong hands ingrained with dirt, grab for their children and wives, both to give and receive strength and comfort, knowing that what little they had will be lost to heartless men of war and fire in a mere heartbeat.

Lord Neville rode grimly through the night at the head of thirty men. This target was the fourth village today that they had attacked. He did not revel in his task, but it was necessary under the will of the god. Killing low peasantry was not his objective. His aim to drive them in fear into the arms of the godless rebels stood a good chance of working. To ensnarl those who pretended to be their saviours. The flaming firebrand held above his head illuminated his hard face in shadows and plains, the wind of their passage, making the flames waver and flicker, casting dancing hell-born shadows swirling among them.

With angry shouts, more to gain courage for their foul deed than to frighten, the raiders hurled the red-hot brands into the dry roofs which burst instantly into flame, devouring all beneath it. Then grabbing their iron swords, they drove their maddened horses at the fleeing figures, slapping them with the hard, flat planes, forcing them into the night. Any, who dared resist would suddenly feel the sharp edge, slicing open soft flesh, sprinkling the parched soil with blood.

***

Earlier that night, as soon as darkness fell, Nat, old Hatch, the fierce leader of the women warriors, Gabrielle, and forty selected members of her troop, slipped silently through the woods. They led their horses, hooves wrapped in rags to muffle sound, and with hands, gently covered their muzzles to prevent any spontaneous neighing. It wasn't difficult, nor did it take long, to evade the Protectorate sentinels, whose minds seemed to be preoccupied with the aroma of roasting meat wafting from the nearby encampment; some poor peasant's confiscated pig, no doubt. Tagging along with them was another group of fifty, consisting of the hardened, professional, queen's mountain assault squad and siege warfare experts led by Tam. At the edge of the forest, they split into small groups and regathered some twenty minutes later, in a dark, sheltered valley. Hereafter some whispered goodbyes and good lucks, they separated, each team, focussing on their given task.

***

'I'll get the men working on some camp defences, and organise the night patrols, Captain.'

'For what purpose, man? The wagons sit drawn up in a nice circle, the mules tethered inside. We have guards on every perimeter. The countryside is crawling with our patrols. The bloody, godless, disturbers of the peace are penned in on their hill by the governor. Relax man! Get some food in you.'

Newly promoted as a field captain, they had put him in charge of a supply train. Not much of an improvement from a depot supply sergeant, if truth be told. In reality, there were many more drawbacks - hard ground to sleep on instead of a soft bed with a soft, pliant tavern doxy to warm it for you.

Not much of a trade-off for a little higher rank. Still, tomorrow his team would deliver the supplies and head back to the city and a good cup of wine. Now, where did that bloody over-keen, sergeant get off to? The fire was pleasant, but he didn't like drinking coffee and eating alone.

 Suddenly, the wild drumming of hooves pulled him out of his grumbling contemplation. He couldn't see a thing as he stared impotently into the night; too much gazing into camp-fires and dreaming, he thought irritably.

'Sergeant!' he yelled. 'Where the hell are you? What the fuck is going on out there?'

 A high pitched, scalp-prickling, aggressive scream, split the night, causing the increasingly frantic captain to spill half of his boiling hot coffee over his face and hands in alarm.

'Shit! Shit!' he yelled, dropping his mug and fumbling to draw his sword which, unfortunately, had become stuck in its scabbard.

'Shit! Shit!' he hissed, stumbling over his feet and falling into the fire, screaming and thrashing about in desperation.

 This act of supreme ineptitude and awkwardness saved his life. Where his head had been moments before, an arrow flew through the now vacant space. With a dull thud, it embedded itself into the wagon behind. Rolling onto his knees, he slapped frantically at his burning clothing, unaware of his close brush with death. This fraught moment was when he saw his vision from hell. Banshees, screaming banshees, bent low over wildly galloping and leaping horses, eyes rolled whitely in the glow of the firelight. And the banshees, long hair streaming in the wind, mouths wide open, emitting an ululating sound that caused him to loosen his bladder, wetting his steaming trousers.

'God, be my protector!'

A harried, dirt-covered sergeant found him there. He was still on his knees where he had been ten minutes before, staring vacantly at the circle of burning wagons. His command destroyed, his men dead, his carefully corralled mules scattered to the four winds, his dreams transformed into a nightmare.

Nat, old Hatch, and the Banshees, similarly struck two other supply trains night. Going in hard and fast, then racing back out into the night. Their luck was holding for, as of yet, they had not suffered any casualties. However, the patrols were now furiously hunting them.

Twice they managed to slip away from three close encounters, due to the darkness, but in a greater measure, thanks to Nat's and Hatch's consummate knowledge of the land and their superb hunter's skills as well as the seemingly innate ability of the women warriors to make use of and meld into any landscape. They were riding hard, zigzagging, Indian-file, up and down little-known fox trails, when they saw the halo on the near horizon of a burning village. Without hesitation, they swerved towards it.

Bursting through a flimsy, field, border hedge, they found themselves slap-bang in the middle of a Protectorate, village raid; a raid designed to burn and destroy. Although taken aback, they did not break stride but ploughed into the sides of the raiding party hell-bent on carrying out the governor's dirty business, yelling and screaming at the top of their lungs.

In a looping arc, Nat's longsword cut right then left, first slicing through the unprotected neck and face of a surprised raider, then severing the hand of another at the wrist as he tried to bring his sword up in a defensive reaction. Then his horse tore on, crashing its chest into the flank of a horse, bowling both it and its rider over, its war trained hooves stamping and its teeth tearing. Then he was through and galloping clear. Swivelling in his saddle, he glimpsed his banshees ripping through the still shocked Protectorate troop in a maelstrom of blood, noise and mayhem, slashing viciously around them with their long, curved knives. Hatch was in their midst, keeping low over his black horse's neck, almost invisible. Then they were thundering after him leaving a bewildered and uncoordinated bunch of enemy cavalry milling about behind.

Dawn found them pounding towards the forest verges that protected the flank of their fortified encampment. Behind them and hot on their heels, were two patrols numbering around two hundred men. As they swerved around the governor's war camp, they could hear the loud alarms of the sentries. Their horses were blowing and lathered, yet they coaxed every ounce of effort out of them, as they tore mere yards away from the waking camp. Even though they were exhausted from their night's endeavours, and two of the women warriors were bleeding heavily, they launched a hail of arrows at the armed men running towards them. Yelling in savage satisfaction when their deadly darts, fired from their short, powerful recurve-bows, found their marks. Nat, Hatch and the warriors raced up to the treeline. They leapt from their horses even before they had come to a halt. Suddenly, a line of men rose out of the bushes where they had been lying in wait.

The morning air hung filled with a whistling, burring sound as the men swirled long raw-hide slings above their heads. Despatched in unison, a deadly cloud of lead pellets hurtled into the following enemy horsemen, dropping the riders bone dead into the bushes and sending the hapless horses crashing. The slingers then spun on their heels and sprinted after Nat and his group as they disappeared into the treeline. The Protectorate soldiers, maddened by this bold affront, surged after them, only to be met by a storm of arrows, shot by invisible archers, hidden by the trees. Organising themselves into a protective shield-wall, they continued the chase, but in the confined spaces between the dark trees, they were unable to keep formation. Frustration grew, as the retreating defenders repeatedly picked them off. Their commanders soon realised that there was no value gained by continuing the pursuit, and the recall sounded. Those who did not heed the signal soon became the first victims of the hidden traps, and inevitably, even the most fool-hardy gave up the useless effort.

The morning sun was already shining strongly when Nat and his night raiders emerged from the forest into the encampment proper. Here, Morgan and his commanders met them, along with a throng of smiling, back slapping onlookers. He was entirely taken by surprise as Morgan strode forward and embraced him.

'Welcome back, son,' he said to him in his deep voice. Then he turned to the usually bent, but bright-eyed Hatch and muttered. 'I see you're still alive, old fellow.' Hatch cackled in response and replied.

'I needed to come back to find out what you've done with that donkey I sold you, sonny.'

An even greater surprise for Nat was when the warriors' leader, Gabrielle, walked up behind him, draped a long, hard-muscled arm around his shoulders and whispered fiercely.

'Great night! Let's do it again soon.'

Nat grinned. They had been lucky.

Morgan's voice, grave and sober, broke in.

'I'm afraid we won't be able to do that again any time soon. The governor will certainly put a heavy guard on our back door. It's all in Tam's hands now. Come Nat, Hatch, Gabrielle. Fill me in on your night's adventures.'

***

It was gone mid-morning by the time Lord Neville wearily plodded into camp at the head of ten straggling men. The surviving remnants of his original thirty strong raiding party, and they all sported bleeding wounds, including Neville, who held his left arm in a make-shift, blood-stained sling. He noticed the tense, angry mood of the sprawling camp, but the cause was not apparent to his eyes. Dismissing his men, he made his way to the governor's command tent.

'Ah, Neville, it's good to see you back. By your look, I do not hesitate to say that all did not go well.'

'Thank you, Excellency. It's not all bad. We decommissioned four villages and confiscated their livestock, but then providence turned against us.'

'In what way?' asked the governor quietly.

'In the mid of night, just as we were taking our leave to return to you with a job well done, we were struck by an unusual enemy troop - a troop of hell-cats, all women, of a particular sort, led by a tall, fast man. They slammed into us before we even knew that they were there. Cut through us, and were gone again before we could react. I lost twenty men and all of the livestock.'

'Never send a boy to do a man's job,' muttered Lord Otto, his face taking on an even more sneering look.

'Nothing unusual has occurred here,' responded the governor without glancing at Otto. 'Ap Heston is doing what stands expected, trying to goad me into hurried action. My only concern is what little tricks he yet has to show us. Reports are still coming in of supply trains attacked and destroyed. He's pissing on fire with this. Our fighting bellies lie fed by our river barges, untouched and unthreatened. Nothing has changed, but quite a night. Come, Lord Neville, have a cup of wine and tell me more of these hell-cats of yours. They flew through here at dawn this morning. Caused quite a havoc among Lord Otto's men I hear. So you are not alone.'

CHAPTER XVIII

 The rise of the early morning filled the spaces with hazy, uncertain light. Opaque mists stretched low over the grey-green river, reflecting the after dawn sunlight, denying the eye the ability to penetrate deeply, dazzling the visual sense. They lay hidden on the sloping riverbank among the damp, dew-covered grass and reeds. Tam, Douglas, the grizzled captain of the specialist team, and two others, were squinting intensely at the looming, indistinct bulk of the round fortress guarding the entrance to the only bridge leading to the city. Below them, and nearer the water's edge, the rest of the squad were painfully inching their way towards the almost submerged and reed-covered drainage mouth. It was an ancient sewage outlet which had not been in use for over three hundred years. How Morgan knew of its existence was still a mystery to Tam. They had been working on cutting through the rusted grill covering the mud-stuck portal to the drainage tunnel, using fine-meshed, metal-toothed saws, since long before dawn; labouring mostly by touch. Now a hole, big enough to allow one man at a time, had been made, and they had to get in before the warming sun, burned the covering mist away. A close eye had to be kept on the patrolling sentries stationed on the stone parapet, while they slowly and painstakingly cut their way through. A soft bird call told them that all was well, and one by one they slipped away, with Tam the last to follow.

The tunnel was pitch black, damp, dank and musty. It took a little while to light the torches they had brought with them, then on hands and knees, they crawled through the slimy, sticky mud, with Tam taking the lead. At times they had to pause to dig a wider passage. More often, they had to lie flat on their stomachs and worm their way through, feeling the earth pressing down on them, fighting down the sensation of being lost, wandering forever, deep in the womb of the goddess. With time lost to the senses, they came upon a cross-section where the tunnel branched three different ways. Keep to the centre, always keep to the centre, Morgan had warned. So, staying on the central passage, they crawled onwards. After seeming ages, impossible to measure, the first torch guttered out, startling the men out of their time out of place, mental absorption. In quick order the remaining two spluttered, extinguished with a dying flutter, plunging them into unimaginable blackness, where the mind guessed at shapes and shadows that did not exist. 'Shit!' someone muttered.

These tough, sturdy men were siege specialist, accustomed to digging their way under walls and battlements as well as climbing their way over. So after a moment's hesitation, where using their fingertips to feel around, they re-orientated themselves, and moved onwards, following each other through their sense of touch.

With time stretching out, they finally came to a dead end. This stop stood expected, for Morgan's description had already led them to expect it. Reaching upwards with blind hands, Tam felt open space; the tunnel would from here lead straight up at right angles into a now disused and bricked-up guard-a-robe, slap-bang at the heart of the fortress. With a foot and a hand each on the smooth stone of the circular shaft, they began the long, challenging, muscle-aching climb to the top. On getting there, Tam pushed forcefully against the rotted board covering the opening and clambered, relieved, into the small room, lit dimly by a slash of an arrow slit, where he immediately started working free the bricks on the left side of the wall. Thankfully, the lime cement was powdery with age, and the bricks came free with relative ease.

In a short time, he had broken through into a rarely used corridor. Over the years, the fortress lay gradually converted into an administrative stronghold, rather than the original military one. Its internal structure, slowly conforming to its new function. Many rooms, once connected to busy passages, now lying almost derelict. Thank the gods for small mercies. A steady file of forty-seven men streamed silently into the corridor, taking up positions of watchfulness, checking and cleaning their weapons. Hours before dawn, Tam had sent three of the strongest swimmers across the Sacred River on a clandestine mission to enter the city and make contact with the Beggar Abbot. He made the sign of the horn to overt ill-luck, for crossing the river with its cold waters, fast eddies, powerful undertows, and sentinel eyes upon it was a highly precarious enterprise. However, a lot was hanging on its outcome. Still, hope was high, as nothing entered or left the city without the Abbot being made aware of it.

Squatting down next to the Douglas' compact frame, Tam whispered.

'Right, two objectives, two teams. I'll head for the castle-gate, jamb the double portcullis, secure it and seize the sally ports. You make your way through the centre of the keep to the storage basements and secure the supplies against vengeful destruction.'

Reaching out, he grasped the older man's forearm in a warriors grip his eyes shining with excitement and energy.

'May the goddess Fortuna walk with you.'

'And with you, young Watcher.'

With a nod the two men separated, leading their teams towards different ends of the corridor, each quickly consulting the sketched, castle plans, mapped by Morgan to guide them.

Tam did not go for caution. He led his squad at a hard, fast pace. On the first flight of stone, circular stairs leading downwards, they encountered two surprised relief sentries, trudging wearily upwards. Like a leopard, Tam rushed forward and leapt at them, stabbing his knife upwards under the chin and into the brain of the first soldier before he could fully register what was happening. Then shoving the body viciously aside, plunged the tip of his sword into the stomach of the second, bursting through the links of his mail shirt and ripping up into his heart. Wrenching free his sword in a gush of blood, he shouldered the dead man back down the stairwell, bounding agilely after it, his men hot on his heels. They crashed into a small, well-lit guard room, where four other soldiers were desperately disengaging from their breakfast and grabbing at their weapons. They didn't stand a chance. The determined squad was on them like flees onto an old dog, stabbing and stomping on them, sending their spirits screaming into death.

'Quick! Quick! Let's keep moving,' Tam whispered fiercely, his eyes now afire.

They sped along a short passage leading to the battlements, their feet flying and faces belligerent, still shrouded in luck, as of yet the alarm had not been triggered. The guards here were more plentiful, and after being momentarily taken aback by the sudden emergence of the grim squad of armed, enemy combatants, all mayhem broke loose.

Deep inside the central cylinder of the keep, Douglas and his team were using stealth rather than Tam's 'hit them hard' method. Things seemed to be working well for them despite encountering a terrified priest or two, who they quickly subdued, tied, gagged and bundled into their robes and dumped unceremoniously into side rooms. They had remained undetected as they wormed their way downwards, inching towards the second-floor level. Suddenly, the loud brass baying of alarm horns reverberated throughout the stone edifice, making them all jump and grip tightly onto their weapons.

'Here's where the plough hits the shit, lads!' said Douglas in a gravelly voice. 'Get ready!'

'Ready!' droned his crew in response.

The goddess, however, still had her eyes on them. As the Protectorate soldiers rushed out of their sleeping barracks, strapping on bits of armour as they went, they automatically reacted to the alarm call by heading for the battlements, not thinking that the enemy might already be yards from them within the keep itself.

'Tam will have his hands full in a minute,' thought Douglas dourly.

Hunkering down, they let the soldiers' race by, and then moved behind in their wake, crawling down the wide, stone stairs onto the second level, the heart of the administrative sector. Here their luck ran out as the goddess looked elsewhere.

One of the soldiers in his hurry, dropped his sword, and while bending to pick it up, caught from the corner of his eye, the sight of an array of grim-faced men behind him with naked swords bared and ready for use. In a panic, he shouted warning to his fellows, falling over in a crash of metal and leather.

Douglas did not wait. As the back end of the Protectorate guards' caste confused glances over their shoulders, he tore a page out of Tam's book and charged with his men close behind. They hit hard without making any shouts or yells to lend courage. They were mountain born and reared. Their attack was like a stone avalanche, compact and inexorable. This unemotional, implacable and savage onslaught, in addition to the sudden surprise of it, was too much for the unprepared guards, and they fled on towards the battlements, yelling loudly for help. Taking full advantage of this reprieve, Douglas ordered his men to abandon their assault and continue with their objective. Moving swiftly, they disappeared into the cavernous stairwell leading down to the next level, jamming the door behind them.

In the meantime, Tam and his squad were having a hard time of it. Assailed on all sides, they had formed into a tight defensive circle on one of the square platforms which every few yards, interrupted the narrow, stone walkway. They fought desperately, all of them bearing bloodied wounds. Tam felt more alive than he had ever been in his entire life. As yet another soldier came at him, he slashed high with his knife hand, aiming for the eyes, glimpsing from his periphery, as the stocky, mountain man protecting his left, blocked the sword thrust that would have surely ended his life.

As the guard in front of him flinched, he surged forward with his sword arm, a straight and true aim that tore up through the unfortunate's armpit, cutting the main artery inside. As the screaming man crumpled over, Tam brought his sword over in a whistling stroke, chopping off the arm at the elbow, of a colossal, brute of a soldier as he was attempting to bring a war axe down on the head of his stocky companion. Twisting quickly back to his right, he saw his companion stationed there, plunge his sword into the groin of a soldier who was just about to stab Tam in the ribs.

With a savage backhand swing, Tam took the man's head off, ending the terrible high keening noise he was making.

 And so the battle raged on for the outnumbered and beset queen's men. They fought on, caught in the moment. Grim determination held them tight intending to send into the other-world as many of the enemy soldiers as they could. Stand together, protect your comrades, and die standing on your feet, sword in hand. Eerily, they battled in silence, with frequent grunts and snarls, sweat pouring from their bodies, assailing their nostrils in such close quarters with its pungency along with the iron scent of blood. For Tam, the mission lay momentarily forgotten, and he expected that death would find him here at any time. The joy of it was overwhelming. Suddenly, a group of panicked and yelling soldiers burst out of one of the portals leading from the fortress proper, just ahead of him. As in all battle situations where men balanced their emotions between flight and fight, anything unexpected could quickly and unpredictably alter the flow of events. In this case, it worked in favour of Tam and his mountain men. Uncertainty filled the minds of the Protectorate soldiers who sensed something unknown at their backs. Some looked around for an avenue to escape into, others pulled back from the dangerous circle of fighting men, and yet others turned to face the still anonymous threat at their rear. Instantly, Tam seized the moment. Issuing quick, terse commands, he set the fighting circle into a flying wedge, and with himself at the point, surged into the packed and distracted enemy, scattering them; the mission was back on again.

With the Protectorate defenders still in disarray, the queen's men, using their forward momentum, aggressively forged their way forward. Some had acquired discarded shields and spears and were using them effectively to push, stab and slash their way down to the battlements on the first level, which would take them to the cogs and machinery in the gatehouse above the gates and the double portcullis. As they neared their goal, a band of archers turned their bows on them. Immediately, those with shields took the lead, raising cover over their fellows, then on Tam's shouted command, charged ferociously, frightening the poorly armoured archers into inaccurate aim.

They weren't allowed a second chance. Those who did not take the immediate opportunity to flee fell, brutally cut down, their bows and stashes of arrows swiftly snatched up. One young, brave archer, or maybe foolish, stood his ground. It was evident that he had very little knowledge of up-close, one to one combat. At the back of his mind, somewhere behind the swirling vortex of adrenaline, Tam felt sadness as his sword sliced open the youngster's stomach, spilling his roped intestines into his shocked, trembling hands. To put him out of his suffering, Tam kicked him off of the battlements to tumble into his death. Picking up the fallen bow, Tam deftly caught a full quiver of arrows thrown to him by one of his men. Then they turned and sent barrage after barrage of deadly darts into the milling Protectorate soldiers; packed as they were on the narrow parapet, accuracy remained no longer an issue.

Their luck was still holding. The governor's men were wholly unprepared for this type of assault on the fortress. The sturdy, iron reinforced doors to the upper gatehouse were pleasantly left unlocked. The queen's men quickly filed in, locking and barring the doors behind them. Taking a deep breath to steady him, Tam looked around, taking stock of their situation. Of the twenty-five men who had followed him, nineteen remained. He felt a moment's deep shame that he had not noticed their fall, witnessed their astounding bravery. He hoped that some others had so that someone would tell their tales in the many years to come. So that for all eternity, their final moments would live on throughout the land. Their deeds preserved forever in the memories of their friends and loved ones. But he was their leader; it is his eyes they should have met as they fell.

 He watched the close group of men, all from the same area, the same background and childhood experiences, the same traditions and ideals, as they got down to the business in hand, destroying the mechanical working mechanism of the portcullis. With a co-ordinated, pounding, wrenching, twisting and banging, they settled into their task. It wasn't long before an enormous boom crashed into the door, causing the whole room to shake, filling the space with dust and falling bits of stone and cement. Everyone paused in their labours then went back to work with redoubled effort. On the third or fourth boom, the hardwood making up the major part of the door cracked.

'It won't be long now,' said Tam. 'Men of the Misted Mountains, it has been an honour to have fought at your side. As the only representative of the Watchers here, I salute you.'

The short, stocky men turned to face him and nodded, dropping their makeshift tools and rolling their shoulders to loosen them, they picked up their weapons and moved to stand beside Tam.

'You are a fine captain, Watcher. You led us well,' replied the man who had saved his life so many times in the fighting circle.

Tam gave him a tight smile, turning back to the door as chunks of wood and twisted metal began to fall from it into the room. They all knew that there was nowhere to escape to and none of them gave much further thought to it. They had completed the task assigned to them by their general, their king of old. Now was the time to show these bastards what kingdom men could do.

The first man to stick his face through the broken door received the point of a sword through his eye. He jerked away, screaming in a high pitched, anguished squeal.

'Nosy bastard,' grumbled the man who always seemed to be by his side. Tam wished that he had asked him his name. Now was not the time.

They had learned quickly. Burning torches stuck on long poles soon shoved through the opening and into the faces of the defenders forcing them to step back, and as they did so, armoured men leapt through with aegis and sword. The first man to land in the gatehouse came at Tam, punching his iron shield boss at him.

Tam did not retreat as expected, but stepped forward, grabbing the top rim of the shield with both hands, pivoting to his left to avoid the anticipated sword thrust, and wrenched his hands clockwise, revolving the aegis. A sharp crack, followed by a scream, told him the man's arm lay broken. Tam then pushed violently on the slackly held shield-guard with his forearm and smashed the rim with a loud crunch, into the nose of the hapless soldier. As he staggered back, his ever-present battle companion kicked the fellow stoutly in the knee, breaking it. Tam shoved the loudly screaming man into the path of the following soldiers, sharing a grin with the mountain man.

 The room now filled with acrid smoke. It stung and burned the eyes of both defenders and attackers alike, their tears running down their cheeks as they hacked at and wrestled with each other. Tam's muscles felt like water and his legs like jelly. Even with his mouth open and his lungs blowing like bellows, he couldn't seem to get enough air, and what air he did get was filled with smoke. He sensed rather than saw the mace swinging for his head and drove himself forward, ducking under the heavy weapon and tackling its wielder to the stone floor. As they crashed with Tam uppermost, he convulsed his body, bringing his knee up into the exposed groin of his attacker. He rolled off and staggered to his feet, once again narrowly avoiding a wildly swung axe, meant for his face. Ducking under the attack, he stabbed up blindly with his dirk, his only remaining weapon. As he shouldered the stabbed assailant away, he saw through the hazy smoke his battle friend, caught from behind in a stranglehold by a gigantic Protectorate soldier, his face purple, and his legs swinging free of the ground. Pressing in on him from the front, was a second soldier, with a short sword in one hand and a curved knife in the other. The mountain man had this soldier's sword arm trapped at the wrist, but the knife hand was slowly inching its way down towards his neck, despite his increasingly frantic efforts to kick his attacker. Without thinking, Tam threw his dirk, watching it fly past his friends face and plunge into the eye of the enormous soldier, a one in a million throw. The release of the constricting pressure on his throat now freeing him, his friend lunged forward head butting the surprised attacker on the bridge of his nose in a gush of blood, then pushing him back against the wall, reversed the knife hand and shoved the blade into his throat. Their eyes met as he looked around, and Tam saw the thanks written in them. Suddenly, they widened in alarm, but before Tam could react, he felt a blow to his back, then a searing pain as he fell to his knees. His lungs felt as if they were filling with water, and he coughed, staring at the bright blood as it flowed from his open mouth and splashed onto the cold stone. At the back of his mind, he thought he heard the loud blowing of another alarm, but then all strength left him, and he collapsed face-first into his pooled blood.

***

'Lord Abbot, we've just dragged two men out of the river. They have asked to speak with you. They say Ap Heston has sent them.'

Swinging his legs out of his cot, Timothy was instantly awake. He gazed calmly at the man holding aloft a softly burning candle.

'Have you brought them here?'

'Yes, Lord Abbot.'

'Blind-folded, I hope.'

'Yes, of course, Lord Abbot.'

'Take me to them.'

Sitting at a table with the flickering light of an open lamp playing around their faces, were two stocky, broad-shouldered, young men. They each had a blanket draped over their shoulders, and their shortly cut hair was glistening with wetness.

'Good morning, gentlemen.'

'Lord Abbot,' replied the duo in unison, beginning to rise to their feet.

'No, please,' said Timothy, 'stay seated. They tell me you've been through quite an ordeal. I would like to hear it from your mouth.'

'General Ap Heston despatched fifty of our number here on a mission led by a young Watcher. Our objective was to infiltrate the keep outside your city and enlist your help.'

'I see, and who might you be? If you don't mind me saying so, your features are strange to my eyes.'

'We are warriors of the Misted Mountains, queen's men, trained for siege warfare. We are part of the kingdom on the other side of your borders over the Black Mountain ranges.'

Timothy peered at them in silence but did not make any comments.

'And how is it that you have come to our aid?'

'It's a long story, Lord Abbot, and incredible for us, but your Ap Heston asked for our queen's help in the name of the lady Elaine.'

'Lady Elaine! Is she alive? You have seen her?'

'Yes, Lord Abbot. She arrived at our borders in the company of Ap Heston and his young companion Nat. She is under the royal protection of our queen. A threat made on her life is one of the main reasons our arm forces are here on your soil. We have come to free you of the grasping Protectorate, Lord Abbot, but we are now in desperate need of your aid for we do not have the resources to accomplish this feat on our own.'

'Even if we wanted to assist you, young man, the governor has us penned in like goats. A sentinel-keep, guarding the bridge across the river, a strong army stationed off Highpoint crossing, where of course, your forces under Ap Heston, stands besieged by a rampant and well-supplied governor.'

'You are well informed, lord, but there you have it. At this very moment, as we speak, the rest of my companions are inside said fortress fulfilling a near-suicidal mission to seize the governor's supplies and jamb the fortress' gates open to hold vulnerable for your entry. I have lost my brother to the river goddess to bring you this news. Ap Heston beseeches you to stir action and storm, bridge and fortress, for we cannot win the day without you and the forces held in hidden guise beneath the streets of your city.'

'It seems that you are the one well informed, young soldier. If we do as Ap Heston asks, what is to stop the governor from turning and crushing us a second time.'

'Everything has risks, Lord Abbot. Our general gambled greatly in getting here. If we cut the governor's supplies by depot and river, he has two choices, attack us on Highpoint hill or attack you. Whichever way, we will catch him in a nut-cracker. I beg you to act now and act quickly, Lord Abbot.'

'Stop sucking your thumb, Timothy. It's time to throw caution to the wind, and move,' rumbled the Earl of Marches, stepping out of the hidden alcove where he had been listening. 'I, for one, would like to get this over one way or another. At least, maybe, I can hold my daughter in my arms again.'

Timothy gazed at the Earl and smiled.

'All right, you old warhorse, let's rally and throw the dice for the jackpot.'

***

Tam opened his eyes to find himself surrounded by familiar faces and the faint sounds of a raging battle. He tried to get up, but his body refused to move, he tried to speak, but frothy blood bubbled out of his mouth. He frowned, forcing himself to concentrate on the nearest face peering down at him.

'We've won the day, laddie. You have led us to victory on this front. The town's folk have risen and come to our aid.'

Tam frowned more deeply, staring up at the face, his eyes desperately forming a question.

'My name is Bruce, laddie. I canna lie to you. You're dying; stabbed in the back. I owe my life to you. Wait for me on the bridge of souls, for I will soon be joining you. I have to fight on a bit longer, and every bastard I kill, I will send over to be our honour guard.'

A mist lifted from Tam's eyes, and the pain disappeared. He saw everything with exquisite clarity; Bruce's face, and beyond his, Douglas and the remnants of the mountain squad. The sky was a sharp, beautiful, azure blue and he laughed, 'What a wonderful day to die,' then the world went black.

A weeping Bruce closed gently the eyes of the young watcher who had died staring at the grey, stained ceiling of a battle-battered gate-house, surrounded by the dead and dying, but also by his friends. His song they will forever sing.

***

Sergeant Cuttlefish was up early. He sat on the back of a moored barge whittling aimlessly with his knife on an old piece of wood he had found, his heels drumming on the side of the barge, whistling tunelessly; once a well thought of squad sergeant, a battle sergeant, now a sergeant of the barges. No one had said that he sat demoted. Still, what in the name of the gods would you call this? He knew what elevation looked like, and this was not it. Brought ill tidings once too often, sarge, you old fool, kill the messenger, that's the idea. What was he supposed to have done? Lie down and die? Silly buggers!

'Sarge, sarge, I think there is fighting up at the keep!'

'Yeah, well I don't blame them. Governor has been commandeering all the food, must be short of bacon up there. Not enough to go around for breakfast.'

'Sarge, I'm serious. You had better take a look!'

'Gods, keep your pants on, would you; you're a pain in the arse!' he muttered, dragging himself to his feet and clambering slowly up onto the roof of the barge to join the lookout.

'Ye god's, I think you're right! What I wonder, are those priest fondling bastards up to!?'

'Should we gather the boys and go and investigate sarge?'

'What! Are you mad! And leave the barges unprotected? Don't be an idiot.'

'Yes, sarge, sorry, sarge.'

 A growing group of barge guards were gathering on their charges, staring up at the mist-shrouded fortress, the din of battle carrying down to them.

Twenty minutes later, as the sun burnt off the river haze, they could see miniature figures rushing around on the battlements, followed closely by a loud booming sound.

'Quite a fucking party,' mumbled the disgruntled sergeant.

As he said this, loud shouting and a banging of shields were heard, emanating from the bridge.

'What now!?'

Shading his eyes with a cupped hand, the sergeant could just make out two opposing shield walls shuffling towards each other.

'What a racket! Why not just get at them!'

'What's going on sarge?'

'Got a rebellion brewing, me old muck. Oi, you bastards, stop sightseeing, loosen those ropes, and pole these barges clear of the banks!' yelled the sergeant, startling the barge guards into action.

The three loaded barges had just about cleared the river bank. They drifted slowly, floating downstream when a group of leather-clad archers, flying kingdom colours, suddenly appeared on the docks and loosed flaming arrows at them.

'Hit the decks,' yelled Cuttlefish, diving for cover behind a clump of coiled rope, his mouth twisting in disgust as his tiller-man fell screaming into the river, a burning arrow stuck square into his back.

Flames began to flutter into life at various points of the barge, and swearing under his breath sergeant Cuttlefish dashed the pilotless tiller, righting the drifting vessel, and yelling at the top of his lungs to the boatmen.

'Fire, you bastards! Put out the fire! Stop playing with yourselves, you idiots! Pole. Pole! Pole as you've never poled before!'

It was with some relief that the current suddenly took the barge and it began to pick up speed, putting distance between him and the archers. Too bad they were heading the wrong way, but who the hell cared. Safety was safety.

***

An impatient Earl of Marches took charge of the first body of armed men to be ready. They hastily assembled in a side street, where the Earl bullied and shoved them into formation, and then they set off at a double-trot, two-hundred strong, followed by a troop of fifty archers. They headed straight for the fortress bridge, passing on their way small groups of armed men emerging from the most unlikely places.

'This bloody city is a warren,' muttered the Earl, suddenly truly realising the huge underground influence that the abbot had. 'The man has been hiding an army under our very feet.'

As his determined squad tramped heavily through the cobbled streets, they passed pockets of armed men fighting savagely, cries of anger ringing from hidden alleyways. Here and there, he saw black smoke rising from various buildings and impromptu barricades sat thrown up at multiple intersections.

'Fools, I hope they don't burn down their very own city!'

It didn't seem long before the heavy stamp of their hobnailed boots was echoing up the gentle incline leading to the river and the bridge. It was almost surreal, as here the spaces were empty and deserted. However, as they set foot on the stone crossing with its guardian statues snarling down at them, a stream of foot soldiers armed with sword, shield and spear, hurried out of the still open fortress gates. Quickly taking on the formation of a shield wall, they came shuffling towards them with a great hue and cry. On the parapets above them, the Earl saw the bobbing of helmeted heads and the flashing glimpses of weapons falling and rising. Below, on the river, he saw three heavily laden barges waiting to start their journey to supply the governor. With quick, terse commands, he sent fifteen archers off.

'Burn the bastards to their hulls!'

To the others, he shouted.

'Cover us! Cut the whoresons legs from under them, and if they peep, stick them in the eye with those iron barbs of yours!'

Then taking his place in the third rank, he called out in his deep, war-voice.

'For Sorrows Hill, boys! For our dead king! For our kingdom! Out! Out! Out!'

'Out! Out! Out!' crashed back the reply in a rolling crescendo, and the shield-wall surged forward, intent on revenge and murder.

The two walls came together in a thunderous crunch of iron and wood. Crouched men were driven back on their heels. Others were caught between the hammer of the enemy's shields and the anvil of their comrades in the second and third ranks, breaking noses and losing teeth in a bloody mess. Both sides heaved against the other, spitting and snarling; any man who was unfortunate enough to slip and fall at the front was quickly run through by hard iron or crushed underfoot. Inch by bloody inch, the kingdom men, were being pushed back by sheer weight and numbers. The Earl, in his element once again, kept calling to them, extolling them to greater effort.

'Hold, you bastards! Hold, or die!'

Despite all, they were losing ground, lungs and muscles screaming to be released. Mouths dry as an old bone in the desert, bodies plastered with sweat, they were shoved backwards, gasping, fighting to keep every toe-hold, slipping, sliding, and cursing. Soon, they were back where they had started, at the beginning of the bridge, the balefully staring statues mocking them and their efforts. The Earl cast a quick look around him and then tucked his head back down. He was a bit worried if truth be told. Things weren't looking too good at the moment. As soon as his men stood pushed clear of the bridge, they would stand encircled by the enemy's superior numbers. Taking a deep breath, he prepared to bellow out the orders to form a defensive circle, a tricky manoeuvre at the best of times with well-drilled troops, but now, with men long unpractised and under deadly duress, the outcome did not look bright.

Suddenly, thundering at the rear boomed the terrifying echo of iron-shod hooves clobbering the cobblestones, bearing down on his flank.

'Flaming, fickle gods!' was his furious thought. 'Why abandon us now!'

Craning his head around, he saw a phalanx of charging lancers galloping up the thoroughfare, then as they hit the open space behind them they split neatly into two flowing streams, racing around the back of his embattled squad. A burst of sunlight crashed into his mind, at their head rode the king on his white charger, arrayed in the splendid colours of the kingdom.

Shouting with sheer joy, he roared at his men.

'Our king is here! Here, with us! Put your backs in it, boys! Let's push these bastards into the river!'

The two wings of the king's cavalry sliced into the flanks of the Protectorate foot soldiers, surprising them, scattering them. A rout ensued. Some in panicked haste to escape climbed the bridge's stone guard rails. Surrendering all good reason, they leapt into the goddess' arms forgetting the weight of armour on their backs. The goddess enfolded them and carried them down.

Like an avalanche of boulders, the Earl and his still intact shield wall, surged forward, grinding over the now disheartened enemy, stomping over the bridge towards the open gates of the fortress. Ahead of them, the king's riders chased the fleeing men, cutting them down mercilessly, releasing the long-held, pent-up humiliation, in an outburst of violent fury.

The running soldiers tried to rally at the gates under the shouted exhortations and bullying of their commanders, but they seemed distracted by what may be behind them as well as what they could see in front. A few threw down their weapons, fell on their knees and held their arms into the air. Like a ripple in the air, the fight fled from the hearts of the Protectorate, and they, under a herding instinct, took the practical course and surrendered en-masse.

A joyous Earl of Marches turned to the king as he cantered up to the gates and shouted.

'We have won the day, your Majesty! Welcome to the fray!'

'A king's prerogative is to protect and defend his people and their city, would you not agree, my dear Earl?' the king replied calmly.

'Certainly, my King, would you give us the honour of leading the way to reclaim your Keep?'

CHAPTER XIX

'We have no choice! We must attack!'

'I am well aware, Lord Otto. Are you of the same mind, Lord Neville?'

'Yes, Excellency, we cannot show our tail to Ap Heston. He would be on us like a terrier onto a rat.'

'Very apt. Very well, the decision is unanimous. If Ap Heston has denied our men a full belly, let him provide us with the sustenance of righteous indignation and justice. Come, let's sound the call to battle.'

'What of the taken city, your Excellency? Should we not guard against another surprise from that end?'

 The two lords watched the governor fight to suppress the anger raging within him. After a brief struggle, he responded coldly.

'Already done, Lord Neville. I've already despatched cavalry skirmishers in sizeable numbers as soon as ill news arrived before dawn's light, with orders to warn, harass and tie-down any forces moving our way. Should have rooted out that grey, fat worm long ago and put him to the question. I suspect his connivance somewhere in this.'

The governor seemed lost in thought for a moment, drumming his fingers absently on the field table.

'The Ruling Conclave will not be happy with this sudden change of events.'

'Then they should have loosened their tight fingers a bit on their purse strings and allowed me to secure fortification at the delta port to guard against this very event and allow quick reinforcement!' snapped the governor. Then with a quick intake of breath, he continued. 'My apology, Lord Otto, all is not lost. As soon as we tear down this anthill, we will use our stationed forces across the river and move on the city rats with a two-pointed attack. They have no stomach to see their beloved city destroyed. Come, let's not waste valuable time in talk; to arms!'

***

'Still no news from Tam?'

'No, nothing. Getting through the governor's blockade will be near on impossible.'

Morgan, Nat, General Hadrider, and the now ever-present Gabrielle, were gathered, as they usually did every morning, to observe the movements in the enemy camp and to discuss options. All possible preparations stood at the ready. In the meantime, the hill defenders drilled around the clock, pushed relentlessly by their squad and division leaders. Morgan wanted everyone able to respond to commands as efficiently and quickly as possible with the minimum of confusion. It also distracted them from their grumbling tummies.

Somewhere around mid-morning, the deep, bass braying of a horn blasted through the exhausting daily routine, emanating from the governor's camp.

'That's a call to arms!' exclaimed General Hadrider.

'Thank the god's for that!' responded Nat. 'Something to do rather than sight-seeing.'

'Let's follow suit, shall we, it's time to assemble. Today's going to be long and hard,' said Morgan, watching men the size of ants, pouring out of tents. They dropped what chores previously engaging them to don their armour - racing off to corral horses, and scuttling into groups to shuffle into formation, the occasional parade ground voices of squad sergeants drifting up to the watching men's ears. The palisade on which they were standing shivered, as warriors began to climb hurriedly onto it to start taking up their positions. In general, though, things were more orderly and sedate on the hill, as the stringently rehearsed defenders moved to their stations. Behind the barrier, on a higher elevation, long-bowmen stood in rows, protected by large, wicker shields. They would add deadly firepower to the slingers, bowmen, and spear-men already on the fortification. Behind them, the foot-soldiers were gathering. They would make up the bulk of the centre, a compact shield wall. On either side of them, were the cavalry and at the crown of the hill, sat impatiently, the women warriors, horse riders and skirmishers supreme, who were the reserves. With a grin and a punch on Nat's arm, Gabrielle leapt from the palisade and loped off to join them. Nat watched after her ruefully and rubbed his arm.

'Wish we had more of those slingers,' said Hadrider wistfully

'You have to be trained from childhood and its tough skill to master. Only men of the mountains practise enough to be deadly these days,' replied Morgan. 'At least the governor is moving to action, so an assumption is that Tam has been successful. General, when the governor breaks through our defences, and he will do this, take command of the right. Nat, you take control of the left. I will command the infantry at the centre. Any questions?'

'No, commander!' they said in unison.

'Nat,' continued Morgan, 'Get over to the palisade at the river crossing. They will hit us simultaneously. I want you to hold as long as you can, but don't risk getting stranded on the opposite bank. Go! Go! And stay alive!'

'Yes, General,' replied Nat with a grin and bounded away, athletic and youthful.

'I'll put in a show on the far side,' said Hadrider, striding off in the other direction.

Morgan nodded and said after him.

'Stick them before they stick you, General.'

Twelve boxes of enemy long-bowmen, three ranks deep, fifteen across, were taking up open positions just outside of arrow range, with wide spaces between each block. Some of his archers began to nock their arrows staring grimly at them.

'Hold, lads! That's not our target. Wait for the horses!' said Morgan, pacing behind them. 'Pair up, lads, one with shield, one with the bow. Slingers and spear-men keep down. Wait for me! Wait for my command!'

With a ripple, men all along the palisade followed his orders, reinforced by Hadrider.

A flaming signal arrow flew in an arc across the battlefield, and immediately the Protectorate long-bowmen ran forward several yards, then planting their feet, launched a hail of iron-tipped shafts at the men behind the parapet.

'Shields up, lads! Take cover! Iron rain is coming!'

The thick shields, triple plated, ready-made for this purpose, absorbed the pelting storm, causing even the highly trained queen's men to cringe under the assault. The loud crack of planks splitting reverberated all along the walkway. Interspersed between this staccato of sound, were the occasional screams of agony as a plunging barb pierced an exposed limb.

Lightly armoured horseback riders on mounts bred for speed and agility, stormed through the spaces between the archers, some twirling ropes in their hands, others sporting light, stream-lined javelins and still others, jars of sealed oil. The attacking bowmen redoubled their efforts, aiming higher.

Peering through a sky, blackened by flying arrows, Morgan studied the oncoming horsemen with steely calm.

'Get ready, lads! Here come our targets! Wait for it! On my mark! Archers! Fire!'

Under the dense, 'thwack, thwack, thwack' of arrows smashing into the wood, the shield-men heaved upwards, followed by the bowmen sheltering under them. The racing, jinxing horse riders below knew their job well, but Morgan timed his command to return fire with perfection, taking advantage of that small margin where a thrown spear is out-ranged by a flying arrow. A wall of deadly shafts struck the first wave of attacking skirmishers. It sent horses and their riders both, crashing into the dirt in a jumble of wildly thrashing and kicking limbs - the teeth clenching sound of broken bones clearly audible to the defenders behind their wooden palisade. Before the satisfied archers could duck back to safety, the second wave of horse-riders hurled their missiles at them, piercing a dozen of the defenders even before their shield-men could angle cover to protect their comrades better. At the very same time, co-ordinated flawlessly, ropes with loops at their ends, swirled out and encircled the protecting stakes pounded into the earth below the parapet. The riders raced downhill, spinning their horses at the edge of the dug pit, quickly tying the other ends of their ropes to their saddles. With a confusion of mixed results, many stakes were ripped free. In some cases, saddles themselves tore away, yanking terrified, screaming warriors into the air. In others, shocked animals were jerked off their legs by stubborn, deeply grounded stakes, crashing backwards and crushing their unfortunate riders - all was bedlam, dust and noise.

'Eyes open! Eyes open, men! Listen to me! Now! Fire! Shields up! Down!' Morgan yelled above the din of combat.

The attacking bowmen chose this time to change tactics. Bare-legged boys, dressed only in short tunics, scuttled forward amongst them, depositing clay jars with simmering charcoal inside, along with stacks of fat dipped arrows. Setting them alight, they quickly filled the sky with darting flames, many of which lodged themselves into the parapet logs, soaked now in oil, thrown earlier by the madly manoeuvring Protectorate horsemen. As many sections of the palisade burst into greedy flames, Morgan snatched a red cloth tucked into his belt and waved it. The archers stationed further up the hill behind their wicker shields responded immediately, releasing wave after wave of highly arced arrows which crashed among their opposite numbers below with deadly accuracy; decimating them. Even some of the young boys, too slow to withdraw, were pinned mercilessly into the dirt; their joy and excitement of childhood adventure turned into a nightmare reality of pain and death, their mothers weeping faces the last image before blackness took them.

Nat, standing on the short length of palisade between the two towers, on the other side of the river, was having an even worse time of it. The Protectorate forces stationed here were made up entirely of cavalry. They came at them in wave after wave of violent movement, surging in, and flying away, throwing up great clouds of dust and confusion. There were no archers present in their number to pin down the defenders with arrow fire, but each tide of furiously riding horse riders hurled javelins, oil, and burning torches in an unstoppable storm. Nat and his men, Watchers all, bowmen and slingers, brought down the first and second ranks with merciless volleys of lead pellets and iron barbs, but in the end, the effect was the same as spitting into the ocean. It wasn't long before they were scampering across the rudimentary, wooden bridge, escaping the raging flames consuming their log defences rapidly behind them. Soot covered, hair singed, and a broad grin spread across his handsome face, Nat stopped at the third tower at the bottom of the hill to survey the damage.

'Well, that was as useful as a nun in a whorehouse!' he shouted over the roaring fire to the two men who had stopped with him.

With a shared grin, they sprinted up the hill, joining Morgan's and Hadrider's first-line defence as they scampered to take up a roving skirmishing position behind the archers, but in front of the infantry shield-wall. The palisade running along the entire hillside was going up in flames, covering the retreating men in a roiling plume of dark brown smoke.

Nat spotted Morgan standing dead-centre of the field, ahead of the foot-soldiers and in clear view. He made his way towards the imposing figure of his commander.

'That didn't last long,' said Morgan, greeting Nat with a smile.

'Let's hope we do better in the second round, General,' Nat replied with a nonchalant, carefree shrug.

'That will be any time now. It will start as the first ended. The whoresons will be busy filling in our hard dug ditch, the bastards. They'll try to catch us with our pants down and feather our backsides before the smoke clears. Let's turn the tables on them, shall we?'

After a short wait, they spotted a man running towards them waving a yellow flag. He was racing up from the still fiercely burning palisade, although sections of it had already fallen over.

'Ah, here we go! Here come my eyes. The time is now,' so saying, he once again pulled out his red cloth and held it aloft for the captain in charge of the long-bowmen to see as he stood there watching and waiting for his signal.

Giving Morgan a nod of acknowledgement the archer captain, Tam's Watcher friend, Trapper, said something to a young lad standing next to him who immediately rolled a slow cadence on the kettle drum draped by a leather strap around his neck. The archers, mostly fellow Watchers, swiftly nocked their arrows and drew back on the strings with muscular arms, pointing the barbs at a high elevation and holding it.

'Their bowmen are back in range and hoping to be unobserved with this smoke. We'll send them a little surprise,' Morgan explained.

The drum roll built into a climax then ended in an abrupt, thump. The archers released their shafts and swiftly pulled another out of the earth and repeated the action; nock, draw, release. Four times this was done by each bowman before the first shaft struck.

The devastation was widespread. In a way, the success of Morgan's strategy was even more than he had anticipated. The governor was going for a hammer blow. Not only were his archers in a forward position, but his infantry stood caught in the arrow storm as they were double marching between the bowmen. They were heading for the smouldering and burning palisade with long spears, twinned with wicked hooks below the tip, designed not only to stab soft flesh but also to pull down burning timber. The first five ranks of the governor's infantry along with the archers received the full, brunt force of the death falling from the skies. Men screamed and sobbed in agony, the pain and the anguish turning fully grown adults into lost children. However, this setback was inconsequential for the governor, as his swollen forces rolled forward over the fallen and injured, trampling them underfoot. On the wings, the cavalry was also on the move, surging ahead of the trotting infantry, towards the row of sweating, toiling peasants, conscripted and sent forth into harm's way, to fill in the ditches made by Morgan's army.

From both the left and the right, Morgan and the defenders were taken aback. The sudden emergence of a penetrating mass of horse riders as they came ploughing up the hillside on their striving, wild-eyed mounts was shocking. Hadrider had already taken his position on Morgan's right flank and quickly moved his forces forward to block and push back the attacking Protectorate cavalry. However, the left held back, looking uncertain about what action to take.

'Bloody hell! Didn't expect that!' shouted Nat, spinning away and racing off to take command of the wavering left flank.

 Cool and calm as ever, Morgan stepped forward and gestured at both the skirmishers and archers stationed below him, pointing left then right. The two mobile groups hastily peeled away from the centre, leaving the field open to the infantry, directing all of their firepower onto the rapidly advancing enemy horsemen, pounding up on both wings. Their numbers were unbelievable, and time and time again, the splicing arrow blizzard, and haling lead pellets, drove them back, swirling and crashing down the slope, but each time they were replaced by another wave and yet another. Under this grinding pressure, the defenders would soon be running out of their long hoarded stores of ammunition. The fast, quick response of these brave bands of bowmen, slingers and javelin skirmishers had temporarily stymied the fearsome and psychologically damaging insurgence of the governor's highly trained horsemen. This disciplined action allowed Nat to steady the left flank, creating a balance with Hadrider on the right, but things were merely beginning.

 From right-wing to left-wing, the centre field sat filled with a solid, impenetrable, advancing shield-wall as far as the eye could see; rank upon rank of crouching, helmeted, faceless men, a grilling machine of death. From its midst reverberated a deep, guttural roar, rising and falling, with each encroaching step, unstoppable. The defenders, as one, experienced a shiver of fear, feeling small and impotent, in the face of this onslaught. Morgan, standing clear on his own, turned his back on the juggernaut of the advancing enemy, and raising his arms, sword held high, glinting in the sunlight, he roared in a deep, bass, parade ground, commanding voice.

'Queen's men! King's men! Listen to me! Are you ready!?'

'Ready!' came a shout from the men directly in front of him.

'Are you ready for War!? Are you ready to Fight! Are you ready to Die!? Are you ready to KILL!!!?'

'READY! READY! READY!'

The hillside exploded into sound and courage.

Spreading his arms wide, Morgan turned to the enemy and spat at them, then slowly walked to the wildly cheering shield-wall and was enfolded within them, taking his place in the first rank.

'Shouldn't you go back a rank or two more, sir?' a voice shouted at him.

Morgan found himself next to a concerned looking squad leader Honeycut.

'This is a good place as any to stand next to honest men, don't you think Honeycut?'

Honeycut gave him a quizzical frown but answered anyway.

'Yes, sir, as you say, sir. We're honoured to have you fighting in our squad, General.'

'The pleasure is all mine, Squad Leader. Are you ready?'

'Was born ready, General sir,' replied Honeycut with a grin.

'Good, for here they come.'

'Ladies!' bawled out Honeycut. 'Let's show the general how we dance with the governor's girls! On my mark! Step! Step! Step!'

The foot-soldiers huddled behind their tight shield-wall, moved crab-like down the hill, like David going to meet Goliath.

On the left, Nat was hurtling downwards on his horse, clumps of baked earth and mud tearing away from its thundering hooves, matching the movement of Hadrider on the right. The skirmishers and archers had done all they could and were scampering back through the infantry lines to escape a massacre. The wind was ripping across his face and whistling through his helmet, he synchronised with the movement of his horse, feeling its powerful muscles bunching and uncoiling, a breath-taking and exhilarating charge towards potential death; he felt wonderfully alive. He spared a quick thought for Elaine, left behind, but an echoing roar of sound coming from the infantry at the centre distracted him and caused him to swivel his head. 'Fine time for Morgan to give a speech,' he thought and grinned with a fondness for the man.

He focussed on the lunging heads of the horses in front of him. With great effort, he tried to ignore the long line churning up the hill and the mass of horseflesh with their riders behind. They were coming together at a terrifying speed. Suddenly, he was on them, and his large, warhorse, maddened and excited by the reckless downhill pace, took a running leap, trying to clear the charging horses coming at him. As it leapt, Nat flattened himself along its neck, and as it crashed down on the backs of the panicked animals beneath it, legs with deadly hooves kicking madly and teeth snapping and biting, Nat swayed back in his saddle, cutting left and right with his sword. All along the engaged line, the Protectorate forces crashed into the dirt, bowled over by the charging queen's men, but now their sheer weight of numbers had stopped that initial advantage dead. Nat's powerful horse, reared and kicked, turning this way and that, trying to open space around it, but the constant pressure was too much.

 Beset on all sides, desperate men used any weapon at hand, and in truth, any part of any armament, to cut, pummel, and strike at each other, teeth gritted and lungs, searing. Many with weapons lost, grappled and wrestled with each other from horseback, many falling beneath the stamping, iron-shod hooves of the disturbed and restless animals, breaking bones and cracking skulls.

 Not bothering with finesse, Nat used speed and brute strength to carve his way into the maelstrom, followed by the rest of his men. Try as they did to keep some type of formation, it was impossible, and soon they were struggling, adrift in individual pockets and sometimes on their own. Nat lost all track of time, caught up in the meat chopping business at hand. He delivered countless blows and received many in return; the pain would come later if he survived this day. Blocking a strike meant for his neck, he reversed his arm, sending the pommel of his sword crunching into the nose bridge of a surprised opponent, and despite the nose guard, the man's nose shattered in a spray of blood. He grinned as his foe toppled off of his mount, but then the feeling of something very wrong dawned on Nat. The Protectorate cavalry commander had a plan. He wasn't blindly trying to bludgeon the defenders into submission using his superior numbers. He was attempting to funnel them to the side. To push them up against their infantry, hampering both in the bargain. As this realisation struck him, he saw a flying wedge of equestrians working their way around and pushing through his defences. If they succeeded, they would flank the foot soldiers formations, and they would lose the battle and the day.

Snatching frantically at the horn at his belt, he blew the three short notes that signalled a recall. Desperately he watched his scattered cavalry valiantly try to rally to his side, but the press was so great, little headway stood made, and he knew they were too late. How Morgan could follow these changing events in the midst of battle, he would never understand. Still, just as frustration and despair were threatening to overcome him, he heard the two sharp, one long sound of Morgan's horn, the pre-arranged sign to Gabrielle to move her warriors to cover any given threat. She, however, must have pre-empted his signal, for before the sound had died away, her fearsome unit careened down the incline and smashed at an angle into the side of the enemy wedge, scattering them and tearing out their souls. No man could match the fury of these women in battle. It was awe-inspiring. And wild as they at first seemed, their discipline was a thing of iron. Having completed their objective, they swirled about, and before they could become ensnared in the trapping tactics of the Protectorate, broke free intact, and raced back to their position at the top of the hill.

Grinning again, Nat spotted the original archers and skirmishes, sprinkled heavily with the ubiquitous Watchers, having managed to reach safety, streaming through the space left empty by Gabrielle and her girls, forming a grim and determined defensive line. With most of his surviving men now rallied around him, Nat re-launched a furious attack, cutting across the middle of the hill, dividing the attacking Protectorate horsemen into two. He had noticed that Morgan had responded to the dire situation by allowing his shield-wall to take on a horseshoe appearance, with horns curling up the hill, behind the striving, hard-pressed cavalry. The Protectorate riders, in the dust and confusion, did not realise that they rode cut off, so intent were they, on gaining the hilltop. They galloped full head-on into a withering onslaught of ballistic missiles, dropping wave after wave of men and horses, bone dead into the dry mud. The skirmishers had found new ammunition.

Over on the right, Hadrider and his cavalry were having a better time of it. The slope here was steeper, slowing the speed of the attackers drastically, making them easier targets, targets for the batteries of hidden marksmen, screened by the thick forestry running alongside the defenders right flank. From here, a storm of missiles, throwing-spears, arrows, stone and lead ammunition slung by whirling slings, pelted the slogging Protectorate cavalry without pity or pause. They sent terrified and tormented horses bucking, sliding, and rolling back down the steep hillside, hampering and tripping their fellows coming after. Their vast numbers worked against them, causing a considerable build-up at the bottom. Hadrider and his men flew down the hill in sorties, striking the distracted and straggling van-guard with hit and run tactics, racing down the slope with lances couched, piercing and penetrating their hapless opponents, swirling about, re-climbing the hill at a more leisurely pace. Still, Hadrider knew that the odds remained stacked against them. From the bottom of the hill onwards, the plain below lay covered with enemy cavalry awaiting their turn to have a go at them. Fatigue, lack of numbers, and a finite supply of ammunition would eventually spell their defeat despite their good positioning and sound tactics. It was only a matter of time. He hoped Morgan's backup plan worked and worked in time to save their skins.

Within the seemingly tranquil forest, old Hatch was leading and coordinating a seething and frantic defence, tricking and repelling surge after surge of Protectorate scouts and foresters. With him were mostly king's men, men and also women, who had either joined the rebellion or had fled to them for safety. Helping Hatch lead these committed defenders were a selection of hand-picked Watchers. At first, the carefully hidden traps did their work, and the screams of dying and severely wounded men shook the foliage repeatedly. However, the governor's chosen men for this task knew their craft intimately. They soon organised a slow, but a thorough sweep of every tree, branch, shrub, leaf, and bare-patch of soil, painstakingly dismantling the ingenious snares planted to rob them of their lives. Hatch did not sit back on his haunches and allow them to complete this task unmolested. He and roving teams of men and women continuously and incessantly harassed them every inch of the way. They shot them with arrows tipped with very painful if not fatal poison. They laid new traps ever before them, knifing them, slitting their throats, whatever means of torture and pain that opportunity presented, a psychological exercise as much as a master class in killing by stealth. Still, they kept coming, with Hatch and his band continually retreating before them. It was only a matter of time, and the sand clock was running out.

With a thunderous crunch of metal and wood, the two sides grounded together, sending a shuddering vibration across the entire line. Men grunted and gasped with the enormous effort. Morgan and his men had the upper ground, and so on the initial impact, they bore the enemy's first rank into the earth. Still, before they could capitalise with a quick downward stab, they had to rear back, defending, as the second enemy line stabbed at their exposed necks and heads. Men swore and spat at each other, eyes shining with vehemence and rage.

'Steady, ladies! Steady!' bawled out Honeycut, almost deafening Morgan. 'Don't let these girls excite you! Push! Push! Push, you bastards! Push them on their sweaty backs! Push them over, and stick them between the legs! Push!'

'When this is all over,' Morgan thought, 'I must buy Honeycut a cup of vinegar.'

Morgan sensed that Nat was in trouble and quickly blew the alert to warn Gabrielle. Then setting his feet, he began walking forward, pushing men who thought themselves immovable, backwards, as if they were children in the playground. He clinically stabbed them with his sword as they were shoved upright by his enormously applied force, the backs of their legs hitting their mates behind them, stumbling and tumbling over their lowered shields.

He glimpsed a look of surprise on Honeycutt's set features as he strode by him, but the professional soldier quickly recovered and adapted. Lifting his shield, he surged forward and locked his outer rim around that of Morgan's and at the same time called out orders to his squad.

'Shields up! Lock! Cover the general! Follow! Step! Step!'

A small victory changes a man's courage during battle faster than it takes a frightened dog to fart. Morgan's advance against the odds, dead centre of the embattled shield wall, sent subliminal messages across to both sides. For the Protectorate, it was fear and sudden uncertainty, for the defenders, exhilaration and re-born self-belief. The men of the hill, as they had begun to see themselves, ploughed into their foe. They sheared through their defences, pushing them, stabbing them, bashing them with their shields, kicking them, stamping on them, even headbutting them with their iron helms, snarling and growling like rabid animals, froth and spittle foaming at the corners of their dry mouths. The governor's men shied back from this naked apparition of violence bearing down on them. They cast their eyes around for somewhere to escape. However, caught as they were, in a press as hot as hell, they could only cower behind their shields, staving off death from the front, and trapped by their comrades at the back. Morgan led his unleashed men forward, pushing the beset Protectorate back down the slope step by step, inch by hard-fought inch, until mid-way down, he held the line. He dared not move beyond where the cavalry on both wings struggled for their lives against insurmountable odds. He dared not push down to the flat plain below, where, with certainty, his bold defenders would be surrounded, overcome, and decimated. Still, the more they killed, the more stood pushed forward on their swords. With over-lapping shields, men stood and dug deep to find their buried source of energy, but inevitably, they will soon come a time when the strongest of them would come up empty. Looking along the battle-line, he already saw the signs, sections of the shield-wall retreating back up the hill, leaving dead bodies bleeding in the grass and churned earth. He needed his miracle, but the sands of time were running through his fingers.

Back up on the knoll of the hill, Gabrielle and her warriors prowled the summit on their sleek, endurance bred horses. Their totem was that of the snarling she-wolf. They were the wolf sisters of the sea of grass, and like wolves they prowled, looking for prey. Thrice they had plunged into the soft underbelly of the Protectorate and ripped out their guts; thrice they had pulled their young, honorary brother out of the shit. He owed them a warrior's dance. Her sharp eyes had long realised that the enemy outnumbered them four to one. What a glorious death dance today would bring. There was no way to win the victory unless that general, the man who was something more than a man, could somehow make his long-shot gamble pay off. He had something of a mudang about him; the ability to see and do things that ordinary warriors could not. The analysis of that thought belonged to others. She and her sisters lived entirely in the here and now - to the fullest extent. From her vantage point, the raging battle and the land beyond sat laid out clearly at her feet. She tried to decide at what point to lead her sisters in one last joyful charge that would take them over the silver bridge into the spirit world when a strange cloud on the horizon arrested her attention. Shading her eyes with her cupped hand, she studied the unusual, but yet familiar pattern.

***

The governor's imposing grey charger pranced in agitation, mirroring the mood of its rider. He had watched with satisfaction the opening stages of the battle. He had expected heavy casualties with the first engagements, and his expectations had run true to form. Still, pride had filled his chest as he watched his holy swarms set cleansing fire to the heathen's defensive palisade and seen it torn down as a symbol of an affront before god. He had watched his vaunted cavalry, righteous swords held high, flying up the flanks of the devil's molehill, wings of victory on their backs, soaring them aloft. He had nodded in approval as he witnessed the cunning of Lord Otto on the right flank, as he dammed the reckless downward charge of the devil's young protégé, channelling it aside deftly under the guise of a hammer advance. Now events were becoming bogged down in the mud of time. His grey sidled sideways, as it picked up its master's frustration, tossing its head and trying to bite the neck of Lord Neville's mare. Otto's brilliant play for quick victory had been smashed to impotence by the wild women of the grasslands, she-demons all, who rode their horses between their thighs in a manner that no man in his experience, could ever equal. The steepness of the slope had baulked his left. So too had the cowardly attack by craven men hidden in the trees. He would flush them out and hang them all from the branches screening their present hiding places, leaving their carcasses to be pecked clean of flesh by the scavenging crows. And his centre; the devil had his centre, holding it stuck half-way up the bloody hill. Bastard time was mocking his ambitions. As if guessing his thoughts, young Neville spoke up.

'Our numbers will still win the day. They are tiring fast, and their ranks are beginning to fray and thin, like old cloth.'

The governor nodded curtly but did not reply. His mood was becoming dark, and he gripped the pommel of his sheathed sword tightly, keeping tight control of the reins in his other hand, riding his mount's high stepping restlessness.

'Look, Sir! A messenger is coming and fast! Perhaps, he brings ready news from the city.'

A dusty, wide-eyed, young scout, coaxed the last, unsteady gallop out of his exhausted, lathered mount, and drew it to a trembling halt in front of the governor and his field staff, throwing his hand out in a poorly executed salute.

'I bring urgent news, General!' he panted.

'Obviously!' snapped the governor. 'Report, man!'

'Yes, sir...Sir, a huge force has been sighted coming from the city, advancing along the river towards our position. Nearly all of the men of this land, recruited to our cause, have fled into the countryside. Our scouts have reported that many are flocking towards their countrymen and negotiating for entry into their swelling ranks.'

'Fickle bastards! I'm not in the least surprised! Such men have no honour. How far away are they from us trooper?'

'About twenty leagues, General!'

'That bastard on yon hill has tricked us; diverted our attention, whilst the rats of the city foment and organise full, foul rebellion! Who leads this worthless rabble, trooper, the confounded Earl of Marches?'

'Ay, General, and the King.'

'The King!? The bastard! I'll cut out his yellow liver myself! Neville, continue this enterprise till this mound is wiped clean! The rest of you prepare to follow me immediately. I have another king to kill!'

'Pardon me, Excellency, should we not first continue to throw our full and combined weight upon these heathens until we tear them from their perch?'

'The job sits almost done, Lord Neville, I will leave you enough men to finish it. Fail me not! Come, let's delay no further.'

 The governor's anger and fury sat felt by all around him - a palpable and tangible thing which would brook no prevarication.

Within the hour, more than half of the attacking force, all cavalry, struck off, racing towards the direction of the city.

It didn't take long after, for the remaining Protectorate army, left fighting desperately on the hillside, to feel the hand of support at their backs, like that of a father on his young son during his first hunting trip, withdrawn. They began to waver. Lord Neville, against the governor's expressed wishes, called upon the mounted force on the opposite bank of the river, blocking access to the ford, to join the faltering hill assault quickly. The commander there took time out to question his authority, and in the pregnant space it took for him to acquiesce, his fellows struggling on the slope had begun to cave in. First, was the feeling of confusion as men saw their commander in chief turn his back on them, taking half of their comrades in arms and at a time when they sat most needed. Second, to follow, was the feeling of abandonment and lost cause. Third, was the unstoppable urge to find a place of safety, anywhere but on this forsaken hill. In the beginning, there was a trickle, and then this trickle became a flood. Men turned and ran; as they ran they transformed from predator to prey, and were hunted down and slaughtered in a primitive bloodletting spree, uncontrollable by any commander, as once sane and just men surrendered to the demons within. Caught against the river, men bled, drowned and died, panic racing alongside their departing souls. The horsemen on the far bank soon became infected by the mood to flee, and their nerves began to shred. In short order, many were seeking the illusory safety of the unknown forests in the far distance.

Lord Otto, the scar across his face a livid red, his helm lost somewhere in the fray, had almost fought his way to the summit. Then, suddenly, the remnants of his fighting force were hit again - this time by the hell-cats who seemed joined to their horses. They struck him head-on, and from behind, came that blasted young, luck-riding commander of the enemy left wing - hammer and anvil. He shied his horse away, as a red-haired banshee came screaming down at him, barely avoiding an axe blade that split the air a centimetre away from taking the top of his skull off. At that very moment, fate caused his horse to slip badly, and he found himself thrown heavily onto the hard-baked ground. Winded severely, but otherwise uninjured, he forced himself to his feet in time to see the massive stallion of the wing commander bearing down on him. 'This sorry caper is it then,' he thought. 'The bastard governor has abandoned me here on this provincial hill to meet my death.' With a sneering snarl, he sprang forward to find his maker and spit in his eye. Shocked, he stopped in mid-stride as the young man leapt from his stallion and stood before him, pulling himself to attention, and saluting him with his sword. With a grin, he returned the salute and flew at his foe, his last thought being, 'Honour amongst fools, idiot!' His head flew one way, and his body stumbled a few more steps in the other before it crumbled to its knees and stuck there. He never saw the sword stroke that spilt him onto the bridge of light.

The change in fortune happened so rapidly that Lord Neville could only sit his horse in shock and stare. Then with a curse for the governor, a man who in the end, could not control his passion, turned his horse and fled into the countryside, taking sound example from the broken army.

The governor, like a thrown spear, was totally unaware of the sudden collapse of his forces at his rear. Unaware of Morgan and his commanders rallying rampaging men to regain discipline and give chase, to remount purpose and bite his arse; unaware that he, by his own volition, had placed himself between a hammer and an anvil.

The inhabitants of the Kingdom of Granehold, who had preferred to run, hide, lose both house and kin, rather than support Morgan, a foreigner. Now flocked like lost sheep to their shepherd, their king - one of their own. Some even chose to believe that it was the old king who had cheated death and returned to lead them in victory over the Protectorate. Whatever the reason, the King marched, resplendent on his white charger, at the head of a considerable force that near matched the Protectorate at its peak.

The governor, with his elite mounted troops around him, and the rest of his cavalry streaming behind him, topped a bulge in the land and stopped stone dead. His army was soundless except for an occasional nicker of a horse and the jingle of a harness. There on the horizon and slightly on the rise stretched rows and rows of the enemy. As soon as they had come into sight, they were greeted by a wall of sound, 'Out! Out! Out!; shaking the earth with its vibrations. The governor turned pale, and then his face became suffused with hot blood as his anger grew to even more uncontrollable levels.

'Prepare to sound the attack!' he roared. 'Let's scatter these stinking dogs! So the god, help me. I have a king to kill!'

'Sir, Sir!' came a terrified voice behind him. 'Sir, look! Our men!'

Irritably, the governor craned his neck around to see what the trouble was and, for the second time in the space of five minutes, his face lost all colour. Men were drawing away on their horses. First slowly and fearfully, then to a quick canter, glancing around nervously, and finally to a full-blown gallop, as they sought to put as much distance between them and the enormous army of retribution waiting to annihilate them.

And so it came to pass. On a dusty, cultivated plain, trampled under by thousands of hooves, Morgan Ap Heston, the king-maker, and his battered army of liberators, came face to face with the victorious, revolutionary army, led by its new king, a king that once was, a king from the past, reborn.

BOOK THREE

CHAPTER XX

'You wanted to die!?'

The feasting hall was a long, stone edifice, with a high, ornate wooden roof. Noise filled it from stone floor to beamed rafters, the echoing sound of laughter, music and shouted conversation. At the far end stood the king's table, perched on a commanding platform, laden with a rich assortment of food, meats of all types, fish, fruit, wine. In front of it was an ample open space, in which servers plaited their way through spinning acrobats, jugglers, minstrels, troubadours, musicians and mummers. All was movement, colour and smells, bad, mixed with good.

On the high table, seated next to the king, was Morgan, General Hadrider, Lady Elaine, the Earls of Marches and Greendale, and members of the Privy Council, stretching from wall to wall.

Set at right angles to the King's table were several long tables, running along the entire length of the hall. On one of these sat Nat, Gabrielle and a few of her sisters, Trapper, Douglas, Bruce, Duncan and some of his engineers, along with Honeycut, Potter and a fair selection of Watchers. A notable absence was old Hatch, who, true to form, had simply disappeared.

'I didn't say that,' responded Gabrielle to Nat's astonished outburst. 'We want the eyes of the Mistress of the Waving Grass on us when we ride out of this world. Dying on their arses is purely for lazy, good for nothing men.'

'So what made you decide not to ride out in glory?'

'We saw the king's army coming and decided to stick around.'

Mugs of ale gripped tightly in hand, the assembled group listened intently, straining to hear, the exchange between the exotic warrior woman and Nat.

'And a good thing too, I, we all, owe you and your warriors our lives several times over.'

'Here, here!' shouted the men, banging the table and downing their ale in one.

Gabrielle kept her face expressionless, but Nat felt she was pleased.

'You owe us a warrior's dance, you foolish man,' responded Gabrielle.

'What in heaven's name is that!' exclaimed Nat.

This time Gabrielle smiled mysteriously but did not comment. Her warriors all grinned.

Nat frowned and looked at one to the other suspiciously. He was beginning to get a bit worried.

Glancing up, he caught Elaine's eyes fixed on him from her perch at the high table. He smiled, holding his mug up to her, and took a drink. She returned his smile with her beautiful eyes twinkling. Noting the exchange, the Earl of Marches glowered down at him, his thick, shaggy eyebrows pulling together as he studied the young man disapprovingly. Nat spluttered into his drink, quickly diverting his eyes.

To add insult to injury, Nat saw from the corner of his eye, the old warhorse bending towards Morgan and whispering something into his ear. Whatever was said, Morgan looked in his direction and smiled, then replied to the Earl. Nat didn't like that one bit. With a deep sense of unease, he returned his attention to his companions, only to find the full complement of Gabrielle and her sisters staring at him.

'I think we may have to negotiate the honouring of his obligations with our sister on the high table,' said Gabrielle.

Nat liked that even less.

He was rescued from his discomfort by the slightly slurred voice of Trapper, as he rose unsteadily to his feet.

'Let's raise a mug to absent friends, old Hatch to name one, but most of all, to my best friend in all the world, Tam, a braver man I have never known.'

Bruce quickly followed suit, rising unsteadily to stand next to Trapper.

'I second that! To Tam, who wore the mantle of leadership around his shoulders better than many a seasoned warrior. Without him, we would not be here celebrating victory.'

'To Tam!' shouted Douglas.

'Here, here! To Tam!' roared the whole table, and some from the others, in unison.

As the din died down, and men reclaimed their seats on the benches, a very inebriated Duncan spoke up in an intense, loud voice.

'Lads, listen up, listen well, I am no coward, and I love brave men, but I got a tell ye, when we came over that bluff and saw that collection of belligerent and rowdy lads on the rise, I hadda stop meself from checking the state of me pants! I tell yee lads, I was shit scared, may the goddess, forgive me.'

'For the love of the goddess, man!' replied Honeycut, amongst the roaring laughter. 'You're an engineer! What madness led you to take the front line in a battle formation? Anyway, since its confession time, I nearly kissed the man next to me, so relieved was I when it turned out to be the King's army, rather than that bloody Protectorate governor; what the fuck happened to him anyway!?'

'He scampered off after his men. Still out there somewhere, I guess,' yelled Nat from across the table, 'and by the way, you bastard! I was the man next to you!'

The table roared on with good-natured, drunken laughter.

'Your men are enjoying themselves, Morgan. They epitomise strong martial unity and loyalty to each other,' said the king, smiling warmly across at Morgan.

'Pardon me, your Majesty, but these are queen's men, under the command of General Hadrider here. They have been through much these last few months.'

'Our kingdom owes them a great debt. My apology General Hadrider, my words were innocent and not meant to cause harm.'

'None, taken, your Majesty, Morgan has led us faultlessly into victory, a better general and commander I have not had the pleasure to serve under. We, the queen's men, see him as one of our own.'

Before the king could even draw breath to respond, the thin, cutting voice of the Lord Chamberlain, newly confirmed, Lord Greendale, spoke up.

'That is a possible conundrum, Morgan,' he laughed, 'a barrel around your sense of loyalty!'

Quickly throwing water on unwanted flames, Hadrider threw his words into the dangerous space.

'Not so, Lord Greendale, our forces will be making the long march home on tomorrow's eve. We have already made our preparations. There are no cross-roads here for your esteemed ambassador.'

'I am sure our Lord Greendale spoke only in jest, am I right, sir?' said the king with a flicker of grey metal reflecting in his eyes.

'As you say, your Majesty, a badly turned attempt to pull Lord Morgan's leg. I shall stick to royal announcements in the future.'

The king frowned but did not say any more on the subject. Instead, he turned another page in the conversation.

'A lot will be happening tomorrow, somewhat of a new beginning. I will be undertaking the short journey to bring my beloved brother back home, to his rightful place of honour. Morgan has revealed his hidden resting place, but a king does not belong there. A king should be where his people can see him.'

'Well said, your Majesty,' said the Earl of Marches, his voice gravelly with emotion.

The king continued.

'My dear Morgan, I wonder if you can spare some time to join with our cherished Earl to cement the most urgent strategy of how to best rid ourselves of the pestilence wandering our countryside; a malady in Protectorate disguise.'

'I would be honoured, your Majesty, if the Earl has any need of my input.'

'I most certainly do, Lord Morgan. It would be like old times, eh?'

The long-time friends smiled at each other, revealing a boyish enthusiasm for the task.

'All is settled then. Let us not bore the Lady Elaine any further with talk of war and politics.'

Raising his silver cup of wine, the king made his toast.

'To the Lady Elaine, my lords, to beauty, music and a bright, new future!'

The guests of the high table raised their cups and saluted their king. All was back to where it should.

Two days later Elaine and Nat were slowly strolling side by side. The early morning was beautiful, the air fresh and clean with the damp smell of the night still in it and the manicured grass, shrubs and ornate trees, cut a bright, green silhouette against the acute blue, cloudless sky. The day hinted to be a hot one, but at this time, the palace garden was cool and tranquil, and the whole city seemed to be still peacefully sleeping.

'Do you miss them?'

'We have shared a lot; mostly hardship and constant danger. Without each other, we may not have found the strength to keep going. Most of us are around the same age. Yes, I miss them.'

'What will you do now?'

'Stay with Morgan. Unless...'

'Unless?'

'Unless, you know...' Nat lapsed into silence.

Elaine smiled, looking very happy.

'So tell me then, what about that scary, warrior woman who seemed to have taken such a liking to you?'

Nat blushed a deep pink and looked away.

'The grass warriors have chosen to ride with General Hadrider. On Morgan's urging, I have heard.'

'And do you miss them?' Elaine asked sweetly, her eyes sparkling with mischief.

'Their ways are a bit strange and...'

Before Nat could finish, his attention was caught by five armoured king's soldiers, led by the Lord Chamberlain, descending the stairs leading from the palace into the garden.

'What does he want?' whispered Elaine. 'I find him a bit creepy!'

They stopped and waited as the armed party headed towards them.

The older man bowed obsequiously to them and said in an oily voice.

'Good morning Lady Elaine, young Watcher captain. What a pleasant time for a walk. Unfortunately, I have to play the role of the bad messenger. Your father, Lady Elaine, has requested your presence on an urgent matter.'

Nat frowned at the way the chamberlain had addressed him, but before he could respond, Elaine replied with a sharp voice, ringing with authority.

'In the company of armed guards, Lord Chamberlain?'

'You embarrass me, lady. These guards stand assigned to protect my poor, old person, not for your escort.'

Elaine studied the white-haired man in front of her for a long, drawn-out moment, then said.

'Very well, Lord Chamberlain, lead on.'

As they fell into step behind the Chamberlain, the guards fanned out on either side of them, and Nat instinctively reached up to check his sword, remembering belatedly, that he was unarmed, as custom demanded when one is a royal guest. He did not like what was happening one bit.

***

About half an hour later, at the opposite end of the palace, Morgan and the Earl of Marches, walked head bowed in deep conversation, heading towards the old cloister where the Earl once bashed swords energetically with the king. It was one of the few places where peace reigned twenty-four hours per day, and they wanted such a space where they could plan undisturbed.

'It may be a good idea to include young Nat in our discussions. I have found his insight to be invaluable in the past.'

'That young scallywag has been playing the Casanova to my daughter! However, if you vouch for him, I'll send out an invite,' the Earl replied with a smile.

Suddenly, from behind them came the steady thrum of hob-nailed boots on stone. They both turned to see the Lord Chamberlain advancing towards them with five armed guards in tow.

'What now?' muttered the Earl.

Without so much as a greeting, but staying well back, the Lord Chamberlain barked out in a cutting, spiteful command.

'Please, come with me immediately, gentlemen, and do not think to resist!'

Morgan sensed another group, also armoured by the sound, approaching them from the other end of the corridor, and was half distracted as the Earl shouted back at the Lord Chamberlain.

'What's this all about, Greendale!? Shouldn't you be somewhere working out how to relieve the tax burden pressing down on the necks of our good citizens?'

'Don't be a fool, Earl; I have your daughter in custody.'

As the Earl of Marches reeled back, startled by this unbelievable and bold assertion, the Lord Chamberlain nodded slightly, a pre-arranged signal, to the guards around him. Swiftly and without preamble, they produced small, deadly at short range, cross-bows, designed ironically by Morgan, from beneath their white cloaks, and fired point-blank at the Earl of Marches. Time stood still for Morgan as his mind and body flew into battle-mode. In movement, faster than the eye could follow, Morgan saw the strategy, the Earl wasn't the target, he was; still, he stood committed. Five killing bolts were tearing through space towards his friend. With his left hand, he caught a bolt in mid-air, an impossible feat, and as his body lunged past, he used his right hand to jerk a shocked Earl sideways and off his feet, feeling a second bolt flying by their heads. His frame jolted as the other three embedded themselves into his body, one just between his right shoulder blade, one in his lower back, and the last in his upper left thigh. As they hit the floor hard, Morgan, despite his near-fatal injuries, rolled smoothly to a crouch, throwing the dirk, always secreted in his boot top, spinning through the air to stick solidly in the neck of the guard slightly to the side of the now frightened-looking chamberlain.

From his crouched position, Morgan surged forward, reaching the nearest guard before he even knew he was there, grabbing him by his neck and head in both hands, heaving him effortlessly off of his feet, and with a wrench snapped his neck, the sound of bones splitting and breaking filling the hallway. With the body of the now-dead guard still in his hands, Morgan threw its dead weight with crushing force into the next in line, hurtling him back into the unmovable wall, where the impact bludgeoned the back of his helmeted skull, bursting the blood vessels in his brain.

Using his momentum, Morgan spun in mid-air flying towards the now terrified chamberlain, who in his terror, stumbled over his own feet and fell backwards. This cowardly circumstance, saved his life, as Morgan crashed instead onto the fourth guard, bearing him down, pounding his head viciously, three times into the stone-paved floor, cracking his skull open. The last guard fled for all he was worth, back the way he had come. As Morgan reached a clawed hand towards the now foul-smelling chamberlain, a panicked but loud voice, brought him up short.

'Stop! Stop! Or he is dead!'

Turning his head slowly, Morgan saw another five, shaking guardsmen pointing their cross-bows at a pale, but grim-faced Earl, who had armed himself with a fallen sword, and was beginning to advance towards the encircling guards.

'Hold, Lord Earl, please, hold!' the guard captain pleaded, almost weeping. 'We do not wish to kill you!'

'You will have to do just that to stop me, you whoreson! What foul deed is this!?' the Earl shouted.

'Take them both!' squealed the Lord Chamberlain, from his place against the wall where he had crawled to hide. 'Put them in chains, you fools!'

Morgan rose to his feet, and although he must have been in great pain, his expression remained neutral, watchful and commanding. The guards all made an involuntary step backwards, then the guard captain, summoning up all the courage he had, stepped forward with heavy shackles and placed them around Morgan's wrist. Seeing this, the Earl, with an oath of disgust, threw his sword down with a clang, causing the guards to jump, and the Lord Chamberlain to whimper, and offered his arms to be equally shackled.

In a hurry to get these two important and perilously dangerous men off of their hands then to wash the guilt of their actions clean, the guards pushed and shoved the captives out of the palace with rough blankets covering their heads. At the rear service entrance, they were hustled into an iron caged, canvassed top, horse-drawn cart, which the nervous jailors bolted quickly, and with relief. A hooded driver and guard then raced the carriage out of the city. They crossed the bridge, where not so long ago, the Earl had fought such an epic battle, then into the keep, where Tam had given his life. The irony lay not lost on the two men. From here, they were dragged and kicked down the steep stairs. Rough hands filled with haste, hustled them past dark, empty storerooms. Then unceremoniously thrown into the dungeons – damp, moss-covered holes chiselled out of the hard bedrock even before the fortress stood adequately built. Here in the dark, stale air, they found cruel imprisonment.

Left on their own, Morgan sank slowly to the floor with a deep sigh. A concerned Earl felt his way over to his friend's side - his life once again, owed to this man.

'Morgan, how badly are you hurt?' he whispered.

'No one can hear us down here, my friend. Badly, I believe. You will have to pull these quarrels out for me.'

The Earl grunted but did not reply. He was in awe of this man. He had seen him wipe out four, armed and armoured, war trained soldiers with his bare hands in less time than it would have taken a man to blow his nose. Now here he was with three bolts in his body, with a voice as steady as a surgeon's hands, telling him to pull them out. This man's strength and will was prodigious, and, he thought with a shudder, possibly not human.

Wrapping his hands around the quarrel in Morgan's thigh, he gripped tightly, as the shaft was slick with blood. Pulling with all of his strength, he felt the reluctant dart, slide slowly from the prison of sucking flesh clenching it. He was heavily sweating as he held the solid quarrel in his shaking hands. Morgan had not made a sound. The Earl suddenly felt afraid of him and was overcome with shame. As if sensing his friend's unease, Morgan busied himself by tearing strips off of his clothing to block and bind the deep wound, not an easy task while shackled.

'Good job! Two more to go, my friend.'

'Shit!' muttered the Earl.

In the dark, the Earl imagined that Morgan might have smiled. 'If I were him, I would definitely be screaming at this point, not bloody smiling,' he thought.

The heavy metal door banged open with an echoing crash followed quickly by a burst of flame and madly cavorting shadows. The damp corridor resounded with the noise of a furious struggle. Four burly guards led by a torch-bearing jailer, wrestled desperately to contain a deadly fighting individual. He fought like a demented devil, stamping, punching, elbowing, twisting this way and that, head-butting, and even biting them with a single-minded commitment to deliver as much hurt as possible to his capturers, without any regard at all, to the pain he received in turn. As the spitting and swearing combatants stormed past their cell, the wavering torch-light revealed the bloodied face of Nat. His pale visage set grimly, he pushed and pulled, using the momentum of his tormentors to jerk them around like puppets on a string, continuously keeping them off balance. Even so, eventually overcome, they flung him into the cell opposite. Whereupon, his disgruntled captors, spat at him and limped away swearing foul words on his head.

'Get back here, you bastards, I'm not done with you yet!' yelled a furious Nat at the men's departing backs.

'Your lad's got a fantastic fighting spirit, Morgan!' chuckled the Earl.

Hearing his voice, Nat stilled and squinted over at them through the darkness.

'Morgan! Earl Marches? They've got you too!? How!?'

'Whoresons abducted my daughter!' muttered the Earl.

At this, all spirit evaporated from Nat. He sagged against the bars and muttered back.

'I know. I'm sorry.'

'You've seen her, boy! Is she unhurt?'

Nat's attempted reply cut short as Morgan suddenly collapsed onto the cold floor.

'Damn!' muttered the Earl, hurrying to his side.

'Morgan!' shouted an alarmed Nat. 'What's happening?'

'Saved my life,' responded the Earl. 'Took three bolts meant for me and one at least, is very grave.'

'Take them out now!' whispered Morgan tightly.

'I'm afraid that if I do that, my friend, you may die.'

'If you don't, he surely will,' said Nat ominously. 'He knows what he is about. Do as he says.'

The Earl noted the command in the young man's voice, and despite the circumstances he was impressed.

'Very well,' he whispered, 'get ready Morgan.'

'Was born ready', chuckled Morgan, an image of Honeycut flashing before his eyes. 'Never did buy him that cup of vinegar.'

'I think delirium is taking him,' muttered the Earl. 'Here goes.'

This time he reached for the most serious one, the one buried in the small of his back. As before, he gripped tightly and pulled, and as before, Morgan did not twitch, not even a groan. As the bolt came out, the Earl quickly plugged the freely bleeding wound and moved on to the final one. After what seemed like ages, it too came free. Morgan lay there unmoving. The Earl, now more concerned than ever, pressed his finger-tips against Morgan's neck. He could detect only a very, very faint pulse.

'I think he is dying!' said the Earl to Nat.

'I doubt that,' replied Nat. 'A harder man in this world, there is not. I've seen him do this before when injured. He has entered a healing meditative state. Leave him alone; time will tell all.'

Sitting back, feeling old, and exhausted, the Earl said.

'What happened to my daughter, Nat?'

'Sly bastard of a chamberlain, tricked us. He told Elaine that you, my Earl, wanted to speak with her on an urgent matter. Thought something was odd, but then again, I also felt that you might have had a fatherly mistrust of the friendship between your daughter and me.'

'Right on that count, you scallywag!' grumbled the Earl.

Ignoring him, Nat continued.

'I relaxed a bit when I realised that we were indeed heading towards your apartments, and then the chamberlain pulled his ace. One of his guards suddenly pushed me aside, and another grabbed Elaine, erh...Lady Elaine, and put a knife at her throat. I had no choice but to let them take me.'

'Bastard fox!'

'Yes, everything lay carefully planned. The king out of the city, the queen's men gone, you and Morgan distracted, forcing Morgan to defend you and leave himself open. The sly bastard seems to be carrying out a purge of political rivals, but what happens when the king returns?'

'Good question,' replied the Earl. 'I think death will soon come for us.'

***

'Was my message delivered to Lord Morgan and Earl Marches?'

'Yes, Abbot, very early this morning and the messenger has not long returned with confirmation that they will meet with you this evening as requested.'

'Good, good, there are still concerns that...'

Suddenly, a wide-eyed, sweating man burst into the small room, cutting off the Abbot in mid-sentence.

'Lord Abbot, armed men are sweeping the corridors, killing our men as they come!'

'Damn! I expected this might happen, but not so soon!' said the Abbot calmly, swiftly getting to his feet. 'Sound the alarm man, and get yourself to the nearest gathering point!'

'Yes, Lord Abbot,' said the man, dashing off.

'Patrick, you did say that the King was out of the city?'

'Yes, Abbot, he has gone to retrieve the body of his brother.'

The two men strode swiftly towards one of the pre-arranged meeting points - a plan for an unhoped-for emergency. The alarm that warned of a breach of the secret tunnels and corridors leading to the hidden underground dens echoed, deafening all within.

Here, appointed escape prefects guided each group into the carefully guarded passageways known only to the chosen few. By now the clamour of alarm gongs, bells and horns were making a terrible, echoing racket throughout the subterranean network.

'Someone is moving on us very quickly, Patrick!' shouted the Abbot, so that his companion could hear him above the noise. 'This is not a good sign! We have to get the word out, and quickly, to our allies!'

***

'You will do as I tell you, sir!' spat the Lord Chamberlain, in a thin but ringing voice.

'But the King...'

'Is not here! I am his hand. Will you, or will you not comply!?'

'Declaring martial law on a people who see themselves as just winning a conceivable victory is the same as holding a snake in your hands.'

'Lord High Steward, might I remind you that we need a unanimous show of hands to past this motion, yours being the only tardy one,' replied the Lord Chamberlain in a strained, sibilant voice, with spittle forming white crusted bubbles at the corners of his mouth. 'With or without you, my lord, the Keeper of the Privy Seal will make his mark today.'

'This action will spark trouble, Lord Chamberlain,' responded the High Steward with desperation showing in his eyes. Nevertheless, his hand reached shakily upwards.

'Well done, High Steward,' said the chamberlain sarcastically. 'Now we can move on to the crucial matters.'

Looking around the esteemed gathering seated at the table with his chin held high, and his jaw clenched, he continued, wiping the beads of sweat popping out on his forehead with a hurried sleeve.

'Our quick actions have nullified the ambitious machinations of certain over-inflated foreigners and their associates. It's now time to sweep them off of the board and secure our kingdom from such opportunists. Remember, we're all in this together, gentlemen. Let's move to our positions.'

'But this is murder in any which way that we turn the glass on it, sir! Is this what we have become; stabbers in the dark?' objected the High Steward.

'Would you prefer it, sir, if our king were to return to find once again, his kingdom stolen!? We are his right hand; we must do what has to be done! Now go good lords, and let's not have any further prevarication and delay. Lord Keeper, your mark on this document please.'

***

Morgan was floating in a world filled with water. Sounds drifted to him distorted and muffled; as if he were once again, back inside the womb that grew him, formed him, and his twin. He was powerless to latch on to any sensation, powerless to think, powerless to act. His mind was adrift, his body locked into profound self-healing. His mortal essence lay severely wounded. He somehow understood this as he had never submerged so extensively before. He heard noises, streams of undulating sound that he recognised at some level, were voices. They pumped through to him in urgent waves, rolling over him, demanding his attention. He knew that he should be concerned, but couldn't be bothered. In another existence, very far away, his body was being moved, dragged by brutal hands. He felt the impotent rage surging from the voices, trying to rouse him, but he remained adrift, lost in time and space. Nothing mattered.

'Leave him be, you whoresons!' shouted the Earl, his face suffused with anger and rage.

He was pressed back against the wall by spear points, some of them drawing blood. Hooded men dressed in black leather pinned him there, while their comrades dragged the limp, unconscious form of Morgan out of the stone cage by his heels, his head bumping and scraping over the rough floor, leaving a smear of blood on it from his newly cut scalp at the back of his head.

'Wherever you are taking him, you bastards, I'll find him, and I'll find you!' Nat threatened furiously from the other prison cell, his hands gripping the bars so tightly that his knuckles were white and bloodless - the light of the torches dancing black and orange shadows around the players in this tragic dungeon scene.

The iron door at the end of the passage slammed shut, plunging the two men left behind, into soulless blackness and bewildering despair. The Earl, all strength fleeing his limbs, collapsed onto his bottom, placed his hands over his face, and sobbed; how could fate have changed hard-earned events so much and so quickly.

***

Anger and rage surrounded Elaine like a shroud of ice, cold and implacable. Her figure was as still as a marble statue, her face impassive and unreadable, except for her eyes, they burned with green fire.

'You will return my Father and my dearest companion to me!'

Her voice filled the space, like frost on arctic stone, cold and dead.

The Chamberlain, his face turned vulture thin by circumstances, laughed dismissively, and replied.

'You are in no position to make demands, lady.'

'You mistake me, Lord Chamberlain, there are no demands here, just a promise.'

'Your opinion of yourself is overrated, dear girl. Your role is that of a broodmare in the service of the kingdom. The Privy Council will decide your fate soon enough!'

'When was it that you became so nasty, Earl Greendale? You stand before me transformed into a vile worm. If I were a suspicious person, I would suspect your bewitchment by an entity of pure evil.'

The chamberlain had the grace to look troubled by this, but in the end, made a sound of disgust, turned his back on Elaine and walked away. At the door, he paused and without turning, threw one last parting shot.

'You will remain here under guard. Please, do not think of leaving or contacting any outside person. When you are needed, we will send for you.'

So saying, he closed the door with a fateful thud; to Elaine, it sounded like the lid of a coffin as it shut.

***

In the dead of night, even when the dogs slept under a starless sky, six dark, hooded men emerged from the black maw of a small sally port cut into the thick walls of the ponderous, brooding keep, guarding the city against those outside, and sometimes from those within. Three of them half dragged and half carried the dead weight of a wrapped body which was dumped roughly into the back of an iron grilled, covered wagon.

'Why are we bothering with all this?' one whispered. 'The bugger is already dead; might as well just throw his carcass in the river.'

'For one, the goddess will have your soul, and for the other, our orders are to take him out of the city, relieve him of his head, and bury them deep. The penalty for our failure is death. Is that good enough for you, mate?' grated the hard reply.

'Only asking boss. I ain't stupid, you know.'

'Really!' was the sarcastic response.

Three miles outside the city, the wagon made its way carefully along the old road that ran parallel to the river, with two henchmen riding on the driver's bench, and the others skulking alongside, all bent on completing the night's nefarious business.

'This is it, boss,' muttered one of the men, at which point, after a moment's hesitation, the leader, who was at the guiding reins, turned the two teamed horses off the main road onto a tree-lined, partly over-grown trackway, which once a year past, led to a now-abandoned farm.

'Are you sure that this is the right place? Can't see shit!' grumbled the leader.

'Yeah, boss, I know it well. The country folk swear ghosts haunt it. Silly buggers. A young widow got herself raped and murdered here some years back. No one comes down this road if they can help it. It's a good place to hide things if you get my drift.'

The other grunted by way of a reply.

Another ten minutes of stopping and starting, muttering and swearing, trundling through what seemed an increasingly angry chorus of cicadas, the wagon came to a sudden halt.

'Did you hear that?!'

Sure boss, can't help but hear them. Bloody beasties never shut up.'

'Not the insects, you idiot! Something is following us.'

The leader's companion chuckled.

'Never expected you to be one of those spooked by a ghost story, boss.'

'What's going on?' whispered up one of the following foot-pads for hire.

'I'm not bloody sure! Keep your ears open, I think...'

Something ploughed into them, striking them hard from behind. From the rear of the wagon came a muffled scream, cut out suddenly, tailing off in a horrible gurgling sound. In a breath, their minds lay filled with a blinding terror, and the leader felt uncontrolled wetness spreading down his trouser front. As part of his brain registered a deep shame, he heard the talkative man beside him spew out a heart-wrenching sob of pure fear. Something compact, dense, and powerful beyond words, leapt onto the top of the wagon, shaking it violently, lurching the carriage this way and that, as if it sat caught up in the mother of all earthquakes. Looking upwards, his eyes wide open, his body driven in a surge of panic-induced hormones, the captain of this night of ill intent, caught a shadowed glimpse of a nightmare creature falling on him with tremendous speed. It was the last image gifted to him on this earth. A crushing blow struck the side of his face, and he had the out-of-body sensation of the bones in his face collapsing and of a flying feeling as he hurtled helplessly through the air. His spirit was no longer there when his broken body crashed into one of the trees lining the deserted track. His companion sat there mewling in terror, as he smelt a hot damp breath drowning his face, then an agonising tug as his throat lay ripped out in a liquid spray of steaming blood. The other three men fled into the black night, their minds torn-out and scattered to the winds.

The creature, tall and lizard-like, dropped the drained and still twitching body, from where it was standing on the driver's box. Then, agile and swift, it sprang after, hitting the grass-covered earth with hardly a noise, and in two gliding strides, made its way to the rear of the wagon where it paused, head inclined to one side, listening to something far too faint for the ears of an average man. Seemingly satisfied, it grasped the grilled gate, and shook it, rattling the wagon. Then with a guttural snarl, it tugged once again, this time with a sudden and prodigious force, and with a squeal of tortured metal, the barred gate was sheared away from its lock and hinges and thrown with inhuman ease, into the overgrown gutter. With a bound, the creature was in the wagon and grabbing the inert, wrapped body within, flung it over its shoulders as if it weighed no more than a small child. With its trophy secured, it snaked off between the trees.

***

'My lord! My lord! The King and his party are approaching the city!'

'What! So soon! We did not expect his return for yet another week! How far out is he?'

'Another two hours of slow travel, my lord. He sends word that you prepare a fanfare for his and his brother's triumphal return.'

'He commands me to organise a Triumph with only two hours' notice! Well, get to it, man! Rouse the Privy Council. We have work to do.'

The Lord Chamberlain, his face covered in greying stubble, and his eyes, bloodshot with lack of sleep and worry, stood there swaying slightly. His frame, always thin, now looked like that of an unkempt scarecrow. He was not ready for the king; he had returned too soon. He still had much to do to secure what he needed to fix. Rubbing a shaking, blue-veined hand - covered with liver spots - over his face, he hurried out of the royal rooms, shouting orders and instructions as he scurried along. He still had to make his bargain with the stubborn, pig-headed Earl of Marches. His position and expertise were too valuable to the kingdom to throw away, and his popularity with those of low base made him as hot to handle as a freshly baked pancake. With Ap Heston now out of the picture, the Earl sat needed more than ever, but he needed him chained to his will.

CHAPTER XXI

The king sat his horse overlooking his city. Here on the last rise before having to descend into the turmoil of necessary politics, the view was splendid. He loved this land, missed it to the core of his heart, and always dreamt during his long banishment, of a triumphal return. His beloved brother had aided him, but not in the manner he had once thought of doing. In reality, he was helping him even now, for the common folk who revered and loved him, would always be thankful to the man who brought him back to them. Morgan was right after all; a king must work through his people, not over them. The king smiled. If the second part of his plan lay executed as planned, he would be in a prime position to write a new and glorious chapter for him and his kingdom. Patience, a king, must use time, not stamp all over it. Clicking contentedly to his horse, he moved back to the head of the waiting cortège, soon to be transformed into a victory parade if Greendale had got his finger out and managed to get things right this time.

In the short space of time given, Greendale had indeed pulled out all the stops and had laid out a spectacular welcome. The news of the king's imminent arrival had spread like a raging fire throughout the city, and the royal road was thronged with a waving and cheerful populace, shouting and chanting, 'Long live the king, our king is back, and here with us, he will always stay.' It was not entirely clear whether or not the people had the king or his brother in mind, but in the end, it did not matter, as only one of them was alive. Soldiers in sand-polished armour stood stationed at intervals along the main thorough way. Horn-blowers and drummers met them at the outskirts. They were now marching energetically in front of the royal personage and his cavalcade. A fitting escort for a king into his city. The royal person rode majestically forward on his white horse, smiling benignly down at the beaming and happy crowd. Winding their way along the cobbled, freshly swept street, the cortège finally arrived at the palace gates where the Lord Chamberlain hurriedly appeared with the rest of the Privy Council members trailing behind him. As they made ready in all pomp and ceremony to descend the stairs to greet and bow down before their royal ruler, the crowd turned nasty, replacing their cheers with boos, cat-calls and jeering. His royal highness looked around him with great unease and then focused his attention on his gathered council, kneeling at his feet. In a loud, stern voice, he said.

'What has happened here in my absence, Lord Chamberlain? My people have just won a great victory. My brother, their king, has been returned to them. Where is their joy? Explain yourself, good sirs!'

The blood drained from the Lord Chamberlain's face, and he took on a look of bewilderment.

'I...we did as you commanded, your Highness.'

'As I commanded! I left you with the charge to secure my city. I am now wondering what steps and actions you have taken onto yourself to alienate my people so! I will have answers from you, Lord Chamberlain, and forthwith!'

With that, the king dismounted, and strode briskly up the stairs and through the royal gates, his face bearing the thunderous expression of royal displeasure.

'You're going to get what's coming to you now, you bastard!'

'What goes around, comes around, you piece of slime!' shouted individuals in the crowd.

A visibly shaken council hurried after the king.

'You did what!?' the king's voice boomed out, echoing around the closed chamber. Every available space stood filled with lords and dignitaries as the king listened with astonishment to the tale given by his Privy Council. It was an impromptu trial in all but name, and all present knew that immediate judgement stood pending. The room was unnaturally calm as everyone seemed to be holding their breaths.

'And every one of you remained voiceless whilst these atrocious acts lay completed in my name?'

Only silence greeted the king's question.

The Lord Chamberlain's distressed face dripped with glistening sweat, his state garments sodden, and he appeared to be shaking uncontrollably, an old, fragile leaf, frayed by the wind.

The king drew in a deep breath, closed his eyes for a moment, and calmed himself, then focussing steadily on the Lord Chamberlain said.

'Every action carries responsibility, my lord, and so therein lies consequence.'

Raising his eyes, he took in the whole audience.

'This man, fallen from my grace, will have deaf ears and blind eyes turned on him from henceforth. Anyone caught breaking this declaration will suffer the pain of death. All of the condemn's land, property, titles and wealth shall fall to the crown. In three days hence, this nameless man shall have his tongue removed, and his hands cut off in atonement for the deeds he has done to this land. And, let us not forget just punishment, for the taking of the life of my beloved teacher and esteemed servant of our kingdom, Morgan Ap Heston. His harsh and unnecessary treatment of our brave and stalwart Earl, without whom we would not be standing here, has also not gone unnoticed and adds to the severity of his sentence.

Not a sliver of sound stood heard from the astonished witnesses. The once again, ex-lord chamberlain looked around him like an old hound, who after long years of faithful service to his master, was handed over to the huntsman to put down, lost, baffled and bemused. No reassurances stood offered.

'But Majesty...'

'Take him from our sight!'

The once-proud lord lay dragged away, tears streaming from his eyes.

Without even a sideways glance, the king continued.

'As for you lot, miserable as you are, led by the nose by someone who should have known better, I will withhold judgement pending your rightful actions from this day on. Leave us! Lord Captain, see to it that our beloved Earl receives his freedom at once, along with the young king's guard. Have them bathed, fed and rested before bringing them to an audience. The crown owes them an apology.'

All those present on that day left to go to their homes not sure of what exactly they had seen but convinced within themselves that it was something good.

***

Morgan's eyes fluttered open, deep brown and calm. He looked around him slowly, taking in his dim, dry, cool surroundings and the blazing, shimmering light outside the opening in the near distance; a cave then. He didn't need to turn his eyes on the presence behind him. He knew already what it was.

'Have you found inner peace yet, brother?' he rasped from his dry, parched throat.

An equally dry, but twice as rough, snuffled chuckle emanated from somewhere behind his head.

'Oohnly wan I Kraal, brarks yourr spindly naaek.'

'Charming. Thanks for the rescue, anyway.'

'Youu arrr Krarl's to kill orr keeep. Eeet is my right!'

'As you say. What now?'

'Eat lital weekling. Sleep, gate strength bark. All men in thes land yourr enemy now. We hunt togeadar one last time. We kill lying men. We aare pack!'

Morgan fell asleep.

***

A loud bang and the bright flickering light of torches woke Nat and Earl Marches from a fitful sleep. They were covered from head to foot in dirt and grime, their mouths felt foul, and their clothes stank. Feeling ashamed, they shrank away from the light and the approaching guards.

'What's it this time!?' muttered the Earl.

Nat remained silent, gathering himself for one last defiant act before the Fates, witches of mischief, sent him to spit in the eye of the devil. He had been told of the death of his second mentor, Aden, and was determined not to die in the same spiritually disciplined manner; he was going out fighting, the end would not find him easy and compliant.

'The King has sent us to free you, sirs. Please rest easy,' said the captain respectfully, noticing the burning fire in their eyes and the flexing of their limbs.

'You have put us here, you whoresons, why should we trust you!' barked the Earl.

'They sent us to you in good faith, Lord of the Marches. The King is righting the terrible wrong done to you.'

'The king has returned then?'

'Yes, lord. Please extend your arms and let me release you from those rusted bonds.'

'Fair enough,' interrupted Nat, thrusting forward his shackled hands.

'Rest easy, young lord,' responded the captain, eyeing Nat wearily. His fighting prowess was well known. Nevertheless, he inserted the key into his shackles and released him, turning back to the earl and repeating the action.

'Lead on then, son,' grumbled the Earl. 'I've had enough of this splendidly luxurious guest house for now.'

They trudged up the winding ramp leading from the dungeons in silence, but when they arrived at the broader passageway on the level with the storage rooms, two grim-looking jailers passed them dragging a bleeding man with tearing sobs racking his thin body. They were unable to see his face as it lay covered by a thick velvet mask, which muffled his desperate sounds.

'Is this king's justice?' asked Nat coldly.

The captain walked on without answering.

***

Two men sat together quietly, eating freshly baked bread, cheese, and onions washed down with sweet ale. They were comfortable in each other's company, and it was some time before they spoke.

'The King is back then?'

The other nodded but did not answer, continuing with his slow chewing.

'Word has come that he has freed the Earl and sentenced that worm of a Greendale to a terrible fate.'

Another nod.

'He had it coming to him, the bastard. Can't imagine Ap Heston dead.'

'Patrick, you must strive to see further than your mortal eyes. There is a stink of politics in all of this.'

'I'm not sure I understand, Lord Abbot.'

'Think back, Patrick. From where did the king suddenly get a troop of cavalry? Remember, his timely arrival saved the Earl and the day on the bridge of stones? We did not supply him with men and resources, so this means he was secretly building his strength, the same way he did when sparring with the Earl.'

'Granted, but what's that got to do with recent events?'

'This king wants to be loved. He wants his subjects to see him always as the liberator who rides in and wins the day. He has learned how to use others towards that end, and he has learned patience. He knows not to dirty his hands, and he lets others do this for him. Our unfortunate Lord Chamberlain, hungry for power as he is, was very loyal to his kings. He does not deserve the fate dealt him by this oh so clever monarch.'

'Do you have any hard proof on this Lord Abbot?'

'No, Patrick, unfortunately not. I just have a keen nose, and sometimes it leads me beyond good sense.'

'Shouldn't we try to do something anyway?'

'Now is not the time. Our network has survived, but we've lost a lot. Like the king, we have to rebuild our strength secretly.'

***

'An old friend says that the time has come for you to find religion, m'lud.'

The pathetic figure huddled in the dark, dirty corner lifted its velvet-covered head, staring myopically through the two cut holes, a mask of silence, a man imprisoned within his very own mind, castrated. In the darkness of his prison, nothing could be seen or heard. Yet, the lingering trace of those strange words, fact, or mockery, real, or imagined, echoed in his lost and frightening thoughts.

Is this madness? To be betrayed, abandoned, discarded and tortured? Tears leaked into the thick velvet cloth as he curled up into a ball, weeping into the silence that was his hell.

Indeterminable time dripped by, marked out by a distant 'plink' of water, falling drop by slow drop into a hidden puddle, drowning, even more, the deadened senses of a once overly proud man, sentenced to be forgotten, trapped in the consequences of his sins.

Rough hands from nowhere jolted him out of his wallowing self-pity. They jerked him onto numbed, unused feet. In seconds, his senses sat flooded with the excruciating pain of renewed circulation. The rude agony dragged his emptied thoughts groaning back into reality - his tormented existence.

'Walk, m'lud. Walk out of this buried place, but forever be covered by the dirt of guilt,' preached the muffled voice.

The ex-chamberlain, ex-lord, bereft of self and titles, stumbled out through the darkness, his fate no longer in his hands, but deeply grateful that these sullied appendages, were still attached.

CHAPTER XXII

Red, livid streaks covered his exposed neck and the backs of his forearms. His sweat-soaked body was dirt-covered, and he stank; stank of swamp water and unidentified vegetation. He itched everywhere. Reaching up with a swollen, thick-fingered and puffy hand, he scratched at his ruddy neck with black, mud-encrusted nails, leaving behind a fresh set of red weals, raw and irritating. From a face turgid from the heavy, boiling heat, he studied with penetrating eyes the squat, broad-shouldered man standing calmly in front of him.

'So you ran again, did you?'

'We all run, Excellency, when our arses are exposed, naked in the air.'

The reply was not said in a presumptuous way, just a statement of fact.

'Lippy as always, eh, sergeant? But I take your meaning. The past is the past. However, I'm more interested in where you've hidden my barges, and even more importantly, the rations inside them.

The governor had been on the run since his troops had deserted him on the battlefield over three weeks ago. He had been hunted every inch of the way and had not been allowed to regroup much-less as draw breath. Fighting a desperate rearguard, hounded by hit and run tactics, he had finally fled, mostly by accident, into the sprawling, cooking pot of a delta; a spreading unforgiving place of savage, unrelenting insects with an unnatural taste for blood. Added to this unsavoury stew, were lurking reptiles bent on pulling any unwary living creature under the briny, fetid waters in which they lived, and sly, silent natives who would prefer to put a poisoned arrow in you rather than spit at you. His prized horses, including his beautiful, mighty, grey stallion had all succumbed to this pitiless environment - quartered and devoured by their riders and a fair number, by the spiteful denizens of this watery hell-hole. Now he was hungry and had lost most of the dominating bulk that had identified him. He and his men had taken to raiding the stilt raised, thatch villages which lay scattered and hidden among the mangroves. Falling on them as righteous men should, they had burnt these rude, offensive dwellings to the ground but not before they had taken everything and anything useful, killing the men and children, raping the women, old and young, then discarding them like refuse. These instances brought the governor alive again, he revelled in his dominance, and anyway, it was a sensible military option where survival mattered. Then he had run into Sergeant Cuttlefish, seemingly calm, well-fed, clean and in possession of two provision barges; luck was turning finally.

'Mostly all spoilt now, your honour, and certainly too little left to feed all your men; perhaps enough for one good meal.'

The governor felt rage breaking into flame and beginning the process of consuming him. Unable to breathe, he struggled to suppress and overcome it.

Sergeant Cuttlefish watched the governor who seemed rooted rigidly to the spot; his body twitching with involuntary spasms, his eyes clenched tightly shut, and his mouth working to gasp in air. He fought the urge to step back.

'Are you well, Excellency?' he failed to hide the alarm in his voice.

The governor's eyes snapped open and after a brief look of confusion, fixed him with a savage stare.

'Don't you ever do anything right, man!' he accused.

The experienced sergeant decided it was wise not to respond.

The governor continued to stare for an inappropriately long time at Cuttlefish who waited patiently under the scrutiny. As the seconds dragged by in silence, an air of anxiety began to rise in the sticky heat. All present were visibly relieved when they heard the sloshing boots of the returning scout as he waded across a shallow rivulet leading to their relatively dry, little island.

With one last stabbing look, the governor broke away and turned his attention to the scout.

'Report!' he barked.

'Sir! We've sighted another village. About three hours west of where you're standing.'

'Good! For what are we waiting? Let's go! Cuttlefish, you too. Fall in!'

Four hours later, their wet clothes steaming into the air, mixing with the fish-like smell of rotting swamp vegetation, five hundred men, the last remnants of a once-proud, elite cavalry force, crawled forward on their bellies. They wormed their way through wet boggy ground, stunted swamp trees, and razor-sharp swamp grass, positioning themselves to surround an as yet unaware village.

'Why are we doing this?' whispered Sergeant Cuttlefish to the man next to him.

'To find food,' the man whispered back.

'Never heard of fishing?' Cuttlefish grumbled back in return.

The man looked him up and down and grinned.

'If he says anything stupid,' thought Cuttlefish, 'I'll thump him hard.'

They were all gathering themselves, waiting for the governor's signal to rush forward when all hell broke loose.

Two forms, moving at unbelievable speed erupted out of the sluggish river behind them in a burst of shimmering spray. Cuttlefish saw them first, doubting what his eyes were telling him. In that knife-edged balanced point in time, before his warning shout could reach the ears of his enforced companions, the apparitions were upon them. The first to get to them was a nightmare out of any madman's dreams. It was tall, gaunt, with a broad, powerful, naked and very hairy chest. As it tore past the first soldier lying face down in the grass, it plucked him up as if he were a doll with one clawed hand. With the other, it grabbed him under his chin, and with a quick tug, ripped open the unfortunate soldier's throat in a gush of gore. Cuttlefish felt his gorge rising into his throat and struggled not to throw up. The man next to him, sarcastic grin forgotten, was staring with bulging eyes. The second apparition was only a hairs breath behind the first. This one, at least, had the shape of an ordinary man, but all comparisons stopped there. He too was naked except for a loincloth, and his whip-hard body moved with an indescribable quickness. He leapt high, soaring over the body flung aside by his companion, landing on another soldier who was trying to rise and face this surprise attack. As he did so, he pinned the man to the ground with his knees, wrapped an arm around his neck, and with a swift casual jerk, broke his back, the loud snapping of backbones raising the goose-bumps on everyone, freezing them. In a heartbeat, he was up and moving again.

 Then a wall of teeth chattering fear hit them. Cuttlefish, through all his long years of conflict, had never experienced such a thing. He lay there, unable to move, his limbs trembling in terror, and watched the soldier beside him roll his eyes upwards, his mouth a rictus-grin, until only the whites showed, then with an agonising groan, passed out, drool dribbling from his now open, slack mouth. Using every vestige of willpower that he had, Cuttlefish strained to keep track of the fast-moving, unstoppable pair as they weaved a path of utter destruction through five hundred men trained for war.

The governor, sword clenched tightly in his ham-like fist, staggered out into the speeding path of the half-naked man, slashing his weapon viciously at his neck. With consummate ease, and without breaking stride, the brown-skinned man melted under the downward stroke of the sharp blade and flung the governor aside, sending him crashing into the undergrowth, with as little effort as it would take a grown wolf to throw off a bothersome pup. So fast did they move, that they were gone into the trees on the other side in what seemed like a blink of an eye, leaving men groaning and clutching broken limbs in their wake; quite a few did not move at all, and the sergeant suspected, some of these would never move again. Still shaking like a leaf in the wind, he pushed himself to his feet, only to have a whizzing arrow narrowly miss his cheek. Spinning around, he saw men streaming from the elevated, straw huts, all sporting bows and without doubt, poison-tipped arrows. This development was one step too far for most of the broken men, and many fled between the trees in every direction. The governor had managed to drag himself from his entanglement. Bellowing at the top of his lungs, he ordered the remainder of his men to fall in around him. Cuttlefish scrabbled over to join this group, knowing that it was his best chance of survival. Those who still had shields raised them defensively, and under the shouted orders of the governor they withdrew in haste into the shelter of the stunted trees, thanking their god that the village men had chosen not to follow. Of the original five hundred who had started this latest venture, only about two hundred remained, and some of these clearly had arrows sticking in them; they were dead men walking, food for crows.

About half an hour later - after passing some of their members in one's and two's with torn out throats and broken necks - the governor called a halt. The overextended men collapsed uncaring onto the sodden, squelching ground, ignoring the crawling, biting, stinging insects as they sought out this new blood feast. Suddenly, Cuttlefish started chuckling.

'What's so fucking funny, Cuttlefish!' bellowed the governor.

'Sorry Gov, I was just thinking, that's all. You see, we are a herd of buffalo. The wolves have split us to see how we run, and then they pick out the weak and the stragglers and bring them down. We are in the hunt, governor, and we are the prey.'

The governor stared at the solidly built sergeant contemplatively, then muttered.

'Shut up, Cuttlefish!'

'Yes, sir.'

Exhausted and frightened, with both their bodies and nerves worn-down to a fraying edge, the soldiers struggled on, now and again encountering a grisly reminder of the sergeant's ominous words.

'Bloody appalling,' mumbled the sergeant.

'I said 'shut it', Cuttlefish!'

'Yes, sir.'

They spent an awful night huddled together. The vegetation was too wet and damp to start a fire with, and many of the day's survivors were groaning under a burning fever, their bodies defences worn down to almost nothing. All those who had been unlucky or maybe lucky, enough to be wounded by the poisoned arrows were now dead; left in the cloying heat to rot and stink.

'Putrefaction,' muttered Cuttlefish in the stinging, biting dark. 'From mud, we comest, to mud we goest.'

'Cuttlefish! I shan't warn you again!'

'No, sir. Yes, sir.'

About midnight, things started happening that caused the miserable group to descend into sheer panic. It began with a soldier who had wandered a little distance away to piss into the blanketing blackness surrounding their makeshift camp. As he fumbled to find himself by touch only, something reached out and yanked him into the trees; his startled shout led to a terrifying scream which ended abruptly, cut off by an ominous silence. Men drew closer together despite the heat, in search of security, but they found none. At irregular intervals men were snatched away, many finding death even before they could call out to their fellows. Fear covered the besieged group in a hot, sweltering, putrid miasma, making any attempts at sleep impossible, and driving the distressed men into a world of hallucinations, into that no man's land where the lost dead lurked.

Morning found their numbers much reduced. Twenty-five men stood taken, and to the horror of those still alive, the early mist revealed them hanging macabrely from the twisted branches all around. Another fifteen, who had found themselves overcome with swamp fever, had died in the night. Their cold corpses propped up between the bodies of their unknowing comrades. Hunger and despair gnawed at the ever-shrinking survivors, and from the look in their eyes, Cuttlefish could tell that more, losing all reason, would slip away and try to run, thinking that their party lay cursed, that the governor sat cursed. He was undoubtedly a man fit to be damned.

Browbeaten into line by a bullying governor, it was apparent that most of the men had already given up and were ready to lie down and die. They made a bedraggled and sorry lot as they filed out. Cuttlefish wanted no part of it and kept a low profile. He watched everything with a keen eye, ready to sway in whatever direction necessary to get out of this septic pit in one piece. The governor could continue to play the great, war general if he wanted to, but although he couldn't accept it, he was already dead, like the rest of his men. It was only a matter of time. The two hunting them were not human, they were exceptionally skilled, incredibly strong and fast, able to see in the dark, and undoubtedly very, very patient. No mercy stood expected from that quarter for whomever or whatever they were. It was clear that they wanted the governor and his war party dead, down to the last man.

'Our best chance is to make it back to the barges, sir.' volunteered the sergeant.

'Oh, finally, you have something useful to say!' replied the governor nastily. 'Lead on then Cuttlefish! Lead us to where you've stashed your stolen golden egg.'

Not bothering to reply, the sergeant squelched forward to take the point on his sturdy legs.

The journey towards the hidden barges was uneventful if you can call boiling heat, sticky, sucking mud, swarms of persistent, stinging insects, and slicing, saw-grass, uneventful. About one-hundred and twenty hollow-eyed, ragged, limping men, trailed down the long gentle slope towards a slow-moving tributary whose banks lay covered with Manchineel trees. One of the now near starving soldiers reached up to pick one of the small apple-like fruits and took a quick, savage bite out of it. At the crunching sound, Cuttlefish spun around and shouted.

'Stop, spit it out quickly, man!'

The soldier gazed blankly at him and replied.

'Fuck off, Cuttlefish! Go and find your own.'

The sergeant watched him and muttered.

'Ah, mi mancinella, my little apple, your kiss is sweet; you burn my heart, and lead me to my death.'

The soldier suddenly stopped chewing, spitting the mulched pulp from his mouth.

'What the…!'

He fell to his knees gagging and spitting, his spittle tinged with pink blood. Then he rolled onto his back, clasping his stomach and moaning pitifully, his eyes wide with shock.

'What's happening to him, Cuttlefish!' demanded an alarmed governor.

'The fruit is poisonous, sir, deadly. Even the tree itself will burn the skin off you.'

Swiftly men edged away from the cooling shelter of the drooping leaves.

'Help him, man!'

Cuttlefish answered in a steady, dead-pan, matter of fact voice.

'Nothing I can do, sir. He is already dead.'

His fellow soldiers stood around in a loose circle and watched their comrade in arms die slowly and agonisingly with slack, expressionless faces.

With a look of disgust passing over his face, Cuttlefish turned away and continued towards the river's shaded edge. The governor trailed after him, followed by the rest of the group, leaving the dying man to find his solitary way to the spirit world.

Walking along the shoreline for another five or so minutes, the sergeant stopped, wiped his wet brow with the back of a dirtied sleeve, stuck two stained fingers into his mouth, and blew a low, melodic whistle. After a short pause, a similar one, but much more rudimentary, flew back.

With a grunt, Cuttlefish moved towards the sound.

Draped and covered by cut and loosely organised vegetation, the curving lines of a barge came into view. Perched on it were two men with longbows drawn and trained on the approaching group.

'You took a long time coming, sarge!' was the greeting.

'Found me a couple of guests. Stand, hup! Welcome, sir.'

'This isn't your damn house, Cuttlefish! These are my bloody barges, which you stole, remember!' barked the governor, pushing his way past the sergeant.

'Yes, sir. As you say, sir.'

The shocked guards, finally recognising the now ravaged looking governor, drew themselves hurriedly to attention and saluted. Ignoring them, he clambered up the steep sides and made his way immediately to investigate the contents of the hold.

'You're a lying bastard, Cuttlefish! There is plenty of good food down here. I'll have you strung up for this!'

'Yes, sir.'

Hungry men swarmed over the sides, and shoving the sergeant aside, lining up behind the governor, peering avidly around him at the salted and preserved provisions stacked in front of them.

Pulling a knife from his belt, the governor stepped forward and cut himself a generous chunk of dry, salted beef, gave it a quick smell, and began to devour it. After what seemed like ages lost in mastication, he finally nodded to the drooling men, who rushed forward to help themselves.

Soon the men were full, their stomachs distended from the gorging. They lay around in heaps, dozing and snoring, happy and feeling safe for the first time in weeks. Cuttlefish sat at the bow of the lead barge in the shade, watching the idle soldiers with veiled eyes. The sweet, scented odour of wood smoke drifted into his nostrils, sending tendrils of irritation into his mind. The stupid bastards are having a cook up on my barge, he thought. Hope they don't burn them down.

'Fire!' he shouted, leaping to his feet in alarm. 'Battle stations, you bastards! They're burning the barges as you sleep!'

Men began to sit up and peer around blearily, and Cuttlefish saw the governor stumble up from the hold sword in hand, but he knew deep down they were too late. These two bastards were patient and bloody clever. They waited for me to decide to lead them right here, he thought, and they waited until we had stuffed ourselves silly. They knew I'd have to bring the governor here in the end.

'Bastards!' he yelled into the open sky, not caring if they all thought him to be a lunatic.

Yes, everything around them was wet and soggy, but these barges were as dry as tinder wood above the waterline, and like tinder, they would burn merrily. Angry flames were already leaping high over the cabin, and the crackling roar dominated the space, driving everyone back ashore to escape the solid wall of heat. As they stood there, non-pulsed, watching the fire, the added, extraordinary heat from the burning barges caused the canopied manchineel trees to blister and burst, releasing white, poisonous sap which dropped onto the heads and shoulders of the gathered soldiers. The viscous fluid burned painfully through hair and clothing, sending the terrified men into a frenzy as they ducked, ran, and twisted this way and that, in a vain attempt to escape the deadly rain. This moment was when the two wolves chose to strike.

From opposite points they came, like dark angels of vengeance, flying on wings of destruction. One came howling, sending waves of fear crashing ahead of him, the other was deathly silent, racing with an implacable will. Which was worse, which was better, none could tell, none wanted to stay to find out. Cuttlefish watched them coming, and he knew their intersection point was the governor. The fool had not yet realised.

The governor was apoplectic with futile rage, shouting and bellowing at the frightened men to stop the bastards, to cut them down, kill them. They instead, stood rooted in indecision and fear as they died. Some were so obsessed with avoiding the dripping poisonous sap that they did not even comprehend the greater danger. The two creatures weaved through the trees, tearing unerringly towards their target. About two dozen seasoned and brave fighters turned to face them. It was all for nothing, for the forces of nature, bore through them, scattering them, breaking bones and rupturing organs, with the fury of their passage. Alone, in the centre, the governor tried to track them both as they flew at him, mouth working soundlessly, eyes bulging in terror. They crossed him at the same split second as if it were a competition, a tied race—the one with man-like form smoked behind the governor. A sinewy arm whipped around its target's thick neck, catching his chin with an iron hand, then viciously yanking as he flew by. The loud crack of breaking neck bones made Cuttlefish wince like a virgin girl. As the governor's body catapulted into the air, the one in beast form, slashed out with a rigid hand, tipped with sharp, black nails, eviscerating him from solar plexus to groin, spinning the body, complete circle in mid-air with a spray of dark blood and uncoiling intestines. The two came to a sudden stop, as one, as the body crashed into the earth, and looked around them, crouched and ready to kill. The remainder of the governor's men fled.

 Four intense eyes came to rest on Cuttlefish; the only one left standing in the poisonous, smoke-filled glade. Swallowing hard, the sturdy sergeant felt an urgent need to take a piss but decided his best course of action was to remain very still. Maybe they would overlook him. They didn't. 'Fuck', he thought.

 Without disturbing a single leaf, the two moved towards him on bare feet, impaling him with their alien eyes. Unable to look at the one in beast form, mostly because of the drool dripping from its maw, he turned to focus on the other, hoping to find more of kinship there. As he looked into his eyes, he saw golden flecks, swirling brightly in the deep brown pools. Cuttlefish blinked, unbelieving, but when he looked again, there were only deep, calm, human eyes regarding him. Before he could think of what to say, a wet snuffling sound emanated from the hairy other, distracting him.

'Sharl we keel and eeet this one, broadarr?'

Cuttlefish wet himself.

The man regarded him steadily for another few seconds, then without a word, turned and floated out of the glade. The other snuffled a bit more, and Cuttlefish realised that it was laughing at him. Then, it too turned and glided away.

CHAPTER XXIII

The Earl of Marches, his daughter Elaine, and Nathaniel Woodsmoke waited in the anteroom adjacent to the king's private quarters. They stood invited to a private audience with the King but sat attired in formal dress. The Earl was troubled as worrying news had been circulating throughout the city for days. It declared that the crown had asked the Earl and his family pardon for the wrongs committed to them. Yet this was the first occasion in which the King had summoned them. The whole thing had the feel of royal public relations about it, and it made his skin itch from thinning scalp to gnarled toe. This king continued to puzzle him.

Something made him look up, and he caught his daughter's shrewd green eyes regarding him. He smiled brightly at her, but he knew she sat unfooled. This one would make a great queen he thought and then winced at the possible repercussions of such an idea. He found himself making the sign of the horn with his fingers behind his back. Nat had been uncharacteristically quiet since he had heard of the execution of Morgan and had an absent, thoughtful air about him. Both his fathers lost, taken away by actions of the state. Elaine kept glancing at him, concern, written clearly on her face. Once again, the Earl frowned. More trouble ahead, he thought, something had to be done about those two.

Their affections for each other were very evident. Both had been through a lot lately. They had grown accustomed to forging their destinies with a joint effort, he noticed. The two of them would need careful handling, careful watching. Morgan was dead, the Abbot had all but disappeared and was not contactable, and he, an Earl of the realm, was kept in the dark, literally in some cases. He chuckled dryly, drawing young eyes to him. Returning the look of the two young people in the room, he shrugged his meaty shoulders, feeling the warmth of great affection for them, settle over him.

They sat in companionable silence for another five minutes until an enigmatic Alfred appeared at the door and summoned them through. The court attendant led them through two empty rooms, and as Alfred opened the door to the third, they caught a glimpse of an angry king, who with a harsh whisper directed at his Lord Chief Justice, stood overheard saying.

'...impossible to walk out from. Find out and bring me answers.'

Catching sight of his invited guests he cut off immediately, his face smoothing over, his angry frown replaced by a welcoming smile.

'My dear Earl,' he beamed, walking over and embracing the older man. 'I've missed you, missed our honest sparring in the cloister. I have begun to look back at those occasions as my happiest times. I'm sorry for not being here to protect you when you most needed me.'

Releasing the Earl, he bowed to Lady Elaine, took her hand in his and kissed it.

'Lady Elaine, the crown will make due recompense to you and your family for this outrageous slight against your status and dignity.'

Finally, he turned to Nat and grasped his forearm in a warriors grip.

'Young King's Protector, you do and continue to do your country honour. We will see you rewarded.'

With that, he turned away and sat in a large, ornate chair, stationed in front of the open window.

'Please, be seated, my friends,' he said, gesturing at three smaller chairs arranged before him. 'Alfred shall bring you some cooling refreshments.'

'Our small kingdom sits at a crossroad. We have never been so vulnerable as we are now. You three stand intimately involved in our difficult and testing struggle to get us to this point, so you don't need my reminder. It stands imperative that we show the people and foreign interest, a united front. You, my dear Earl, and you, Lady Elaine, are representatives of one of the last great houses still standing, free of reproach, alongside my own. We will have to join together.'

The Earl's craggy face creased even more into a frown, Elaine visibly stiffened, and Nat, although his expression did not change, grew more focused. Clearing his throat audibly, the Earl asked.

'Pardon me, your Highness, but what exactly are you proposing?'

'I'm proposing that we unify our great houses, dear Earl - to elevate you to the title of King's father, protector of the realm! This suggestion is a great honour. It is a great opportunity for both our houses and for the future of the kingdom. No, No, do not give me any hasty answers. All I ask is for you to go away and think over my royal offer. I need you at my right hand, my dear friend; now more than ever.'

An unhurried Alfred drifted in with a silver tray of refreshing wine and spiced cakes with honey and hovered in the background, as the three guests took polite bites and sips. An air of discomfort had settled over them as they listened to an outwardly chatty and happy king outlining his plans for renovating the poorest quarters of the city and a new aqueduct already under construction, to bring fresh water to every citizen. He didn't seem concerned about how he would obtain finance.

After about half-an-hour of this, the king begged his leave regretfully, on other urgent matters of state, giving them the royal invitation to attend a formal state gathering on the following eve. This time, he kissed Lady Elaine on both cheeks before grasping the arms of both the Earl and Nat, looking them in the eye and smiling fiercely with apparent joy.

As they walked through the rose gardens on their way back to the Earl's quarters, Nat broke the silence and said.

'What was that all about? Did he just suggest that Elaine should marry him?'

The Earl pretended not to notice that his daughter had immediately reached out to hold the young warrior's hand.

'His aim is just to secure the kingdom', muttered the Earl absently.

'He aims to seize your daughter's hand and legitimise his rule, cornering all the claims to the kingship!' responded Nat, with heat in his voice.

 Elaine remained silent, holding on to Nat's hand tightly and gazing up at him.

'What do you suggest we do, young fighter? Challenge the king? Look, the king has made a legitimate proposal. We, Elaine and I, shall give it due consideration and return his answer.'

 Nat clamped his jaw shut and didn't say any more.

***

'You took a great personal risk.'

'The past sometimes dictates our actions.'

'Is he worth it? All our contacts and influences in the prisons now sitting nullified?'

'As far as my honour is concerned, yes, in other things, we will have to wait and see. Sometimes a high price has to be paid for information, and if he possesses what I suspect he does, then we hold a treasury full of gold in our hands. Remember Patrick; information is our trade.'

The two men were looking across at the slumbering form, curled up on a cot in the corner.

'Should we try and wake him? He has been sleeping for two days!'

'It's a good sign, a healing sign, but yes, let's rouse him. He has been through much and has fallen far. He now has to face the world that he has created for himself. Wake nameless one! It's time to see again!'

The Abbot shook the thin, dejected bundle gently, but firmly, by his emaciated shoulders, eliciting a snort, then a fitful start. His eyes flew open and seemed to take ages before recognition replaced the glassy, displaced look.

'Timothy? What? Why are you in my bedchamber?'

'On the contrary, my old friend, you are in mine. Humble as it is.'

The man with no name or title frowned in puzzlement, then memory flooded into the empty spaces in his mind, revealing itself by the look of horror on his face.

'The king. I must see the king - make him understand. He has made a mistake. I must explain it!'

'Easy, old friend, you can see him later. What mistake did his Majesty make?'

'You don't understand! I only did my duty.'

'Of course, old friend, duty is everything.'

'Yes, yes! Tell the king. I did what he asked! I did my duty.'

Tears ran down the thin cheeks of the once again, ex-chamberlain.

'The king surely should have rewarded you for your act of service.'

'Yes, yes, you have it, this is why I must see him, explain.'

'Explain what though, my lord? Did you do things which ran contrary to his instructions? This lapse may explain why...'

'No, no! He told me exactly what to do, and I did it all, the goddesses forgive me.'

'They see everything, my friend. The king has delivered the Earl from the place you put him and asked forgiveness on behalf of the crown.'

'Yes, yes. The Earl was not to be hurt; we need him, just kept out of the way for a while.'

'Kept out of whose way, my dear friend?'

'I wanted to help the king; he was worried about the intentions of self-styled king-makers. History must not be allowed to repeat itself. I saw his pain, his hands tied to friendship and loyalty. Only I could help. I knew what was required. I must make the King understand this.'

'So the king did not specifically order the execution of Lord Morgan?'

'No, but I saw his pain. A king must not have blood on his hands.'

'No, he should not!' whispered the Abbot softly.

***

The audience chamber stood filled with the buzz of formally dressed dignitaries and nobles. Palace servers were threading their way through the expectant and mutely festive crowd with laden silver trays of sweet-meats, honey cakes and cinnamon flavoured wine. The Earl of Marches wanted to, but could not find the right opportunity, to approach the king who seemed to be in his element, circulating from one party to the next, putting people at ease and drawing light laughter from them. Nat was irritated and was only being kept calm by a serene and beautiful Elaine, who spent her time stuck to his side, leaning delicately on his arm. Once again, the Earl could not help but think of how much of a queen she looked, however, he was not sure if the closeness of the young couple gave out the appropriate signals to the king, bearing in mind the circumstance. Finally, his Majesty seemed to be heading their way, and the Earl quickly rehearsed the words that he and his daughter had prepared for this occasion. The King, without establishing any eye-contact whatsoever, suddenly swerved away, trailing his sycophants. He turned and clapped his hands loudly, stepping up onto the podium.

'Noble Lords and Ladies, gentlemen of the court, please, give me your ears, I have wonderful news of great import which I am overjoyed to share with you.'

A hush fell over the gathering, all smiles and rapped attention, except for a trio of creased and cautious brows.

Holding his hands up and open as if in blessed benediction, the king continued.

'One of the greatest, most loyal, stalwart houses of the realm, headed by a lord most popular and highly regarded by the people, and by his liege; a lord whose strong and brave actions have been integral to us standing here today, proud and free. This lord has consented to join hands with the Royal House of Kings. A symbol of this union will be my marriage to his beautiful daughter, the Lady Elaine, a better queen of this realm there will never be.'

The crowd broke out in rapturous applause, craning their necks around to have a look at the lucky bride to be. The Earl had the look of one who had been pole-axed, Elaine's face was as white as a sheet, drained of all colour, and anyone looking at Nat's grim face would have heard the word 'bastard' mouthed through his tight lips.

Raising his silver cup, the king shouted over the cheering.

'Join me in a royal toast to this happy and momentous occasion, for our future royal houses and the future line of the kingdom.'

He drained his cup in a flamboyant flourish and without further pause, turned and disappeared through the closely guarded door at the rear, a door through which only kings could pass.

With a face of thunder, the Earl headed for the main exit, scowling at any who dared approach him, closely followed by Nat and Elaine. As they stepped into the hall outside the Earl turned to them.

'Go back to our quarters and pack quickly. Only essentials mind. Events are moving faster than the north wind. We should return to our estates sooner rather than later. Nat, I would like you to guard my daughter with your sword and life if necessary, and I would be most honoured if you were to accompany us to our home.'

'I would do so even without your asking, sir!' replied Nat. 'And I would be honoured to ride by your side, but may I ask what your immediate intention is?'

'I am going to see the king. If I don't return within the hour, flee.'

With a nod, the Earl was gone, and Nat and Elaine hurried off to do his bidding.

As they made their way along an echoing corridor on the way to the Earl's palace quarters, Nat suddenly grabbed Elaine's hand and veered away, exiting onto a little-used courtyard.

'What are you doing? This route isn't the way.'

'It is now. This king will already have thought through the consequences of his actions. Neither you nor your father will be allowed to leave, especially you. We need to move faster than his planning.'

'Sounds like old times,' said Elaine with a grin. 'What about father, though?'

'The old man knows how to look after himself. Besides, the king may try and detain him, but he can't hurt him. The people dearly love your father and, if this king fears anything now that Morgan is gone, it is the will of the people. In a way, you are the Earl's Achilles heel. If we spirit you away, the king loses his leverage over your father.'

'Let's pray he doesn't gain leverage over me. You've become quite the politician! What happened to my violent ruffian?'

'My guardians always taught me to take my time, watch, listen, then act quickly, and with vigour.'

'Oh! I can't wait!' said Elaine. 'Show me this vigour you speak of as soon as we are married, maybe even before!'

Nat turned a bright red and sped on, lengthening his stride.

***

'The King sends his regrets, but he is unable to see you at this time. Maybe I can schedule a meeting with him within the next few days on your behalf?'

'Don't treat me for a fool, Lord High Stewart, and more importantly, don't act the fool! Fortunes rise and fall on a whim. Remember your predecessor.'

'Be careful with hot words, Lord Earl. We may mistake them as treasonous.'

'Those who live by the sword will always choose to die by the sword, enemy to the front. Your arena is that of the sharpened feather. Watch your back well, sir.'

With his expectations confirmed, the Earl turned his back on the High Steward and headed off to his quarters. He knew what he would find there. His only hope was that young Nat had picked up the hidden message in his words and acted swiftly.

As he walked along the same corridor that Nat and Elaine had not so long ago been hurrying along, he was unsurprised to see a troop of king's white-cloaks marching towards him.

'Greetings, Earl of the Marches,' said their captain bowing respectfully.

'What can I do for you, son?' replied the Earl calmly.

'Our King has asked that we protect you with our lives.'

'Very generous of his Majesty, but pray-tell, captain, who or what are you protecting me against?'

'From all danger, my lord, these are uncertain times.'

'They are, indeed, captain. It is hard to believe that we have just thrown out the Protectorate. Were you at the Battle of the Bridge, captain?'

The captain looked momentarily embarrassed but replied evenly.

'I was in the rank next to you, great lord.'

'A day to remember, eh, captain? The king saved our arses on that day. Pray, he continues to do so.'

The captain did not comment.

'Well said, captain. I planned to return to my estates within the hour - a long, tiring journey for a man of my years. Will you be escorting me there, captain?'

'Such a journey is dangerous and unpredictable, Lord Earl. Our advice would be to return to your quarters and remain there for now. The stable situation will allow us to protect you better.'

'This is wise advice, dear captain. Please, lead the way.'

CHAPTER XXIV

The two boys ran naked. Sweat running in rivulets down their backs. Their lithe, long-limbed, sinuous bodies, gifted with the excess energy of youth, sped them on, racing each other through the long grass, dodging trees, ducking under low hanging branches, leaping streams without hesitation or thought. As they ran, they pulled and pushed at each other, trying to trip and hamper, laughing with the pure joy of running free and wild. The hot mid-day sun blazed down on them, burning their already nut brown skins to an even darker hue, but they were immune to its heat, oblivious to the fact that the children of the nearest village were dozing in the shade, waiting for the baking oven to cool. They did not belong there, had no desire to be there, were not wanted or welcome there; they had each other. They were brothers born from the same womb, just an hour apart. Created by their fathers from the best, the strongest, the fastest, the smartest, cut, spliced and joined - their uniqueness forging them as one.

'They are evenly matched.'

'Yes, almost; mentally and physically, they score evenly, with slight divergences.'

'They seem to love each other.'

'Each other is all they have, but only one can fulfil our purpose.'

'But each is a great achievement in its own right. They both strive so hard to please.'

'Yes, but their natures are too far apart. They will represent disharmony rather than harmony. Only one can go forward. Karl has the force of nature smouldering in him. He hears only its call. Everything else is a distraction even though he is capable of mastering all the disciplines.'

'He may learn to control it in time.'

'He can now, but he doesn't want to. He tolerates the training only to stay near his brother.'

The two men, both of indeterminable age, studied the racing boys with narrowed eyes, their long, blue robes, flapping in the stiff, hill-top breeze.

'It is inevitable then?'

'Yes, it is. Now is the time; the sooner, the better.'

The boys were on their third circuit, but their breathing was smooth and easy, their legs light and free of lactic acid build-up.

'Yu run lirrk gurl!'

'Maybe, but I'm still ahead of you,' was the laughing reply.

'Not fuur long, little bruudar,' responded Karl, lashing out with a naked foot, striking his twin behind the knee. As the leg gave way slightly, he sprang ahead, giving out a howl of humorous victory.

'Cheat!' gasped his brother with a throaty chuckle. *'May I remind you once again that I am the first-born; little brother, my backside.'*

'Yup, but youu ah wimp! Scrawny wimp; Krarl strong!'

Morgan threw himself forward in a flying leap, catching Karl around his thighs, bringing him down, plunging both of them laughing and rolling in the soft grass, where they began a wrestling match, Karl drawing on pure energy, fast and muscular. In contrast, his brother utilised his training, trying to summon up the techniques drilled into him by their instructors, suppressing his natural instincts. Suddenly Morgan stopped, dropping his defensive posture, listening to the air. A blow heading for his head, froze, centimetres from causing him injury.

'What is mattar, brudaar?'

'Old limp foot is worried about something. I felt great sadness coming from him.'

'Reerre,' growled Karl dismissively. *'Thart one too soft. Like yuure.'*

'Ha! He kicked your backside in the training circle yesterday!'

'Jarst Lurky.'

'Come on, tough bum! Catch me if you can!' shouted Morgan, racing off again, closely followed by his brother. They still had another ten laps to do before they could eat.

That night, exhausted after yet another day of constant, unrelenting training, the two boys lay in a deep sleep on their bare mattress on the stone floor of a Spartan room. The only item in the chamber was their stuffed mattress, no boyish collections, nothing personal, nothing that revealed who they were.

As from birth, they lay with their hands touching, drawing strength and comfort from each other, even in slumber. Lines of concern, worry even, etched themselves into Morgan's smooth, unblemished brow. His breathing increased, pulled through his nostrils in rapid snatches. His face began to twitch, and then move side to side, as if he were trying to avoid something threatening and unpleasant. A grunt burst through his lips, and his eyes flew open, immediately focused and aware.

'Brother, wake! I feel danger!'

Karl's eyes fluttered open, black pools boring a hole into the world. He did not ask questions. Trust was everything; he just waited for clarification and a course of action.

'We must hide, run. Our fathers are coming for you! They mean to end your life!'

Karl felt rage burning in the pit of his stomach, like smouldering coal, dark and hot, its sole purpose but to burst into flame.

'Foar mee, little bruthaar? Not urss?'

'You brother, but we are one. They have forgotten this!' Morgan snarled, fighting down the flood rising dangerously within him.

'Quick, they are here! We must hide!'

They bounded from their bed, through the door and into a room where the fathers stored extra things. Here, they leapt into the rafters, blending their bodies and minds into the dark, becoming as still as a fell shadow.

Below them passed three hurrying shapes, and a fierce, admonishing whisper flew up into their sharpened ears.

'I warned you to block your thoughts. You're a leaking bucket of conflict! We will be too late!'

Hell fell from the rafters.

Ten years cut from the floating womb, but ten years of hard lessons, absorbed and assimilated, combined with a mixture of genes stolen from nature herself, re-inserted in a manner alien to her, the boys did what they did best, what they had to do, what they created them to do; fight!

First, a wave of fear descended on the three men like a flock of vengeful crows. One buckled and fell to his knees, grabbing his head between his hands. The other two, swirling swiftly about, deflected the mind attack as easily as a grown man deflects a fly. A demon of retribution dropped onto the back of the kneeling man. Before he had time to defend himself, a black-tipped talon, ripped across his throat, opening the jugular like a knife through an old wine-skin, shedding its dark contents onto the stone floor, a splash of finality. The other two leapt nimbly back as a falling Morgan tore through the shadowed space they were just in. Without missing a beat, he attacked low, going for their vulnerable nether regions, striking to the left then to the right. Missing his targets for the second time, he leapt high without hesitation, driving stiff-fingered hands for the throat. Despite his bewildering speed and aggression, the men melted away from his attacks, and his efforts met only thin air. Morgan fell like a coiled spring into a crouch, ready to uncoil again into deadly action. The two tall, robed figures drew themselves up to their full height, extended their hands towards him, palms open, and concentrated on him with eyes of ice. Morgan felt cold tendrils drilling into his mind, taking his breath away, and leaching his will away. With superhuman effort, he turned to his twin, words of warning grating through his clenched and chattering teeth.

'Run, brother, run!'

Without hesitation, Karl fled into the night, his anguished howl tearing the darkness.

Morgan opened his eyes. Krarl lay on a bare section of rock directly across from him, fast asleep. He seemed as comfortable as if he were on a feather bed, his mouth hanging open, his overly long tongue lolling out at the side, the soft buzz of a snore emanating from him. Suddenly, he slopped in his tongue, made a slobbering sound, and snapped at something invisible with his yellowed, prominent teeth. Seemingly satisfied, he then rolled over and farted loudly. Morgan shook his head and almost smiled.

They were resting on a dry promontory sticking out of the ubiquitous wetness, where a rare warm breeze blew, easing the oppressive stillness of the swamp. Whereas Morgan had spent their period of rest, cross-legged, contained, deep in meditation, Krarl had sprawled himself on the nearest dry spot and had immediately fallen into sleep. Discipline and Krarl did not go well together. He refused; in fact, he didn't see the point, in bending his nature and placing it behind bars. Morgan saw his reasoning, and at times, during the many years, had felt a bit envious of the blatantly simple philosophy. Krarl knew from the very first betrayal of the fathers that he would never belong. Why waste a lifetime, long as it may be, trying?

Since being rescued by his brother from certain death, a service, done for each other time after time through the decades, Morgan had guided them along the Sacred River intending to reach the coast. From there they would run until they hit the Black Mountains and follow its looming range until finally reaching the old, hidden passes. Here he would wait in the hope that Nat and the Earl had escaped their fate and would try to flee to the Queen. Krarl didn't care where they went; he just wanted to run with the elements, to approach everything with the joy of the challenge.

The swamp proved to be just one of those challenges. Finding the governor there, terrorising and preying on the water-folk, had added the sauce to the adventure.

Krarl just wanted to hunt them down, but as always Morgan had a plan. Krarl couldn't care less, once he could get his teeth into their necks, so he had happily followed his brother. Now the governor was dead, and the survivors of his band scattered, prey in turn to the vengeful villagers. The twins had decided that it was an excellent time to take a rest before moving onwards. Morgan felt refreshed, refreshed of mind, of spirit, and body. He needed Krarl just as much as Krarl needed him; as he had said well over two hundred years ago when their odyssey had first started, 'they were one.'

'Thenking agarn, little brudaar? Yu thenk too much! Stupid!' Krarl's harsh words interrupted his thoughts.

'A little thinking before rushing in and messing things up might do you a world of good, Mr tough bum.'

Krarl chortled, then both of them fell silent and listened to the noisy insects.

'Yu still arngry cuz I blow up crazy makers? Boom! Serve barstards right!'

Morgan looked up at his brother with a steady, thoughtful expression.

The Masters had assembled together on the tenth day, as they had always done, to pool their psychic strength through joint meditation. Morgan flexed his eighteen-year-old form, feeling the supreme power of his youthful limbs and firm, torte torso. He watched the last of them, old Limp-Foot at the rear, file past. They had all ignored him, except for Limp-Foot, who glanced enigmatically at him with the ghost of a smile teasing the corners of his full lips.

A slight twitch pulled at his cheek muscle as Morgan felt once again the lash against his bleeding back, interspersed with the tearing mental agony of the mind probes, one smoothly melding into the other, a throbbing heartbeat of pain. Limp-foot had refused to take part, the only one. Morgan marked that action forever. He had revealed nothing, even whilst they trampled all over him with their power. Still, he had chosen to stay and not run, forging a discipline around him like an unbreakable diamond chain, bright, rare, and compressed. He sometimes saw the awe in many of the Masters' eyes and in some, fear. He had excelled, progressing beyond the reach of many. At the back of his mind, he sensed the essence of Karl, prowling, trying to mask his mind unsuccessfully. He still wasn't good at it, a tricky feat without daily, careful instruction, but he was getting better. In the dead of night, Morgan would sometimes slip away to run with his unfettered brother, as he had done since that fateful day. Punishment meant nothing to him, and the Masters had long since given up on it as a method of a deterrent. In the beginning, he had brought him stolen food, forbidden knowledge, helped him to survive, brought him companionship, comfort, a salve from loneliness and isolation. He had watched the hurt and confusion in his brother's eyes turn to resentment. The tendrils of jealousy began to take root, growing through time slowly, but embracing and overshadowing the birth of all these negative emotions was the over-riding presence of implacable hate, hate for the makers. This hate, this negativity, made him stronger, but also, sadly, much weaker, transforming him. Morgan and Karl were linked from before birth and tied they remained. Karl was like a satellite, running an elliptical orbit around his twin, unable and incapable of breaking away. The makers were aware of him and had tried on many occasions to seize him, but he always eluded them, like black smoke, visible but untouchable. Karl had never made any overt, aggressive or harmful move towards his betrayers, but today something felt different.

Over the past two years, Karl had become increasingly coy with his thoughts, trying to hide them, never looking Morgan in the eye, and if he had to, only briefly, sliding his gaze away. Morgan tried to put aside the feeling of unease that was crawling inside his head, but it refused to fade. He did not want to try to enter Karl's thoughts, which would just be yet another act of betrayal, a grave disregard for his brother's right to privacy. He felt the urge to pace, but sat down instead under the shade of a tree and waited, opening himself. If Karl experienced a high emotional thought, it would slip out and come to him. He could only hope that he would be fast enough to divert potential disaster. With Karl involved, that was a very high expectation.

Suddenly, a surge of animal elation and triumph flooded over him. He leapt to his feet in one smooth movement and began running towards the arched entrance of the meditation hall. A force of power and noise struck him like a wall, blowing him like a straw doll off of his feet and slamming him into the unyielding tree trunk. He fought with all his will to stay conscious, and through a ball of roiling flame caught a glimpse of Karl streaking off like a fox with its tail on fire. Struggling to his feet Morgan, staggered towards the hall, his legs felt like jelly, and there was a muffled roaring in his ears, his senses disorientated. He ducked under the precariously propped, broken stone and crawled on hands and knees through the thick smoke and shattered debris, the nauseating smell of sulphur and chemicals burning into his lungs, as he tried to avoid flaming roof beams scattered all over the stone floor. Bodies and parts of bodies lay strewn here and there, all dead. As he began to inch his way back out, a faint groan broke through his abused ears, and he caught the slight movement of a blue sleeve.

'All but one, brother; you missed one.'

A feral gleam sprang into Krarl's eyes, and he fixed Morgan with a glare of malevolence, his hands formed into hooked claws and the muscles of his body tensed on the point of violent action.

Morgan watched him calmly.

'Something is bothering you, brother?'

Krarl was unnaturally still, a part of the rock on which he perched, a gargoyle of pitted stone. Only his eyes burned, mirroring the heat of that incident, two hundred plus years past. Almost as if he had never reacted, Krarl relaxed on his rock with studied nonchalance, absently licking the tips of his talons.

'Wheech one, bruudar?' he asked innocently, turning over and lying on his back as if sun-bathing.

'The best of the lot, brother; he who did not deserve to die in such a manner.'

'Ahrrr! Limp-foot, soft foot, pain in arse foot.'

'As you say, Karl, he survived your design and lived for many more years.'

'Tharnks to yuu eh, brudaar? Arlways the fartful sorn.'

Morgan did not allow himself to stand baited and remained silent.

CHAPTER XXV

Speed was everything; the speed of thought, speed of action. But caution and cleverness must also play their part. Nat represented decisiveness, executed with a novel and keen edge; Elaine was a planner, working through the hidden and intricate designs of others and overcoming them with an unexpected sleight of hand. They made a formidable team.

'We can't just escape the city dressed as party-goers! We might just as well light a fire on our heads.'

'What do you suggest?' breathed Nat, carefully surveying the seemingly quiet streets ahead.

They had made it out of the palace grounds by being bold. With eyes ahead, they side-stepped any questions with pure authority and rightness of action. An attitude mostly carried off by Elaine, supported by a ram-rod straight and dangerous-looking Nat - a lady of high standing with her body-guard. Even those who had orders to detain them hesitated, and before they could decide their next course, the duo had swept by them.

'Let's find ourselves a dirty beggar.'

'What! Oh, okay.'

Walking quickly forward, they slipped into a narrow, shaded alley, at which point Elaine's hands flew up to cover her mouth and nose, giving out a choking, retching sound, as an over-powering stench of pungent, stale urine assailed them. In the late afternoon, in the hot, closed space of the alley, the smell of it felt thick, the stink permeating into their clothes and hair, even into their very pores.

'Goddess help me!' she gagged.

'Welcome to the world of the Beggar Abbot,' muttered Nat.

It wasn't long before they encountered a dirty, rag-wrapped figure huddled at the corner of an intersection of alleyways.

The smell of urine was nothing compared to the odour emanating from this figure which had the uncertain look of being possibly female, an old woman, would be anyone's guess. Unwashed clothing mixed with several unmentionable and unsavoury things drifted up into their labouring nostrils, forcing them to try to stop breathing. This conscious act attempted to stop them gagging, was successful for a brief moment. Unfortunately, despite their best efforts, they soon had to open their mouths to obtain precious air, only to have the nauseous sensation of tasting things that would be repulsive even to step on in thick, well-heeled boots.

'A coin, sir, m'lady, a coin for the poor wretch that I be. A coin, please, for bread?'

Dipping into her purse, Elaine hurriedly dropped a silver coin into the offered, coffee and soot-stained metal cup.

The putrid-smelling beggar stared at it in amazement for a split second, then with a snatch that would have made any magician envious, made it disappear from her cup.

'Take us to the Beggar Abbot.'

'I be the only beggar here, missy. A coin?'

'For the love of the goddess! I've just given you one! Tell us where we can find the Abbot.'

'Don't know anyone by that name, missy. A coin, missy. A coin?'

'Look you!' whispered Elaine fiercely. 'No more coins until you tell us something useful!'

'Don't hurt me, missy,' whined the beggar, cowering down, and partly covering her head. 'I be old, don't hurt. A coin?'

'Come,' said Nat. 'She's not entirely there', he continued, pointing his index finger at his head. 'Let's go before we attract attention.'

As they gathered themselves to move on, shadows began to emerge from the swiftly falling twilight; shadows draped in rough, torn and dirty rags.

'Oh shit!' said Nat under his breath, reaching his hand to where his sword should have been, finding nothing. 'Shit!' he said again.

'Shit!' Elaine echoed at his side.

The figures all had glinting blades in their hands, small, curved knives designed for cutting and slicing in close, deadly work.

'Coin, missy?' came a voice from behind them, and a cursory glance by Elaine revealed a grimy, outstretched palm and the black, rotten stumps in a horribly grinning face.

'Shit!' she said again, but this time with more vigour. Nat briefly frowned down at her.

She felt his body relaxing, his centre of gravity lowering. Inappropriately, she remembered his half-naked body training in the garden. It felt like a lifetime ago. There were too many. Even for a superb fighter like Nat, trained by the best, and they all had knives. They, in turn, were weaponless, out-numbered, friendless, isolated and hunted. He was her man, and she would fight by his side, despite the odds; she would die by his side if that were to be her fate. She dug into her purse and pulled out a tiny knife, made to cut thread. Well, this day it will cut flesh. Nat was as still as a lizard on a rock, waiting for the first move against them. She stayed next to him, waiting for his explosion into violent and deadly motion.

'Shiny, you should not bring bright silver coins into alleyways. And if you do, keep them well hidden.'

Everyone froze.

'Today, it seems, is your lucky day,' again the invisible voice, soft and cultured.

'There are many, some here included, who want what you have. Regretfully we will have to start with those silver coins, miss. Everything, I'm afraid, has a price.'

Nat replied, his voice even, strong and deadly.

'You may have the coins. Anything else you will have to bleed for.'

After a quiet pause, the voice returned.

'I believe you, Nathaniel Woodsmoke, last of the guardians of the true realm. A fair number of us will die this evening if we move against you. Your skill is well known. On my word, none here shall do you harm or the Lady Elaine. We honour her father above all.'

'As a start, you can come out where I can see you then!'

The semi-circle of ragged, night thugs, parted slowly, allowing a bald, rounded, short man to float through them. Nat noticed that his naked feet made hardly a sound as he moved towards himself and Elaine, perfectly balanced. He frowned, for this man, whom he guessed to be the elusive and influential Beggar Abbot, walked with the semblance of an accomplished fighter, but everything else about him seemed to deny that incongruous fact.

'You seem puzzled, young Woodsmoke, I admit, so am I. It is an odd circumstance only that has led me to be passing through this quarter on this day, at this time. What though, brings you here, and with the royal bride to be in tow?'

'News flies very fast to your ears, or so it seems, Abbot!' spat Elaine.

'The poor, the downtrodden, the dispossessed, and the overlooked are my ears, my lady. This reality is our true strength. The strength of the people, and when a king announces the unthinkable, the people may need to secure its last champion.'

'My father?'

'Your father.'

'So that's why you happen to be so close to the palace. You are a bold one, Sir Abbot. The king wants you dead.'

'The king wants many things - not all of them with the people in mind. But come, your coins, please, so as to win the affections of these hungry men. We need each to go about our businesses, and quickly.'

'What will you have us do? We need to flee this city. All we have heard so far by those we hold close is that you are a man to trust. Are they right, Lord Abbot?'

'Here is a token of that trust, Nathaniel Woodsmoke.'

With that, the Abbot produced from within his grey robe, a strange, slightly curving sword with a razor's edge, wicked and beautiful, designed for cutting and slicing men. With a flick of his hand, he tossed it to Nat who caught it neatly, plucked from mid-air.

'I had intended to give it to your father, Lady Elaine, but it would probably find more work in your lover's hands.'

Both Nat and Elaine turned a bright shade and were grateful for the falling darkness.

'You will want to change your palace fancies for more suitable gear. Follow these men. We will guide you through the lesser-known paths and out of the city. After that, you are on your own. I apologise for not accompanying you, but I have pressing matters to attend to, and the window into the palace will not remain open for much longer. Farewell and good luck.'

Turning his back, the Abbot melted into the gloom.

Minutes after midnight, Nat and Elain found themselves escorted to a copse of trees at the edge of the city. This outcome was a relief, after spending many hours skulking in dirty back alleys and hovering at the entrances to questionable buildings waiting impatiently while shadowy figures tapped intricate codes on thick, wooden doors.

They now wore brown, nondescript trousers, rough tunics which itched the skin and worn threadbare cloaks.

'Down this road, you will find a man waiting with two horses and a day's supply of rations. That's the best we can do for you,' said the one-eyed leader of their clandestine, little party of guides. 'You'll need to hurry. He won't wait for long. The king sprinkles his gold among us like water to thirsty plants. It is irresistible for us, and many are already hunting you. Now go!'

Without a word of goodbye or a thank you, the two turned and trotted off down the narrow, tree-lined, cart track. They understood that information on their whereabouts would soon be traded, maybe even by their guides. The world of the Abbot was one of swirling, shifting alliances and expendable commodities. He controlled absolutely but was not in absolute control. Now the king himself had become one of the players.

True to the guide's word, they encountered an old farmer, sheltering under a rock-outcrop with two sturdy horses which appeared to be more suited to pulling ploughs than taking part in a mad-dash escape across rugged countryside. 'Still, beggars can't be choosers,' thought Elaine, and giggled. Nat once again looked down at her and frowned. Quickly clearing her throat, she dug into her now battered purse and dug out her last four copper coins. These she handed over into the swollen, calloused hands of the silently waiting old, farmer.

Nat set a steady pace, and they plodded through the peaceful night on their two plough-horses which were undoubtedly strong, but stamina and speed were probably not in their repertoire. At a pitch, he thought, they might squeeze a lumbering gallop or two out of them. As dawn began to twinge their world with grey, Nat broke the monotonous, clopping, but somehow reassuring noise, by suddenly standing and balancing like an acrobat on his saddle. With his sword, he cut free long strips of a fibrous looking vine which were hanging high and had intertwined itself, from the branches of the shrouding overhead trees. Whistling softly, he settled back down and proceeded to slice strips in both directions, away from a bare central patch.

After a few minutes of peering across at him with narrowed eyes, Elaine finally asked.

'How can you see what you're doing in this dark?'

'Don't need to see; can just feel my way.'

'You're beginning to sound like Morgan. And feel your way into doing what, oh great sage?'

'I wish I had my bow. I itch all over at the thought of it, but Morgan used to say that there was no point in fretting over what you didn't have. Fashion something new and bend it to your will.'

'Yes...and?'

'And what?'

With a very audible sigh to demonstrate her frustration, Elaine continued.

'What magic and novel instrument are you bending to your will?'

'Oh, this? It's a sling-shot,' replied Nat, sounding pleased with himself.

'I see,' responded Elaine, sounding a little doubtful. 'You know how to use one?'

'Oh, yes. Morgan had me practising every day when I was a boy. Wish I had leather, though.'

'You've made two wishes so far. Not fair. The third one is mine.'

Nat smiled.

The birds were commencing to sing busily in the trees, and the light was now crystal, and dreamily pleasant, with the sky a beautiful rosy colour. The cart-track was beginning to take a winding ascent, climbing gently out of the trees, and Nat started to twist in his saddle occasionally, checking behind them for open patches of road where the trees lay thin in places.

Suddenly he swore.

'The picnic's over! Look, there are four runners on our trail already. It bloody well didn't take them long!'

'Shall we run?' asked Elaine, frowning at the trotting figures in the distance, marking their speed. Nat noticed that there wasn't a trace of fear in her voice.

'Nope, we surprise the bastards!'

After another five minutes of more urgent plodding, the incline began to level out; Nat grunted and stopped his horse.

'Here's the plan. Ride on till you think those cut-throats have got to this point, tie off my horse, then turn and ride back and as soon as you sight them, gallop full tilt down their throats.'

'But...where shall you be?'

'Behind them!' once again, Nat stood on his saddle and pulled himself with ease into the branches above. 'Go now.'

It didn't take long before the four panting bounty hunters padded by under Nat's aerial hiding place, intent on over-hauling their quarry. After a slow count of ten, he dropped silently from his perch, and jogged quietly after them; the hunted had become the hunter.

As he turned a corner behind them, the earth started shaking, and the heavy drumming of hooves shook the trees. Nat saw the four men hesitate and stop, spreading out along the road with naked swords in hand. They stood wholly focussed on the oncoming sound, and Nat broke into a sprint, flying like the wind at their unsuspecting backs. Suddenly, Elaine, astride and bent low over the powerful neck of a charging horse who probably thought that finally, he was heading back home, burst around the corner ahead, her red hair streaming behind her and a look of steely determination in her green eyes. The men crouched, ready to confront the incoming assault; surprising, yes, but quickly dealt with. Nat struck them like a whirlwind, fast, concentrated, and uncompromising. His razor-sharp sword, sliced through the first man's leg, just below his buttocks, severing his hamstring, and dropping him with a scream into the dust. The others glanced around, alarm written on their faces. Nat flew through without pause, changing direction uncannily in mid-movement, his sword-arm continuing in the same flow, slashing a second man across his face, shearing through the very bone, his garbled scream was horrible to hear in the fresh morning air. A third was already leaping to meet Nat's onslaught, his notched blade aimed at Nat's neck. Spinning like a dancer, Nat ducked smoothly under the attack His sword, held close and low, cut deeply into the man's unprotected thigh, so deep that the femoral nerve snipped in two and the artery ruptured; although he had not yet realised it, he was already dead. The last man, a street-tough out of his element, back-peddled desperately, fear etched in every line of his face. He dropped his pitted and uncared for sword, and turned to flee. Nat was merciless. The tip of his blade, ripping across in a horizontal stroke, surgically dissected the spinal column at his neck, dropping him paralysed into the dirt, staring with uncomprehending eyes, mouth working piteously. As Elaine galloped up, pulling the horse's head downwards and around masterfully with the reins, the deadly work lay already done. Nat stood there, eyes still lost in battle-trance, breathing deeply and evenly.

'Nat...Nat, are you all right?'

Nat blinked.

'We should go. Things are only just beginning.'

Without a spare glance, he turned and loped off. Elaine hesitated, looking at the four men now lying like debris on the leaf-strewn forest road. Two were already dead, dark blood pooling beneath the glassy-eyed corpses. The other two were drifting near death's door. She caught the eye of the thug with the severed hamstring and stared back at him coolly, then clicking to her reluctant horse, turned and followed Nat. By the time she caught up with him, he was sitting already mounted and waiting. After a brief reassuring look into each other's eyes, they continued on their way. They had hardly covered twenty yards when an arrow lanced out of the trees, narrowly missing Elaine's neck as she bent to pat her horse's neck. As it is, its barbed head sliced her flesh, drawing a thin line of leaking blood. Nat pivoted in his saddle and with a lightning movement, slashed a second arrow from mid-air as it flew towards Elaine's back. Reversing the stroke, he hit her horse's flank with the flat of his sword, lurching it forward into a cumbersome gallop. At the same time, he glimpsed the silhouette of a horseman plaiting his way through the trees, trying to get onto the road behind them. He didn't wait to see if they were more; he took it for granted that they would be.

'Bandits!' he shouted. 'Ride!'

They thundered off in a stately gallop, with Nat thinking that he would be better off running on his own two legs. He cast a frustrating look behind and swore as he saw at least seven bandits on rangy looking horses on the road behind them. Elaine was lying almost flat on her mount's neck, whispering words of encouragement to it. Whether or not the big animal was listening, he couldn't tell, but it was pulling slowly away from his. Quickly he unrolled his newly made, make-shift sling-shot, and rummaged around in his saddlebag to find his collection of round stones. Fitting one he swirled it expertly around his body and head, then when he felt the whirling momentum was right, he twisted again in his saddle, ending the revolving motion in one mighty heave, sending the stone flying backwards. A rewarding thwack reached his ears, and he glimpsed one of the leading bandits toppling from his horse, falling under its thrashing hooves and trampled underfoot. He gave a whoop of satisfaction, not caring if it was just good luck or skill that had guided the missile.'Six now, you bastards,' he thought.

Although now more cautious, the bandits were drawing closer, and their wildly shot arrows were getting nearer to the mark. Their luck would not hold forever, and the horses were now blowing like the bellows in a blacksmiths shop. Scanning the verges of the forest on both sides, Nat spotted a break where a wild-game trail intersected the road. He quickly veered off, trusting that the fast thinking Elaine, would see his intentions and stick with him. She did, and they crashed into the undergrowth, their muscled mounts powering their way through.

 Now the bastards could only come at them one at a time. The drawback, however, was that the path was too constricted for him to use his sling-shot. For now, they would just have to keep running, to stay ahead. As they began to enter the forest proper, the underbrush started to thin out as the older, larger trees cut off the light reaching the floor. This fortuitous space allowed Nat to change places with Elaine, as he was better suited to protect their backs. He could hear the bandits shouting to each other as their horses thrashed their way after them. Suddenly, they plunged into a leafy clearing, and Nat swiftly selected another stone, pulled his horse around, viciously twirled his sling-shot, and sent it slamming into the first bandit to emerge. The stone struck him full in the chest and Nat could have sworn that he heard his breast-bone crack. Anyway, the fellow grabbed at his chest and slumped over his horse which veered back off into the bushes. With a savage yell, Nat pulled his sword free and charged at the next bandit in line before the rest could get into the clearing. His big horse, heavier by far than the bandits' mounts, barrelled chest first, into the oncoming horse, bowling both it and its rider over in a tangle of thrashing legs and terrified whinnying. Bulldozing forward, he slashed at the next man, who yanked back on his horses head in a panic causing the animal to rear upwards. As it did so, Nat's blade, meant for the rider, cleaved through the animal's throat in a shower of blood. Before the bandits could recover from the confusion caused by Nat's wrecking assault, he pulled his now angry and willing mount around once again. With one last wild backward kick, the wild-eyed beast thundered off to catch up with its mate which was bearing Elaine even deeper into the forest.

The unlucky bandits had had enough. They hadn't bargained on such resistance. They much preferred it when their intended victims keeled over and gave in, hopefully without a fight.

Some hours later, the pair were still picking their way beneath the perpetual twilight gloom of the forest. Their bulky mounts hung their powerful necks in exhaustion, their mouths covered in a froth, and their bulging musculatures, damp with sweat, constantly twitched, causing them to stumble now and again. Nat called a halt.

'We're lost, aren't we?' said Elaine quietly.

'Not at all,' replied Nat reassuringly.

After a drawn-out pause, he added.

'Well, yes, we are a little bit lost.'

'A little bit?'

'A lot.'

'Ah!'

'We might as well camp here. I can hear a stream nearby, and the nags are knackered.'

'No arguments from me, sir knight,' said Elaine tiredly, sliding from the broad back of her mount and walking bent and bow-legged over to a log, where she promptly, but gingerly sat.

'Let's not do any spanking tonight, okay?'

Nat looked momentarily shocked, then grinned broadly, shook his head, and proceeded to unsaddle and care for the horses. He then led them to the stream for a well-deserved drink. By the time he returned, he found his alluring companion curled up on the forest floor with only a blanket under her, snoring softly.

Something woke Nat. He lay there unmoving, listening. It was very still under the trees, but up above, in the canopy, the leaves rustled restlessly, whispering to each other in the slight breeze. A soft purr drifted to his ears from Elaine's deep and peaceful sleep. There was nothing unusual so far. He concentrated on the horses, and they, except for an occasional stamp of hoof and a whisk of a tail, were calm.

He relaxed, intending to drift back to sleep, thinking that maybe he should light the already banked and prepared fire, when as sometimes happens, the wind gusted, changing direction for a brief space of time. The change was dramatic. The horses suddenly became restless, twisting, stamping and churning. He could hear them pulling on their tethers, trying to escape. A very faint, almost imaginary, musky smell, teased his nose; there then gone. He rolled to his feet, feeling Elaine waking. He reached to his waist for his flint, but the horses began to rear and whinny in terror.

'Quick, up, up! Climb! Get up this tree, now!' he whispered urgently to Elaine.

He felt her warm breath on his face as she hurried to comply, and forgetting courtesy and down-right good manners, he placed his palm underneath a firm, rounded rump and heaved her upwards. She didn't complain or object, but clambered up quickly, feeling her way from branch to branch. Nat heard a woofing sound, followed by the noise of an unstoppable, beefy and colossal body moving at an incredible velocity towards him. Using all the speed and skill in his youthful body, he dived to the ground, balling into an acrobat's roll. Even so, something of inconceivable power swatted at him in passing, connecting with the heel of his boot and sending him spinning like a ragged doll along the forest floor.

'Nat! Nat!' yelled Elaine urgently from somewhere up in the trees.

This disembodied voice must have distracted the monstrosity for a split second, for it swerved off slightly, then with renewed purpose, thundered off towards the now panic-stricken horses. Nat didn't wait. He bolted to his feet, feeling a sharp stab of agony in his ankle, and made a herculean leap of faith in the darkness towards the sound of Elaine's voice. Luckily his hands struck a branch, and he hauled himself rapidly upwards. The thing, whatever it was, must have reached the horses for they were almost screeching in fear. Also, from the tumultuous sounds of struggle, they must have been fighting back for after a few moments of this, the somewhat terrified couple, heard a solid, wet, meaty whack, followed by a dead thud, the thunder of racing hooves, then silence. From this silence came a second woofing noise and a very, deep, nasal, snuffling. A heavy tread marked the beast as it made its way back to the foot of their tree refuge. After more snuffling noises, they felt an almighty shaking, forcing them to cling on for all they were worth. Nat could hear a desperate gasping coming from Elaine and reached out an arm, clamping her to him. The force of the shaking was teeth-rattling and unnerving, like the elemental force of an earthquake. Just as they thought that they could no longer hold on and started to believe that it would be easier to let go and fall to their fate, the onslaught stopped. With an annoyed snuff, the beast lumbered off and settled down to its meal. Trying their best to hold their breaths, Nat and Elaine listened to the macabre crunching, cracking, swallowing and slobbering for what seemed an endless period. Finally, as grey dawn lightly painted the sky, the feast stopped, and with a satisfied grunt, the monster of the night began dragging away the remains of its hunt to stash it in some hidden larder for future use.

'By the goddess, what was that?!'

'The mother of all bears, I think. What good luck we're having! I didn't think I had it in me to show a pretty girl such a grand time.'

'So you think I'm pretty, do you?' teased Elaine, looking up at him. Her eyes were deep pools of emerald, and he fell into them. Then he realised that he was still holding her close, and cleared his throat, releasing her from his embrace.

'Better see if the big bugger is gone, good and proper,' he said clambering down.

Elaine followed more slowly, but just as nimbly. As she at last placed both her still shaking feet on the ground, balancing on a network of gnarled roots, she found Nat frozen there, staring through the grey, muted world in which they stood lost. Following his intense gaze, she witnessed a scene taken straight out of an abattoir.

'It's eaten our poor wee horses,' said Elaine, a deep, weary sadness in her voice.

Nat automatically reached out and took her hand in his.

'Only one, the other got away.'

As they stood there, drawing whatever comfort they could from each other, a hair lifting howl, penetrated the colourless morning, echoing moan-fully between the silent trees; they both jumped, startled.

'Bloody hell, what next!' Nat muttered grimly.

'Bears, now wolves! The goddess is testing us, surely!' responded Elaine, with a fire burning in her eyes.

'Yes, this is our forging. We will meet it head-on, as Morgan would have! Come, let's gather our things. They're coming fast.'

'Shouldn't we climb back up in the tree?'

'Not this time. They may decide to sit it out, and we don't have any water or food.'

Moving swiftly and efficiently they gathered up what they could easily carry from the shattered campsite and loped off, putting as much distance between them and the scattered pieces of raw horse meat and intestines as they could. With luck, the wolves would be content with the scraps or might choose to follow the bear's trail to its hidden stash. They stood mistaken in that hope. The pack gulped down the remains and surged after the duo, instinctively deducing that they were the weaker and more vulnerable option, a meal with fewer risks of becoming injured.

It wasn't long before Nat was limping. His obvious lameness wasn't slowing them, but the pain was evident by his visible limp.

'Let me have a look at that!' Elaine said, snatching at his arm to stop him.

Seeing sense in it, Nat immediately stopped, sat down on a log, and pulled off his boot. As he feared, his ankle was swollen double. Elaine prodded it delicately, moving the joint gently back and forth, seemingly listening with her fingers.

'Twisted, not broken,' she muttered. 'Let's bind it tightly and keep going. We haven't got a choice.'

Nat nodded, and in three minutes, they were up and running again. They might have been trying to run from Father Time himself. The end was inevitable.

Grey, lean, wraiths glided soundlessly on either side of them, floating around the trees with effortless and timeless grace. They regarded them with luminous eyes, assessing their form, calculating opportunities. Their movements weren't outwardly aggressive, but their intent was clear. Elaine's breath was rasping harshly in and out of her lungs, tearing through her throat. Quick as a mongoose, a small, low ranking bitch, slunk in low, darting for the back of Elaine's thigh, slavering teeth bared, fangs ready to tear, in then out. Nat spun, unsheathing his sword in a lightning-fast flow, slashing at the bitch, who jinxed away with fluid agility, the blade nicking an already tattered and scarred ear, dripping bright drops of blood, which went unnoticed. As Nat moved to defend the weaponless Elaine, a young male running on his side, tore in behind him, again aiming to rip the muscles of his leg, as Nat reversed his sword in a reverse slash, it bounded away, to join its mates, unperturbed.

'Catch!' called Nat, flicking his sword to Elaine.

She caught it deftly, her spirit rising to the dire situation. Nat swooped low, snatching up a stout branch which would serve well as a fighting staff.

Now they were both armed. The wolves observed all with calm, intelligent eyes. They were supreme hunters, gifted with infinite patience. They knew that eventually, their prey would make a slip, one fatal mistake. That's all they needed to disrupt defence and make a clean kill. They had seen it time and time in the past; pack memory.

Nat was now beginning to limp badly and felt the attention of the wolves shift to him. The big, battle-scarred, pack leader checked his forward position, dropping back, and began to criss-cross behind the struggling pair, making them try to track him and lose sight of the treacherous terrain they were running over. One trip and a fall and that would be the end of the hunt. However, the two they were trying to chase to the ground were not bovine; they were members of the ultimate predators on the planet and were capable of exterminating entire species. By some unconscious signal, Nat and Elaine suddenly switched sides, just as the alpha female was angling in on Nat, who now stood out as the weak link. Expecting to bring down or at least injure her intended target, the lead female unexpectedly found herself face to face with the sharp point of Elaine's sword. Whereas Nat would have slashed, Elaine simply stuck the blade forward, which seemed to have surprised the attacking wolf, as the point sunk deep into her shoulder. With a yelp and a snarl, she leapt clear, but it was too late. Although not seriously injured, the wound would inhibit her hunting prowess in weeks to come.

The big male, hearing the yelp of pain from his mate, sprang forward recklessly, only to feel the full force of Nat's staff, which knocked it off its feet. In a flash, it was back up, shrugging off the blow, and taking back up its original position at the head of the pack.

Nat's limbs were like lead weights. If he felt this way, he couldn't begin to imagine how Elaine was feeling. He had made a mistake; an error that had put Elaine's life in great danger. The wolves, he knew, were still not yet committed. They had caught them on the run, and of course, this had excited the wolves into treating them as prey. It was only their age-old weariness of man that was keeping them undecided. This bit of luck, he also knew, would not last for much longer.

The wolves were becoming bolder, increasing their testing forays, beginning to make them more pointed. Nat was casting about, looking for a place where they could protect their backs and make a stand. Elaine was now shuffling along, her eyes hollow with exhaustion. He saw a large stack of boulders with an old gnarled tree sitting atop it and was about to signal Elaine for them to make their way to it when a rushing, roaring sound came to his ears. He immediately headed towards its source.

As they edged their way towards the thunderous, still yet unseen, surging water - ducking under and dodging around the sentinel trees with their unwelcome lupine companions funnelling them - the alpha male suddenly snarled, and jinxed away, distracted. Almost immediately, several of the other junior members of the pack began to behave uncertainly, whining, tucking their tails between their legs, some even turned to go back. Only the lead bitch sprinted forward, with fangs bared and a thick, savage snarl rumbling in her throat. Ahead of her arrowed rush, a massive, shaggy form emerged as if from nowhere, in a spray of incandescent water. It was the biggest, meanest looking bear that Nat had ever seen, its fur matted, thick, wet, and it was lumbering belligerently towards them. It had the full attention of the wolf pack, which anyway, seemed to have forgotten them. Seizing the opportunity gifted ironically by fate, Nat grabbed Elaine's hand, and with their last vestiges of energy, raced desperately for the river, legs pumping. Bursting out of the trees, they found themselves on a high bank, with a rapidly flowing, white water river yawning beneath them. Unable to check their onward rush, they tumbled untidily off of the steep side in a tangle of ungainly limbs and crashed into the cold, racing, dangerous waters. Immediately, they were pulled under and yanked downstream by a tremendous force; their breaths sucked out of their shocked bodies. The water gripped them, dragging and throwing them about helplessly. They clung together, riding a vortex of power, their consciousness suspended, as if they were mere spectators to their fate. Pulled downwards at a breakneck speed they crashed into a rock, disguised by the fountain of violent liquid spraying madly over it. Nat felt his shoulder wrench, pain surging across it and up his neck. His clawed hand, locked onto Elaine, loosened involuntarily, and then the surging current ripped them apart, separated by the cascading torrent. The last thing he saw was her green eyes, reflecting the river, holding onto to his as she was borne away by the swirling downward flow. As he twisted to reach for her, something heavy smashed into his head, and blackness took him under.

 Nat came to in a world of pain. Blinding light seared into his eyes, causing him to squeeze them shut in agony. Water filled his lungs, trying to drown him, making him splutter and cough. His ears filled with a clamorous cacophony of noise, and he felt as weak as a newborn kitten. Something or someone was dragging him through the water, slowly, inexorably. He tried to fight back, but it was useless. 'Shit!' he thought.

Elaine spiralled out of Nat's grip; she felt that she was losing touch with reality, drawn away from that constant anchor in her life. She relaxed into the flow, into the deep rhythm of the river, joining with the goddess. This act of surrender, of spiritual trust, saved her life. The goddess held her to her breast and carried her down to a gently swirling pool, where she left her as the will to live returned. Turning over, she began to slowly paddle for the shore, changing her direction as she saw Nat's limp, unconscious form gushing down between the rocks on a stream of fast-flowing water, only to be dumped unceremoniously, almost in front of her. Circling her arm around his neck and gently supporting his head, she pulled him steadily through the eddying water. Without strength left in all her body to get them both to the shore, she used what was left in her limbs to push and manoeuvre his dead weight onto a convenient flat rock.

'Thank you, goddess,' she whispered her prayer.

Finally, she heaved herself up next to him, and collapsed with utter exhaustion, not caring in the least, what would happen next. She lay her head down on his shoulder and let sleep take her.

Elaine awoke in the glow of the warm, late afternoon sunshine. A night and a day had gone by since they had fled the city. It seemed like a lifetime. Her skin stung a bit from lying in the sun for most of the day, but her long hair and clothes were dry. Her boots had disappeared, but her feet felt cool and fresh as the cold water caressed them. She propped herself up on her elbows and looked carefully at Nat. He was breathing with relative ease, but he was still in a deep sleep. She sat up and began to examine him slowly, starting with his head. Under her probing fingers, she felt a large lump at the back of his skull. That was concerning, but she moved on to his right shoulder, which felt unnaturally hot and swollen. That was worrying as he would probably be unable to wield his sword. With a gasp, she realised that she had dropped the thing when they had fallen into the river. Well, that solved that problem. There would be no sword for him to wield. Lastly, she checked his ankles. One was, as expected, inflamed. With a sigh, she sat back to contemplate her next action.

'Please, don't stop now. I was enjoying that.'

Elaine started, glancing happily down at Nat who was wearing a slight smile on his face.

'You'll have to earn it, you scallywag! And wipe that silly smile off your face. Makes you look like a simpleton!'

Belying her words, she flung herself down on him and hugged him tightly.

'Go easy, tiger,' he chuckled. 'A wolf got to me first.'

'Don't forget paid killers, bandits, a bear, and a river,' she replied wistfully.

'Ah, yes. This river, I know where we are now.'

'Not lost anymore, then?'

'Nope, I think we should rest and recuperate here for a day or two then move on.'

'Rest and recuperate are beautiful words.'

Nat spent the rest of the afternoon fashioning a platform high in the trees, lashing small, sturdy logs together with a fibrous vine. It would provide a relatively safe place to sleep, an excellent defensive position, at least from wild animals, and serve as a reasonable look-out. He also made a selection of light spears along with an atlatl to throw them faster and further. As the sun was going down, he made his way to the river. He stopped at a place where an overhanging rock caused the water to cascade down in a mini-waterfall. Stripping, he sat under the tumbling stream of water and settled into meditation. Soon he was deep under, working, as Morgan had taught him, on healing his injuries. Suddenly, he became aware of a presence behind him, and two naked arms circled his chest. They were not the only things that were naked. He could feel Elaine's firm breasts against him, her nipples, hard as two marbles pressing into his back. His body immediately responded. Confirming this with her hands, she swivelled around him, placing one long, smoothly muscled leg over his hips, and ever so slowly, guided him inside her. With her mouth sweet and hot, she kissed him deeply and began to move her hips against his, muscular and sinuous, enveloping him in the heat of her body. He became lost, lost in a void where no amount of years of meditation could ever have taken him.

Nat awoke hungrily and with the sound of Elaine's voice drifting into his consciousness. He had slept like a log, curled up on their tree platform, next to Elaine, enjoying the soft caress of a cooling night breeze. As realisation cleared his sleep-fogged mind, he bolted upright - talking? Who was she speaking to in the middle of a forest?

Her voice was low, sensual even. Nat crawled to the edge of the platform, cushioned by the thick fronds laid down in layers under their only surviving cloak, and craned his neck over the side. To his surprise, he saw Elaine far below, stroking the face of a large, powerful horse, and speaking to it in the low tones of a lover. The horse seemed entranced; he didn't blame it. In reality, he was a bit jealous. Not wanting to spook the animal, he lay there silently watching the two of them. How did the big fellow survive in the forest after having known only the life of a farm? It seemed that theirs was not the only incredible story that lay forged in these last few days. He still wore his halter and Elaine now had one hand firmly on it while the other stroked his quivering neck, soothing it. He smiled, recalling the night, she knew horses and how to handle them.

Soon the animal was cropping contentedly at clumps of vegetation and Nat climbed down taking care to go calmly and slowly. He joined Elaine in watching the munching horse.

'It's a wonder he survived.'

'It's a wonder that he found us; a sure sign from the goddess.'

'Breakfast?'

'Why not, I can eat a horse,' said Elaine, giggling softly.

'I think we will have to settle for rabbit and river trout.'

They did the rounds together, checking their snares and traps. They hadn't caught a great deal, but it was enough to fill their stomachs.

'Old horsie showing up is a bit of a bonus,' said Nat. 'The king's coin will have found the professionals by now, and they won't give up until they've finished the job.'

Elaine sighed.

'We leave today?'

Nat nodded.

By late morning, riding double, they left to continue their journey with a heavy bitter-sweet emotion enwrapping them as if it were a shroud. With a last glance behind her, Elaine said.

'This place, this time, will live in me forever.'

Nat nodded and replied.

'Now for the Badlands.'

They turned their eyes forward and set their minds, neither looking behind them again.

CHAPTER XXVI

'Last I looked, it was I who wore the crown! It is the king's right to protect his subjects!'

'It is a father's right to protect his daughter. No king has the remit to usurp that.'

'You are insolent, Lord Earl, have a care that you do not go too far!'

'You know full well that young Nathaniel Woodsmoke did not kidnap or seize my daughter by force. Yet, despite this, you have issued a bounty on his head. So which of your subjects are you protecting, my King?'

'On this question of subjects, Lord Earl, may I remind you that I am not subject to your questions.'

'No my King, but a king, in the end, is subject to his people.'

'Yes, yes, Earl of the Marches, and I have not forgotten that you are the darling champion of the people, but the people will not always be able to protect you.'

'Do I need protecting, my Lord King?'

'No, no, of course not. I didn't say that, but surely, people should see their king as their protector and their champion.'

'A crown is a heavy burden, my liege, but it sits unneeded for a king to wear every hat.'

'I will have those two young rebels brought back before me, Lord Earl, and Nathaniel Woodsmoke will have to answer for his audacious crime against my person and my will.'

'And I am Lady Elaine's father. It is I who is to say yea or nay where her fate is concerned, and if you attempt to take this right from me, I have legal recourse, as an Earl of the realm, to claim king's justice through peer-selected counsel.'

'Yes, I know the law as written by my fathers, Earl, and we both know who whispered in their ears, but I am the one left sitting on this throne.'

'As you say, it is not my place to rebuke a king.'

'No, it is not!'

'May I ask your leave to return to my estates, Lord King?'

'No, your request is denied. I need you near me during these troubled times.'

'As you command, my Lord King.'

'Leave me, Lord Earl. I am bone-weary, and in need of some rest.'

The court stood astonished, shocked by this unprecedented exchange between one of the most influential, highly regarded and loyal nobles in the land and the king. They gave way quickly as he departed through their ranks, fury burning in his eyes.

The first winds of a civil war were beginning to gust, and they were afraid.

The Earl knew that someone was following him. Although confined to his quarters, the Abbot had still reached him - beseeching him to seize the opportunity given and take a new stance on his provincial estates, on a firm and familiar stomping ground. The Earl had refused to be a sneak thief, slipping around in the dark. He would leave in bright daylight with a king's sanction or not at all. The Abbot had given him one of his long, delving looks, then nodded, gliding unhurriedly away as if he were in his parlour. It was only until the next morning that he had learned that his stationed guards had been found unconscious in a back room, surrounded by empty jars and smelling strongly of alcohol. Since then, shadows had attached themselves to him and followed him everywhere. Thanks to the Abbot, he also now knew what had happened to Nat and Elaine since departing the palace. He even knew that the king was now habitually pay-rolling cut-throats and alley thugs to carry-out special projects for him; projects that no king should sully his hands with. Dirt sticks, and left unwashed, one becomes dirty. He was pleased that he had manoeuvred his Majesty into having an open court discussion. This display, in a way, had gained him some immunity from royal manipulation and allowed him to publicly air his opposition to the king's intentions to force Elaine into being his bride. It also exposed the wrong behind making Nat an outlaw and hopefully, as a result, offer him some protection. The Abbot was an astute conductor of mass emotions, and already he was orchestrating the subtle strains of discontent. With a heavy heart, he recalled the uncertain days just after the old reunification king died, and his eldest, the present king, had taken up the reins of responsibility and leadership. Power was a dangerous drug. Taken too quickly, it floods the brain with its induced headiness. In some, it becomes an obsession; enough is never enough. Now Morgan, a strangely, long-lived man, accustomed to power, and practised in controlling the powerful, was no longer there, and he had found himself in the unenviable position of being the linchpin of the nation, a pin on which everything was finely balanced. It was not to his liking, but his life lay dedicated to serve and serve he would until the end of his time. His father, and grandfather, before him, had done no less, and they had died for their country in selfless acts.

As he strode along, the Lord Exchequer of the Privy Purse fell in silently beside him. He was the oldest of the king's council and had acted in his capacity for two other kings before this present one.

'Lord Privy Purse, are you well?'

In his usual non-intrusive way, the introspective man replied.

'I fare better than the nation's wealth, my lord.'

'You are a magician with commerce and numbers, old friend; I hope you are not going to tell me that we are impoverished.'

After an overlong pause, when the Earl was beginning to think that either the old fellow had not heard him or would not bother to reply, the Exchequer softly said.

'We are impoverished in more ways than one, Lord Earl. Our king fritters coin away on the backs of questionable things.'

'Careful, my lord, treason, flies far too quickly to the lips in these disturbing times.'

'Yes, disturbing. It reminds me of a time gone by when our nation teetered on the edge of internal division. We need a much loved and steady hand on the tiller before we run aground once again.'

'Every man is born to play a role, and mine is to lead men in battle. A sword in my hand is much better than one resting on my neck. I have a great fondness for my much-loved head and would stand dearly gratified if it were to remain attached to my body. Go whisper intrigue in more fertile ears, my lord.'

'Battles come to us in many forms, dear Earl. There are many ways to serve from the front. A man cannot run from destiny.'

'No, but he can run away from dangerous whispers. Good day to you, old friend.'

Oh, Morgan, thought the Earl, why did you sacrifice your life for mine? Was it just to show me the dark, ambitious hearts of men?

***

Krarl was becoming more and more irritable. His moods, fluctuating, a pendulum flicking back and forth, but unpredictably so, following rules and being triggered by events that only Krarl could explain and discern. Always savage in the hunt, he was becoming more so, revelling in the pain and bloodshed of the prey. He would lash out at the smallest of perceived infractions, real or imagined. It was becoming clear that the differences in temperament and training between the two brothers, from boyhood to now, were becoming starkly evident with each passing day. Morgan was beginning to stand back, giving his twin as much space and forbearance as was possible. The ironic reality was that Morgan felt their kinship deeper than ever. They were unique in a hostile world. Krarl was jealous of his brother; jealous of how he could move and live in a world of men; a place where he could not comfortably follow. Humankind saw him as an abominable beast whereas Morgan stood thought of as a wise and measured man, a leader, a teacher. Yet, here they were, both hunted, both ostracised, both unwanted. Still, despite decades of learning, discipline, restraint, sophistication and courtly manners, in the end, Morgan had had to leave every place he had called home, and in some cases was driven out. Not much different from the fate experienced by his brother.

 Yet Morgan's character continued to grow, personifying ultimate gravitas, his personality steady with humour threading its way through every facet, cultivated, enlightening humour. Krarl, on the other hand, was becoming a thing twisted. So much so that it was gradually etching itself into his very features, the outside mirroring the inside. Still, they sat fashioned from the same elements with equal measure. Morgan needed to run wild with Krarl, as they had done in the beginning, allowing his caged nature to burst out, his eyes changing to a burning sun, his heart pounding in his chest, the limits he had set himself, broken like the chains of a slave. Krarl needed his brother to ground him, to help him remember who he was, to keep him from falling off of that cliff, from passing beyond the veil of anything human. Yet now, as in countless times before, their time together could only be short, before their differences overwhelmed their similarities, before what they took from each other, overpowered what they gave to each other. Krarl would become impossible to be near, quarrelsome, snapping and snarling, his passion for blood and conflict approaching the outrageous. To avoid mortal combat between the two, separation would become the only course, with Krarl, unable to completely break away, falling into an orbit around his brother, entering into any and every type of mischief to gain his twin's attention.

They had run along the burning coast, the surf pounding incessantly, white-water breaking far out, seagulls diving and calling raucous protestations from above, the abrasive, coarse sands beneath their feet, saturated with salt, both cleansing and toughening their soles. The briny, hot winds scoured their skins, howling around them both night and day as they hunted, picked, dug-up, and brought down whatever they found in their path, surviving by drinking brackish water, thirst their ever-present companion. In this desolate, sticky landscape, they hardly spoke, communicating by a look and a nod, Morgan with a destination in mind, Krarl wanting only to fill his time with motion and challenge.

On the eight-day after leaving the swamp-lands, they came up to the foot of the cloud-shrouded, glowering black mountains and turned inland to follow their majestic, god-like presence. They ran tirelessly among towering pines and piled boulders, silently ranging along wild game trails. It was here that they stood attacked. They only had themselves to blame as they had become self-absorbed and over-confident in their prowess. As they trotted along a narrow track with cracked and broken boulders looming over them, they stood struck hard from above.

Morgan was in the lead with his brother panting smoothly on his heels, running single file. A split-second warning saved Krarl's life. Whatever had alerted him he could not tell, but he was twisting swiftly in mid-stride when one hundred and seventy pounds of muscle, claws and tawny fur fell on his back. With primitive reflexes honed by nature and many near-death experiences, Krarl caught the mountain lion by its throat with one taloned hand, narrowly avoiding its fatal bite to the back of his neck. Even so, he stumbled on the uneven path, and cat and man crashed to the ground in a spitting, snarling heap, gravel flying in every direction. Morgan spun, and in a heartbeat, was on the cat before it could cause any severe injury to his twin. Grabbing the furiously thrashing animal by the scruff of its neck with one hand and by the loose skin on its shoulder with his other, Morgan heaved quickly backwards before the angry beast could sink its fangs into his arm. It flew through the air, its claws tearing free of Krarl's skin, leaving behind bloodied slash marks. The force of Morgan's throw sent the creature slamming into a pine tree, where it swiftly rolled back onto its feet and rushed back at them. The twins were ready and leapt together to meet the challenge. Quick as a striking snake Morgan slipped under the swiping paw, with its deadly sharp, retractable claws, slicing the air above his head.

 His balled hand struck, deep and powerful, into its underbelly, then, gripping with clawed fingers, yanked the beast side-ways as he streaked by its flank. Krarl, a hair's breadth behind, slipped to the other side, wrapping a roped forearm around the off-balanced cat, catching its head in a vice-like grip and wrenching it around. There was a loud audible snap, and the animal fell limp to the ground. The brothers did not even pause to look at the dead beast but continued on their barely interrupted run. Together they were a thing feared. Wolf-packs, resident in the area, sensing their approach, detected something other in their scent, and loped away, not wanting or daring to elicit contact; their essence hinted at something not entirely formed by nature and lay best avoided. Even the large and solitary grizzly bears, top of the food chain, hesitated, and moved on, disturbed by the duo's presence.

 If wishes were wells, thought Morgan, the deserts would lie filled with people. Together, he and his brother were near-invincible; jointly, they could have led an empire, but it was not to be. The Masters had realised this since the near beginning. One alone could still achieve their dream to forge a better world, but two would be a distraction since their natures were so different, and their fears had borne fruit. Instead of building in harmony, the two had brought disharmony and interruption; unsettling many societies and cultures throughout the intervening years. He knew that Krarl understood this, for even today he referred to Morgan as 'the one' - another thorn digging into the festering flesh of his jealousy. Even so, nagging at the back of his brain, was his old mentor's firmly held assertion. 'The secret lies within both of you, Morgan. Together you are the One. Solve this puzzle, and you will find the answer to your destinies.' He missed old Limp-Foot.

He sent his mind out, hoping to find even a spider's web of a trace of Nat. He sincerely wished that his adopted son had made good his escape from the clutches of ambitious and faithless men. He was confident in the young man's ability, but fate had a way of catching even the best of men by surprise. Still, Nat had the Earl, and that man had more of a noble spirit in him than the majority of kings he had encountered in his long life. He wanted only to serve, but surely he must have understood that serving is the highest calling of a true king. This fact seemed to have remained hidden from his forthright and honest old friend.

Morgan could feel Krarl trying to work his way into his thoughts. He smiled grimly. His brother was always mediocre at this skill; he lacked discipline and patience. Even with the rambling terrain, Morgan entered a semi-trance and insinuated his mind around his twin's childish attempts to read his mind, lulling his brother towards sleep. A crash, followed by a snarled curse behind him, told him that he had succeeded. With a laugh he increased his speed, becoming even more amused as Krarl scrambled hastily to catch up.

CHAPTER XXVII

'I'm afraid that we haven't got a choice. We will have to go through High Point Crossing.'

'The king will have his goons there waiting.'

'I know. Have you got a plan?'

'I'm working on it.'

The big horse was plodding slowly along - his hairy fetlocks like some strange costume. They were sitting on his broad, swaying back following the fast-moving river which would eventually join and empty itself into the Sacred River just below the crossing.

'The village should have returned to normality by now,' mused Elaine. 'It's always been a place of busy trade. Maybe we could take advantage of that somehow.'

'Yes, but how?'

'Ask yourself for what will they be looking? I'm quite sure they have neither met us nor seen us before.'

'Almost certainly. Those paying for our blood will order our unscrupulous hunters to look out for a tall, blond warrior travelling in the company of a young, red-headed, green-eyed beauty.'

'Why, thank you, sir! Yes, spot on the mark. We could start by changing that.'

'We can begin the show with our hair then. I noticed some walnuts back along the trail. If we find more ahead, we can boil down the shells. It should turn our lovely locks brown.'

'Where, by the goddess, did you learn such a thing!?'

'Morgan!' they said in unison, laughing a bit with his memory.

'One question for you though, my genius,' said Elaine after a short pause.

'Uh-huh?'

'What do we use to boil these magic shells in?'

'Ah, you see this rolled-up deerskin? From that poor creature, we managed to bag with our trusty sling-shot? Well, we'll fill it with water then throw hot rocks in it. Should do the trick, I think.'

'I see. What about our eyes?'

'Well, we'll either have to remove them or enter the village at dusk.'

'I prefer the second option. Shall we pretend to be traders?'

'We've got nothing to trade, so I suggest homesteaders, me being from a long line of foresters. And you'll be my sister. Our Pa has just died from the forest flux. We've had enough of bad luck and are going back home to where we've come from.'

'Bloody hell! Worth a try, I guess. Don't too much like the sister bit though. It has a wrong feeling to it, bearing in mind what we've recently been up to.'

They had spent a whole day lingering at the fringes of the forest, surreptitiously casing the small, trading village. It had a new palisade built around it, the logs still green, oozing resin. Over the double-hinged gate was a covered platform, stationed with two burly looking guards, wearing an assortment of armour.

'They haven't wasted much time. When last I was here, this place was a smoking, charcoal ruin.'

'You haven't told me much about the battle. Why?'

'Not much to tell. There is no helping it. We'll have to go through that gate. Got anything to offer up as a bribe?' Nat replied, quickly changing the subject. Recent memories of Morgan still tended to hurt.

'Nothing that I care to give,' she answered back, earning a frown from Nat.

She noticed it and smiled inwardly. He was so easily shocked she couldn't resist doing it. His hair was now a dull, brown colour, like hers, she supposed and was cut short. He had fashioned a pointed hat made from forest leaves and looked the part of a rough, yokel, and woodsman very much. He leant on a long, sturdy staff held firmly in his hands, then shrugged.

'We go in this evening. Let's get some rest till then.'

At dusk, they approached the roughly crafted gate, and Nat thumped heavily upon it with his staff. A small shutter slid gratingly across, and a creased, dirty face appeared.

'Hey, yup there! Wat de ye be wanting here?'

'Shelter for the night. We seek shelter.'

The dour-looking, one-eyed, gatekeeper, studied them suspiciously.

'Ye be not from these here parts, are ye? Not seen ye before.'

'We tried setting up in the woods. It hasn't worked out for us. We're heading back home.'

'Just ye two?'

'Yes, good sir. Here is a token as a show of appreciation for your kindness.'

To Elaine's surprise, Nat fished out a small opal attached to a rawhide cord and placed it through the slot into the grasping hand of the gatekeeper.

The keeper eyed it in the dimming light and then slipped it under his patched cloak. Then grumbling to himself, he pushed open the gate.

'There be a small inn, suitable for ladies, along the main street, called the Maiden's Dance. Nice food and a comfortable bed at a reasonable price.'

'Thank you, sir, and may the goddess grant you a good night.'

The keeper grunted and pushed the gate back, firmly closing it behind them.

The owner of the Maiden's Dance turned out to be a stout, blustery woman, with shoulders and forearms to rival Nat's and put him to shame, and a bulbous face which it seemed, a smile was afraid to visit. On seeing Elaine, she immediately took her under her wing and gave Nat a flat stare when he proclaimed them to be brother and sister; especially after he asked for a single room for the night. He had to stop himself from squirming under her gaze, reminding himself that he was no longer a little boy. Despite this minor setback, the formidable woman was fair in her business transactions and met his request for a room, food, and some boots for Elaine, with a few coins thrown in for the ferry crossing, in exchange for their horse. Elaine was reluctant to part with him even though Nat explained that he was not suited for the Badlands and would surely perish. The innkeeper seemed more than happy for the trade as she said that she was badly in need of a big, healthy horse to pull her new wagon. Business concluded, she whisked Elaine away for a hot bath, pointing out to Nat that he could find a bucket and a well in a corner at the rear courtyard. He was beginning to suspect that the shrewd woman had some inkling as to whom Elaine might be.

After an indeterminable period, Elaine reappeared. She made her way over to Nat, who was seated at a corner table, opposite the entrance. She was rosily scrubbed, with new, clean clothes and boots designed for the outdoors. Eyes shining, she sat down next to him and proceeded to chat away non-stop.

'Nat, what was that jewel you gave to the gatekeeper?'

'Something I did not want to give...except to a special person, on a special occasion. It was the last I had of my mother.'

'I'm sorry, Nat.'

He quickly ordered their meal, a delicious meat stew and hot bread, washed down with sweet ale, which they devoured like starving wolves, then retired to their room. They were so exhausted that they lay down next to each other and immediately fell into a deep sleep.

Nat awoke with a start at first light. To his surprise, Elaine was already up and peering through the curtains at the grey dawn.

'Come on, sleepyhead,' she said softly. 'It's time to go. There are two shadows down there, watching the inn. Why? I dread to think.'

He didn't bother to look, but rolled out of bed fully alert, picked up their small bundle of things and headed for the door, where down below, yet another surprise awaited them. It was in the substantial form of the innkeeper, who without any type of greeting, shoved a sack towards him saying.

'You'll need these. Don't go out the front. You will find a small door behind the courtyard. Follow the little alley to the town wall. Hidden behind a pile of burnt timber you'll find a ladder.'

With that, she turned to Elaine and swept her up into a big embracing hug.

'The goddess go with you, mistress.'

Nat blinked but didn't dare say a word.

They hurried out the back door following the innkeeper's instructions and were soon dropping down outside the palisade. They found themselves in some bushes about two hundred yards uphill from the river. Nat quickly checked the contents of the gifted sack and had his third surprise for the morning. Inside were two long, and very sharp hunting knives, snug within their accompanying sheaths, along with a finely crafted throwing axe, and some journey cakes. With a soft whistle of amazement, he handed one of the knives to Elaine who immediately secured it to her belt.

'I won't lose this one,' she said with commitment.

 The ferryman was half-asleep on his floating platform, and without comment he took the offered coins in a crocked, calloused hand, and began hauling steadily on the rope, pulling them across to the other side. As they neared the far bank, a watching Nat detected three shapes emerging from the shadow of the village wall. They each led a horse.

'Shit!' he muttered.

'Nat, since I've met you I've constantly been running from someone or something!' Elaine panted. 'I'm beginning to get suspicious.'

'Not fair! You were already on the run when I met you!'

'True, we both were!'

'Life never changes; so boring.'

They were trotting at a fast clip, trying to get into the woods beyond Highpoint Hill before the ferry could make a return trip. Nat hoped that some of Hatch's traps were still unsprung and operational. If so, they would buy them some time as they made a dash across the chalk hills and with luck, down into the Badlands. Signs of the past titanic battle still visibly scoured the earth as they scampered towards the waiting trees. He shut down his memory and concentrated on the task at hand. As they disappeared into the fringes of the forest, two more horsemen came galloping up along the King's Road where they had been lying in wait for days. At the crossing, the two groups of riders intersected each other and became engaged in an animated altercation. After about five minutes of this, they appeared to have agreed on something. For they then proceeded as one, setting out on the trail of their marks.

Jogging single file, Nat carefully picked their path through the trees and undergrowth, zigzagging along, sometimes going hand over hand through low lying branches. Elaine copied whatever he did without question, literally following in his footsteps. They heard the large group of men and horses clumsily entering the woods in the distance, but kept to their steady pace; haste would most certainly lead to disaster. It wasn't long before the scream of a panicked horse in terrible agony crashed into their ears, followed by a violent commotion, and the shouts of confused men. Breaking through the other side, they raced on. This disturbance was their opportunity to gain some ground on their pursuers.

Like it was with the wolves, they were running with the odds stacked against them, but this time they were leaner, fitter, their muscles trained for stamina. They maintained their lead on the now four horse riders who dogged their trail. Nat did not make it easy for them, and many times he caused them to lose their tracks, at which point the king's bounty hunters found themselves in a dead-end where they had to double back, losing precious time, or stood forced to circle for hours trying to pick back up a lost spore.

On the third day, early morning found them dog tired, looking down on the sleeping camp of one of the king's patrols. They had run through the night, regaining some of the lead they had gradually lost over time. Now they stood almost spent. However, the sleeping soldiers below were an unexpected boon.

'How is this a good thing!' demanded Elaine, her face grey with exhaustion.

'Horses, my princess, horses.'

'Oh, I get it! How romantic!' she said, perking up. 'I've always fantasised about being a horse thief.'

Nat looked at her and frowned.

'Okay,' he said slowly. 'Now is your chance to make it real.'

They were lucky. The change of sentry had not yet occurred. And, fortunately for them, the soldier on the graveyard shift was nodding off on the job.

'Here's what we'll do,' whispered Nat. 'I'll silence the look-out. You are good with horses, and they like you. Gently make your way over to the picket line and soothe them till I get to you. If something goes wrong, grab one and ride hard.'

'I'll take that as a compliment, Mr Tactful,' replied Elaine with an edge of sarcasm in her voice.

They split on their separate objectives, easing down through the long grass only when the wind blew.

The hapless sentry was in mid-yawn when Nat reared up behind him, grabbed him by chin and head and yanked viciously. With a loud crack, he went limp. They both froze. After an all-clear, Elaine approached the horses, making sure that they had all seen her, whispering to them. They nickered softly in return, a few tossing their heads, and stamping their hooves, but none showed alarm. She moved along the line stroking and whispering. Gently she unhitched two of the best, and guided them over to Nat who picked up the stroking and soothing, then making her way back she loosed the rest, they were ten in all. When they sat safely mounted, they kicked their mounts into a full gallop, launching themselves at the bunched and uncertain horses, driving them towards the sleeping soldiers. The latter woke in startlement to find themselves amid a nightmare of thundering hooves. Alarmed, they scattered, rolling and shouting, trying to avoid getting trampled; not all were successful. In a cloud of chalky dust, Nat and Elaine were gone.

Bent low over their horses' necks, Nat and Elaine rode filled with elation. Their desperate gamble had paid off. The upside was that they were now mounted and on equal terms with their pursuers. The downside was that they would now have another five riders on their tail, as soon as they managed to recapture their mounts, but cavalry horses stood trained to stop when they became riderless, so that wouldn't take long. Four soldiers were dead or too injured to pick up the chase, and another sent to raise the alarm, but Nat and Elaine did not yet know this.

After two days of hard riding, they began to descend from the chalk hills into the Badlands proper. Here they stood a much better chance of evading their angry and determined pursuers. Using every trick that he had learned from both Morgan and Aden, Nat led the posse behind them on a merry chase, but they were eating into their lead, closing the gap, mile by mile. On more than one occasion he spotted dust clouds on the near horizon which may have been signs of others joining the chase. They couldn't escape them all without help. Already thirst was weakening them, and more importantly, was exhausting the horses. On foot, they wouldn't stand a chance.

'We can't make it on our own. They're closing down on us. We need help.'

'Don't tell me. You're close friends with a coyote,' Elaine's attempt at humour failed. Her lips were cracked and dry, her beautiful eyes dull, their lustre faded.

Nat studied her calmly with grave concern.

'Of a sort. Hang in there, princess. We still have cards to play.'

'I was never a good gambler. Don't worry, my love. I won't let you down.'

He smiled into her eyes, leant over, and kissed her gently.

'Come, let's play our last hand.'

The effect of the moonlight on the rugged landscape of the Badlands was always dramatic, and this chilled desert night was no exception. The otherworldly scenery was breath-taking. However, both Nat and Elaine were so stretched, psychologically and physically, almost beyond their coping limits that they only drew from the vista what was functional and necessary to survive. They had had little sleep, always had to be alert and watchful, continuously trying to out-think their hunters, planning ahead, covering their tracks, careful, careful, ever vigilant, coupled with the need for speed, driving them onwards. Their reserves of youthful energy were almost empty. Their horses stood blown, heads hanging dejectedly, tails motionless. In another mile or two, they would keel over if not allowed to rest.

'Out here time seems just to stand still,' Nat said, his voice croaking. 'Nothing changes.'

The village looked the same as when he and Morgan had first looked down on it.

'When we get down there,' Nat continued, 'wait by the little temple with the horses. From there, you can escape in several directions; better to be safe than sorry.'

Elaine simply nodded.

Before the road branched, they dismounted. Elaine took the horses and led them towards the white, glowing, ethereal temple. Some of the village dogs were already beginning to stir, a bark here and there, as Nat moved, wraithlike, along the main village road.

Soon a pack of barking, howling dogs surrounded Nat, but he had been taught well on how to deal with these nocturnal guards, and before long, had them whining happily and wagging their tails, most of them drifting off to curl up somewhere warm once again.

He quietly made his way to a sizeable, white-washed cottage, and eased open the top half of a two shuttered door. As he opened his mouth to call out, a calm voice drifted to him from the darkness.

'Stay very, very still, sonny. One more move and this iron bolt will split your skull.'

'Hatch, is that you?'

'Who else can it be, sonny? Last I looked this was my home. Whom you be expecting, the king?'

'Hatch it's me, Nat.'

'A bit late for dinner, aren't you, sonny? Last time I saw you, you dragged my old bones into a war.'

'Hatch I need your help.'

'If it's marital advice ye be after, I'm all yours. If it's another war, ye can bugger off. Where is that Morgan fellow anyway? Hope he isn't behind me with a knife at my throat.'

'Hatch, Morgan is dead.'

After a pause, the aged voice came back.

'Dead, you say? Seen the body, sonny?'

'No, not exactly. Well, no.'

'That man isn't the normal kind, sonny. Until you see his cold body, he ain't dead.'

Nat stood, transfixed at old Hatch's door, a bit shocked by the older man's words.

'I hope you're right, Hatch.'

'What do you want with me, sonny?'

'We need your help, Elaine and I.'

'Tell me you don't mean the Earl's little daughter!'

'I'm afraid so.'

'What's the matter with you, sonny? Can't you get into trouble on your own?'

'The king's men are barking and snapping at our heels, Hatch. He wants to marry her to secure his reign.'

'Did her father give his consent to this?'

'No. It is he who asked me to spirit her away.'

'The Earl is the last man of honour left standing in this broken kingdom. Who's after you? King's soldiers?'

'Yes and his bounty hunters.'

Hatch whistled through his remaining teeth.

'What's your status?'

'Bone weary, exhausted. No food, no water, no sleep. Two clapped out horses, fit to drop. Elaine is waiting by the temple. Riders about one hour behind us.'

'I'll rouse the men. Becky, you can put down that crossbow now, and prepare some travel food and some water skins.'

Nat jumped. He had no idea that Hatch's wife was there next to him. He made a quick reassessment of this unassuming woman.

'Go and fetch the Earl's daughter, young man. I'll arrange things here.'

Without a word, Nat leapt to obey.

Within the hour, Hatch had ridden out in pairs with a few men from the village. The intention was to criss-cross Nat and Elaine's trail, muddying and confusing the issue, sewing doubt into the minds of the pursuers and making them lose precious time.

In the meantime, the running couple were making their way at a swift but steady pace on two fresh horses, supplied with food and water. Rest would come later if their luck held. Hatch's quick-thinking actions had granted them a new lease of life, hope reborn; they had no intention of squandering it. They weren't in the clear yet. At most, they would gain a day's march, and then the bastards would be back onto them like ants on a caterpillar.

Nat's thoughts, unfortunately, carried the day. Twelve hours after leaving the village, high on a sandstone bluff, he saw them in the valley below, at the far end of his vision, what appeared to be at least four riders.

'Damnation!' he muttered.

'They're on us again, aren't they?'

He nodded, clicking his horse into forwarding motion.

'Much sooner than expected. We can only keep moving.'

An hour later, they were working their way even higher, up a narrow pass. It lay covered in dangerously loose sand and scree. Their horses, slipping and sliding, the relentless sun, baking and boiling them at the same time, their breaths steaming in their lungs, sweat soaking every inch of their tormented bodies. Suddenly, Nat pulled his horse up, staring ahead.

'What...?' said Elaine. 'Oh, please, goddess, no!'

Standing at the top of the pass, almost naked in the blazing heat, stood two men, watching them. One was exceptionally tall, and stood, still as a tree, in a boneless unnerving way; the other, although much shorter, gracile in comparison, but with broad shoulders, radiated raw power, an aura of invincibility. They were both unnaturally motionless, like statues waiting to come to violent life, fictitious guardians of old.

'Caught between a rock and a hard place,' Nat muttered.

'What shall we do?' whispered Elaine.

'Always face what is in front of you,' replied Nat grimly. 'Both my teachers, my fathers, were firm on this.'

'My father believed the same.' She reached out and touched his arm. 'We will always have each other.'

Nat looked deeply into her eyes and saw rock-hard resolve.

'I love you,' he said simply. Her smile reached into the core of his heart.

Releasing all that had gone before, their cares, hopes and dreams, they set themselves and advanced into the broiling wind to meet their fate. An unexpected gust peppered them with grit and dust, causing them to look down, blinking to protect their sight. As they glanced up again, rubbing dirt-streaked hands across their eyes, only one figure remained, shimmering, almost swimming, in the heat haze. Expecting ambush, Nat hastily scanned the red walls of the canyon pass, feeling the heat like an oven roiling back at him. Nothing. He reached down and slid his hunting knife into his left hand and grasped the throwing axe in his right, sensing Elaine mirroring his actions. The bastards would bleed before they could get their hands on them. As this thought flew through his mind, his mount suddenly buckled, collapsing from the climb and heat exhaustion. Without missing a beat or removing his focus from the still unmoving figure, Nat threw a leg over the front of the saddle, and smoothly, almost gently landed on his feet, poised and balanced. Without a sign of warning, he burst into action, his right arm blurring forward, hurling the axe in a motion impossible to track. As it flew a deadly path, spinning through the thick air, Nat surged after it, tearing up through the intervening space, closing the gap with mouth-dropping speed. Elaine caught unawares, watched the unfolding scene as if in slow motion.

The waiting man, who she could now see quite clearly, had thick, long, dark hair on his head, and the growth of a grey-streaked beard covered his face. His sinewy body was naked, except for a loincloth, and completely hairless, burned to a deep brown, with a reddish hue, the muscles of his torso and legs set in hard, clearly outlined, bands of corded muscle. He remained calm and unperturbed as Nat flew at him, watching him coming with a steady gaze. As the axe's blade tore unerringly towards his face, he flicked his head, almost nonchalantly, to the side, allowing it to spin by harmlessly. By then, Nat was on him, his left hand, knife held low, ripping inwards towards his groin. Pivoting slightly from the waist, the bearded man brought his hand down in a reverse circular motion, a blur of speed, intercepting Nat's wrist with his, then with a smooth pivot, brought Nat's arm up against the joint, and hurled him, head-over-heels, onto his back. Elaine was astonished, astonished for two reasons. First, the shock at seeing her man so easily negated was chilling. For the second, the bearded opponent did not display any aggression whatsoever, but stepped back, and chuckled in a deep, pleasant voice, down at her floored and winded lover.

Nat rolled over and got groggily to his feet.

'What took you so long, son?' she heard the bearded man say.

A broad grin of uninhibited joy broke out on Nat's handsome face, revealing the boy that still lay within him. He staggered forward and pulled the sun-browned man into a huge embrace, lifting him off of his feet, spinning him around with whoops of laughter.

'You old bastard!' he shouted happily.

Elaine frowned down at them, confused by this unexpected circumstance and strange, out of place display.

Seeing her look, Nat dropped the man back onto his feet, looped a long arm around his shoulders, and laughing still, shouted up to her.

'Elaine, Elaine, can't you see?! It's Morgan!'

Elaine blinked.

'Morgan...but?'

'Yes, yes, I'm supposed to be dead. It's a long story, girl.'

'Morgan,' Nat interrupted. 'We've got bad company close behind us.'

'Not for much longer, I would say,' replied Morgan enigmatically. 'Come, let's get down out of this heat.'

Down in the valley, the four hunters had the full scent of blood in their nostrils. Their prey was almost run to ground. They were confident, tough, highly trained, and skilful, the best of their kind, professionals, expensive man-killers for hire. They were a team, knew how each other thought, and knew each other's strengths and weaknesses. They had been working together for ten years and had never failed to deliver. Their leader, a scarred and grizzled man of about forty years, lifted his head and surveyed the winding path leading up to the pass.

He cocked his overly large head to one side and listened to the faint sounds of horses labouring up the steep and slippery track.

'They're trying to move too fast. Horses will never make it in this bloody furnace.'

It was a statement of fact.

Dismounting, he set out on the steep incline, leading his mount. The others followed suit.

About halfway up, strung out in single-file, concentrating on every footstep, as the inferno tried to suck every bit of moisture from their flesh, a demon dropped into their midst. Experienced as these manhunters were, they could have never expected such a misfortune. Before the surprised man in the middle could look up, his throat sat ripped out. His blood, steaming onto the sandy slope as his lifeless body rolled under the hooves of his startled and terrified horse. In terror, it lashed out with iron-shod back legs, striking the next man in line, full in the chest, breaking his chest bone, and cracking his ribs. The other two spun, backing clear of their kicking horses and drawing their swords, facing this unexpected enemy ambush as one. They might have just sat down and whistled. Krarl, sending a force of fear ahead of him, vaulted clear over the back of one of the bucking horses. He landed on them, one gnarled hand catching the wrist of the closest bounty hunter, breaking it with a twist. Then smashing the heal of his other hand into the face of the screaming man, he bore him to the ground. With his full weight centred over one knee, Krarl crushed it onto his neck, snapping it like a dry twig. He bounded back and onto the side of the sandstone wall corralling the path, avoiding the wild slash of the team leader, who overbalanced as he overcommitted in his stroke, fuelled by unreasonable fear. It was his last mistake in life and knew death when Krarl landed on his back. Anguish and fright contorted the face of the hunter with the broken ribs as he hauled himself desperately back down the track, watching the demon who followed behind him slowly with wide, panicked eyes. He drew a hunting knife from his belt and waved it shakily in front of him. A wet, snuffling noise emanated from the creature's maw, and he had a horrible sensation that it was laughing at his efforts. The last thing he heard was a snarl, and then blackness took him.

With a chilling howl, Krarl rose from his crouch over the dead body and raced headlong down the path seeking more prey, filled with the heady joy of bloodlust.

'Bloody hell, what's that!' exclaimed Nat.

'Merciful goddess!' Elaine whispered in alarm.

They were sheltering in a shallow cave, a large overhang really, just big enough for the two exhausted horses and themselves, trying to stay cool under the sticky attention of hot, prevailing winds.

'Our saviour,' muttered Morgan.

Nat studied him for a few seconds.

'I may have been exhausted and drained, but I distinctly saw two men standing on a ledge.'

'So did I,' echoed Elaine.

Morgan stared into space, taking his time to answer.

'Krarl.'

'Who?' said both Nat and Elaine in unison.

'Krarl, a once man fashioned from the wildest of the elements.'

'How did you come to know this Krarl?' asked Nat. 'I've never heard you mention him before.'

'That is a very long story. However, if it weren't for him, I would not be here today. And now, he is destroying those who are chasing you with ill intent. In a way, I feel sorry for them, for Krarl is very, very good at the art of destruction. In truth, he revels in it.'

'Will he be coming back?' asked Elaine, looking a bit worried.

Morgan smiled.

'No, we have parted company for now.'

The two young companions studied him for a while, but none ventured any further questions or comments.

As the sun started to drop behind the high ridges, the trio emerged.

'It's so wonderful not to be hunted,' commented Elaine. 'Your mysterious companion must have been successful.'

'There is no doubt,' responded Morgan, leading them to a hidden rock pool, where they slaked their thirst in preparation to continue on their journey.

'We must get to the Queen,' said Nat. 'It is the only place left where we can find refuge.'

'Yes, you both must. I would not be welcome there. Therein lies too much of an uncomfortable history. And besides, I am responsible for squandering her largesse. She lent me an army of liberation and I used it to install an egocentric dictator wearing a crown as a disguise.'

'You cannot blame yourself, Morgan,' said Elaine. 'You acted in good faith, and in truth, none of us owned all the facts at the time.'

'Yes, what stands done has been done and cannot be changed. We must bathe in the tub of tears that we have created and look to the future, be ready. I will come with you until the Black Mountains pass, then we must go our separate ways.'

'But Morgan, where will you go? And how shall we find you when we need you? Nat has promised to make an honest woman of me. We will need you.'

Nat turned a deep red, and Morgan's face broke into a wide grin, a thing rarely seen.

'In that case, I will be honoured to make an appearance. Send word to the Watchers when you both are ready. With the Queen's leave, I will come.'

With hearts and minds much lighter, they moved on through the blasted landscape.

EPILOGUE

King's scribe and memory

If a King

Like a mountain range, morals strong,

Is the backbone, a mighty binding thing,

Holding this land bonded, the line of a song,

Then it lies broken.

If a King

Like a body, sturdy in health, limbs long,

Is the heart, an engine, central to everything,

His people's blood, flows no longer, dry, life energy gone,

Then, our land lies broken.

There, in his tower, built wrong

THE HIDDEN KING

The king lies dead, Kingship fled,

His Kingdom

Hidden from destiny.

In a one-roomed cellar, hidden under an open-fronted tavern, three men sat, two of them hoping that their last few places of refuge would remain undiscovered, the other had no hope at all. It was the last command post of a once intricate and extended underground network. Now this once vast web sat reduced to a few dimly lit rooms scattered here and there. Ignoring the muffled din filtering through the thick floor-boards above their heads, the once famed and feared Abbot of Beggars and Thieves listened to the thin, lilting voice of his longest and most trustworthy friend and adviser.

'This king is besieging his very own kingdom!'

'He wants so much that through the grasping, loses for the wanting.'

'The people are turning against him more and more with each passing day.'

'Paid mercenaries are placing their boots on their necks with each new declaration; the people are without choice. I cannot blame them.'

'The Earl has become the gate that holds back the flood. Should we not declare for him?'

'This would be his death sentence, dear Patrick. The king knows what is obvious, but we dare not give it a name. Shadows constantly threaten a mind filled with dark thoughts.

'He is unintentionally creating a kingdom that is the mirror of his mind?'

'It certainly looks that way. His mind is under a siege of his own making, and he hunts us mercilessly, day and night.'

'What shall we do?'

'We run...we run and hide!'

The Abbot and Patrick glanced over at the emaciated and stooped over figure - forlorn and rocking in the corner.

'We can only wait, Patrick. Wait for events to run the course, come full circle.'

'The noose is a circle, waiting to squeeze our necks,' the figure quavered, cackling hysterically at the end. 'A king never dies for there is always another, waiting and hiding. Long live the king!'

The two men stopped their discussion and watched the almost unrecognisable ex-Lord Chamberlain as he laughed and laughed, seeing humour lying in the corner that no-one else could see.

'Has he lost his mind, do you think?'

'I think that he is not the only one, dear Patrick. Our land stands ruled by a king who is mad with power. Maybe our Lord

Chamberlain here sees more clearly his intentions than all of us who think ourselves to be sane.'

'Is this the end then?'

'No, Patrick, once we remain alive and breathing, we await the right elements to make ourselves a new beginning.'

The end

ABOUT THE AUTHOR

Over many close years, the author shared a love for movies and fantasy books with his son. As his son grew into manhood and blessed retirement presented itself, the author gained long lost spare time and freedom to reacquaint himself with his imagination. With the wish to thank his son and present him with a gift, the author started to write a novel with one of the characters modelled after him. From this, 'The Brothers of Destiny' series was born with 'The Hidden King' being the first.

You can follow the author's work on

https://www.amazon.com/author/jcpereira

https://www.amazon.co.uk/-/e/B07B1KSP6K

https://www.smashwords.com/profile/view/jcpfountain

or visit his Facebook page, 'Something to Read'.
https://www.facebook.com/jcpSomethingToRead/?modal=admin_todo_tour

Printed in Great Britain
by Amazon